THE DEAD HAVE NO VOICE

A TENTERDEN MYSTERY

The Dead Have No Voice

A Tenterden Mystery

Paul Ryley

First published in Great Britain in 2024

This book is a work of fiction, set in a real place and time. However the actions and words attributed to real historical persons in that setting should not be taken to mean that those persons actually did or said those things or held those opinions. The protagonists are fictional, and any resemblance to real people is coincidental.

ISBN 978-1-3999-9002-8

Typeset in Goudy by Falcon Oast Graphic Art Ltd.
www.falcon.uk.com
Printed and bound by ImprintDigital.com

1 3 5 7 9 10 8 6 4 2

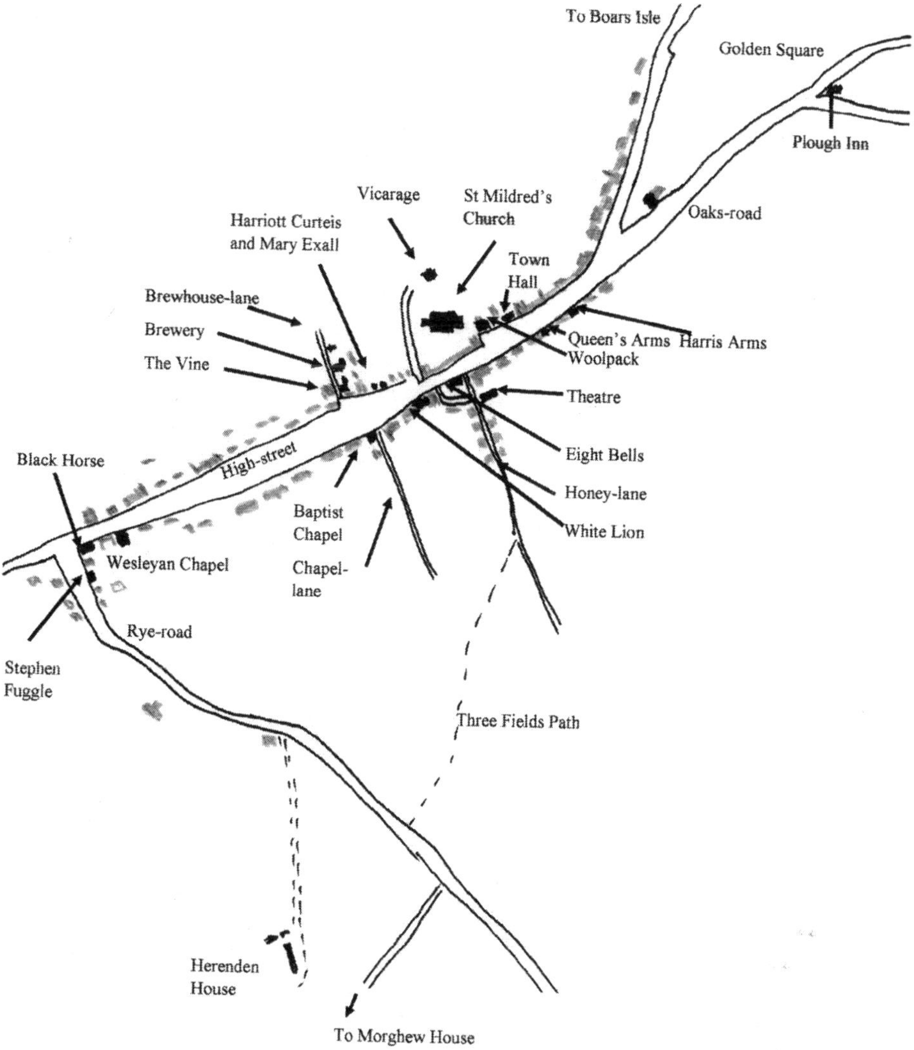

Map of Tenterden

CHAPTER 1

THE TIMES THEY ARE A-CHANGING

Wednesday 30th June 1830

'THE KING IS DEAD. LONG live the King!'

Mayor Virgil Pomfret stood on a low platform outside the Town Hall, dressed in his red robes and tricorn hat, with his serjeant-at-arms in attendance bearing the ancient mace of office. He rumbled on with the proclamation in a stentorian voice, but Mary Exall turned to her friend Harriott Curteis and pulled a face.

'Doesn't he relish being important, eh, Harry?'

'They all do, don't you know, but hush, don't say anything against him: I've got news for you.'

'How be?'

'Well, Mr Pomfret,' she nodded towards the speech-maker, 'he's going to offer me a job. I've to see him tomorrow morning at eight, and if I suit, I'll be his secretary. How about that then?' She folded her arms across her chest, and grinned.

'Never! Secretary to the gentry? I thought all such were men?'

'Yes of course, they are, usually. But Father says Mr Pomfret came to consult him for advice about a new clerk; seems his last one left under quite a cloud, but Father wasn't saying anything about why. So,

Father suggested me, being as I'm,' she puffed out her chest and put her nose in the air, 'perfect for the job.'

'But how can you?'

Harriott tilted her head back and forth, and crossed her eyes at her friend.

'And anyway, Harry, could you do that sort of job? It's a bit of a change from serving at the Bells, don't you think? You write a real pretty hand, now, but what of the other things? What does a clerk do anyway? I mean, a private secretary?'

Mr Pomfret was in full flow, announcing the details of the regnal name of King William IV, attesting the town's loyalty to him, and all the other details of a proclamation of accession. The girls stood a little way up the road from the Eight Bells tavern, by Mr Martin the auctioner's house, so as to be able to see the spectacle, but both wore aprons and clutched their dishcloths, in anticipation of being summoned back to work at any minute.

Harriott waved at Mary to be quiet for a moment, as the party across the road readjusted itself, and someone else began to speak. Then she continued,

'Well, seems I'd have to look after his library, and open his correspondence, and write his letters, and such like. I'm not quite sure myself, but I expect I'll find out.'

'I'd be too scared to do something like that, Harry. I mean, what if he . . . I don't know, told you to do something you didn't know about?'

'Well, I'd ask him to explain,' she retorted, with a flick of her head, followed by tucking a loose strand of hair behind her ear. 'He can't expect me to be a mind-reader, can he?'

'No, but he might be angry.'

'Then I'd leave, and he'd be back to the first square.'

'Ooh, you are brave. I couldn't do it.'

'Your writing is a scribble, anyway, Mary, it'd never pass.'

'No, it's true. If only I could print everything, like on one of Father's presses, but it would take too long.'

'They'll probably invent a machine for that some day, I expect. There's all sorts of new contraptions coming. Have you heard, they've nearly finished the new rail-way from Manchester to Liverpool? Stephen Fuggle was telling me all about it. They're going to open it quite soon, and the carriages will be pulled by steam locomotives.'

'What are they?'

'They're engines on wheels, so you don't need horses, and they can pull more carriages than even a big team.'

'How does Stephen know all about this?'

'He gets the London newssheets from Mrs Croughton at Herenden when she is finished with them.'

Someone close by hissed at them to be quiet, and they dropped their voices.

'Everything's changing so fast, isn't it? Is it true that we're to have a new vicar?'

'It is. He's called Mr Ward. But I expect Mr Temple will take all the services, like before for Mr Coombe. Anyway, it doesn't make any difference to me, down at the Wesleyan.'

At this point, a barman from the tavern tapped them on the shoulders and recalled them to their work, and they trudged back, glancing several times behind them at the continuing spectacle, the members of which seemed to be moving into the Woolpack next door, business having concluded. As they did so, the church bells began pealing out, celebrating the new King.

Harriott was kept very busy serving the horde of new drinkers who had flooded in once the announcements had finished. She dealt firmly with some of the more lively ones who tried to flirt with her, but after about forty minutes the ringers came in, and she was approached by the tower captain, Richard Marshall.

'Afternoon, Harriott. All the better for seeing you again, of course. Thirsty work, ringing. What have you got for me today?' He gazed into her eyes, then slid his gaze down over her bosom for a moment, then winked.

'Just ale, Richard. Just ale.' She in turn couldn't help noticing his muscular shoulders, and strong forearms showing with his rolled-up sleeves, and shivered internally. 'What'll it be this time?'

'Old ale,' he said, 'unless anything else is on offer?' with a slight lift of his eyebrows.

'Not today, Richard,' she said regretfully, remembering what a reputation he had as a Lothario. 'I wouldn't want to jump the queue, it's pretty long.'

'Queue? You'd go straight to the head, you would, young Harriott, no problem.'

She shook her head. 'Tempting, but, the Good Book tells us to resist temptation, doesn't it?'

'Well, maybe another time? I'll be seeing you.'

She watched his back as he went over to the other ringers, and sighed again. He was such a . . . well, she wouldn't mind being held tightly by those muscular arms, just occasionally.

It was not until mid-afternoon she and Mary could meet again, once Mary had finished washing the dishes from lunch and Harriott had been relieved from serving the crowds.

'What are you going to wear tomorrow, Harry? You can't go in that gown, it's serviceable for here, but not for a gentleman's rooms.'

'Of course not. I shall wear my Sunday best.'

'You mean the dark red stripe, with the demi-gigot sleeves? Won't they be in the way if you are doing much writing? And wouldn't the neckline seem a bit frivolous? Even with a pelerine?'

'I hadn't thought of that. You're right. Well, what about the black, that I had when grandfather died? That would be sober and serious.'

Mary considered this, rubbing her knuckles together. 'I don't think so. Too gloomy. How about your dark blue; it's only two seasons old? It's got a higher neckline, and the sleeves are only puffed a little? I'd say you'd look sensible and reliable in that.'

'Ideal. But I'd need to mend the cuff, it got torn when Edward

Wickens was messing about in the Queen's Arms. Look, I'd better hurry home, I've got lots to do before the theatre tonight. It's the Rivals again, I've seen it twice, but I don't care.'

'Who are you going with this time? John?'

Harriott pulled a face. 'No, I got tired of him, he was boring. I met this new man, he's called Daniel Cousins, he just arrived in town from London, he's so good-looking, and tall, and wears such fashionable clothes. He's staying at the Woolpack. He seems most exciting.'

'What is his trade?'

'I don't know yet. We're to meet in the Harris Arms at a quarter after six.' She did a little dance for her friend.

'What about a chaperone? If he's from London, you know.'

'Huh! I can take care of myself. And they all know me there anyway of course.'

'But your reputation?'

'What do I care for reputation? Anyway, I must be off. Come on.'

The following morning extra early, Miss Harriott Curteis, smartly and soberly gowned, bonneted and gloved, crossed the great width of the High-street opposite her house, and walked sedately down towards West Cross. Her calm demeanour concealed two anxieties. The more pressing of course was her forthcoming interview with Mr Pomfret. However, she was also unsettled by the memory of the behaviour of Mr Daniel Cousins after the theatre. Rather than heading back along Honey-lane toward the High-street, he had conducted her along the alley adjacent to the theatre entrance and there in the dark tried to kiss her, grasping her shoulders with force, and who knows what else might have followed.

Really! Outrage hardly covered it. Firstly at his impertinent behaviour on a first encounter, but more so at her own poor judgement in allowing such a situation to arise. It was a good thing she had known how to discourage a man – with a well-placed knee. Not very ladylike, but . . . well, that was the last she was going to see of him, for sure.

As she passed the Black Horse and turned into Rye-road a familiar voice hailed her.

'Harriott? What are you doing down here so early and all dressed up?'

It was Stephen Fuggle, standing on his threshold, just leaving the house for work, with Mr Ducksbury who had clearly called for him.

'Come to that, why are you so late?' she retorted.

Stephen shrugged. 'I do what Mr Ducksbury tells me, you know that.'

'You at Herenden today, then?'

'Thursday, Herenden, yes, I'm surprised you know.'

'I know lots of things, Stephen.'

'We have the lawns to cut close, see.' The three of them set off down the road, Mr Ducksbury tactfully preceding the youngsters by a few paces. 'And it's no use starting too early, they'd be wet with the rain we had last night.'

'Oh, yes.'

'Have you heard, there's a new machine just been invented, you push it over the grass and it cuts it nice and even, and a lot shorter than we can manage with our scythes and that. I hear we might be able to get one, but it's all hush-hush at the moment.'

'It's not been in the papers, I haven't seen about it.'

'No, Mr Ducksbury saw it in the gardening sheets. They've applied for a patent, so it won't be sold until that is dealt with. Anyway, you haven't said where you are going.'

'No, I haven't, have I?' she replied, screwing up her nose at him teasingly.

'?'

'I,' she said, swaggering a bit, 'am visiting Mr Virgil Pomfret, Mayor of this esteemed borough, to consider accepting a post as his private secretary.'

'What, at Morghew House?'

'Where else would I be meeting him?'

'I meant, Mr Pomfret of Morghew? Why would he want you?'

'Thanks very much, Stephen, and I wonder why Mr Ducksbury wants you too.'

'Sorry, I didn't mean that, and you know it. I mean, secretaries are men, surely?'

'Not this one. I gather from Father he wasn't happy with his last man secretary, so he was open to Father's suggestion of considering me.'

'Very well. Will you have to give up your other work, then?'

'I don't know. Nothing has been said about hours, I'm going to see if I would wish to take the post.'

'Don't take that hoity-toity line with Mr Pomfret, Harriott, he won't like it.'

'Take me for a fool? I shall be all deference and amiability when I see him.'

'You can act a part, then?'

'Huh! I can, and a great sight better than those fools at the theatre last night.'

'You were at the theatre?' Stephen looked away. 'Who did you go with?' he added carelessly.

'Noone you know,' she replied. 'So, tell me, did you see Mr Pomfret doing his speech for the new King?'

'Not us, we were working, remember? We did see him leave Morghew in his carriage, though. We were edging the drive; had to doff our caps as he passed, he likes that courtesy.' There was a brief pause. 'Anyway, if you're going there, why didn't you go down Honey-lane and Three Fields path? Much quicker.'

Harriott flinched internally at the mention of Honey-lane. 'Much muddier too, remember the rain last night? I need to look my best.'

'You always look perfect, you know.'

'Don't be silly. I have a spot on my nose and my hair won't stay curled with the damp air.'

'Whatever you say, Harriott.'

The two gardeners turned up the drive past the Herenden gatehouse and Harriott continued along the road, rehearsing the sorts of things she might say to Mr Pomfret, and turning over the things he might ask her. She felt for the sample of her handwriting in her pocket, and fiddled with the sleeve of her gown, where the mending last night had not gone quite as well as she might have wished.

At last, she was at the door of the big house. She pulled the bell, and waited. After something of a delay, the door was opened by a young footman, who blinked at her in some surprise. Harriott, in spite of her nervous state, still was able to appreciate his height, his fine calves and broad shoulders emphasised by his uniform, and smiled faintly at him.

'Miss Harriott Curteis, by appointment with Mr Pomfret,' she said, aware her voice sounded a mite squeaky.

'We aren't expecting a lady,' said the lackey, 'only a gentleman for the post of clerk to the master.'

'That would be me,' Harriott explained, 'I know it is not usual, and I expect I am rather early.'

The footman looked at the clock on the wall of the hall, then back at her. 'Matter of twenty minutes, that's right you are.' He looked her up and down, curiously. 'I'll be putting you in the Yellow room. Happen Master'll see you in his library.'

Harriott sat in the Yellow room, remembering to set herself on the edge of the sofa and keep her back straight, unlike her usual mode of slouching on furniture at home and with friends. She could see, or thought she could see, Herenden across the fields, and wondered how the men were getting on with the mowing. Then, by association of ideas, she wondered if Mr Pomfret might object to her walking out with his footman, if he was as enticing in mind as in his physical form. But then, he did look quite young. But not *too* young, she considered; and variety was important after all.

She wondered if she ought to be occupying herself, but there seemed to be no books to look through, or newspapers or anything like. There was a fortepiano, but it did not seem the time to pick out a melody with her limited skill on the instrument. Harriott did not do well with inactivity, and she found she was getting more nervous by the minute, glancing out of the window, then at the door, and then to the painting over the mantel, in spite of what she had said to Stephen.

Eventually, the hall clock struck the hour. Almost as soon as the strokes had died away the door opened to reveal Mr Pomfret himself. 'Come,' he commanded, and straightway led her to a room lined with books, with a huge desk, some leather-upholstered arm-chairs and a matching settle. A Turkey carpet was on the floor, and as Mr Pomfret drew back the curtains fully, light flooded in, glinting off a number of brass ornaments.

'I keep the curtains almost closed to protect the books from the light,' he explained, 'it damages their spines; and fades the chairs and carpet too. Now, do have a seat, Miss Curteis.' He indicated the chair nearest to the desk, and took his seat behind it. Harriott obeyed, and perched there, awaiting the first question. He held off speaking for several seconds, then,

'Your father said you are a capable woman,' he opened. There was a pause, and Harriott supposed she ought to say something.

'That is generous of him,' she said, 'but he is after all my father.'

Mr Pomfret smiled, slightly lopsidedly. 'Of course. But we shall test his opinion, I think. Your handwriting, now.'

Harriott fumbled in her pocket. 'I have brought a sample, sir.'

Mr Pomfret took it, and inspected it closely. 'Indeed, extremely neat. However, any such effect can be produced by enough time and chances to repeat a smudged attempt. Come over here, take my chair, and write to my dictation.'

Harriott got to her feet, and did as he said. The pen resting on the pad was a steel nib, most modern, and the inkwell plain and utilitarian. 'Sir, I am unused to your pen, so may I try it a little first?'

'Sensible girl. You may.'

After a few lines had seemed to flow quite smoothly, Harriott looked up. 'I am ready, sir.'

'Very well. "My dearest Mr Smith, I am in receipt of yours of the 26th inst., and have noted its contents. I find myself unable to meet your proposal for the price quoted, however, and would suggest a sum of ten guineas less. I look forward with anticipation to your agreeing this adjustment and beg to remain yours, etc."'

Harriott scratched away as fast as she might, only asking for a pause once, to allow her to catch up. To be fair to him, Mr Pomfret dictated at a moderate speed, and as she finished, she paused, looked up and asked, 'Sir, how do you usually like your salutation to read? Yours faithfully, Yours sincerely, or some other; and your name and titles?'

'Good girl. I use the simple, "Yours, V. Pomfret", normally. Unless the man is a close friend, in which case I use my Christian name too.'

Harriott finished off her writing, sanded it and held it out. He read it through, nodding, and h'mm-ing occasionally.

'Good, very good. A clear hand, and neat. Also, you have punctuated "inst.," correctly, and spelt receive properly. And well laid out, though I prefer there to be a gap after the greeting and before the signature. You were not to know this. Good. Please take your seat again.'

There followed a catechism of what she knew about publishing, and books in general, which was simple for her to deal with, her whole life at home having been spent with printing and books. Then about confidentiality, which was a little more tricky.

'So, how can I be sure you will be absolutely discreet about any matters you read about or hear about here in this building? Can you call witnesses to vouch for your conscientiousness? As Mayor, and magistrate, I cannot have rumours being spread, nor information useful to my competitors in business.'

Harriott paused. About everyday things she knew she was anything but judicious in her sharing of information – well, gossip, she ought to say in all truth. But in matters of business?

'Sir, I am not regularly involved in matters that need to be kept . . .

secret, or private. But,' she was struck by a happy thought, 'we live next door to Mr Exall, who is also a printer, like my father. You must know him, he is responsible for the poorhouse?'

'Indeed.'

'Naturally my father and he are in competition, although they are also good friends. You might ask him if I have ever passed on information useful to his business, and I think he will deny it.' She wrinkled her brow and added, 'Even though I have been close friends with his daughter Mary since birth, almost.'

After a number of other questions about her education and knowledge of business, Mr Pomfret leaned back in his chair and put his hands behind his head. 'Now, Miss Curteis, have you any questions yourself?'

'Yes, sir. If you find me suitable, what would be my hours of work? And the rate of pay? I have other employments at present, and would need to adjust them.' A thought struck her. 'About your earlier question: I have just remembered, I assist Mr Knowles the Wesleyan minister by writing up his sermons from his notes, which are quite, well, quite untidy; and I make them presentable so he can read them in chapel more easily. He would give me a good character, I believe.'

'Thankyou. Well, your hours would be mornings from perhaps eight to one, four days a week would suffice at present, I think. Although, your mentioning Mr Knowles, reminds me that I would also require you to attend the parish church with me each Sunday, together with the rest of my household. Are you then a dissenter?'

'I attend the chapel, yes, sir. But these things can be accommodated.'

'And your pay would be, as a non-resident servant, let me see. My previous man worked twenty hours a week, for 16 shillings, but as you are a woman, say, 14 shillings. But we should have to see how we went, as you may be slower than he. Or possibly,' he mused, almost to himself, 'quicker?'

Harriott began to object, then caught herself, and bit back the words before they escaped. Time enough to address such matters if she was taken on.

The interview was at an end. As he showed her out into the hall, to the care of the footman, he had one final query. 'You are a Curteis, Miss. Are you connected to the landowning family of this town, of which I myself am honoured to be a sprig?'

'Not as far as I know, sir, but my family has lived in the town many years, I understand.'

The library door closed behind him, and Harriott spent the next few minutes in idle conversation with the footman once they were on the threshold, so as to admire his physique again, and learn his name. George Bunn, he was, and from Suffolk. Not long in the post, and only just eighteen. Well, she would have to see. Might be worth a try, some time soon.

'So, I kept my mouth shut, and didn't say what I wanted, and sat neatly on his settee, and behaved,' she finished off, as Mary Exall put the last lot of tankards into the sink at the Bells.

'So, what was he like, as a person, I mean?'

'He's quite old, thirty-five I think, and he's important and knows it. But he was straight with me, really. And he didn't sneer or anything.'

'Do you think you'll be taken on?' she asked over her shoulder, bending to the pots as the cook came into the room.

'Ought to, if he's any sense.' She stretched, and wriggled her shoulders: perhaps she had been a little tense at the interview after all, she considered.

'They don't always have sense, these men, though, do they?'

'Hardly ever. Except perhaps in business; and I'm a square buy, I believe.' She leaned against the jamb of the door and frowned.

'He would want me to do four mornings, until one o'clock, Mary. Do you think Mr Paine would let me alter my duties to suit?'

'Can't see why not. Everyone says you're his best barmaid, the reason they come here rather than the Lion or the Woolpack. You wouldn't want to miss out on the chance to meet men, is that it?'

'No, of course not.' She shrugged. 'I can meet men anyway. No, I was just trying to fit all the things I have to do into the week. Which reminds me, Father wants me to help with the latest job, it's a set of notices I think . . . no, I shouldn't say what they're for, I need to practise being confidential. Oh well, better get on, but I wanted to let you know how the interview went.'

'When are you next working here?'

'This evening. Must rush. Bye.'

Harriott went through to the print room at the back of the house, looking for her father. 'Do you think you could help with this new job?' he said. It's a bit fiddly: the customer wants the paragraphs in alternating typefaces, and lots of italics and capitals and specials. My eyes are bothering me today, I'm afraid.'

'Of course, that's why I came home early, Father.' Harriott took the forme over to the print cases, picked up her composing stick, and began to set the letters in place, carefully checking the instructions on the side of the handwritten text about which typeface to use. After a few minutes, she paused, looked up.

'What exactly is this sheet?' she asked. 'It seems, well, just a collection of unrelated snippets.'

'I can't say anything: I've been sworn to secrecy. It's a kind of newssheet, just for the town and roundabout. I'm looking out some of those wooden letters we haven't used for ages, for the heading: I'll give you them when I've found all the characters. It's to be called "Dear Tenterden", and it's a kind of scandal sheet, I suppose. People can leave juicy bits of gossip at the Queen's Arms, and they will pass them on to the author, to use as . . . he, or she . . . sees fit. I get paid extra for the secrecy, so please don't ask.'

'Fair enough,' she said, turning back to the typecases. 'How many are we doing?'

'A thousand to start with,' he said, 'to be delivered to every shop for people to pick up for free. The shopkeepers will get a small payment for taking them. After that, well, I'm not sure.'

'This little bit here, I'm sure lots of the butchers will want to know who is being referred to, and will clamour for you to tell them the author.'

'I will be as silent as the grave,' he said. 'But anyway, I'm not to put our name to the papers, like we usually do. And see who is to be credited as the author: look, at the bottom of the manuscript.'

Harriott looked. '"Lady Susan"?' she said. 'Who? . . . Oh, I see, a *nom de plume*. Or *de print*, anyway.'

'Yes. I believe it will also carry some local news, and charge for the advertising, like a regular newssheet.'

Harriott carried on composing, frowning, and quite often having to take out letters and replace them, when she found there was a variation in how they were to be displayed. Yet another new thing to be taken on board, she supposed. Whatever will people think of next?

They worked in silence for a while, and Harriott wondered when her father was going to ask her about her interview. However, he held his counsel until the forme was complete, with the heading in place, and he had fitted it on the press. Only then did he speak.

'You seeing that young man again tonight?' he asked, his tongue poking out of the corner of his mouth as he inked the forme.

Harriott hesitated. 'Not . . . No, Father. He was a bit too . . . forward, I found.'

Mr Curteis looked up. 'Everything all right, Harriott? You weren't . . .'

'No, Father, I'm fine. Just didn't appreciate his treating me like he did.'

'Glad to hear it. Now you be careful mind. Young men these days . . .'

'Yes Father.' She sighed, and carried the paper over to the stack.

'This old press is getting a bit cranky, you know. I'm thinking of buying a more modern one. It's called the Imperial, it's a London invention. Ought to give us faster and cleaner production, we need to keep up with the times.'

'Have you the details?'

'No, I wrote to them, I'm expecting their pamphlet soon.'

'I'd like to take a look at it when it comes.'

'You're a good girl, Harriott. Now come on, out with the real news, how did you fare with Mr Pomfret? You've said nothing about it since you came in.'

'Everything was fine, Father. He's going to check up with a few people who know me, like Mr Exall, and Mr Knowles, and I expect he'll tell me in a few days what he's decided. It sounds interesting, and different. Plus, there's the money. I can contribute more at home with that sort of job.'

'Don't you worry about that. You have gowns to buy, and bonnets and so forth, and amusements to pay for. Now, just pass me that other platen and we'll begin.'

CHAPTER 2

I STILL HAVEN'T FOUND WHAT I'M LOOKING FOR

THE FOLLOWING WEDNESDAY, HARRIOTT TURNED into the Morghew drive and was greeted by Stephen, turning around from weeding a flower bed. She started, being lost in thoughts of what might be expected of her that day, and almost dropped her reticule.

'Morning, Madam secretary,' he called, and standing up, took a few steps towards her.

'Don't get any of that mould on me,' she told him, shrinking away, 'Mr Pomfret wouldn't like it.'

'Chance would be . . . am I likely to?' He halted, a couple of paces away. 'So, first day, eh?'

'Surely. And I don't want to be late.'

Stephen rubbed his nose with the back of his hand. 'Can't see the clock from here, but you're plenty early, I reckon: I know you, you would never let yourself be late for anything important.'

'Yes, but . . .'

'I know, I know, you want to be all settled and ready before time. Good for you, Mr Pomfret'll be pleased about that.'

'Tell me, Stephen, you might as well be useful, where is the servants' entrance? I used the front door last week, but I think I ought to be more self-effacing now.'

'Round to the right. You'll see a water-butt outside. Not that you'd ever be self-effacing, I reckon, not really.'

'Huh!' She hesitated, made to set off, turned back, brushed her hands over her skirt. 'Stephen, am I . . . well, do I look all right?'

He paused, shifted his weight to the other leg. 'I think you look splendid,' he managed, eventually. 'The perfect secretary.'

'Good. I don't want anything to go wrong, not today. I mean, I'm sure I'll make some mistakes sometime, but I want to start off well.'

'You will be the best he's had. And, what time do you finish?'

'One o'clock, I believe.'

'Be sure to let me know all about it before you go. I'll like as be in the glasshouses around then, round the back. I'd like to hear.'

'Well, I don't know . . .'

'If you can, I mean, don't put yourself to trouble.'

'I'll see you sometime anyway, and be sure to tell you about it.'

'Break a leg.'

'What?'

'It's what actors say to each other before they go on stage; it's supposed to be unlucky to wish another actor luck, if you see what I mean. Dunno why.'

'Oh. Bye then.'

'Goodbye, Harriott.' And as she walked on, head high, he added, under his breath, 'Lucky Mr Pomfret.'

Harriott walked out of the mansion at ten past one, by the clock over the stables, and strode off down the drive. Her full skirts flicked from side to side, and she looked at the little fluffy clouds in the blue sky as she went, conscious of a successful morning. She didn't see the figure of Stephen in the glasshouse, watering can in hand, gazing after her, she was only thinking about how she had negotiated her tasks, and earned a pleased nod from her employer.

'How was your first day, then, Harriott?' asked Mr Curteis, wiping his hands as he came into the kitchen. Harriott looked up from the fireplace, stretched, and grinned at him with her head on one side.

'Fair to middling,' she said, 'nothing disastrous at any rate. He is a punctilious man: he showed me the way he likes his correspondence opened and what to do with it once I have read it; how to detect letters that are of a private nature; there are several boxes of books he wants cataloguing and inserting into his library in alphabetical order; and he gave me a number of standard letters so I may reply on his behalf once he has told me what he has decided. I took dictation twice, and for the rest of the morning acquainted myself with the room, where everything is kept, and so on.'

'And how was he to you?'

'Everything correct, Father, you need have no concerns in that regard. He lives with his sister, another Harriott, who I only spoke to briefly when he introduced me during the morning. She may sometimes need me to do things for her, it seems. I also met his other servants, and they seem all quite happy with their positions. There is a cook and two maids, a footman and a groom. He has two gardeners coming in two days a week. You know one of them, don't you: Stephen Fuggle?'

'Yes, of course. Nice lad, knows what he wants in life. And how is he?'

'He seems well, I don't really know.'

'Oh. I see.'

'Anyway, I'm getting your dinner ready, we'll have to eat early as I'm due in the Bells at five.'

Mr Curteis looked at the fireplace. 'I read there's a new kind of cooking invention being made, called a range. It's made of cast iron, and it makes better use of fuel than a regular fire, and is less smoky. It has places for several pots, but I think it might be a bit big for our kitchen. Shall I find out a bit more about it? Would it help you?'

'Can we afford it? I mean, it sounds a good thing, but I can manage.'

'I'll see what I can find out. You're a good girl, Harriott, but you have a lot to do.' He turned to go back to the print shop. 'You know, that pamphlet about the press hasn't come yet, the post is terrible these days. I'll look out the newssheet where the range is advertised, see what you think.'

Harriott rushed into the tavern, threw off her bonnet and took her place behind the bar.

'Late, Harriott,' said Mr Paine. 'Not like you.'

'No, Mr Paine, I'm sorry, I was getting the dinner for my father, and the fire wouldn't draw. I'm not very late, am I?'

The landlord put his head out of the door. 'Only five minutes by the church clock, but it's been running slow for the last few days, I must have a word with Mr Milsted about it.'

'I'll make it up tomorrow, sir, may I?' She turned to serve a customer.

'That's my girl. But don't make a habit of it, now you're going up in the world.'

Harriott looked around at him. 'What do you mean?'

'That story of yours about changing your hours to fit in with your father better. Didn't believe it for a moment. I hear you're down at Morghew now. Not sure I hold with that sort of thing, but as long as it doesn't affect your work here, fair's fair.'

'Yes, Mr Paine.'

Once the flow of customers died down Harriott was able to speak with Mary. She was agog to hear the news, but mostly wanted to know about Mr Pomfret.

'So, come on, what is he like, I mean, really?'

'Well, he's well-dressed, of course, and quite particular, but he is most civil in manner. He is, well, of moderate height, and average build, but you know what he looks like. He's often away on business, that's partly why he needs a secretary. He has a lot of land, and other properties, and interests in a bank, and so on. But I'm not allowed to discuss anything in detail, he is very particular about that.'

'Do you like him?'

'He is perfectly polite, as I said.'

'No, I meant, do you find him attractive? He is unmarried, I know.'

'Mary! He's thirty-five! And a gentleman, not to mention my employer.'

'That hasn't stopped you before, remember Mr Elphick?'

Harriott winced. 'Don't; that was so embarrassing. Anyway, it was ages ago. But no, I don't find him attractive, for your information.'

Mary sighed, dreamily. 'I've seen him in church, he looks kind. As far as I can tell from up in the gallery, I mean. But . . . I wish there were more men around that I might like, you know. Do you know of any? And not that John Catt, from Boars Isle, before you say anything. He was in here yesterday with his friends, and I overheard him saying such horrible things about some poor girl he'd been chasing.'

'I thought you liked the look of him?'

'Well I did, but looks ain't everything, now.'

'Well see, I'll be in church this Sunday, I'll have a look around and see who might be a likely lad for you. Or rather, we can have a look together.'

'But won't you be in chapel?'

'Not for the time being. Mr Pomfret wants all his staff to greet him as he rolls up in his carriage, we have to stand on the path as he arrives, and I have to sit together with them. I don't mind, it's no big imposition.'

'But you're Wesleyan, aren't you? Are you allowed in church?'

''Course I am, anybody is. It's Father that's the convinced Methodist, remember; I'm quite happy with it but I can swing whichever way the wind blows. Makes my job that much easier to go along his ideas. Mind, I'll have to explain to Mr Knowles when I see him on Saturday, as to why I won't be at the service on Sunday.'

'I'll wait outside church to see you, then, Harriott. I'd like to watch the procession.'

'If you must.' She turned away to serve a customer. 'But there won't be much to see.'

*

Sunday was overcast and dull, but not cold. Harriott stood on the flagged path with the other servants, and waited. She was dressed in her red-striped best gown and her new wide-brimmed and beribboned straw bonnet, which looked like a Leghorn but wasn't, not that she could have afforded a Leghorn, of course. She could see Mary hovering a little way away among the gravestones, but she kept her eyes demurely downcast, however against her nature that might be.

A chariot drew up: but it was yellow and white and contained a lady with four middling-sized children. The cook whispered to Harriott that this was Widow Croughton, from Herenden, which she had already deduced. Then, two other light gigs deposited their mistresses, and the servants took the vehicles around to the yards of the Woolpack or the White Lion.

At last, Mr Pomfret and his sister arrived, dignified, nodding to those watching. The servants bowed or curtsied as they passed, drawing a smile from Miss Pomfret, and as soon as they had entered the church, the little group followed them in to secure their pew. Mary hurried after them, and waved to Harriott as she scurried across to the gallery stairs in the north aisle.

Mr Pomfret's sister of course sat in a pew close by the pulpit, but the servants were to sit in the south gallery, opposite where Mary and her parents were accustomed to sit. The box pews filling the nave were tall and made it hard to see who was in which, but from the vantage point of the gallery Harriott had a chance to inspect nearly all those attending divine service. But where was Mr Pomfret? Why was he not with his sister?

The organ fell silent, then began a new voluntary. Mr Temple processed in, preceded by the cross and the churchwardens with their staves, and the service began. Harriott realised at this point that of course, as well as being a magistrate, and Mayor, her employer was also churchwarden, together with Mr Milsted from the Woolpack. He had a wide influence, and plenty of power. If she could please him, she might find it a help in furthering her ambitions, wherever they might lead her.

Having come without a prayer book, she had to share the cook's, although her wide sleeves got rather in the way on the narrow bench. She told herself off for omitting this simple preparation: next week, she would be fully ready. At least she knew the hymns, for the most part, and the large clear windows made it easy to see the small print in Cook's missal. When the sermon came, she concentrated on comparing it with Mr Knowles' style (as amended by herself), and thought it a poor second best. The rest of the time she spent running her eye over every young man between eighteen and thirty, who did not appear to be accompanied by a wife. Some she knew, and others she did not, but it was a pleasant way to spend the time. George Bunn, seated on the opposite end of the bench from her, had a most satisfying profile, she thought.

As soon as the service ended, having conferred with Cook to check this was in order, she descended to the aisle and hurried across to Mary. The Pomfrets had left almost on the heels of Mr Temple, and were talking with him in the porch. She half-overheard something about ". . . your position when Mr Ward arrives . . ." but was focussed on finding her friend.

Leaning in close, she began, 'Seen anyone likely yourself?'

'No, I haven't. But my eyes aren't as good as yours, everything's a bit blurry more than twenty yards away.'

'Well, how about that chap there?' she indicated, discreetly. 'He's fine-looking, and well-turned-out.'

'No, that's Jed Mason, I know him, he's a bad boy. Rumour has it that he's the father of Jane Mills' bastard, but he's denying it.'

'There's Martin Fellowes, over there. He's harmless enough.'

'Possibly. I knew him when I worked at the circulating library for one summer, he delivered books and things. He might do . . . if there isn't anyone better.'

'I'll tell you what, you need to see if you can work in the bar, rather than the kitchen at the Bells, then you'd see more men.'

'No, I'm too shy. Anyway, they don't need me with you there.'

'I'm not doing so many hours, now, am I? You can but ask.'

'No I couldn't. Really I couldn't.'

'I can go with you, if you like, to speak to Mr Paine?'

'No, no; that'd be too embarrassing. I'll think of something.' She hesitated, and leaned closer. 'I didn't see him in church, but I did meet someone new, when I was on an errand to get beer for father from the Woolpack, he likes their porter. He was staying there, a Mr Cousins, he's from London. He seemed very attentive, but I don't know. London folk, they might be anyone.'

'Daniel Cousins?'

'I don't know his first name. He was tall, and had a quite long nose, and a very ill-judged waistcoat. Well, I thought it too gaudy anyway.'

Harriott scowled. 'I should stay clear of him; I went to the theatre with him and he was most improper. Keep away, if you take my advice.'

'Ooh, I will, thankyou.'

They left the church, dipping a small curtsey to the curate, and outside there was Stephen Fuggle.

'Good morning ladies,' he said, bowing exaggeratedly.

Mary, giggling, made a deep curtsey suitable for meeting an earl or marquis, at least. Harriott just inclined her head, and said, 'Wotcha, cully' in the manner of an urchin.

'I haven't seen you since Wednesday, Harriott. How did your job go?'

'Everything was done in the proper fashion to introduce me to the task,' she said, tucking a stray ringlet behind her ear, 'and I think I acquitted myself to Mr Pomfret's satisfaction, at least so far. But it's only been three days.'

'Glad to hear of it; not that I would have expected anything else. Do you have to deal with his sister?'

'I have been told so, but she has asked nothing of me so far.'

'I have the paper about that mowing machine I told you about.

Would you like to see it?' He pulled out a folded newssheet, and offered it to Harriott.

'Not just now, Stephen, I don't want to get print on my best gown.'

'Oh. I'm sorry. Well,' he said, brightening, 'how about I show you the new tree we planted in the churchyard this week? It's a holm oak, *Quercus ilex* is the proper name.'

'Quercus what?' asked Mary.

'*Quercus ilex*. I'm learning all the special Latin names for plants. Mr Ducksbury said if I want to get on, it'll help me. He can't be doing with them himself: he says the old names are fine, but I want to get to be in charge of a big estate some day.'

They walked a few steps along the path towards the Woolpack, and there it was, a small sapling, supported by stakes.

Mary reached out to feel one of the leaves. 'That's a Holly-oak,' she pronounced. 'Not what you said.'

'Well, there's the advantage of the Latin name, you see. Some call it holm-oak and some holly-oak, but there's always only one Latin name, so you can't mistake which plant is meant.'

'I'm impressed,' said Harriott.

'And I'm leaning about soil types too,' Stephen added, looking at the gravestones behind the sapling. 'The scientific gentlemen are finding out all sorts of things about why some plants do well in sand, or clay, or compost, and so on, and I want to know as much as I can about it all.'

'And about machinery too?'

'Yes, that's why I brought you the paper, I thought you might be interested.'

'Well, leave it at our house, and I'll have a look later.'

The following Saturday afternoon, Harriott was at the Exalls' next door, helping Mary and her mother who had become entangled in how to use a paper pattern.

'I was given it by Mrs Avery,' Mrs Exall explained, 'she got it from a periodical, but she didn't give me the instructions, and I'm all turned around. Perhaps it would be better just to try and do it the old way?'

'Let's not give up, Mrs Exall; I'm sure we can get everything in order. Now, first, can we clear the rest of the table so we can lay all the pieces out properly and see how they go?'

She and Mary did as she said, and all the flimsy bits of tissue were eventually set down. Set down, that is, until Mr Exall came into the room, bringing a draught with him, and sending them all over the floor.

When order was again restored, Harriott stood back and surveyed the pieces. She looked over them, seeing if there were instructions printed on the papers. She moved them around for a while and then pronounced.

'I think the problem is, that you are missing several parts. We need . . . oh, now I see, there is one piece of paper, but you are supposed to make two pieces of fabric from this one . . . and four from this . . . and I think, six from that one, for the skirt, it is to be made with them sewn along the long side, to create the shape, the fulness at the hips, if you see what I mean.'

'I see now,' put in Mary, 'and that little bit I thought was waste, must be the collar part, do you think?'

Harriott inspected it. 'I believe you are right,' she opined, 'but it is most damaged. I think it would be better to trace it on some more paper and use that, or else you'll have a crooked neckline.'

'Oh, now I understand,' said Mrs Exall, 'I thought this was the whole gown. And I believe I shall trace out these other torn pieces onto new papers too: at least that is something we don't lack in this house.'

They set to work, tracing, pinning, and cutting. As the girls sat back to sew seams, they were at last able to talk.

'Did you manage to talk to Martin Fellowes?' Harriott asked. 'Oh bother, my thread's snapped.' She reached out for the scissors.

'Yes, but he's seeing a girl from Leigh Green, so there's no prospect there. Besides, he's a bit rough for my liking.'

'And did you speak to Mr Paine? You told me on Thursday you'd do it yesterday.'

Mary went red. 'No, I couldn't. I . . . he'd look at me in that way he has, and say something rude.'

'Hmm, well then. What shall we do with you?'

'I shall die an old maid, I expect. At least I have my cat, she loves me.'

The cat, whose appearance had triggered this sentiment, rubbed itself against Mary's legs and departed, presumably to look for mice, or some other inscrutable cat errand.

'Did you make that red striped gown of yours from a pattern? You seem to know all about them? It's very splendid, and so fashionable.'

'No, I had it made for me by Mrs Relph, down past Brewhouse-lane. I know, I know, but I can't be bothered with all that sewing, and I haven't a mother to nag me to do it like you do. Look, I can't even get this simple seam straight, I hope it won't show too much.'

'I wish I could afford to do that too. Still, sewing is one thing I'm good at. And I suppose I can cook, too.' She sighed.

'You'll find some lovely man, don't you worry. You have a heart of gold, Mary, and you're a good friend.'

'Well, maybe.' Mary concentrated on her seam for a few minutes, and then, looking up, said, 'Have you seen that new newssheet that's appeared all over town? "Dear Tenterden", by Lady Susan?'

'Yes, but I haven't taken much notice of it, it's all gossip.'

'I know, but what did you think of that piece about the butcher?'

'I didn't read it properly: what did it say?'

'Well, you should. It didn't mention names, but I think it must be Mr Simons they're talking about, he had such a row with his wife, the whole alley heard it, the other week. Or so Mrs Collins told Mother, when I was helping her bake.'

'I'm not too keen on hearing gossip, that sort of thing. Well, really, I can't be bothered with other people's business, I suppose.

'Oh.' Mary deflated, and went back to her needle. Sighing, she finished off a seam, and looked over at Harriott unpicking a piece she'd somehow pulled too tight.

'Did you ever look at that mowing machine paper Stephen left for you?'

'No, I forgot all about it.'

'You ought to, you know. He'll be upset if you don't.'

'Very well, I'll look this evening. Can you pass the white twist?'

Harriott set off down the High-street to collate Mr Knowles' sermon, once she had made dinner for her father and herself, but was intercepted outside the chapel by Stephen.

'Oh, hello, Harriott, you going to see the minister?'

'Of course, Saturday evening, as always. Where are you going yourself?'

'To have a look at a book Mr Assiter has on soil types. He lives up there: Mr Ducksbury told me about it, but says he doesn't want to let it out of his sight, so I'm to read it at his house.'

'Well have fun.'

'Harriott, are you . . . will you be in church tomorrow?'

'Yes, with all Mr Pomfret's staff, like last week.'

'Oh. Good. Well, I'll see you then.'

CHAPTER 3

THE FINAL CUT

'YOU THINKING OF GOING TO the theatre this Friday? They have a new play on, it's a melodrama called "Black-eyed Susan", by a Mr Jerrold. It's just finished a run in London, at Drury-lane, and it's the first time it has been performed here. It'll make a change from the usual round of plays.' Harriott lolled against the kitchen door in a lull in serving at the bar.

'No: who are you going with?' Mary banged the pans as she scrubbed at them.

'Oh, you don't know him.'

'Tell me.'

'Well, . . . it's the footman at Morghew, he's called George Bunn, I finally persuaded him. He has the most gorgeous rump. I'm not sure about his brains, mind, but we'll see.'

'Won't you get into trouble, being seen out with Mr Pomfret's staff?'

'He's away tomorrow, until Saturday afternoon, on business. And it's George's half-day.'

'What about the dance this evening?'

'Is there one? I hadn't seen the notice.'

'Yes, at the theatre. It's an Aid dance, for the family of that man who was killed on the farm out at Broad Tenterden last month. You know, the one who fell under the haycart wheels?'

'No, I'm not. Anyway, I'm working.'

'Of course you are.' She turned away from the sink, picked up the bucket and paused on her way out to draw water. 'I wish I had someone to take me to the theatre.'

'What about Stephen Fuggle? He wouldn't mind, I shouldn't think.'

'No, I meant, someone to go with, properly, just for me.'

'Hmm. I'll have another think, but it's hard to please you. You might like this play, though, it's about a sailor, and his horrible captain.'

'Ooh, I do like a sailor, all those stories of foreign places. Remember that man who came up from Rye, and used to get drinks bought for him on the strength of his tales?'

'I do. Made out he had been a pirate, didn't he?'

'That's him. Well, I could go on my own, I suppose . . . or with Mother?'

'You'll think of someone.'

Harriott, flushed with the success of completing the first two weeks in her new post and being pronounced satisfactory by Mr Pomfret, decided to watch the play from the gallery, rather than the pit as she would normally have done. Tickets were admittedly cheaper up there, but she felt George might like the view better, and she fancied a change. George was impressed, it seemed he hadn't been to theatres much if at all back in Lowestoft. Having met by the Black Horse, it being the nearest landmark to Morghew, for someone as yet unfamiliar with the town, they had walked up the High-street, with Harriott regaling him with snippets of local history. He had said little, and nodded a lot.

They arrived early, and took their places, having first scanned the pit and the boxes opposite to see who was there. Harriott, even at this early juncture, began to regret her judgement in inviting George, as he seemed lacking in conversation. However, it was perhaps only that he was overawed by the unfamiliar, as when she enquired after how things were in Lowestoft, he became suddenly communicative, and she learnt a lot more about the intricacies of sea fishing and the ways eels could be caught in the rivers than she perhaps anticipated.

She felt mildly guilty for Mary having been left out of the amusement, but after a few minutes saw her entering the pit with Stephen Fuggle, and sitting on the very front bench on the far side. It was quite a novelty, being up high: Stephen looked about the same height as little Mary from here. Although to be fair, he was three or four inches bigger in reality, which was hardly taller than herself.

And over there behind them in the stage-side box was a party of what looked like the Haffenden family, from Homewood, who must be on one of their rare visits to the town. She nudged George, and then pointed out two other families with whom she was slightly acquainted. George's round face seemed full of admiration for the whole ambience of the place, the profusion of candles, and the buzz of expectation in the audience. And then some family friends came by behind them and she had to introduce George to them, without of course mentioning who he was, just in case.

The imminent commencement of the play was announced by the lighting of extra candles on the stage, and the extinguishing of others in the auditorium. The pitch of the hum of conversation rose, but gave no signs of quietening. Then, the door below them flew open and the actors entered with a flourish.

"Tut! If you are inclined to preach, here is a milestone. I'll leave you in its company." And they were off, Mr Doggrass and Mr Gnatbrain, sparring away. The set was rather plain, just a chest on one side and a few upright chairs around the back. The scenery flats seemed to indicate the inside of a cottage, and with a little imagination, the two men could be thought to be arguing outside it.

Then, the sound of doleful singing, and the entrance of the heroine, lamenting the absence of her husband and then weeping at the news she was to be turned out of her cottage. George was entranced, but Harriott had yet to be caught up in the emotion of the piece, and continued to try and see who else she might know in the place. Was that Daniel Cousins over in the opposite gallery? He hadn't been there when the play started, she thought, and who was with him? It was hard to tell in the dim light, and the shadows cast by the bright stage.

The action swirled back and forth across the stage. Pleading, iron intransigence, threat of destitution: all the stock characteristics of melodrama were there, with the nautical theme yet to become apparent. And then, Mr Doggrass strode across the stage, threw open the chest to see if there were any possessions he might distrain, and fell back in horror.

This was no acting, however. From her elevated vantage, she could see the chest contained not some few keepsakes of great sentimental value, but a white-faced woman in a diaphanous gown. Mr Doggrass' reaction made it clear at least to Harriott, that this was not in the script, and that the person in the chest, whomever she may be, was not going to play any part in the drama.

The actor playing Doggrass fell in a heap, clutching his chest. There was a second's silence, then a woman in the audience shrieked. Harriott heard gasps from those in the gallery near her, from where people could see the contents of the chest, and murmurs of puzzlement from those in the pit. Old Dr Bishop clambered stiffly over the sill of his box to attend to the fallen actor; others began to climb out of the pit onto the stage, to see whatever had caused the calamity, and the hubbub rose in volume with every second.

Harriott, consumed with curiosity as to who it was in the chest, tried to get to the stairs but was thwarted by the press of people trying to do the same, blocked by a tide of others trying to ascend to get a better view. She returned to George's side, and attempted to contain her frustration, while tutting at all the people now crowding around the corpse who blocked her view.

'What is the commotion?' George asked. 'Why has the play stopped?'

'Didn't you see? The body in the chest? The dead body?'

'Dead, did you say? I thought that must be someone who was to take a part in the scene. And what has happened to Mr . . . that actor on the ground?'

'I imagine, George, he has had such a shock he has had a heart-attack. That is Dr Bishop is with him: he is a surgeon from down near West Cross.'

She then noticed Mary, sitting alone on her bench, shoulders hunched, and shaking somewhat. At length she managed to make out in the press, the back of Stephen's head as he bent over the chest, arms outstretched, trying to keep others from touching the body.

For several minutes chaos reigned. Eventually the theatre manager came to the front of the stage with a bell, and, ringing it as violently as he could, was at length able to make an announcement.

'Would all our valued customers please leave the premises immediately. As you will be aware, there has been an unfortunate occurrence, and the performance will not be able to continue as scheduled. Rest assured that your tickets will be honoured for the very next performance of "Black-eyed Susan", as and when that might be possible. We thank you as always for your patronage.'

This statement had little immediate effect, although some of the ladies in the boxes gathered up their belongings and disappeared through the curtains to the corridors behind. A number of men, some in theatrical costume, tried to shepherd onlookers off the stage, with difficulty. Stephen held to his post, explaining by gesture to one dressed in nautical garb what he was doing to protect the body; and in a few minutes the stage was clear but for three or four men bending over Mr Doggrass, and Stephen by the chest, which, after rubbing his nose in thought, he closed, carefully and reverently.

Harriott and George descended the spiral stairs with reluctance, and only once all the other theatre-goers had left the gallery. In the hallway, Harriott turned toward the pit. George attempted to detain her, saying, 'Hadn't we better go? The man said to leave immediately,' but she wriggled past the last few stragglers and made her way to the stage edge, and Stephen, still on guard.

'Who is it?' she called up.

'Don't know,' he told her, 'but I reckon Mr Doggrass there knows her, the way he reacted.'

'What do you think killed her?'

'Can't see, but there's a smell of blood. That's partly why I closed the lid.'

'What can we do?'

'Nothing for now; they'll be calling the parish constable, I expect. Not that he'll do much except tell them to take the body to the mortuary, and then, I don't know.'

'How's Mr Doggrass?'

'Can you go over and look? I ought to stay here by the chest.'

Harriott made her way to the other side of the stage, and saw that the actor was sitting up, looking flushed. As she watched, the others helped him to his feet, and the little party left by one of the rear doors, through which "Susan" had entered only a few minutes before.

The manager reappeared and told Stephen to leave, indicating Harriott should do the same. Stephen hopped down into the pit and together they made their way out, down the corridor into Honey-lane, and looked around.

The lane was swarming with people and raucous with chatter, but after a little while they saw Mary, who seemed to have made acquaintance with George Bunn, standing by a cottage opposite, and pushed their way over to her.

'What happened?' she asked, 'is everything all right?'

'Not really. Well, the actor who collapsed seems fine, but the other . . . the lady in the chest, obviously, not so.'

'Is she really dead then? Mr Bunn said she was.'

'Please call me George,' he put in, 'and yes, Harriott told me she was.'

'Very much so,' said Stephen, but that's about all I know. She was dressed in an unusual costume for a lady, all thin white muslin, quite out of the fashion. Not that I'm an expert,' he added, hurriedly.

'It's odd coming out of the theatre in daylight, isn't it,' said Harriott inconsequentially. 'It's just struck me.'

'Why don't we go and sit in the Bells and have a little refreshment, settle down?' said Stephen, 'it'll be easier to talk there.'

The Eight Bells however was heaving, so the four of them decamped to the Harris Arms, and sat over glasses of porter. They talked and speculated and guessed, but to no end. George said he didn't really want to know much about it, it sounded horrible, and Mary was yet more nervous, but Stephen and Harriott came up with wild suggestions as to whom the lady might be. For example, an heiress, fleeing from an unwanted marriage to an old and fat minor nobleman; or a theatrical spy, out to learn the company's secrets; or an unhappy girl driven to suicide. Although as Mary pointed out, it would be most odd to make away with oneself in a chest on a stage.

At length, they had exhausted their imaginations and departed the alehouse. Mary told Harriott she didn't feel safe out, if there was a murderer about, and would she come home with her. Stephen said they'd all walk on with her, and he'd continue with George, as his house was on the way to Morghew, while looking as if he would rather another arrangement. However, that was the result: the four went together as far as the adjacent printers' houses, where the two men left the girls outside their doors and headed down the High-street.

On Sunday at church there was talk of little else. Harriott heard so many rumours that she decided not to believe them in the main. However, one recurring theme was that the woman was a member of the theatre company, but nobody knew who, as the company had departed to give a performance in Hastings the following night. This identification seemed entirely possible, given the reaction of the actor.

As for the church service, she could not have said anything about it afterwards, except that Mr Temple preached on the plagues of

Egypt, which she thought scarcely relevant to the news of the day, but charitably decided he had probably prepared his address some days previously. She had wanted to ask Mary what she thought, but she seemed to have disappeared. Stephen was there, of course, but she hurried away without speaking to him, as she wanted to get on with her household chores. She thought she heard him calling after her, but pretended not to hear.

On Monday Harriott arrived at Morghew and began her usual work. Mr Pomfret entered his library about noon, and after going through the routine work, told her that once he had been informed of the fatality at the theatre on his return on Saturday evening, he had notified the coroner, who had arranged an inquest. Hence she would be required to accompany him in his capacity of magistrate, to the Town Hall at 10am on Wednesday, to make a record of the proceedings, separate from the official one. He said she should meet him there half an hour beforehand, and if proceedings ended as expected quite quickly, return with him to Morghew to make up her hours. Remembering that she would not be at the great house again until after the inquest, she gathered up her pen and ink, collected some paper, and took it home with her.

On Tuesday, Stephen called after work to see if she had finished with his paper about the mowing machine, and she handed it to him, saying she had not had a chance to look at it, which was only a mild untruth. He then asked about the death, and she was unable to give him any more details other than that she was attending the inquest with her employer. He said he would love to be there, but he had to work. Also, he imagined, the town hall would be full to bursting with the curious public. He left, taking his paper, and she caught him looking back at her after a few steps down the road with an unreadable expression on his face.

*

On Wednesday she filled the time until half past nine in doing household jobs she had been putting off for days, though she kept being distracted by thoughts of what she would likely see and hear later. After changing her gown, she made sure she arrived at the town hall in good time, and waited outside for Mr Pomfret's carriage to arrive. She followed him in and settled herself at his elbow in the court room. However, he left his place almost immediately and began to converse with various official persons as they entered: she recognised the theatre manager, and later Dr Bishop, but many of them were unfamiliar to her. When he returned to his seat she asked Mr Pomfret to identify each person as they spoke, so she could record what they said correctly, although this proved unnecessary as the coroner took details of name and occupation before hearing evidence.

The coroner was a man from Maidstone called Mr Ludlow. He arrived late due to some problem with his carriage, and seemed flustered and hurried. The twelve jurors were sworn in, although a replacement had to be found at short notice because one refused to swear on the Bible, saying he was a Quaker, which delayed things further, and seemed to annoy Mr Ludlow unduly.

The first witness called was the theatre manager, a Mr Brooke, who identified the deceased as one Philadelphia Burton, who lodged in Golden Square and had performed comic songs for the company as well as taking minor roles in a number of their plays, especially the farces. Then, Dr Bishop gave evidence that the deceased perished from a single stab wound to the rear of the left chest which would have penetrated the heart. He had not performed an autopsy, as such had not been authorised or funded. He had not been asked to examine the body until the Saturday afternoon, and when he saw it at about 3pm there was no evidence of rigidity. The body at that time was still in the chest, and there was a great amount of blood soaking the cloths therein and slightly staining the rather decrepit bottom of the chest. He had extracted the deceased, removed all clothing, and made a superficial examination. No, such a wound could not have been self-inflicted, unless Miss Burton was a contortionist in addition to her other talents.

No, he could not give an accurate time of death. In view of the fact that there was no rigidity, and twenty hours had passed since the body's discovery when he saw it, death was likely to have occurred, say, before 11am on the Friday, but it could have been at any time before that. As no post-mortem examination had been performed, it was hard to say how much before, but perhaps a maximum of three days? Now was too late to perform such an examination as the internal, particularly abdominal, organs would have liquefied, the weather being so warm, and in any case the cause of death was only too apparent.

Next, Mrs Robberds, part of the company, explained that Miss Burton was from Northumberland, had no known relatives, and certainly none in this county; that she had come to Tenterden after an unsuccessful period trying her luck in theatres in the United States of America, and that she had no reason to think why anyone would wish to harm the poor young darling (*verbatim*). She had no savings, or other valuable assets, as far as she knew, and often had to supplement her income by other work (*sensation in court*). This response seemed to fluster her, but she clarified, by saying poor Philly used to do sewing for the company, and help in the kitchen of the Plough Inn which was near her lodgings.

The coroner then seemed to remember something, and recalled Dr Bishop to ask him whether the weapon was still in the wound when he examined the body. It was not, he said, which accounted for the great effusion of blood. The wound was about one inch in breadth. The caretaker of the theatre, a Mr Elias Carpenter, gave evidence that no dagger or sharp knife or similar implement had been found in a search of the theatre that had been made, and that all the knives and swords used in dramatic productions were wooden and incapable of causing such an injury.

Several other persons were called, who gave varying accounts of the character of the deceased. The only feature on which they agreed was that she was a quiet and gentle person, except when performing songs, when she could generate a splendid volume, and produce the most overwhelming emotional effect, so out of keeping with her normal self. Her landlady Mrs Tamkin said she paid her rent on time and was never any trouble. She was not accustomed to having gentleman callers, and she knew of nothing to her disadvantage. She had not seen her since the Wednesday morning, as Miss Burton had her own key and Mrs Tamkin was a heavy sleeper who retired early.

No suggestions were made even under rather leading questioning from the coroner as to anyone who might be suspected of eventuating the death (*verbatim*), and indeed it seemed that the theatre had been constantly visited by all manner of people, on the day of the calamity as well as the one before it was discovered. For example, the chandler had delivered a quantity of candles; Mr Wickens from the brewery had delivered a firkin of his best beer for the refreshment of the cast; more than one seamstress had brought costumes that needed attention, there had been people painting scenery, and so on.

It seemed likely that the body must have been placed into the chest after 10pm on the Wednesday night, when the Aid dance was concluded; and probably some time after around 6pm on Thursday when the stage was first set for the Friday performance. No, the chest had not been opened in the dress rehearsal on Friday, as the cast needed to hurry through the play in order to practise the minor feature scheduled for the end of the evening, after the songs, which had been sadly neglected previously.

The coroner summed up briefly. The jury were taken to see the body, and returned with expressions consistent with the deterioration of the corpse likely in the warm weather. They duly took no time at all to return a verdict of murder by person or persons unknown.

CHAPTER 4

WE CAN WORK IT OUT

'SO, TELL ME ALL ABOUT the inquest.' Stephen Fuggle, still in his working clothes, sat on the bench in the Curteis' kitchen and looked eagerly at Harriott. Her father busied himself with the fire but was clearly listening carefully.

'It was all quite, I don't know how to say it; cold, really. I mean, not the people giving evidence, the ones that knew the lady, but the whole process. Mechanical, I mean, like one of those machines you keep telling me about.' She shuddered.

'Who was she?'

'Philadelphia Burton was her name. She sings, sang I mean, at the theatre. I must have seen her sing when I went there some time, but I don't . . . but you know, I think I might have met her, once.'

'Met her?'

'Not at the theatre, but somewhere. I mean, I didn't have to view the body, thank goodness, like the jury, but the name . . . it's quite unusual. And she was from Northumberland, so she'd have a different accent from folk round here.'

'It'll come to you, Harriott. Let it surface, you'll remember.'

'And, well, they couldn't say when she died, or when she was put in the chest, but now I think about it, it must have been the evening before the play, or perhaps during the night. Because, on the Wednesday there was that dance, so the pit would have been floored over, and they'd have taken all the boards up on Thursday, and then set out the stage.'

'Could she have been in the chest before, though?'

'I don't think so. They said the chest had a quite weak bottom, so unless the murderer had several others helping, to hold it underneath, he wouldn't have been able to move it onto the stage from wherever they keep it normally, not with the weight of a body inside.'

'That sounds sensible to me. You don't want to kill someone with lots of witnesses watching you.'

'No. No. I mean, I don't want to kill anybody, except sometimes that David Godden, when he's in the Bells drunk, and even then not really. But you're right, they could tell on you, or blackmail you.'

'How did she die?'

'She was stabbed from behind in the chest.' She shuddered again.

'What with?'

'Some sort of dagger or knife, they didn't find it anywhere in the theatre. So perhaps the murderer has it still.'

'Or he's got rid of it somewhere.'

'Yes. The whole business was quite horrible, actually, and I had to just sit there and take notes for Mr Pomfret. To be fair, he asked me afterwards if I felt alright, which was kind. I was a bit surprised at that, really.'

'So what happens next?'

'I'm not sure. I don't think . . . well, they didn't say anything about what anyone does now. They said it was murder, which anyone could see, but then . . . well, that was it.'

'Will they look for the murderer?'

'I don't know. I mean, she wasn't anybody, was she, and she has no family, or close friends; well, she might have some in the acting company, troupe, whatever they call themselves, but nobody to press for justice.'

'I see.'

'Let's see. They might get someone to . . . but there isn't anybody really. Not like in London where they've got the Bow Street Runners, and thief-takers and suchlike.'

'Didn't I read that they set up a new police force in London, just last year?'

'Did they? I must have missed that.'

'Yes, I'm trying to remember, they have proper constables, not like old Hugo, who's so lame he couldn't catch more than a cold.'

Harriott shook herself. 'I need to forget about all that for now. You can read my notes if you want to know any more. I have to write them up for Mr Pomfret later, because he said to go home and finish it up when I felt better, rather than come with him back to Morghew. Now, I need to eat something. I felt too sick at lunchtime.'

'I've got broth on the fire, Harriott,' put in Mr Curteis. 'Shall I put some in a bowl for you?'

On Friday Stephen caught Harriott as she arrived at Morghew. She stopped, reluctantly, as she was only just on time for her work.

'Any news of the murder?' he asked.

'Nothing, I'll let you know as soon as I hear, if I hear.'

In the library, she set down her parcel of notes, and laid out the fair copy ready for Mr Pomfret. She collected the post from the footman George, and began to open it. Laying the letters on the table she opened them carefully, easing up the seals with her penknife as instructed. Then, she read through each, and set them in piles according to type, and started to write out covering letters for the bills which Mr Pomfret would pay by cheque. She then entered the meetings to which he had been invited into his diary in pencil, awaiting his decision about whether he would attend. She had not realised before she took this job, just how much he was involved in so many enterprises.

Her master came in about eleven o'clock, and dealt with the correspondence most rapidly, without even reading some of the letters. She smiled internally, knowing this meant he already trusted her to respond appropriately to each one, since he had relied on her summary of the contents. Then, she handed him the two missives that had seemed to her likely to be private, and the notes of the inquest, and as he turned to go, asked him in her sweetest voice,

'Sir, have you any further news about the murder? I just wondered . . . will anyone be able to investigate it, and look for the murderer?'

'Hmm. I should not think so, Miss Curteis. In such a place as this, who might perform the task? There were no persons suspected, that anyone put forward at the inquest, now were there? And she has no family to press for justice.'

'No, sir.'

'And although the Metropolitan Police is now a reality, the long arm of the Law does not stretch out of London as far as little Tenterden, does it?'

'No, sir, I do not suppose it would.'

'So, I imagine the poor woman will remain unavenged. But in a few years, I would expect we will have police even out here in the countryside. Maybe ten years, maybe twenty, but eventually. And a good thing too. Too many cases of drunkenness and fighting and all sorts of evil behaviour come before my court as it is. Good morning to you, and well done.'

Knowing Stephen was so interested in the death, she decided to take a moment after work to seek him out. He was again in the glass-house, and she quickly told him what Mr Pomfret had said, before scuttling off in case she ought not to be seen hobnobbing with the outside servants. He asked her if she had remembered where she had seen Miss Burton before, and she had to admit she had not.

She cudgelled her brains that evening at work, but to no avail. It was not until she arrived at Mr Knowles' house the next day after dinner, that any light was thrown on the matter.

'Come in, come in, Miss Curteis,' the minister greeted her. 'And are you well? I saw you at that dreadful inquest on Wednesday: I felt it essential to attend, although the whole matter turned my stomach.'

'Why so, sir, if it was distasteful to you?'

'The poor lady, Miss Burton, you know. A member of my flock.'

'Your flock . . . you mean, she attended the chapel?'

'Yes indeed. A recent arrival, but sincere. And most helpful in small matters of service. She had offered . . . no matter, now she is dead, I should not speak.'

Harriott paused at the door of his study. His maid stood waiting patiently: her job was to be busy with housework in the hall while she was there, so as to act as chaperone, the study door remaining open.

'So . . . I might have met her? How long had she attended the chapel?'

'Only a matter of two months or so, I should say.'

'And could you describe her? I did not view the, er, the remains.'

'No, indeed, of course not. Well, she was a small woman, not as much as five feet tall: I believe she had had a very hard childhood, with little food on the table. She had a fine head of dark hair, and a rather blocky build, if one may use such a term of a lady. I am told that was why she had such a resonant voice, it is to do with the volume of the lungs.'

'And a strong accent?'

'Well, sometimes. When she spoke normally, it was quite a usual kind of voice, perhaps a little echo of the North in her vowels. But when asked to use her childhood tones, she was almost incomprehensible, I felt, though I did not say anything, naturally.'

'I think . . . yes, I believe I spoke to her once, only briefly, after a service. But I cannot recall her face for now. No matter, Mr Knowles, no matter. But it is all very sad.'

'Most sad, and most outrageous, that this could happen in our town. I cannot but think it will be to do with the amount of strong drink that is consumed by the men, and the unwholesome atmosphere around the area of the theatre, and the sinful behaviour that goes on there. And the new Beerhouse Act will only encourage this, by the abolition of the duty on the drink, and the great profusion of breweries that will no doubt spring up.'

'And now that dreadful newssheet, Dear Tenterden, is spreading salacious rumours about the poor woman's morals, and speculating as to which upright gentleman of this town might be responsible for her death. My servant showed me the piece, she felt quite rightly that I ought to know about it. I of course had not taken any notice of it before. Utterly unfounded accusations, I am convinced. The woman was an abstainer, and most moral, I am sure. Such publications are most unhelpful to all of us.'

'Yes, sir. But, well, we cannot be responsible for what others may do, can we?'

'No, that is true.'

'So, sadly these things have happened, but we must continue with life. Have you your sermon notes ready for me?'

Stephen approached Mary and Harriott as they stood talking after church the next day, and waited patiently until they had finished their conversation about the completion of the gown they had started two weeks earlier. There were difficulties, occasioned by the imperfect state of some of the paper pieces and the lack of instructions, which needed resolving, and Harriott, though far less able with a needle than Mary, had more ideas about the management of recalcitrant templates.

When the topic had been exhausted, she turned to him. 'So, Stephen, what can we do for you?'

'I've been thinking.'

'Really? Is your head sore?'

'No, don't fool with me, I've been thinking about this poor Miss Burton.'

Harriott sobered, and nodded her head. 'I too. I discovered she was a member of the Wesleyan chapel, and I had met her briefly once, it seems.'

'Yes, well, you know she is said to have no family?'

'I do. It was in those notes I made.'

'So, nobody to press her case, to find out who did the wicked act? She can't do it herself, of course.'

'Quite. I told you Mr Pomfret said there would likely be no discovery of the murderer, in the absence of a police force.'

'Well, why couldn't we look into the matter? I mean, I know we don't know much about that sort of thing, but you are very good at organising information, and writing things clearly; and I . . . well, I just want to do something about it. she looked so . . . sad, in that chest, all pale and defeated.'

'But how could we?' put in Mary. 'We can't go around asking everybody questions.'

'Well, I think we could,' said Stephen, his eyes gleaming, 'I think anyone would be glad someone was doing something. Well, not the murderer, obviously, but others.'

'I'd be too shy,' she said.

'I bet Harriott wouldn't.'

Harriott put her head on one side, and thought. 'Could we? I haven't any . . . actually, I don't see why we couldn't, you know. It makes it more real, somehow, having met the poor woman once. I would like to . . . Mr Knowles said he felt quite responsible, even though he knew he couldn't have stopped it.'

'Excellent,' said Stephen. 'When shall we start?'

Harriott considered. 'I have to get lunch for Father, but that isn't for an hour or so. The first thing to do, I think, is to put down on paper everything we know, and work out what we need to find out. That's what I'd do, anyway.'

'That's what these scientific folk do when they are deciding what to plant where,' Stephen agreed. 'They survey the land, and test it; and then work out how they could improve it, or what would suit it as it is.'

Harriott began to like the idea more and more. 'Well, no time like the present. Shall we go and get some paper, and start now?'

*

'So, then, what do we know?' began Harriott, settling herself at the big table in the printshop.

'Let's start with all we know about the poor woman,' suggested Stephen.

'Very well. Item: Philadelphia Burton, age not known, from Northumberland, lately in America, in Tenterden about two months . . .'

'We don't know that, it was just about two months at the chapel that Mr Knowles said, wasn't it?' objected Stephen.

'Very well, at least two months; lived in Golden Square; singer and sometime actress, height five feet or less, stocky build, mass of dark hair. Anything else?'

Neither of the others could think of anything, so they progressed to more items: murder method, which was straightforward; then time of murder, which was undetermined; then place of murder, that's the theatre of course. Lastly, why should she have been killed, which had to be left blank.

'There are a lot of gaps,' said Mary.

'Of course, there are bound to be,' said Stephen, 'we haven't begun to find out anything yet. But we could put in some things for the time of the murder. Like, well, it must have been after the dance on the Wednesday, mustn't it? And before, well, before they started rehearsing on the Friday?'

'That's something,' admitted Mary.

Harriott wiped her quill. 'Next, we need to have a list of what we don't know at all.' She fiddled with her pen. 'This quill is breaking up: I wish Father would change to steel nibs, like Mr Pomfret.' She selected a new one.

'Well, we don't know who did it,' suggested Mary.

'Item: list of suspected persons.'

'Nor why.'

'Item: the reason for the murder. No, we had that earlier. What's a better word for reason?'

'Motive?' suggested Stephen.

'Good.' She scratched out the line, and rewrote the word above. Then crossed through the first version above. 'I'll rewrite this tidily when we have finished.'

'I don't know how anybody could kill someone,' said Mary. 'It's just not . . . well, right.'

'Indeed,' said Harriott, with a grin. 'Not at all a nice thing to do. But think, even if you wouldn't do it, why might you wish you could?'

'No, I couldn't even think it.'

Stephen guffawed. 'I could. How about, anger?'

'That'd be on the spur of the moment, then?'

'Yes, but then a theatre isn't a very sensible place to choose on purpose, is it?'

Harriott inscribed, Anger; and then waited, pen poised.

'That man who died last week, I think it was in London, wasn't it, I saw it in the newspaper, I think, he was killed over a lady, wasn't he?' said Mary, hesitantly.

'Jealousy,' said Harriott.

'Or Love?' Stephen suggested.

'Lust. One of the deadly sins,' agreed Harriott.

'I know those.' Mary counted off on her fingers. 'Pride, greed, wrath, envy, lust, gluttony and sloth.'

'Very well. We have Lust and Wrath: how about Greed? People are killed to take their money.'

'But she didn't have any,' Mary objected.

'She might have been an heiress, you know,' said Harriott. 'We can find out about that. I'll put it down for now; greed for what? Money?'

'Yes,' said Stephen. 'And you can have Pride: she might have inadvertently seen through some pompous person or embarrassed them in some way.'

'Or she could have seen someone doing wrong, and been killed to keep her silent. I read about that in a novel, I forget which one,' said Mary, with a shiver.

Harriott counted through the seven sins again. 'I think gluttony and sloth aren't really reasons, are they? Not to kill, at least.'

'Unless someone stole your share of dinner,' said Stephen with a grin.

'Stephen!' said Mary. 'We shouldn't joke about it.'

After a few more minutes' discussion, they had no more ideas, and moved on to what to do next. Harriott said she would visit Miss Burton's lodgings, and talk to her landlady about what sort of woman she was, because she thought she wouldn't have said all she knew in the court. Stephen said he would see Dr Bishop, and ask if he could say any more about the weapon used, or be more precise about the time of death.

'My father once had to consult him, so he'll know me,' he said. 'And he lives quite close by our house.'

'What about you, Mary?' said Harriott. 'What would you like to do?'

'I don't know. Somebody needs to talk to the people at the theatre, but I couldn't dare.'

'Why don't you come with me to start with? After lunch, we could go up to Golden Square and talk to Mrs Whatsername, the landlady, it's on my notes.'

'Yes, please. And we could see if anyone else around there knew her well.'

'Right. After lunch then. And Stephen?'

'I'll go around tea time, after I've done my chores at home. These doctors like to sit down to tea don't they? They eat dinner late and they get hungry.'

'And we can meet up this evening, say, at seven. Here?'

'Good.'

CHAPTER 5

TOO MUCH INFORMATION

MRS TAMKIN WAS AT HOME, and most ready to talk about her poor lady. She invited them into the tiny front room, sat them down, and wanted to fetch refreshment, but Harriott and Mary politely declined, saying they had just eaten. The furnishings were threadbare, but the lady seemed quite respectable.

'Such a good lodger, she was,' she expostulated. 'Never a moment of trouble, even with her late nights at the theatre. I gave her a key within the week, once I saw how reliable she was. I suffer with my rheumatism, see, and I goes to bed real early, with a draught.'

'How long was she with you?' asked Harriott.

'She came in Whit week, that she did, I recall, on the Monday.'

'And do you know where she came from?'

'No, she never said, she just arrived, I think someone at the theatre sent her, knowing as I kept a clean house.'

'Was she someone who had a lot of friends?' asked Mary, feeling she ought to contribute.

'Not as I saw, Miss, but then she might have had them and not brought 'em here, if you see, it being quite restrictive for space, as you can see.'

'And, I think they said, she worked at the Plough as well?' Harriott, consulting her notes.

'That's right. Though I never seen her tipsy, and her language was always proper. Some of the men over the road come out blaspheming and cussing fit to be struck down where they stand, sometimes.'

'Did she leave much in the way of possessions behind?' put in Mary.

'Not more'n the suitcase of clothes she came with, that's God's truth, poor mite. The men came from the theatre to see if she had any of their things, not that I trusted 'em, and I kept a close eye on them looking through the little dresser in her room, but they didn't take nothing. And before you ask, there was no money neither, the man from the cor. . . what's his name?'

'Coroner,' supplied Harriott.

'Him, anyway, he came to see. She hadn't a penny, except maybe if she had anythink in her pocket, but they'd have had that already, natural.'

'No possessions but clothing, then?'

'Only her Testament, and I've kep' that, hope it wasn't wrong, to remember her by.'

'May we see it?'

'Certainly. Not as I can read, mind, but it has some pictures, and I like to hold it, you know. And Mrs Elsom next door sometimes will read me a bit, for comfort, like.'

She produced the book, and Harriott looked inside. It was inscribed, "To Philadelphia Burton, for good attendance; Morpeth Wesleyan Sunday School", and dated 1819.

'Thankyou. Now, Mrs Tamkin, can you tell me what sort of person she was, other than reliable and quiet, and well-spoken? Such as you might tell someone who wanted to know if they might be friends with her?'

This Mrs Tamkin found more difficult. 'Well, she was a very short woman, to be sure, and quite, well, rounded, if we're being polite. She had a little snub nose, and masses and masses of almost black hair.'

'How might she comport herself? Was she always fidgeting, or very still? Or did she have little mannerisms, like, I don't know, rubbing her knuckles together?' with a glance at Mary.

'Nothing like that. She was more a still kind of person, I should say. But she did have a laugh, once she found something funny. A real, belly laugh, I should call it.'

'Was she a fit woman? Or subject to illness?'

'Well, she hadn't been here above two months, so I don't rightly know. She did sometimes have bouts of dizziness, though I never saw one, something where she had to sit down sudden, poor thing.'

Mrs Tamkin was unable to offer any more information beyond this, and thanking her, the two girls took their leave.

However, in the Plough Inn opposite Mrs Tamkin's cottage, the landlord Mr Cruttenden was more forthcoming.

'Good worker, Philly,' he said. 'Couldn't often work evenings, of course, and she was away with the company for two or three days from time to time, but she always gave good notice, and when she was here, she did everything I asked of her.'

'What was she employed to do?'

'Anything and everything,' he replied. 'She was mostly needed in the kitchen, mind, being she usually worked midday and round'bouts; but she'd take a turn on the bar if I was in the cellar seeing to the barrels, and clean, and serve tables, and if there was a man who was getting a bit lively, like, she was onto him, and clearing him off the premises, never mind she was only knee-high to a grasshopper. Fierce stuff, our Philly, and a voice that'd put the fear of God into a man.'

'Really? I thought she was a quiet sort of person.'

'Well, you're right, for the most part, but when she needed to be she could take the hide off you with her tongue. Not that you'd understand a word she said then, but you could tell by the tone.'

'How so?

'Well, she'd slip back into her old accents, from up North, you see, and it sounded like she was strangling you, or herself, maybe.'

'Did she have friends?'

'She was very pop'lar here, I'd say, but I couldn't name anyone she was partic'lar friends with.'

'Did other members of the theatre company come here with her?'

'Can't say they did, now. But they'd have drunk nearer the middle of town, the Bells is closest to their work, I'd say.'

'And what did she usually drink?'

'Nothing. Nothing at all. She said she'd taken the pledge, that's what she called it. She'd been in America, and it's a much bigger thing over there than here, she said, she'd joined a Temp'rance Society, whatever that is. And she was chapel too, of course.'

'Really? She didn't drink? But she worked in your alehouse?'

'She said, it was her choice not to partake, and she didn't try and tell others what to do, unless of course they were out of order. I think her father had been a drunkard, that's my understanding as to why she was like that.'

'And do you know how she came to be in Tenterden?'

'None. I'd ask the theatre folk, I expect it was something to do with that.'

The girls thanked Mr Cruttenden and took their leave, walking back along Oaks-road quite slowly, trying to make some kind of picture of the woman who had died.

'So, we have a lot more information, but do we know any more?' asked Harriott.

'Of course we do, we know all sorts of things about her,' Mary said. 'I feel I almost know her, in a way.'

'Perhaps, but do we know the sort of thing about her that might get her killed?'

Mary's head dropped. 'No, I don't suppose we do.'

That evening Stephen reported to Harriott that Dr Bishop had been unable to make the matter much clearer. He had said that Miss Burton was not a regular patient of his, and none of his colleagues had mentioned that they had been consulted by her, adding that of course this was confidential, out of courtesy to the dead, of course.

He said the knife wound was cleanly incised, and about as wide as the last joint of his thumb, and just under the point of the shoulder-blade. There were no preliminary cuts or stabs, it was a single blow. The deceased had been dressed in a white muslin high-waisted gown of the style of about 1810 or so, with very light stays over a short chemise and no petticoats, and there would have been almost no resistance to the blow, especially as the gown was not fully fastened at the back and the wound was located between the lacing of her stays. He should have said it would have been too chilly to wear such a flimsy gown outside, unless on a very warm day, and it was more suited to a ball, or suchlike.

His brow had then furrowed, and he said that it had puzzled him at the time, but her hair was not arranged in keeping with the style of the gown. He had attended such balls when he was rather younger and the ladies would have had their hair up and ringleted, not just bundled into a large bun as Miss Burton had it. Also, she was wearing white face paint, which was popular at the time of her costume, but no other cosmetics or jewellery. He did not know what this meant, but it was odd.

He would not be drawn as to the condition of the actor playing Doggrass, saying that such information was between him and his patient, other than to say he was alive when he last saw him. And of course, he had not seen the body until the next day, being concerning with his living patient, so he could not comment on its condition at that time.

Stephen had asked about the rigor mortis that Dr Bishop had mentioned at the inquest: he had seen the words on Harriott's notes but not understood them. Dr Bishop said that after death, the muscles stiffen, starting in the face, and extending downwards, beginning after perhaps two hours, and complete after about eight hours. Around twelve hours later, it passes off in the same order as it came on, so after thirty hours approximately, the body is flaccid or limp. That is why, having seen the body only the next afternoon, he was unable to use the phenomenon to estimate the time of death, as it had passed off completely at that time. Thirty hours before 3pm on Saturday took us to 9am on the Friday, but he had given 11am as the latest possible time of death. This was because the process of stiffening and relaxing is quicker in warm weather, such as we have been having, although to a varying degree.

All in all, Stephen felt more rather than less puzzled by the additional information.

At this point, Mary hurried in, out of breath, and full of apologies for being delayed.

'Where have you been?' asked Harriott. 'Finding out more information for us?'

'No, well, not really. I've just been . . . out.'

'Out?'

'Yes, out. Now, come on, what have you been talking about?'

Harriott looked at her with narrowed eyes, but ran over the information from Stephen quickly for her.

Stephen, looking puzzled, added, 'One thing, you know, I'm not sure about. Dr Bishop said she was wearing white face paint, whatever its proper name is, and I saw that too when I was by the chest in the theatre, but she'd put it on rather badly. And there wasn't any other cosmetic like that red stuff ladies use.'

'Rouge,' supplied Harriott. 'So what does that mean?'

'I've not any idea.'

Harriott looked down at her paper, and said, 'Now, what do we do next? I know it'll be harder tomorrow, because we have to work, but we can fit things in around it, can't we? But what should we do first?'

'Can I see your paper?' asked Stephen.

Harriott passed it over. 'It's a mess at the moment; I'll write it out neatly this evening, when we've finished.'

Stephen read it carefully. 'Your idea of a mess is my idea of tidy,' he commented, 'but I think, the next thing to do, is talk to the people from the theatre. About Miss Burton, and what she was like, but also, don't we want to find out exactly when she died?'

'Of course. And who was in the place, to have a chance to do it.'

Mary shuddered. I wouldn't want to go there, where someone died.'

'You live in an old house, don't you? Lots of people have died there, over the years,' said Harriott.

'Yes, but it's different, being murdered. What if the man is still there, and looking out for people being nosy?'

'Or woman,' put in Stephen. 'Don't forget it might be a woman.'

'Would a woman stab someone like that?'

'I admit, it's more likely to be a man, but she was a small person, and it wouldn't take that much strength if the knife was sharp.'

Harriott thought a moment. 'Will there be anyone at the theatre? Aren't they playing at Hastings or somewhere?'

'Oh, yes,' said Mary. 'That's what they were saying in church this morning.'

'Well, I'm at Morghew tomorrow until one o'clock, and Stephen's at Herenden until four; what are you doing, Mary?'

'I've to help Mother finish that gown, we just have the trimmings to do, and some buttonholes to neaten. And then just general house jobs. And then I'm working at the Bells from three. But I could . . . well, what do you want me to do?'

'Could you run up and see if they are back from Hastings yet? And if so, see if we would be allowed to have a look-around inside, when it is convenient to them?'

'Ooh, I don't know if I'd dare. Can't I do it with one of you?'

'Well, I could go after work, before I'm due in the Bells, if you don't want to.'

'No, I'll go, I will. I'll just ask at the front cottage, you know, the one that you go through to reach the boxes on the far side.' She screwed up her nose at the thought.

'Good for you,' said Stephen. 'And I'll put my head in the Bells once I'm home and cleaned up, and perhaps you could tell me what you find, and I could go in and have a first look round, if they say that's bene when you ask 'em.'

Stephen leaned on the bar and asked Harriott for a nip of ale since he was there. 'It's been monstrous hot in the sun today, I spent most of it barrowing manure from the stables to the beds, and digging it in around the roses.'

'I'll fetch Mary: I haven't had a chance to speak to her, so far.'

Mary reported that yesterday she had knocked on the door of the cottage, which was labelled "Theatre Cottage", but in very small letters that she hadn't noticed before, and spoken to the woman who answered, a Mrs Carpenter. The party from Hastings were due back this evening, Monday that is, she said, there was only her and her husband, the caretaker, here presently. She didn't think she ought to say anything about people coming in without Mr Brooke's say-so. She was sorry, but there it was. Mr Brooke ought to be back with the others, she thought, later, perhaps she'd like to come back around supper-time?

Stephen rubbed his nose. 'I was all set,' he said. 'What can I be doing until then?'

'Well, we want to know when the murder took place,' said Harriott. Which means, I think, we ought to see if we can find out the last time anybody saw her alive.'

'Good thinking. Hmm. So, where should I start?'

'Ask around here, I should. I'll do the same with the men that come to the bar, I should have thought of that before.'

Stephen, carrying his ale, set out to tour the tavern and try and get into conversation with the groups of drinkers, as best he could. Harriott saw to the two who had arrived at the bar in the meantime and were tapping their tankards on the counter for service. Mary went back to the kitchen, and her sink full of plates and tankards.

Harriott watched Stephen as he went the rounds of the public bar, getting rebuffed by some, and welcomed by others, who perhaps thought he might buy them a drink for their information. Then he disappeared to the saloon, and she got on with her task of interrogating customers as they appeared, most of whom could tell her nothing, but some of whom were most interested in why she was asking, or wanted to know all the details of the tragedy in the most ghoulish fashion.

At length, Stephen reappeared, and ordered another fill of his tankard. 'Thirsty work, talking,' he observed, 'will you have one yourself?'

'I'd better not,' Harriott said, 'I get very sleepy if I do, and Mr Paine wouldn't like that.'

'Maybe later?'

Harriott put her head in the kitchen and asked Mary to come out for a moment.

'Anyway, I found out a little. Miss Burton was at the dance on Wednesday, she was seen by that carter over there, and two men in the saloon who danced with her. They said she stayed until the end at ten o'clock, and was most lively.'

'Ten? I've been putting Mr Pomfret's appointments in his diary, and the ball he's going to doesn't even start until nine.'

'That's gentry for you. It was even earlier than usual this time of year, as most of the folk were farm labourers and had to start work before six the next day, to make best use of the light. Anyway, she was still alive and well at ten.'

'Anything after that? Did they say who she went to the dance with?'

'Apparently. they didn't see her arrive. She danced with lots of people, anyone who was willing. And everybody was willing it seemed, she was a good dancer.'

'Was it just labourers, and the like, there?'

'No, I don't think so. There were people sponsoring the fund-raising, and a few what you might call, middling folk. I'll go back and see if my men in the saloon can give me any names.'

'Do you think it's not likely to be a labourer?' asked Mary.

'Not really, but he had to have had access to a dagger or long knife, and I don't know, it's a place to start.'

'Who was the organiser of the dance?'

'Again, I didn't ask. I'll go back, like I said.'

'I've just thought,' said Mary. 'We never asked Mr Cruttenden at the Plough when he last saw her.'

'No, we didn't. Bother, I'm stupid.'

'No, come on Harriott, we are all new at this; you're too hard on yourself. I'll go up there after I'm finished here and find out.'

'Mrs Tamkin said she hadn't seen her since Wednesday morning,' said Harriott, 'I heard her at the inquest.'

Stephen returned to the saloon and the girls to their work. He must have slipped out without them seeing him, as the next time he appeared it was late evening.

'Firstly, the dance was organised by Mrs Phoebe Morris, from Pittlesden Cottage, you know her husband is a brewer, and they donated a barrel for the dance. She took subscriptions, and there was a lottery, and so on.'

'Well done. I'd better go round and see her sometime.'

'Also, I've been to the Plough, and Miss Burton was due in work on Thursday about three o'clock, and didn't appear.'

'Right,' said Harriott.

'And one of the men in there thinks he saw her that morning, in the town, with a smart sort of fellow, one he didn't know.'

'Interesting.'

'He was very vague as to the time, just that it was between breakfast and noon. But nobody saw her on Friday at all. Nothing after the sighting in town on Thursday.'

'So, we narrow it down. What was she doing with this man?'

'My fellow said he just saw them, walking together, in the High-street, opposite the Harris Arms.'

'And who might he be?'

'Indeed. Was he the last person to see her, I wonder.'

'We need to get in the theatre, and ask them there.' A thought struck Harriott. 'What did the man say she was wearing?'

'He didn't say anything, I assume a regular gown; why do you ask?'

'Because in the chest, she was wearing a high-waisted muslin from twenty years ago, remember?'

'Oh, yes, I forgot.'

'Never mind, I should think your informant would have mentioned it if she was in costume like that.'

'I'll go back and ask. If he's still there.'

Mary came out of the kitchen, wiping her hands on her apron. 'Finished at last. What now? Shall I go and see if Mr Brooke is back yet? But, would one of you come with me?'

'I will,' said Stephen, 'I'm heading back to the Plough, I forgot to ask something, but you can do the talking at the theatre. And then you can go home, if you need to.'

CHAPTER 6

WE'VE ONLY JUST BEGUN

MR BROOKE HAVING RETURNED, BUT having quit the premises immediately, further investigations had to await his attending the theatre the following day. The task fell to Harriott, Mary being otherwise engaged at home, and Stephen again at Herenden. She decided to wear her dark blue gown, as she wanted to look more authoritative, and once admitted by Mrs Carpenter, spoke to the manager in his tiny office in the front cottage.

After introducing herself, she began: 'Sir, I must first offer my commiserations for the sad loss of Miss Burton.' She sat erect on the edge of the chair, feeling she had to be as correct as possible. 'And I trust that your performance in Hastings went well, even in her absence.'

'Yes, yes,' he responded, 'but I am a busy man, what do you want?'

Harriott sat back slightly at this, but rallied. 'Sir, it seems to me and to my friends that nobody is attempting to find out who killed Miss Burton, and bring him or her to justice? She has no family who would seek justice, she has no voice? Am I correct?'

'I suppose so. But how could anyone discover the man? It is now ten days since, and nobody has been named as suspect.'

Harriott smiled deferentially at him, her head slightly bowed, and suggested, 'Sir, if you would be amenable, my friend Stephen Fuggle and I, and another, would wish to try and unravel the mystery. But we should need to be allowed access to the theatre and permission to speak to the people who work here.'

'That would be most disruptive to our members,' he replied, 'I do not think I can allow it.'

'But sir, just think: is it not possible that the murderer is one of your own company? I know it would likely be someone from outside, but as the body was found within, would it be safe to continue with the possibility of a murderer in your very midst?'

Mr Brooke harumphed a little and pulled out his handkerchief, blowing his nose noisily. 'I see what you mean, Miss. But are you qualified to make such an investigation?'

'No, sir, only in that I and my friends have our native wit, and a desire to see the miscreant caught. We should be very careful not to upset your rehearsals, and speak with people only when convenient to them.'

'Well . . . But you are a woman. How can you do such a thing?'

Harriott swallowed her irritation. 'I have found that people, especially ladies, are often more ready to talk to a woman, as they find our sex less, well, less intimidating than a man. And for those who would prefer to talk to a man, there is my friend Mr Fuggle.'

The manager hesitated, then decided. 'Very well, Miss, I can see your point about the murderer being at large among us is most disquieting. I had assumed it was someone from the town, but now . . .'

'Thankyou sir, thankyou, you are a trump. You will not regret this, I know.' She paused awhile, as if in thought, then pulled out a paper from her pocket. 'Now, as I am here, can I ask you a few things?'

'What sort of things?'

'Well, firstly, do you know how Miss Burton came to be in Tenterden, after she returned from America?'

'Ah yes. Well, we here in this little theatre have strong links with Drury-lane, that famous establishment in London, and she applied there at first, was rebuffed, but advised to try her luck her with us. I must say, their loss was our gain, her singing was something marvellous to hear.'

'I see, sir. And now, could you tell me your own movements within the period from after the dance on the Wednesday before the discovery of Miss Burton's body, until that time? You may wish to consult your diary, I understand, it is some few days ago.'

Mr Brooke looked startled. 'Oh! I see. Am I suspect too?'

'Well, sir, without being unmannerly, every person in the town could be considered, before being excluded as innocent by some proof or other. The first thing we believe we have to do is determine as far as we can, the time of her death. The times I mentioned are the extremes of when it might be, I mean, after ten o'clock on the Wednesday evening, and before seven on the Friday.'

Mr Brooke thought a while, and pushed his glasses up his nose. 'As for Wednesday, I was in the building, and saw Miss Burton at the dance. I was not involved with the affair, you understand, but felt I ought to be on the premises during the evening in case of need. I left to go home soon after ten, and did not return to the building until the Friday morning. Let me see . . . we had some business to transact then, there were a lot of deliveries, and creditors to settle with. Mr Wickens brought a firkin of ale for the green room; the chandler was here, as we had run low on candles after the dance, and I think others, but I misremember; there were charwomen cleaning, and I made up a bill to advertise the next performance, and sent it to the printer by a boy.'

Something seemed to strike him, as he said, 'Your father is a printer, is he not? Well, we use Chambers, I am afraid, very reliable they are. No matter. Where was I?'

'At the end of Friday morning, sir.'

'Oh yes. Well, then, we rehearsed Black-eyed Susan, but quickly, as we were confident in it. We were interrupted by men bring in flats they had painted for our scenery, it was most annoying. Then we had a short break for a rather late lunch, sandwiches, that sort of thing, we stayed on the stage to eat, I recall, time being short. Oh yes, while we paused, I had to go and deal with some people delivering costumes, it quite unsettled my stomach moving around so soon after eating. After that, we went through the farce for the end of the performance, The Lying Valet, which we were much less sure of. The Valet took up much more time: in fact, until the doors opened at six to admit the audience. And after that . . ., well, I was in and around the green room until the start of the show, as you would imagine.'

He frowned. 'I think that was when I first noticed Miss Burton was not with us: she was due to sing in between Susan and The Valet. I asked around but nobody had seen her that day, and I just hoped she would arrive before she was due to go on. Most unlike her, I thought: she was usually extremely reliable.'

'I see. And, sir, do you recall when you did in fact last see her?'

'On the Wednesday, at the end of the dance; and then, not . . . no, I did not see her on the Thursday, I was at home all day, reading, and learning a new part for a production next month, with the assistance of my wife. Just a minute, I think I have told you false. Some of those people I said came on Friday, they were on Thursday, I now recall, because they sent a boy to fetch me, to deal with Mr Wickens and Mr Cloute's payment: I was cross about being interrupted. And the charwomen were there then too, because they left at twelve or twelve-thirty, and I had to pay them as well. But the sending of the playbill I did do on Friday, and the flats and the costumes did come then, and there were people buying tickets all morning, and all sorts of folk in and out of the office.'

Harriott made adjustments to her notes. 'So, just to make sure I have it right: you saw Miss Burton at the dance; and that was the last time you saw her?'

'Yes. Wednesday, that was the last. Poor Philly. Poor, poor woman.'

Harriott took her leave, after taking down the names of the charwomen and the chandler; and having Mr Brooke promise to tell the caretaker and other staff that she was allowed to look around and question people in the theatre.

'But if I find you have been upsetting people, or causing a disruption . . .' he said.

'I shall be as diplomatic as can be, she assured him.'

Harriott repaired to the Bells to sift through what she had heard, and sat in the snug, deserted at that hour. She made a list of names of people who had been in the building on the Thursday, people who she ought to talk to. She realised that Mr Brooke had not been able to narrow down the time of the murder at all, and they would have to seek other witnesses. Finally, she put her head out to check the time on the church clock, and seeing it was past ten, decided she would have to go home as her father needed her for a print run, and then she had cooking and cleaning to do before she was due behind the bar.

The first, or next, thing to do, she thought, was to speak with Mr Carpenter, because he would likely have been in and around the theatre throughout the period, and have seen whatever there was to see. When could she do this, she wondered? Not until the evening, it seemed. Well, Mary and Stephen would be free then too. They could decide together what to do, and who would do it.

As she came out of the tavern, she was accosted by a young man. It was James Maynard, from Goodshill. He was tall, and broad in the shoulder, and had good prospects in farming.

'Miss Curteis,' he said, 'may I say you look simply splendid today?'

'You may,' she retorted. 'Why so, do I not always look splendid?'

'Indeed. But at present, all the crack, prodigious splendid.'

'Why the sudden flattery, Mr Maynard, may I ask? Not that I don't deserve it, mind.'

'Well, it's like this, I have this group of fellows, we're going to fish Breeches Pond this evening, ladies coming too, all above board, and we will have supper, and it should be great fun, if you would care to come.'

Harriott was torn. James was very attractive, he had this kind of lopsided smile that made her insides turn over, but on the other hand, she ought to get on with their investigation.

'Peter Parton's joining us: I know he's only fifteen but his father said he ought to be with us if we want to use his water. And ladies, well, there's Jane Chalmers, and Ann Barton, I think you know them?'

Harriott smiled. Jane was a bene girl, and Ann was fair, too. She decided. 'Yes, please. What time? I'm working in the Bells this afternoon.'

'We thought about half after six, it isn't properly dark until about half after eight, and the fish like the twilight. My father has let me use his chariot, I could collect you from home if you like? We have all the tackle and things, and lots of lanterns.'

'I'll look forward to it, I really will.'

'Till then, then.'

Stephen called for Harriott about six o'clock, and told her of his return visit to the Plough. His helpful drinker had left, but he found another customer who had also seen Miss Burton, walking with the man in question around lunchtime, and said she was dressed quite normally. The man, he said, had a fancy waistcoat, but he didn't know him from Adam.

Harriott, frowning, and nervous about her anticipated visitor, explained briefly about her visit to Mr Brooke, and showed him her rewritten sheet. He perused it carefully, and grinned at her with enthusiasm.

'You're a treasure,' he told her. 'This is wonderful. So clear, the way you've laid it out. What now: do we go up and interrogate Mr Carpenter right away?'

'Well,' Harriott dropped her eyes, and fiddled with her skirt. 'I've been . . . someone has invited me to go to a pic-nic this evening.'

'Oh.' Stephen's face fell. 'I see. Who . . . no, never mind; I can go with Mary. She'll like that, doing something without being on her own.'

Harriott brightened. 'Yes, let's go and fetch her.'

But Mary was not at home. Mrs Exall said she had gone out about ten minutes before, and she had put on her best gown, and dressed her hair, but would not say where she was headed. She had contented herself with an admonition to be careful, and watched her cross the road and disappear down Chapel-lane.

'Wherever can she have been going?' asked Harriott, in surprise. 'That's not like Mary.'

'No, not at all.' Stephen rubbed his nose. 'Oh well, I'll go and see Mr Carpenter on my own, then.'

'Thankyou, that would be good of you. I'm sorry for . . . well, for letting you down.'

'I'll see you tomorrow then, Harriott, at Morghew?'

'Surely.'

As it turned out, Harriott did not see Stephen at Morghew, she being engaged with the library all morning in the absence of Mr Pomfret and his sister on a few days' visit to his cousins the Stilemans in Winchelsea. Becoming embroiled in rearranging the books in a more useful order, she lost track of the time, and before she knew it, it was gone two o'clock and she was almost late for her work in the Bells.

Hurrying away, she did catch sight of Stephen in the distance, and gave him an apologetic wave. But on the walk home her mind became filled again with thoughts of the previous evening's entertainment, and the romantic atmosphere of the growing twilight and the twinkling lanterns, with the various young people moving to and fro between little groups, trying their hand with the rods, or tying on hooks and lures, or sitting on blankets eating the delicacies that had been provided. And, it must be said, drinking some very potent punch, which she only recognised as being strong after becoming somewhat tipsy. She had sat and chatted with Ann and Jane, and been introduced to another girl, Elizabeth, and chaffed the men for any imagined fault, and laughed heartily when one of them managed to fall in the pond.

All in all, a lovely evening. And James Maynard had been very attentive, collecting her and returning her in the chariot, admittedly along with others; and his profile against the skyline when at the reins had quite made her heart flutter. She had not actually caught a fish, though others did, but she thought she might have caught the attention of her host. She would have to wait and see if anything came of it, whether he thought fit to visit her again. If he did, she believed she would be quite amenable.

Once home she changed her gown rapidly and made her way to the Eight Bells. She took her place behind the bar, and began serving. Was Mary on duty today, she wondered? And if she was, ought she enquire as to where she had gone the previous evening? Or would that be too intrusive? Mary was quite a shy person, and she didn't want to upset her.

Stephen, now, he had been tactful and not asked about her pic-nic. He was a good sort of fellow, really. And most keen on this venture, which she felt was quite exercising her brain. James Maynard though, he was so . . . Oh well. She served another rush of customers and let the matter go.

It was not until much later that she saw Mary. She looked considerably more cheerful than usual, well, ebullient really. She didn't like to enquire as to why, but in the event, Mary saved her the trouble.

'I spoke to Cook just now,' she said, 'and guess what?'

'You have lost your job?' hazarded Harriott, grinning at her excitement.

'No, silly, nothing like that. She said I can help with the cooking, I do like cooking, and it'll be much better than washing dishes and scrubbing and peeling vegetables.'

'How has this come about?'

Mary tossed her head, airily. 'I just thought it was about time I asked,' she said. 'She knows my mother, so she knows I'm not just cracking myself up.'

'Excellent. You see, if you don't ask, you don't get, Mary, like I said.'

'I mean, it's only preparing basic stuff, for the men in from the fields, and that, but it's a step up, and I'm chuffed.'

Harriott smiled, and wondered where this change had come from, but she hadn't any ideas. 'So, how about our mystery, then?' She wondered if Mary would volunteer any excuse for why she had not joined them last evening.

'Oh, yes, I want to do something more. Did you see Mr Brooke?'

'I did, and he agreed we could look around and talk to his company; and Stephen has been to see Mr Carpenter, the caretaker, but I haven't heard what happened.'

Mary frowned. I think I overheard . . . Mary Jukes in the kitchen, she lives near the Fuggles', and she said to one of the men at Jackson's out back that Stephen had to go help his father after work with a house out on the Rye-road. It's going to rain tonight, and he has a job he wants to get done before. So I don't expect we'll see him this evening.'

'Oh.'

'I think Mary's sweet on him, but, well, he's not interested.'

'He's a good man, Mary, its' a shame.'

'Yes, well, there it is.'

'So, what shall we do after work, this evening?'

'It's hard to know until we hear from Stephen, isn't it?'

'I do have one idea. He told me that someone at the Plough said he saw Miss Burton walking in the High-street with a man in a flash waistcoat. On the Thursday, that is. I have an idea who that might be, but I don't want to talk to him alone. Would you come with me to the Woolpack and see if he's still there?'

'Of course. As soon as we finish here?'

'That's right. He may have left town, if it's who I think it is, but we need to try. It's just . . .'

'Just what?'

'Well, let me say, I last saw him in rather awkward circumstances.

I'd rather not say what. In fact, I'm hoping he won't be there, but anyway . . .'

'That's fine, I'll see you later.'

Unfortunately, or fortunately, Mr Daniel Cousins was still in residence at the Woolpack, and graciously agreed to come down to interview Miss Mary Exall, for that was the message that was sent up to him. It seemed any unmarried lady was irresistible to him, from the alacrity with which he descended from his room.

He entered the saloon wreathed in welcoming smiles, and began to say, 'Miss Exall, I do not think I have yet the honour to have . . .' when his eye fell on Harriott. His expression changed, and he became wary.

'Ah, not only Miss Exall, but Miss Curteis too, I see. A veritable deputation. How can I . . . be of service? And will I be subjected to physical violence if I remain?'

Harriott blushed, but gathered herself. 'May we put that incident behind us, sir? I . . . we . . . are here on another matter. It concerns the late Philadelphia Burton.'

'Philly? Indeed, a very sad affair. But how can I assist you? And why should I desire to?'

'So you do . . . did, know her, then?'

'I do not deny it. We had walked out together on more than one occasion.'

'Did you see her a week last Thursday, sir?'

'Let me see. That would have been . . ..'

'The day before her body was found at the theatre,' supplied Mary.

'Indeed. Well, then, the answer must be yes. I took her for a drive, by arrangement. She joined me for breakfast here, and we left immediately after. We took a hired gig, and went out to, let me see, a place called Stone, on the Isle of Oxney, to see a curious carved Roman stone, at the Black Ox, by the old ferry to Appledore. It is used as a mounting-block, but I heard it was found somewhere in the churchyard centuries ago. We had a drink there, the porter being most pleasant, and then I returned her to town, and we separated.'

'You say you both had a drink? May I ask what Miss Burton drank?'

'Gin, I recall. She said she had been most nervous since the night before, and she hoped it would settle her.'

'Once you returned to Tenterden, to the Woolpack, did you walk anywhere before separating?'

'I should say I staggered a few steps, yes. I am not entirely unmanned by recent . . . events.'

Harriott swallowed, but persisted. 'Where might you have gone?'

'Only so far as to see her safe to the theatre, as a gentleman should, where I understand she was needed for some purpose.'

'Did you go into the theatre with her?'

Mr Cousins seemed to hesitate, just for a moment. 'I cannot exactly recall,' he said. 'I may have slipped inside briefly . . . no, I left her at the door, the back door, and returned to this inn.'

'Thankyou, Mr Cousins,' said Harriott, 'for being so open with us.'

'Yes, thankyou very much,' added Mary. I am sorry if we deceived you by my message, but we need to find out as much as we can about this tragedy.'

'I must thank you, ladies. You have given me some very useful information.'

'One last thing,' asked Harriott, 'can you say at what time you last saw her?'

'The church clock here is most unreliable,' he said, 'but it struck the half hour, I recall, as we crossed the road to the theatre. That would be half past twelve, I should say. Now, may I leave you ladies? I am sorely in need of my dinner.' He paused, and turned back. 'Though, perhaps, Miss Exall might care to join me?'

CHAPTER 7

I WANT YOU TO WANT ME

'THAT MAN HAS A VERY forward manner,' declared Harriott as they walked along the path through the churchyard. 'Even though he was ill-treated by me, he was unabashed.'

'He is very charming,' Mary observed. 'And handsome, to some, I should say. I was quite tempted to take him up on his offer of dinner, you know, Harry, in spite of your warning.'

'I did wonder. The way you looked at him, I thought you might be smitten.'

Mary blushed. 'No, not smitten, exactly, but it might have been a pleasant way to spend the evening, and I might have found out more for our puzzle.'

'Blast!' Harriott stopped in her tracks.

'Harriott! Such language!'

'No, I do apologise, but I should have thought of that myself, it would have been most useful to us. And, a free dinner for you, of course.'

'Never mind. Let us sit on this bench in the last of the sun and decide what next.'

Harriott arranged herself elegantly on the seat. Mary noticed this, and frowned.

'Harriott? What are you doing?'

'Oh, nothing, just getting comfortable.'

Just then, James Maynard came up the steps from Vicarage-lane, and headed for the two girls. Mary leaned in, and whispered, 'Now I see. You must tell me all about it,' before he reached them.

'Ladies,' he said, 'charmed to meet you again.'

Mary giggled.

'We are just taking a little sun,' said Harriott. 'It is a lovely evening.'

'All the more lovely in your presence.'

Mary whispered, but loud enough for James to hear, 'I think Mr Maynard could be an admirer, Harry.'

'Where are you headed, James?' Harriott said.

'Meeting some fellows at the Harris Arms,' he said. 'Card school.'

'Then may I wish you the best of luck.'

He took his leave, and Mary turned to Harriott. 'Tell me all, every last detail.'

Harriott, still a little ruffled by the encounter, told her about the previous evening at the pond, and how attentive James had been. She carefully left out any mention of how she had felt about it, or what thoughts she had had about him subsequently, but when Mary's questions became too pressing, she turned the conversation around:

'How about you, Mary? You haven't said where you were yesterday either.'

Mary frowned. 'No, I haven't. But then you haven't asked.'

'I'm asking now.'

'I think . . . yes, I'm sure, that I shall not disclose my whereabouts, just yet. I shall be a woman of mystery, like in that book I just read where Miss . . . Fairfax, I think she was called, turns out to be more than she appears.'

'Oh. I see, I think; though I don't think I have read that book.'

'Anyway,' said Mary briskly, 'what do we do next?'

'We need to speak with Stephen, he interviewed Mr Carpenter, like I said. That should lead us to our next step.'

'But he is at work.'

'It is so frustrating.'

Mary cocked her head. 'I've just remembered, something Mr Cousins said at the end of our talk. What do you think he meant by, "You have given me some very useful information"?'

Harriott hadn't noticed this, having been engaged at the time in making Mr Cousins aware she had seen him gazing at the top of her gown. 'Did he say that? Well, I don't know at all. Do you have an idea?'

'Not a thing.'

Harriott ran through the conversation again in her mind. 'One thing, did you notice, he said Miss Burton drank gin at the Black Ox. And Mr Cruttenden told us she had taken some pledge or other to abstain. Curious.'

'Indeed.'

'Do you think we can trust what Mr Cousins told us? I mean, he isn't a very . . . he doesn't seem a really trustworthy sort of man.'

'I can't tell.'

'And why is he still in town? What is his business here, that detains him for over two weeks? Dare we ask him?'

Mary shrugged.

'No matter, let's go home, and see if Stephen has sent a note around, or anything.'

There was no message from Stephen that evening, and Harriott's frustration grew. Grew to the extent, that she was a little tetchy with her father at breakfast, and spilt water over her gown when drawing water, and had to change it. Later in the morning she dropped a pan in the kitchen with a loud clatter, spilling some broth, and let out a smothered curse. Only once she was free from household duties, and had helped her father run off some advertising flyers, and looked with him through the pamphlet about the new Imperial press, which had finally arrived after almost a month's delay, was she able to go next door to look for Mary, but she had gone with her father to Cranbrook on some errand. Restless, Harriott decided she would amble down to West Cross and hope Stephen was not delayed at work. Last night's rain had stopped, though it was still overcast. She would be a little early, to be sure, but she was on thorns.

As she passed along the High-street she remembered that she had meant to visit Mrs Morris, who had arranged the Aid dance, so, feeling a pang of guilt, she diverted to Pittlesden Cottage and knocked on the door.

'Yes? What do you want?'

The lady of the house looked hot and flustered, and kept glancing behind her.

'I'm so sorry to bother you, Mrs Morris, I just wanted to ask you something about the Aid dance you organised two weeks ago.'

'Can it be quick? I've got a mash on the boil.'

'Just this, Mrs Morris. I'm Harriott Curteis; my friends and I are trying to find out who killed Miss Philadelphia Burton. You know, the lady who was murdered? What I want to ask is, did you see her at the dance?'

'That I did, she was the life and soul, like.'

'Did you see who she came with?'

'She arrived with a stranger, a man in a foppish sort of outfit, with a waistcoat I'd think belonged on a clown. Didn't know who he was, but he paid for his ticket, and for the lottery, so that's all right.'

'And at the end?'

'Well, I was clearing up, so I was running around like a headless whatsit, so I couldn't tell you. But she took part in the last dance, that's for sure, she couldn't stop laughing at something someone said.'

'Did she leave with the same gentleman?'

'Couldn't say. Now, if you're done, I've to get back to my mash.'

Harriott carried on down the street, thinking hard. Perhaps Mr Cousins had known Miss Burton better than it seemed? She turned into Rye-road and knocked.

Mrs Fuggle greeted her warmly. 'Ain't seen you in weeks, Harriott. You should come round more often, we love to have you. Can I get you a bowl of tea?'

'That would be most kind, Mrs Fuggle.'

'You'll be after seeing young Stephen, I'll wager,' she said as she put the kettle on. 'He'll be back shortly, I should think. Anyway, while you wait, tell me the news. I hear you're looking into the death of that poor woman at the theatre?'

'Well, yes, Mrs Fuggle, but it isn't common knowledge.'

'I've eyes in my head, and ears that work too, love. Word gets around.'

'We are trying our best, but we don't have any experience, so it's a bit hit and miss at the moment.'

'You've got a good brain, that I'll say. And our Stephen's not short of wits, either.'

'He's been most helpful.'

'He's a real Tommy Tit with machines, and knows so much about soil it makes my head spin when he talks.'

Stephen's young brother and sister rushed in, looking for a crust to feed the hens.

'Hallo, Harriott,' said young Mary. 'When are you and Stephen getting married?'

'Er, what do you mean?'

'He likes you, you know.'

'He's a good friend, but . . .'

'Anyway, the choockies want us,' and they dashed out.

Mrs Fuggle raised her eyebrows, but said nothing.

'Where's Sarah?' asked Harriott. Is she around?'

'She's gone into service,' said Mrs Fuggle proudly. 'With Widow Croughton, at Herenden, so she can see us easily on her half day, and on Sundays of course. Service is the best thing to train a girl up to be a wife, that's what I say.'

'How old is she now?'

'Fifteen, and a bonny lass. Here you are now, here's your tea.'

Harriott wondered about all this, but decided to change the subject.

'Stephen had a paper about a mowing machine, he wanted me to look at it, but I didn't get around to it. Do you know where it is?'

'It'll be in the box where he keeps all his papers,' she said. 'Let me look it out for you.'

Harriott settled herself at the table and read the paper carefully. It was quite amazing what men came up with these days, she thought. Maybe some day they'll invent one of these mowers that has its own steam engine to drive it?

As she pushed the paper away, Mrs Fuggle put another sheet down in front of her. 'This is something he was working on last night, no matter he was dog tired after finishing off that wall with my William till dark. He means it for you to see, I know.'

Harriott looked at the paper. On it was a plan of the theatre, carefully labelled, showing all the various doors and the staircase. It was most neatly drawn, and she was greatly impressed. The location of the chest on the stage was marked, and the green room as well as the backstage area, that the public never saw, were laid out clearly. She leant over it, seeing how the backstage area was laid out, and how the building backed onto the rear of the shops and houses on the High-street.

A moment later she became aware of a warm something close by the back of her neck, and twisted around, knocking her head against . . . Stephen?

'I didn't hear you come in,' she said, rubbing her forehead, 'you startled me.'

'I am cunning as a fox, and silent as death,' he said, grinning.

'Yes, well, that's as may be, but you're also very good at draughtsmanship. This plan is wonderful.' She picked it up and held it at arm's length.

Stephen grinned again, foolishly, and stuck out his tongue. 'Praise

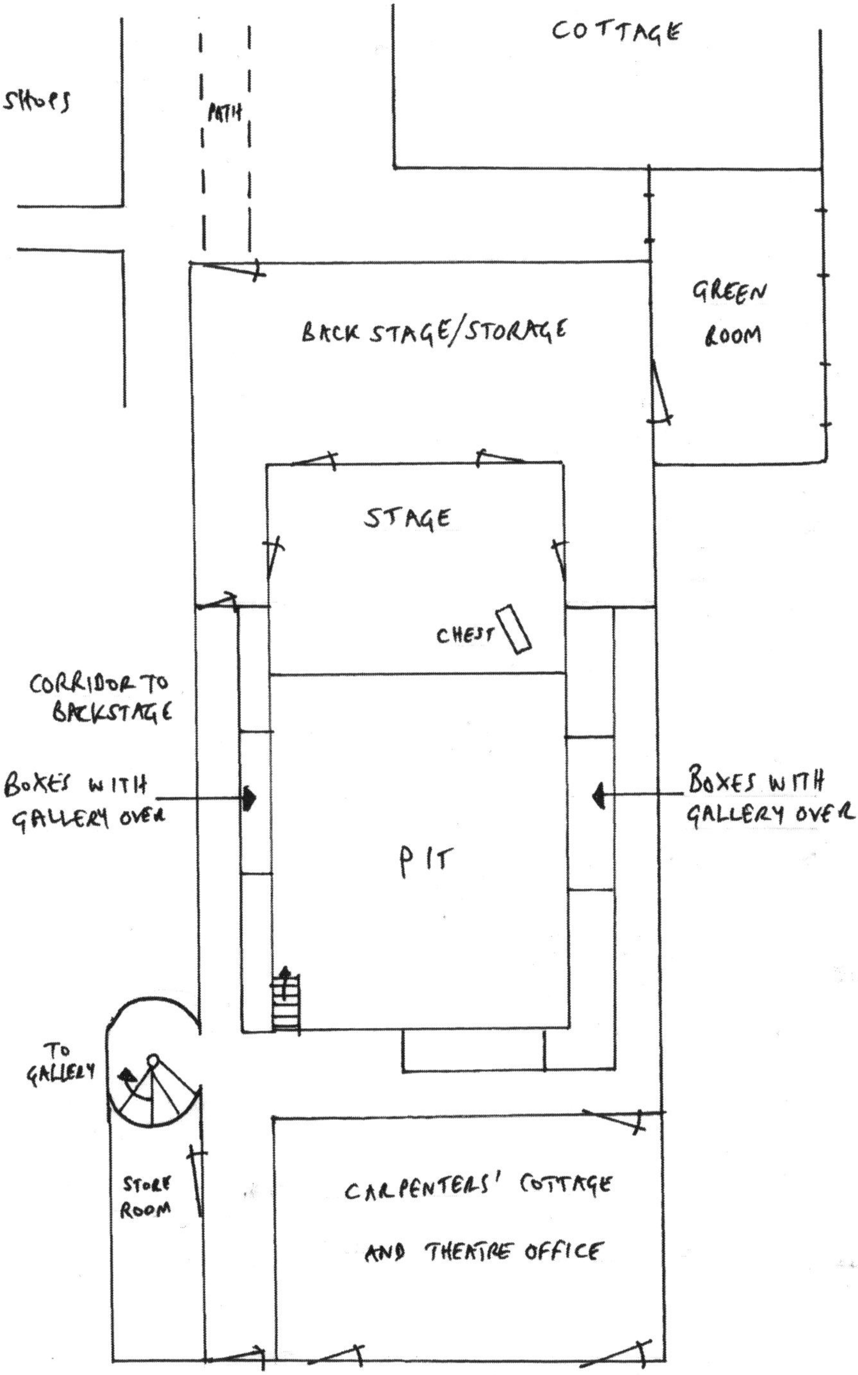
SHOPS
PATH
COTTAGE
GREEN ROOM
BACK STAGE/STORAGE
STAGE
CHEST
CORRIDOR TO BACKSTAGE
BOXES WITH GALLERY OVER
BOXES WITH GALLERY OVER
PIT
TO GALLERY
STORE ROOM
CARPENTERS' COTTAGE
AND THEATRE OFFICE

from you is a pearl beyond price,' he said. 'I must say I was quite pleased with it.'

Harriott set the drawing down, and turned around on her chair. 'Now, out with it, I'm dying to hear what Mr Carpenter told you.'

'Shouldn't we wait until Mary is here? And perhaps go somewhere . . . more private?' with a glance at his mother.

Transferring to the back yard was out of the question, with the younger children involved in some game which seemed to consist mainly of persecuting the chickens. Slightly awkwardly, Stephen invited Harriott into the front parlour, normally only used by his parents for respite from the family.

'So, tell me.' Harriott leaned back inelegantly on the sofa, and cocked her leg up over the other knee, which caused Stephen's eyebrows to rise somewhat.

'Well; I was not made exactly welcome, but when I reminded Mr Carpenter about Mr Brooke's instruction, he was more-or-less cooperative, in a surly kind of way. He says that he wasn't there at the dance, he was at home: he and his wife live on the premises, in Theatre Cottage, and he got in about eight the next morning and began taking up the floor.'

'Oh, yes, I know, the dance floor, it covers the pit, doesn't it?'

'Yes. He took me to show how it works, though I had to press him to do so: there's a set of joists that sit on the pit benches, along the length of the room; and they fit into notches at back and front. Then there are crosswise planks that are screwed into them at intervals, they come up flush with the stage. It's all very neat, really. He stacks them at the two sides when they're not in use, funny how I'd never noticed them.'

'Hmm. How long did that take him?'

'Upwards of three hours, he said. I got the impression he resented not having any help; I can understand that, some of those joists looked heavy. But I suspect he took his time over the job. Anyway, he says Miss Burton came in about lunchtime, looking upset.'

'Did he say she was alone, or not?'

'No, he said she was with this man with a London accent, a posh sort of blighter was his expression. They looked around the stage for a while: he was in the gallery at the time, collecting up rubbish, things the people had dropped the night before, you know how it is, so he didn't actually see her come in the building. He'd done the boxes; well, I forgot to say, he'd gone home for a spot of lunch after the floor was all done, and he'd just come back and started upstairs. He had some sort of bucket, he was putting things in it, you know, bits of sandwich, cups with dregs of tea, bottles, that sort of thing left over from the night before.'

'Harriott sat up slightly. 'And what was she wearing? Did you ask?'

'Of course, take me for a fool? She was in her normal clothes, just a skirt and bodice'

'Oh.'

'Yes, Oh. So they went onto the stage, and looked around a bit, then they disappeared through the door on the right, which he called, stage left.'

Harriott consulted the plan. 'So towards the green room? Why is it called that?'

'I asked him that: I thought it might make him feel clever, and settle him, he wasn't exactly keen to answer my questions. He said they used to be painted green, to be calming, actors get all up and in a state over the least thing, he said. Theirs though has patterned wallpaper. So there, he said.'

'Did he see them again?'

'He says not. Not until she was found the next day.'

'And when was the chest put on the stage?'

'Good point. He moved it there that evening, and no, there was no body in it at the time. He seemed most offended I asked such a thing.'

'What about the people making deliveries?'

'They either left their things with Mrs Carpenter at the cottage, or they came round the back. There's a path to a back door, it passes behind the butcher's and the grocer, and comes out on the High-street a few doors up, before Martin's auction house. If they wanted paying, they went through to Mr Brooke, he has his office in the Carpenters' place. He complained about that too, he says they don't have room to swing a cat in their cottage, and at the back of the theatre, everything's piled up in the backstage, they need a bigger area, it's a devil to find things, pardon my quoting him.'

'So, who came?'

Stephen took a list from his pocket. 'Mr Wickens with beer, the boy from Mr Cloute with candles, they both wanted paying. The two charwomen you already know about he says they were there in the morning, they start in the green room and the backstage area, and then do the auditorium. He has to sweep the pit, and he had a moan about that too. Mrs Relph from Brewhouse-lane came to leave some costumes, a man to look at pricing some repairs to the ceiling, he didn't know his name; and there were people in and out of his cottage wanting tickets all day. He said they should have a proper, separate office to sell them, but Mr Brooke won't have it. Can't call a man's house his own, he said.'

'Hmmm. Seems a delightful fellow. Now, what did he do when he'd finished cleaning?'

'He claims he went and took a walk to get some fresh air, and ease his back, but he was very vague about where he went. I think, mind, he went to one of the inns, and left the rest of them to it.'

'When did he say he came back?'

'About half past three, by the church clock, he says, but I thought it might be a lot later, by his manner. And anyway, that clock is never right these days. Then, he saw to unpacking some costumes from trunks they keep backstage, and laying them out in the green room, it's more a changing room too, there being so little space.'

'Did he say who else was there, from the company I mean?'

'He couldn't exactly say, but I'm not surprised. People are in and out, and if you see them most days you don't take notice much. But he remembers Mrs Robberds being there, sewing something of hers; and Mr and Mrs Gregory came by, to ask for parts of the script for the Lying Valet that they'd lost, somehow, and Mr Bosworth, that played Doggrass, that found the body, remember. He wanted to practise his entrances with Mr Gregory, but he wasn't having any, said he was busy, and they had a bit of an argument. And they all took no notice of Carpenter, as if he wasn't there, seems he has a real grudge about that.'

'What about the evening?'

'He says he was with his wife at home. And the next day, well, he spent it in bed, claimed his back went on him, soon as he got up. It's done it before, he said. He was still there until the theatre opened up at six, when he had to get up to direct people, keep order, and so on.'

'That would be too late to be moving bodies, when people were in the theatre, of course. Did you ask who he thought might have done it?'

'He said it'd like as be one of those rich men that frequent Honey-lane looking for ladies of the night. These young actresses, they have to supplement their income in any way they can, he said, and maybe someone didn't want her to be telling about where he'd been, to avoid embarrassment. Or maybe she would be blackmailing him in the same way. He thought that would be who the "posh blighter" was, maybe.'

'Really? That doesn't fit with what we've learnt of Miss Burton so far.'

'No. But I think our Mr Carpenter has no opinion of women in general, actually of people at all, but particularly women. I must say I didn't take to him, the old curmudgeon.'

'I think,' said Harriott, biting her lip, 'we ought to get Mrs Carpenter's version of all that. I wonder how much was true, and how much he . . . made up. Doesn't sound as if he was that keen on hard work, does it?'

'Well, he said his bad back was because of all the lifting of the joists and planks, and shifting trunks to get the right costumes out, and then moving the chest onto the stage. That might be true.'

'What time did he say he moved the chest?'

'He didn't really say. Just, in the evening, sometime, just before he went home.'

'There's such a lot for us to do, isn't there? Do you think there's anything in his idea of a rich man protecting his reputation, after an illicit liaison?'

'I simply don't know. And how does one find out that sort of thing?'

'I reckon we ought to stick to talking to the people we know were there. I'll see Mrs Relph on my way home, and the two charwomen some time. And, oh yes, I haven't told you about what Mary and I did yesterday.' She filled him in on Mr Daniel Cousins, and on Mrs Morris at the dance; and then tried to make a list of who next to see.

'Mr Wickens, the boy from Mr Cloute, Mrs Relph, the ceiling man, Mrs Robberds, Mr and Mrs Gregory, and Mr Bosworth. And Mrs Carpenter, mustn't forget her. And we could see if Mary's back from Cranbrook yet. Coming?'

'I've not had my dinner yet. Can I come up later?'

'Very well. I'll see Mrs Relph on my way home, and see you later.'

'Yes.' He paused. 'Harriott?'

'What is it?'

'Oh . . . no, nothing.'

CHAPTER 8

CRACKED ACTOR

'I'M SO SORRY, FATHER KEPT me all day in Cranbrook, what have I missed?' Mary was round at the Curteis' almost as soon as Harriott had entered her house.

'Well, Stephen's coming up when he's had his dinner, and we have some more people to see.' She brought her up to date on what they had found out, and showed her the list she had made of those that they should talk to. 'Stephen's drawn this beautiful diagram of the theatre, he's so clever.'

Mary smiled the smallest of smiles to herself.

'And Mrs Relph just told me she had been to the theatre twice that day. First she delivered some costumes in the morning, and then she was due to meet Miss Burton at two o'clock to see about some alterations to a high-waisted gown which was too long and too tight, but Miss Burton was nowhere to be found, so she went home again after waiting about fifteen minutes.'

'Where did she check?'

'On the stage, where she was due to meet her; backstage; and in the green room, where they said she'd been in and taken her gown. Then she went and stood on the stage again for a while, and called her name when nobody appeared, and after a few minutes more, gave up.'

'Had the others from the company seen Miss Burton before two?'

'Yes, there were some players in the green room: Miss Burton came in and fetched her gown, but then disappeared, saying she was going to change somewhere private.'

'I see.'

'And that's about it.'

'Hmm. So we know she was alive until, perhaps, somewhere between one and two o'clock on the Thursday?'

Harriott consulted her notes. 'I've still got to write down what Stephen found out, but yes, if we believe the actors. And that does fit with Mr Carpenter, if he is right. He said, I think, he saw her on the stage in normal clothes with a man, just after he'd had his lunch, and then she left towards the green room.'

'So, we ought to divide up the people we have to talk to. How about you see Mrs Carpenter, as you already spoke to her; and did you see the charwomen yet? And I will talk to Mr Wickens and Mr Cloute, because I know them? And you can ask Mrs Carpenter who the ceiling man was, and what she thinks of her husband's truthfulness, or how hard he works, or something? And then Stephen, well, he could speak to some of the actors. Or maybe you two could do that together?' She raised her eyebrows just a fraction, but Harriott didn't see it.

'No, he'll be fine on his own. He's very good at this, you know, I'm surprised how good.'

'I'm pleased you've noticed. I think he's great, isn't he?'

'Well, yes, but, he's just Stephen.'

'Well, you could do it together or separately, it was just a suggestion.'

'So, when can we see them? Tonight?'

'I could; but aren't you working?'

'Oh of course, I forgot. And tomorrow I'm at Morghew, and the Bells after; and Stephen's at Morghew too.'

'I've just thought of someone else: Daniel Cousins, we ought to see him again.'

'Oh yes. And I'm not very keen on doing that.'

'Maybe Stephen could?'

'Good idea.'

'But what about this man from Honey-lane, who Miss Burton could supposedly be blackmailing?'

'I don't know.'

'And the mysterious stranger, of course?'

'What mysterious stranger?'

'It's just that there's always a mysterious stranger in the books I read, someone who is beguiling and seems charming but really . . .' She tailed off, and made a grotesque face.

'If he's that mysterious, we haven't come across him yet, have we?'

Mary sighed. 'No, I thought it might be Mr Cousins, but he just seems to be a rake.'

'You haven't heard what he's doing in Tenterden, have you?'

'No: perhaps I ought to ask around?'

'Good plan. And I will at the Bells this evening.'

Stephen did not appear in the tavern, but his brother Thomas turned up with a note saying he had to help his father again that evening. Harriott fretted that they needed to get on with the investigation, and she wished Stephen could have come up and helped. And she was tied up in the Bells until after dark. Still, she could ask customers about Mr Cousins, and whether they had seen any "mysterious strangers" as Mary had put it. And no doubt Mary would come back with what Mr Wickens and Mr Cloute had said. But, why couldn't Stephen be there too?

Mr Paine was in a bad temper, and banged about upsetting people. She got a rebuff when she asked him to change the barrel of old ale, and mostly tried to keep quiet if he was near. This meant she wasn't able to talk to many of the customers about their suspected persons, and those she did, hadn't met the Londoner, or were more interested in drinking. There was one man, however, who said he had heard there had been a foreigner in town a couple of weeks ago, he spoke

English but with a funny accent. Maybe this was Mary's mysterious stranger. If so, she ought to hear more about him.

Mary came by about eight o'clock and reported that Mr Wickens had brought the beer on a handcart, taken it to the green room where there had been some of the players talking, and then gone around to see Mrs Carpenter; but that he had had to wait for Mr Brooke so as to be paid, which had delayed him. He had not gone into the theatre proper, just the backstage area, so as to reach the green room door, and then taken his handcart around outside. He hadn't seen anybody except the players; and then Mrs Carpenter and Mr Brooke of course, but various people had come into the cottage while he was waiting, to buy tickets, he couldn't have said who.

Then Mr Cloute, he had been even less informative. He found out his boy that ran errands, and he said he just left the candles with Mrs Carpenter, and waited for Mr Brooke, and took the payment from him, and saw nothing else of interest. Both of them were gone in any case before twelve, by the church clock, which they didn't quite trust, but there it was.

'So, can we do something tomorrow evening, Mary? We're all free, as far as I know.'

Mary looked down at her feet. 'I'm . . . well, Harry, I can't, not really. I'm busy then. I could see some people earlier if you like, but I'm busy in the evening, well, after about three in the afternoon really.'

'Whatever are you doing?'

'I can't say. And don't push me about it, I'll just get all muddled.'

'Oh. Well, I suppose . . . I'll have to see what Stephen says, maybe I'll see him at Morghew.' She looked sideways at Mary. 'Busy from three, eh?'

Mary shuffled her feet. 'I didn't like to go and see Mrs Carpenter, because you said you would do. And, well, I think I'd better go home now, see if Mother wants me to do anything. I'll see you . . . I suppose on Saturday?'

'Saturday afternoon, Mary, I'm at Morghew in the morning.'

*

Stephen was apologetic when they met the next day as she came into work. He had had another summons from his father to help out with a building, well, the same one, to be fair, and he was a bit fed up, he was tired as it was after a day in the gardens. Anyway, he would definitely be around to the Bells by five, when she finished, and they could go across to the theatre together. There wasn't a play on, was there? Harriott thought not: it was on Saturday this week.

It was nearer half past five when he appeared and Harriott, more and more agitated, was just about to go to Theatre Cottage on her own. Mumbling apologies, he explained he had a bit of a disagreement with his father who wanted him to go out again to help with the building for a third night running, which he had refused to do. He would have been on time, else.

'I'm sorry, Stephen, I've just been getting frustrated about this mystery, we don't seem to be making any progress.'

'No, that's not right, we've found out a lot. I think your lists and so on are great. Now, do we need to wait for Mary, or do we go?'

'Mary's busy, she said, from about three. Most mysterious, not like her at all.'

'A man?'

'Not Mary, surely? She's not . . . well, not very good at finding someone to appreciate her for what she is.'

'What then?'

'I've no idea. Anyway, let's go.'

Mrs Carpenter answered their knock. 'Ticket, is it you want? They're selling fast.'

'Er, no, Mrs Carpenter. I just wondered, could I have a word with you about, well, Miss Burton?'

'You've arsked Carpenter a mort of questions, what do you want with me?'

'Well, we like to know what each person saw, you understand. Ladies often see more than men, don't we?'

'You're not wrong, there, now. Well, you'd better come in, then.'

'And, Mrs Carpenter,' put in Stephen, 'would it be in order if I went around to the green room, would it disturb the actors?'

'They'll tell you straight if it does,' she snorted, 'in no uncertain terms. Side door's open, or do you want to go through here?'

'I'll go around,' Stephen said. 'Disturb you less.'

'Well,' said Mrs Carpenter, once she was settled in a chair, 'what do you want to know?'

'Really, just who you saw on the Thursday and Friday before they found Miss Burton's body.'

'That's two week since, my memory's not that good.'

'I think you'll find it's better than you expect, Mrs Carpenter. Now, in the morning, there had been the dance the night before . . .'

'And Carpenter moaned and moaned about having to take up the floor. He moaned before he left after his breakfast, and he moaned the next time I saw him for his spot of lunch. At least I didn't see him again then until the evening, but he moaned again, saying his back was playing up, and so he went to bed early, where at least I couldn't hear him carrying on.'

'So, you are saying you only saw him three times that day: breakfast, lunch and early evening.'

'That's right. Good thing too. Bad back my mutton. Just don't like work, that's his problem.'

'What sort of time was his lunch? And his dinner?'

'Lord if I know. I don't keep a watch on the clock, not that we have one in here.'

'Very well; who came by between breakfast and lunch?'

Mrs Carpenter screwed up her face in concentration. 'There was Wickens, and Cloute's lad, I remember those, because I had to send a boy to fetch Mr Brooke out to pay them and he wasn't best pleased. And there was Mr Joseph came to look at the ceiling, from Woodchurch, not that there's anything wrong with it, if you want my opinion. He had a good old chinwag with Mr Brooke about it. And then there were people in and out wanting tickets, so's I couldn't get on with my jobs, but they didn't go into the theatre itself, if you get my meaning.' She paused. 'And the actors were in and out, couldn't tell you which ones, Mrs Robberds though, I remember, she wanted some tankards, and so I gave them her.'

'All these people were before Mr Carpenter came to lunch?'

'That's so. He wasn't here above fifteen minutes, and then he was off, saying he had to clean up the Pit, or summat. If I know him he'd be off to the Harris Arms more like, which is where he probably is now. And then in the afternoon, who was there? Well, lots of people after tickets, it was very popular, that play, on account of it having been a big thing at Drury-lane earlier this year. I can't put my finger on anyone special, though, it was mostly regulars.'

'Wasn't there any ticket-buyer who caught your eye? Anyone who looked a bit . . . well, different, maybe spoke like he wasn't local?'

'There was one fellow, now you mention it, said he was from Noo Yark, least that's how he said it, thought it a great thing to be able to go to a show in such a small kind of place as Tenterden. Looked like a regular fellow, but he did talk funny. Oh, and he had a kind of straw hat, like; not seen one like that before.'

'Was he on his own?'

'Yes, but he bought a ticket for the gallery; and now I think of it, there was another stranger, with a nasty kind of waistcoat, who bought two tickets, for the gallery too, he didn't say where he was from but he looked like London to me. And before you ask, he was alone as well.'

Harriott consulted her list. 'Did you see Mrs Relph?'

'Not that day. But she would have gone straight to the back, she wouldn't need to come in here.'

'What sort of time did Mr Carpenter come home?'

She considered. 'Might have been about five, five thirty, six maybe. Told you we don't look much at the time, 'cept on play nights.'

'And did either of you go out in the evening?'

'Not us. He set to snoring in the big chair, and I went out back to do my chores, and then he took himself off upstairs once he'd had his dinner.'

'And was he there all night?'

''Course he was, snoring fit to bust, too.'

'And Friday?'

That seemed to be harder to recall. 'I don't rightly remember,' she said, scratching her neck.

'Your husband said he stayed in bed all day?'

'That's right, so he did now. Which meant I could have a clear run at getting the place tidy, for a change. And there were tickets to sell, and Mr Brooke mithering about this and that, and actors coming and going. But I didn't stir out of doors, and that was that, till I rousted Carpenter up and told him he had to see to the public, back or no back, which he did, at least.'

After thanking Mrs Carpenter profusely for her help, Harriott was shown the door into the theatre, and went in search of Stephen. At first, surprised by the dimness, she felt her way along the wall toward the rear of the building, but found herself in a dead-end, where the furthest box which looked out directly onto the stage on the right of the auditorium, had no door through to the back. After considering hopping over the sill onto the stage, she decided to be more circumspect, and found her way around to the opposite side, where at length she found the connecting door and picked her way through the crowded corridor to the actors' domain past heaps of trunks, costumes, and unidentifiable boxes. She wondered as she went, whether the famous chest was among them, but decided not to start to rummage.

However, struck by a thought, she opened a door which as she expected led onto the stage, and looked about her. It was still daylight outside, of course, but the auditorium was quite dark. There were no windows on the ground floor, only in the galleries, and she recalled these had been shuttered when a play was performed, to create a better atmosphere, she supposed. At present, the only light came from them, and the whole place was wreathed in shadows. Curious. How did the actors, or indeed Mr Carpenter, perform their duties without the benefit of innumerable candles? She must find out.

In the green room, Stephen was just finishing questioning the four actors present. He introduced them: Mrs Robberds, Mr Gregory, Mr Bosworth, and a younger woman called Miss Rebecca Chester, a girl of about her own age. Harriott curtsied to each, and then, feeling a little odd, sat down on a rather rickety chair.

'Mr Bosworth and Mrs Robberds agree that Miss Burton came into this room, alone, a little after lunchtime, and collected a costume that was too tight and too long for her, the one in which she was found, and left, saying she was going to find somewhere private to change. So they support each other in this. Mr Gregory is sure that the chest was not on the stage until after five o'clock when he left on the Thursday, as he had been practising his lines there for about two hours previously. Miss Chester, who is quite new here, but plays our heroine Susan, says that Mr Carpenter came by to lay out costumes at around four thirty, and that he seemed to have been drinking. She kept away from him for that reason, but he left the green room and did not return.'

'None of them was in the building after five o'clock, but all of them came the next morning, and there were several people on the stage all the time from about eleven o'clock on Friday, running through various parts, and then the main rehearsals of Black-eyed Susan and the Lying Valet. They only left the stage just before six, when the doors opened to the public. They agree nobody could have put a body in the chest after eleven on Friday.'

'And the theatre is locked, from when in the evening?' Harriott was attempting to calculate times in her head.

'Ah, there's a point. Yes, it is locked up, but the back door has a very bad catch, and anyone can open it if they just fiddle around with it for a few seconds. Also, several people have keys too: Mrs Robberds, Mr Gregory, Mr Brooke, and of course the Carpenters.'

'Do we know who locked up on Thursday? It wouldn't have been Mr Carpenter, he was snoring in his chair.'

'Mrs Robberds here thinks it may not have been locked that evening, as the back door was unlocked, not just loose, when she came by on Friday morning about nine o'clock.'

'Ah.'

'Yes indeed, Ah. But we still have not established when Miss Burton died, so the idea of someone coming in to murder her during the night is still a possibility. The only thing would be, where would she have gone between say, two on Thursday and eleven on Friday? It looks much more likely she died on the Thursday afternoon, so far.'

Harriott looked at the four actors. 'And none of you saw her after she picked up the gown at around lunchtime? Perhaps, about twelve thirty?'

They all nodded. 'It might have been a little later than that,' said Mr Gregory. 'Maybe nearer one, I would have thought. Mrs Robberds had fetched some tankards so we could try the beer, but it hadn't settled, and it was after that. Perhaps even as late as half after one? You lose track of time rather, when you're involved in your Art.'

Harriott turned to Mr Bosworth. 'Are you quite recovered from your shock, sir?'

'Why yes, I thank you. It was but a trifling heart-attack. I hope to be able to recreate the part of Mr Doggrass in due course, when we can fit the performance into our busy schedule, and I have recovered from the emotional shock. Without untoward elements, naturally.'

Harriott and Stephen thanked them all, and left by the back door, so Harriott could get her bearings concerning the rear entrance. They examined the lock, and saw how the catch was very loose. Then, they set off along the narrow path by the rear of the shops, towards the lane, Harriott looking over to her right where the window of the green room could be seen, and thinking that anyone in that room might notice who was approaching the door.

'Ow!' There was a clatter; Harriott stumbled and nearly fell, but

Stephen reacted quickly and caught her before she hit the cobbles. He cradled her in his arms for a few moments, and looked into her eyes, before he set her gently upright. 'What was that?'

Stephen turned round. 'You kicked the butcher's pail, where he puts the offal and blood and stuff when he slaughters an animal. Are you alright?'

'Of course. Nothing wrong with me. The noise just startled me. I'm fine. No, I don't need your arm; let me go, will you? We can go to the Bells and see what we've found out.'

CHAPTER 9

STRANGERS

'SO WHERE DO WE GO NOW?' asked Harriott in the Eight Bells, nursing her port and lemonade.

'Keep on keeping on,' said Stephen. 'We're going great guns, aren't we?'

'But we haven't found out anything yet.'

'We've got lots of stories, only we haven't solved it yet. But we've only been trying for a few days.'

'Yes but, I thought we'd know more by now. It feels all confused, and out of control. And Mary's gone off somewhere, and won't say where.'

'Leave her be,' said Stephen, equably. 'She'll tell you when she's ready.'

'I like to know things, though.'

Stephen grinned. 'Don't you just. Still, we now know Miss Burton was alive at around half past one on the Thursday, and her body had to have been put in the chest by eleven on the Friday. And was probably not put there until after five on the Thursday, because the chest had not been placed until then.'

'Yes,' said Harriott slowly, 'I think that's right. But then, what about all that time we haven't any witnesses for? It's nearly,' she counted on her fingers, 'twenty-two hours.'

'Better than the several days we started with, though? I think we're doing fine. We just need to plan our next move.'

'I'm tired. I just . . . I don't know, I'm not feeling very . . . Can we go home, now? I think I ought to go to bed.'

Stephen looked like he was going to ask something, then sat back, and took a gulp of his beer. 'Alright, as soon as we've finished these.'

'I don't fancy mine after all. I think I'll go now.'

'No, don't, I'll walk you home, if you wait just a moment.'

Harriott got up. 'No, I want to go, I don't need taking.'

Stephen quickly downed the rest of his pint, and followed her. 'Come on, Harriott, it's on my way, I'll just come with you.'

'Oh alright, if you must.'

Harriott felt a little better in the morning, but it was still a struggle to get herself off to Morghew. She was clumsy, and spilt ink on one of her letters, and had to find a rag to clean it up with, which annoyed her. Mr Pomfret didn't seem to notice, though, when he came in for a book, and she was left to get on with her work.

Mary was around to the Curteis' house while she was finishing her lunch, and trying not to think of the jobs she had left to do around the house.

'What are we going to do this afternoon, Harry? Have you and Stephen solved it yet?'

'Nowhere near, Mary. Not by a country mile.' She ran through the things Mrs Carpenter and the players had told them, and Mary quickly picked up on the mention of the American gentleman.'

'I said there ought to be a mysterious stranger, didn't I? Now we just have to find him.'

'Yes, well, maybe; but he's probably left town if he has any sense.'

'He might have, but we can find out about him. Remember, Miss Burton had been in America.'

'We don't know where though, do we? America's a big place, it's not just New York.'

'Don't be a grumpy-guts, come on, let's go and ask around.'

'But where are you thinking of asking?'

Mary considered. 'Well, first of all at the inns. He has to have stayed somewhere, and we can try the Lion, and the Bells, and the Woolpack, to start with. Tenterden's not that big, it'll be quite easy.'

Harriott groaned. 'Not the Woolpack; or at least, you can do that one.'

'Come on, let's start. The Lion is nearest. And if we don't find him there, they might know about him, he probably drank in one of those places. An American with a strong accent shouldn't be too hard to turn up.'

'Oh alright.' She levered herself up, and stretched, and rubbed her back.

'You don't have to come, you know, if you're feeling poorly, Harry. I can go on my own.'

Harriott frowned. This was so unlike Mary.

'No, I'll be fine, come on, let's go.'

The landlord of the White Lion, Mr Collins, limped slowly over to them when they called and enquired at the bar. He was a veteran of the Peninsular War, and Harriott was never sure if his limp was exaggerated for effect, or whether he really did have the damage from the same cannon shot as killed Sir John Moore at Corunna that he always told visitors about. Whichever it was, he seemed to manage his cellar and organise his establishment efficiently.

He recognised their description immediately. 'American fellow? From New York? Of course, he was here a couple of weeks ago. Left, let me see . . .' he consulted his ledger, 'on the twenty-fourth of last month, that was a Saturday, left early, for the 6:45 coach to London. Said he had had some bad news, and needed to cut his stay short. Man by the name of Higgins.'

'When did he arrive?'

Mr Collins looked again in his book. 'On the Wednesday before. That's right, he arrived by the London coach, but the Woolpack was full, he said, so Mr Milsted sent him on here.'

'What sort of time did he arrive?' asked Mary

'That coach gets in around mid-evening, doesn't it?' he told them. 'It's supposed to arrive at eight, but it's often held up for one reason or another. I'd say he got here about nine, or thereabouts.'

'And do you know what he did then?'

'Not me. I'd be busy with the cellar, or the bar, or something. You could try my housekeeper, I passed him on to her, she might know.'

The housekeeper, when summoned, was a young woman of about twenty-three, who seemed to be harassed, as seemed reasonable in a busy inn. She screwed up her face in thought.

'Higgins you said his name was? Oh, yes, the American? I put him in number three. I recall, I think, that once he'd got his bags up and looked around the room, he was asking about places to go in town. And . . . that's right, I directed him to the theatre, seemed he wanted to try and find someone. But it was late, and I said there would likely be nobody there, because I thought the dance would have finished by that time. Anyway, he said he'd go and look, and that's all I can tell you.'

'That was on Wednesday two weeks ago? The night of the Aid dance, is that right?'

'That's right: I'd wanted to go, but there was nobody to take my duties, so I had to miss it, which was a big shame, I love a dance. No, that was definitely the right night. And I didn't see him again, not until he was leaving on the Saturday, he asked to be woken early, for the coach, I mean. I remember especial, because he left me a present in his room, which we don't always get, usual.'

'What was he like, this gentleman?'

'I couldn't rightly say. I mean, I only saw him for a few minutes, a couple of times. But he was a tidy sort of fellow, left his room all neat and that.'

'Did he drink in the bar here?'

'Couldn't say. You can ask 'em if you like.'

In the bar, nobody seemed to remember the American gentleman. Mary asked the staff in both the saloon and public, and also put her head in the snug and checked with the men in there, taking their time over their stout porter. Nothing. Undismayed, Mary led the way out of the inn and started up the High-street.

'Mary, hold hard, where are you going? And what's got into you?'

'I'm just going to the theatre, to ask if anybody saw Mr Higgins that night.'

'Good idea. But, . . . well, you're not usually this . . . you don't like talking to people on your own.'

'I'm not on my own, am I; you're here too.'

'Yes, but you know what I mean.'

Mary shrugged. 'You're always telling me to stop being so shy, so, well.'

The theatre was busy, very busy in fact, with the play to be performed that evening. The actors were all rehearsing, or making last minute alterations to their costumes, or trying to find Mr Carpenter who had disappeared. Nobody wanted to stop and answer questions, and Mary and Harriott withdrew, defeated.

'Oh, well, we can try again later,' said Mary philosophically. 'Let's go and ask about Mr Higgins in the Bells, the Harris Arms and the Woolpack shall we?'

'If you say so. But I'm staying outside at the Woolpack.'

Nobody recalled Mr Higgins in any of the three inns, which Mary thought odd. In the Harris Arms, though, the barman, though not remembering Mr Higgins, pointed out Mr Carpenter, who was snoozing over a tankard, and told them he was in the inn most afternoons. On the day of the murder, though, he couldn't recall when he might have come in or left, it was too long ago, and he was too regular a customer.

They were just heading back towards the Eight Bells, to plan their next move, when a large coach, piled high with luggage, passed them, and drew up at the Woolpack. One of the men climbed down from the perch, and went inside the inn. Presently, Mr Milsted came out, and spoke to the people inside. Then, the coachman started up again, took the vehicle through the toll gate and turned into Vicarage-lane, while Mr Milsted went inside briefly, then hurried off along the path to the east of the church with one of his female staff.

'Who do you think that is, Harry?' asked Mary. 'They have a deal of luggage.'

Harriott thought. 'I'm not sure, my mind is a bit muzzy today. Could it be . . . well, the new vicar is coming soon, might it be him?'

'Let's go and see.' Mary set off at a fast pace, across the road and through the churchyard. Harriott followed more slowly. Quite a crowd of people had the same idea, and by the time she reached Mary at the wicket gate to the vicarage, there was a veritable welcoming party on the drive and along the churchyard wall.

She watched as the family descended from the coach. She counted four children and a baby, as well as what must have been Mr and Mrs Ward. There was no sign of servants, as the coach would have been very crowded as it was. Mr Ward stood talking to Mr Milsted, who looked as though he was singing the virtues of the vicarage, while Mr Ward looked unimpressed.

The three older children ran off to play in the garden, while a small child clung to his mother's skirts, and the baby cried fit to raise the nearby dead. Mrs Ward, a tall and handsome woman, looked drawn after the long journey with restless children. Nonetheless she took a keen interest in proceedings, and pointed out to her husband the corner of the house, where the weatherboarding was rotten, and how there were streaks of green coming from defects in the guttering.

Mr Milsted opened the front door and conducted the parents in, indicating to his servant to go and keep an eye on the children. Harriott thought this exceeding sensible, knowing the garden to be most overgrown, and that there was a deep pond somewhere in the thicket.

'Don't they look splendid?' said Mary. 'And quite a young couple, too, after Mr Coombe. It looks as if they are actually going to live here, so what will become of Mr Temple?'

'I expect Mr Ward will keep him on, like before, don't you?'

'I don't know: he has five children, so he has expenses, doesn't he?'

'Children don't cost much, though?'

'Father seems to think they do.' Mary pulled a face. 'Now, tell me, is it true that Mrs Ward is the daughter of Admiral Nelson? The cook told me she was, but I didn't know whether to believe her.'

'Yes, I believe so, they met in Norfolk where Mr Ward was curate; but isn't she elegant and collected after that long journey?'

There was a lull in the entertainment, while presumably the Wards inspected the rooms and facilities. The crowd gradually grew as the news spread, and the buzz of conversation rose. Harriott, feeling suddenly tired, thought about going home, but Mary kept her back, saying it would all be over very soon.

When the three came out of the house, Harriott could see that the inspection had not gone well. Mr Milsted appeared to be apologising, and Mrs Ward climbed back into the coach with the baby who was still crying. The coachman handed the small child up to her, and shut the door. The two men stood for a while deep in conversation, punctuated with many gestures.

Just then, a horse cantered up, parting the crowd. Mr Pomfret dismounted, handed his horse over to the other groom, and joined in the discussion. He was taken across to see some of the dilapidations, and shook his head decidedly.

'What is Mr Pomfret doing here?' asked Harriott. 'I thought he was supposed to be having visitors this afternoon, and taking tea in the garden with his sister and them.'

'Silly, he's a churchwarden, like Mr Milsted, he'll have been fetched to welcome Mr Ward.'

'Of course. So, what is he going to do?'

'Mr Ward doesn't look happy, does he. Do you think the house is in too bad a condition? Nobody's lived there for ages.'

'Hmm. Look, Mr Ward's getting back into the coach, with Mr Pomfret, and Mr Milsted is hurrying off. Come on, we need to move, he's coming through here.' Harriott stood back and opened the wicket.

Mr Milsted hurried through without a word, looking harassed. The coach turned, slowly, and set off back to the High-street. The crowd, once it had passed, followed in ragged bunches, talking, speculating, wondering. Harriott, in spite of her curiosity, decided she was just going to have to go home, and said as much to Mary.

'Very well, I understand, I'll tell you all about it when I next see you. Do you need me to come with you?'

'No, I'll be fine.'

'Do you think you'll be well enough to go to church tomorrow?'

'Oh yes, I usually rally quite quickly. I'll be fine, really.'

'Good. Or maybe I'll be round later, if there's anything juicy to report.'

It was not until after church the next day that Mary had a chance to talk to Harriott, having decided to let her be for the evening. The church was extra full, because, no doubt, of the new vicar, and possibly also the excitement of the identity of his wife. Both girls had eagerly watched out, as had everyone else, for the appearance of the Ward family in church, but they were disappointed, as only Mr Ward was in evidence, and he did not take any active part in the service, neither processing in, nor sitting in the vicar's stall but in a pew with the Pomfrets. He was however dressed in his cassock, which gave them some interest.

Mr Temple led the service as usual, but did announce that Mr Ward would be installed as vicar on Tuesday, and inducted by himself to the living on Saturday. He would therefore be present in church in his new role next Sunday, but the exact arrangements had not yet been decided. Harriott thought Mr Temple looked a little nervous when preaching, but then she was rather far away to be sure.

'Let me tell you what I discovered,' said Mary, meeting up with Harriott in the churchyard, looking flushed. 'Mr Ward and his family are staying at the Woolpack at present, and there was such a commotion as their boxes were taken in, and the children brought around from the vicarage garden, and then guests who had booked a room had to be sent down to the White Lion, because there was not enough space, and they were most put out. And then the wagon with their heavy luggage and furniture and servants arrived in the middle of this, and there was such a to-do with the carter arguing that it all had to be unloaded, because he was wanted elsewhere, and it blocked half the High-street, until someone decided the furniture could go in a barn for now.'

'Did this all happen in public?' asked Harriott. 'Oh, hello, Stephen, did you miss the Wards' arrival?'

'Yes I did, being at Westwell. But I heard a few things in the Black Horse, after work. Is it true that Mrs Ward is Lord Nelson's illegitimate daughter?'

'So Harriott says,' said Mary.

'And that the vicarage is uninhabitable?'

'I heard it was,' said Mary. 'And Mr Pomfret is most annoyed, and is finding them somewhere else to stay until repairs can be done.'

'Mr Milsted looked extremely harassed yesterday,' observed Harriott, 'I think they both ought to have seen to the vicarage being in good repair before this.'

'I wonder why they didn't?' asked Mary. 'It seems wrong.'

'Also, what is this installation on Tuesday, and then an induction on Saturday, that Mr Temple told us about? Why two ceremonies?'

'I don't know.' Harriott was put out at this lapse of intelligence. 'I must find out.'

'You could ask Mr Pomfret tomorrow,' suggested Mary. 'If he's not in too bad a mood.'

Harriott considered. 'I might,' she said, 'but I might just leave it.'

'What, you being tactful?' grinned Stephen.

Harriott turned her back on him, and tossed her head. 'Now, Mary, did you find anything else out about the American man, what was his name?'

'Higgins,' she said. 'Stephen, we have a new person to find out about. My "mysterious stranger".'

'Really? What about him?'

'He arrived just about the end of the Aid dance on the Wednesday, and stayed at the White Lion, and left by the early coach on Saturday. And we know he bought a ticket on Thursday for the play, for the gallery, and nobody has seen him in any of the inns Harriott and I went to, which we thought odd.'

'So why is he connected to all this?'

'He is from New York, and Miss Burton had recently been in America.'

'It doesn't signify, does it?'

'Well it might. I forgot to say, he asked to be directed to the theatre, to look for someone, according to the folk at the Lion. So, after Harriott had gone home, I went to the other inns, well, the ones on the High-street, you know, the Gardener's and the Black Horse, and no luck. So I thought of trying Mr Avery's wine shop, and maybe the Queen's Arms, though I don't like going in there, or perhaps even going up to the Plough. But then I met Mr Cousins by the Town Hall, and I thought, why not ask him, he is the sort of man who goes all over the place, and sees things.'

'I thought you wanted to avoid him?' said Stephen.

'We are investigating, that's more important. Anyway, I made him a little curtsey, and smiled my best smile, and asked. And do you know what?'

'He hadn't seen or heard of him,' suggested Harriott, pulling a face.

'No, of course not, or I wouldn't be telling you. He said,' she paused dramatically, 'he saw someone who was likely our man, after the dance on Wednesday!'

She looked at the other two for a reaction, but all she got was a 'Go on,' from Stephen.

'Oh alright, anyway. He didn't really see him, but he was leaving the theatre with Miss Burton a little after ten o'clock, and there was a man in the shadows in Jackson's-lane, who called out, "Philly?" So they both stopped, and Miss Burton looked shocked, he said, and said, "Who is it?", and the man said, "Surely you can't have forgotten me already, Philly?".'

She looked at them both, and was pleased to see both faces were rapt with attention.

'Mr Cousins said he advised Miss Burton to carry on walking with him, but she said she had to face this sooner or later, now he was here, or something like that, and she told Mr Cousins to please go, and she would see him the next morning for breakfast as they had arranged. And he did, so that's all he could tell us.'

'Why do you think he's come out with this story now?' asked Harriott.

'I should think it's because he's worked out he is suspected, being the last person to see Miss Burton alive, as far as he knows,' said Stephen.

'Yes, I wondered that myself.' Mary twisted a lock of hair round her finger. 'Anyway, Mr Cousins said he thought the man might have had an American accent, but he didn't actually see his face, but it has to be him, Mr Higgins I mean, doesn't it?'

Harriott looked at Stephen. 'It certainly seems like it,' she said, 'but what did they do next?'

'I don't know,' said Mary, 'but isn't it exciting?'

'You've done wonders,' put in Stephen. 'Good work.'

Mary smiled broadly, and waited for someone to suggest the next move.

'I think,' said Harriott slowly, 'we ought to go and see the players, if anyone is in on a Sunday. We were going to do that yesterday,' she explained to Stephen, 'but they were rehearsing.'

The three of them crossed the road and tried the side door of the theatre, but it was locked. Then, they went around the back, past the rear of the shops, and found that door locked, but as they had been told, it opened to a very small amount of jiggling. Inside was dark and empty of people. The green room contained a barrel of beer, propped up at an angle that indicated it had been almost finished, and a lot of empty tankards, but no players. They retreated, closed the door as best they could, and returned to the High-street.

There, almost opposite, was Mr Pomfret coming out of the Woolpack accompanied by Mr Ward. They seemed deep in conversation, as if important matters were afoot. Mr Ward looked quite calm, although Mr Pomfret showed signs of anxiety that Harriott had not seen on him before: he mopped his brow below his hat, and fidgeted with his coat tails before taking his leave. He climbed into his carriage, in which his sister was waiting, and drove off.

CHAPTER 10

TALK TALK

THE NEXT THING TO DO seemed, to Harriott at least, to collate all the information in one place by rewriting her lists. Mary wanted to go and make more enquiries, but could not say of whom; and Stephen, wishing to keep the peace, kept silent in their discussion. So they found themselves at the Curteis' house, and sitting at the big table again.

'What do we need to find out next?' wrote Harriott on a fresh sheet of paper, and looked up expectantly at the others.

'I think we need to ask about my American,' said Mary, 'he sounds most suspicious.'

'Mr Higgins,' said Harriott, writing his name. 'Where shall we enquire, then?'

'Well, we want to know if he has been inside the theatre, apart from buying his ticket on the Thursday, so we should ask the players and Mr Carpenter.' Stephen frowned. 'Why has nobody seen him in the inns, though?'

'I know, I know, I've just thought,' put in Mary excitedly. 'He'll have taken the pledge like Miss Burton, won't he? So he doesn't drink.'

Harriott nodded. 'Of course, that'd explain it. So where would he frequent, if not inns?'

'Coffee houses,' said Stephen promptly. 'Except we don't have one here, like they do in London. Er, I can't say where else, people generally take tea at home, don't they?'

'We do serve tea at the Bells sometimes; certain ladies prefer it to ale. Hmm. Well, leave him for now. What about other people?'

'Mr Cousins,' saids Mary, promptly. 'He is just the sort to be a murderer, don't you think?'

'Also,' put in Stephen, 'he was the last person to see Miss Burton alive.'

'No, Mr Higgins was,' said Mary frowning.

'That was on the Wednesday night, though. Remember, Mr Cousins took her out in a gig and delivered her to the theatre on Thursday lunchtime.'

'For that matter, Mr Carpenter saw her after that, you said.' Harriott pursed her lips.

'And after him, all those actors in the green room, when she picked up her costume.' Stephen looked out a paper with the names of those he had spoken to.

'Very well, I shall put down Mr Higgins, Mr Cousins, Mr Carpenter . . .'

'And Mrs Carpenter, she was around all that day,' said Stephen.

'. . . Mrs Robberds, Mr & Mrs Gregory, Mr Bosworth, Miss Chester. Anyone else?'

'There are other actors in the company,' said Stephen, 'we need to find out their names. And don't forget Mr Brooke.'

Harriott looked up from her list. 'That's a lot of people to find out about. What can we do today?'

The others sat back and considered.

'Who has a reason to kill Miss Burton, do we have any ideas?' asked Stephen.

'We don't, do we?' Harriott looked most dissatisfied. 'She was a quite, how should I say it, unexceptionable person. Didn't really give offence to anyone.'

'Could she have upset Mr Higgins so much he wanted her dead? I mean, if he was an old flame who had tracked her down, and she rejected him again?' said Mary rubbing her knuckles together.

'I suppose so,' said Harriott slowly, 'but then . . . why did he not leave Tenterden that day, or at least on the Friday morning; why wait until the Saturday? And if he killed her after he bought the ticket for the show, why did he go to the performance and watch the discovery of the body?'

'Maybe he thought it would look too suspicious going so soon?' Mary's eyes brightened. 'Or maybe he wanted to gloat over the result of his foul deed?'

'Or there might not have been seats on the coach that morning,' Stephen put in, 'not to put a dampener on your idea, Mary.'

'Well, that is something,' said Mary. 'We could find out when he bought his coach ticket, couldn't we?'

Harriott made a note of this on a separate paper.

'And we could ask Mrs Carpenter how he seemed when he bought the theatre ticket on Thursday afternoon,' she added. 'I mean, was he in good spirits after his interview with Miss Burton the previous night, or downcast and angry, or something.'

Harriott nodded. 'Yes, and we could see if Mrs Carpenter could be any more clear as to just when he bought his theatre ticket, couldn't we?' She added this to the new list.

'He must have gone somewhere when he wasn't at the theatre, though,' she mused. 'But where?'

'Let's leave him for now, and think about the second person on your list. Mr Cousins,' Stephen suggested.

Harriott brightened up. 'Yes, let's. I really don't like that man. I'd love it to be him.'

'Slow down, you can't judge him because he upset you, or whatever it was,' said Stephen.

'I can and I will,' she replied, nose in the air, 'but I agree, we need to get something a bit more solid to point the finger at him.'

'How about, what is he doing in Tenterden for all this time,' suggested Mary. 'He's been here nearly two weeks, hasn't he?'

Harriott considered. 'No, it's longer . . . more than a month, isn't it? I met him first the day before the proclamation, he came into the Bells and invited me to the theatre.'

'Did something happen then?' asked Mary.

'I don't want to say.'

'But, well, it might help our investigation,' said Stephen, diffidently, addressing the air.

'Well,' she pursed up her lips, 'I . . . he was most improperly forward, after the performance, and I . . . dissuaded him.'

'How did you do that?' asked Stephen, trying not to seem too inquisitive.

'I, well, I . . . I kneed him in the ballocks, if you must know.'

Mary gasped, but Stephen grinned. 'Good old Harriott, knows her own mind.'

'Anyway,' Harriott continued, brushing a hand over her skirts, 'I don't like him, and I suspect he, me.'

'So why is he in town so long?' asked Stephen.

'Good point.' Harriott wrote it down on her new list. 'How can we find out?'

'Ask at the Woolpack,' Mary said. 'Or ask anyone, really, he's noticeable with that horrid waistcoat, isn't he?'

'Now, what about the actors?' Harriott looked back at her first paper.

'Ask Mrs Carpenter for the name of the ones we haven't seen, and speak to them all one after another,' said Stephen promptly.

'It's an awfully big task,' she said.

'Not like you to give up easily,' he pointed out.

'No, I'm not giving up, I'm just being realistic.'

'We have some things to do now. Who's going to do what?'

'I'm not going to do any of the things about Mr Cousins,' Harriott stated. 'That's flat.'

Mary pulled the papers toward her. 'How about I go to the Woolpack, and find out when Mr Higgins bought his coach ticket, and ask about Mr Cousins' business?'

'Good. And I can go and see Mrs Carpenter about when Mr Higgins bought his theatre ticket, and get the names of the other actors, and maybe where they live?'

'What shall I do?' asked Stephen.

'You can go with Harriott,' said Mary, with a small smile. Then if you find out any more names, or addresses, you can split them between you.'

'Very well. Let me fetch us some lunch, and then we can go.'

'Mrs Carpenter, we're sorry to bother you on a Sunday,' began Harriott.

The lady of the house stepped out onto the doorstep, and pulled the door closed behind her. 'Carpenter's asleep and snoring after his lunch, and to be honest I'd be glad of a breath of air. What do you want now?'

Harriott explained about Mr Higgins. 'So, we were wondering if you could think back, what kind of time did he come by and purchase his ticket? And how did he seem in himself?'

'Mrs Carpenter thought briefly. 'Can't help you, I'm afraid, it was a long time ago.'

Stephen tried again. 'It was, of course, but can we jog your memory? He was saying he'd come from New York, wasn't he? Did he say when?'

'No, just that. He said it funny too, I recall.'

'Yes, you told us he said, "Noo Yawk", didn't he?'

'That's about it. And he called me Madam, which I liked, and made a little bow, he did.'

'When he did this bow, did he seem cheerful?'

Mrs Carpenter put her head on one side. 'Not exactly cheerful, no. More, determined, I s'pose.'

'As if he was unhappy?'

'No, as if he just had to go through with summat. Like I feel with Carpenter, mostly.'

'I see. And had Mr Carpenter left long when he bought the ticket? Or perhaps, had he come back?'

'No, he was well gone, good riddance. It might have been an hour or two since, I suppose. Mr Brooke had finished and left well before, and the cleaners; and I went and had a little sit-down after this American gentleman had gone. So it was probably about the middle of the afternoon.'

'You say he was a gentleman? Was he well-off, would you say?'

'Not really, but he treated me nice, that's why I called him that. Very polite he was. He said, he particular wanted to see one of the performers, that's why he was coming to the play, and I asked which one, but he didn't say. Then he went, and I never saw him again, that I'd swear.'

'Thankyou so much, Mrs Carpenter. There's just one other thing: can we ask for the names of all the actors, we have met some, but not all.' She pulled out pencil and paper from her pocket, and waited.

'Well, there's quite a few, ain't there?'

'We know of Mrs Robberds, Mr and Mrs Gregory, Mr Brooke, Mr Bosworth, Miss Chester . . .?'

'Mr Robberds, Mr Sharpe, Mr and Mrs Roland; and Miss Brown of course. There's others, but they don't live in Tenterden, of course, being as they perform all over the area, Rye, Hastings, Folkestone, all over.'

Harriott noted these down. 'And could you tell me where they live, please?'

'Not offhand, I couldn't. Well, Mr Brooke; but he wouldn't thank me for telling you. Miss Brown though, she's just down Honey-lane there. See that cottage with the little bow window, just there?' She pointed.

Harriott nodded.

'That's her: she was to play Dolly Mayflower. She won't mind you, she's a nice girl, not like some down there.'

'How do you mean?'

'Well, it's not a secret is it? Ladies who ain't what they ought to be, you know. And all sorts of fellows coming to take advantage of their services, of course.'

'Yes, I see, and thankyou, Mrs Carpenter, thankyou a lot.'

The two of them walked a little down the lane, and before knocking on the cottage door, conferred.

'Do you think Mr Higgins might have gone into the theatre after he had bought his ticket?' asked Stephen.

'I hadn't thought of that. He might have, if he wanted to see Miss Burton again, mightn't he?'

'He was new in town, though, so he wouldn't know about the broken lock on the back door.'

'No, but that and the side door were open all day for deliveries, weren't they?'

'Of course. What we need is someone to have seen him inside, then.'

'Mr Carpenter? He'd have said, surely.' Harriott frowned.

'Not if he was at the Harris Arms at the time, though.'

'No, you're right, and it would have been about then, because he was out somewhere, or in there, from about half past twelve until half past three. Or so.'

'So, what are we going to ask Miss Brown?'

'If she ever saw Mr Higgins or Mr Cousins in the theatre at that time. If she saw them down Honey-lane? If she knew Miss Burton?' Harriott bit her lip.

'And whether she ever saw her, Miss Burton I mean, down here too? Remember, Mr Carpenter thought she might have added to her income by a little, extra activity?'

'Prostitution?'

'Well, it sounds so horrid to put it like that.'

'It is horrid, isn't it?'

'Yes, well . . .'

'Will you start or shall I?'

'You: women are less troubled by another woman. I'll stay in the background to start with.'

Miss Brown turned out to be not so much a girl as a woman in her mid-thirties, but still with a striking figure, and a welcoming smile.'

'What can I do for you, this fine Sunday?'

'I am Miss Curteis, and this is Mr Fuggle. We're looking into the death of Miss Burton at the theatre, and Mrs Carpenter told us you work there.'

'From time to time; when they'll have me, yes.'

'Er, shall we talk here or would it be better in private?'

'Of course, come in, do.'

Once settled, Harriott began: 'Miss Brown, did you know Miss Burton at all well?'

'Not well, I had met her of course, but we had not acted together as yet. She mostly sang comic songs, between the main play and the farce, though she did do some acting; and I was usually just a farceur. Though I had a good part in the Susan play, I must say.'

'What was she like?'

'I couldn't really say. Short and barrel-chested, with a miraculously strong voice; otherwise quiet. Kept herself to herself, I think.;

'It has been suggested . . . I mean, I don't wish to be rude, but did you ever see her down this lane, making use of the facilities for ladies who wish to earn a little extra?'

'In the brothels, you mean? No, never. She wasn't like that, not at all.'

'Good. And, we have two gentlemen who seem to have known her. First is a Mr Daniel Cousins, staying at the Woolpack. Have you come across him? He wears a gaudy waistcoat most days. He's been in Tenterden about a month.'

Miss Brown took a moment to consider. 'Can't say I have, sorry.'

'Or an American by the name of Higgins, from New York. He was only here from the Wednesday until the Saturday around Miss Burton's death, staying at the White Lion. We think he might have known her in the United States.'

'I might have. Would he be looking for her?'

'He might have been.'

'Well, I met a gentleman in the corridor stage right, on the

Thursday afternoon. I don't spend much time in the building normally, except for rehearsals and performances, living so close, but I had to fetch something I'd left in the green room after the last show, and he was coming out as I went in.'

'The corridor?'

'Yes, the passage behind the boxes, between the spiral stairs and the backstage.'

'Oh, I see.'

'It's rather dark there, unless Carpenter has hooked the curtains back, which he never bothers to do, so I didn't see him properly, but he spoke as we passed, just a good day, and I thought he might have had an accent. Either way, he wasn't one of the usual tradesmen, I don't think, or people who have a reason to be in there.'

'When might this have been?'

'Midafternoon? I can't be sure, it was a while ago.'

Stephen asked, 'Was he carrying anything?'

She shook her head. 'I wouldn't have seen, unless it was quite big: there's not much room to pass in that corridor.'

'Were any of the others in the green room when you went in?' Harriott tried to recall who was on her list.

She stopped and thought. 'Yes there were, but I can't recall who now. Mrs Robberds was one, though, we're pretty good friends.'

'You didn't see Miss Burton?'

'No, not that afternoon.'

'And, did you see Mr Carpenter?'

'No, he was probably in the Harris Arms, he usually is.'

Stephen added, 'How about outside the theatre? We think there may have been a disturbance on the Wednesday night, late, after the dance.'

'There's always disturbances in Honey-lane, what with the theatre, and the ladies having arguments with their gentlemen about money, and so on. I'd not have noticed.'

Harriott paused to think. 'And, lastly, do you have any idea why anyone might want to kill Miss Burton? Did anyone in the company dislike her enough?'

'No, nobody disliked her; in fact the ones who knew her at all thought she was lovely. And she had nothing of value, I know people get killed for that sort of thing.'

They took their leave and stood outside, puzzled.

'That means we have one more person who had a chance to do the deed,' said Stephen, 'if it really was Mr Higgins Miss Brown saw.'

'Yes. And we're no nearer the answer, are we?'

'Let's see how Mary's got on, shall we? Unless you'd like to come in the Bells with me for a swift one?'

'No, no, not now, let's find Mary.'

Mary was just crossing the road as they came out onto the High-street. They went into the Bells after all and sat in a corner by a window.

'You first, Mary,' said Stephen. 'Have you solved the puzzle for us?'

'No, silly, but I think I might have made a little progress.'

'Well done: what did you find?'

'So, they wouldn't say what Mr Cousins was doing here in the inn, or else they didn't know. I asked the bar staff, and the housekeeper, and Mr Milsted even. And I had to fend off James Maynard, who wanted to know where you were, Harry. I said I didn't know, because I didn't think you would like to be disturbed when you were investigating.'

'Thanks,' said Harriott, with a grimace. 'Thanks a lot.'

Stephen saw the grimace, but said nothing.

'So, I went out to the stables, and asked them about him there. There's a very good-looking groom there, if you ever feel led in a horsy direction, Harry. Anyway, he said that Mr Cousins is out most days, on horseback, not in a carriage. I asked how often, and he said, maybe four times a week, and he's gone all day. He didn't know what he did, but he always takes a big leather satchel slung around him, and he often asks the way to places. When he first came, it might be

Appledore, or Rolvenden, but nowadays it's much further places, like Staplehurst, or Lydd even.'

'Really? What ever is he doing?'

'I couldn't make head nor tail of it, Harry. So that's that one. The other . . . oh yes, Mr Higgins' coach ticket. That he bought on Friday evening, late. The agent couldn't say when exactly, but it was twilight, or thereabouts.'

'Did you meet Mr Cousins while you were there?'

'No, and I'd have avoided him if I had, like you.'

'Don't do that, Mary,' said Stephen, 'he might have useful information for us.'

'Well you can find it out, not me, then. So, come on, what about you two?' asked Mary.

Stephen gave her a clear and concise summary of what they'd been told, and Harriott glanced at him with what might almost have been an admiring expression on her face. Mary noticed this, but kept her face impassive.

'I'd better get home now and start on Father's dinner,' said Harriott. And I'll put down what we've found on my papers. Can we do anything tomorrow?'

'What though?' Mary looked puzzled.

'Visit the theatre and talk to the other actors, if they are there.'

'Oh, yes. Well, I can after I've finished my work; and Stephen?'

'Surely, in the evening.'

'Fair enough. Let's hope it gets less confusing soon, not more.'

CHAPTER 11

EVERYBODY WANTS TO RULE THE WORLD

AT MORGHEW THE NEXT DAY Harriott found Mr Pomfret still somewhat agitated. Not that anyone else would see it, she thought, but she could tell: his manner was different from previous weeks. A matter of tone of voice, and the clipped nature of his speech. However, once he had given her instructions, she beamed at him and handed over a letter that had been delivered by a messenger, rather than the regular man from the receiving office.

'Sir, I rather think this letter will be welcome to you.' She looked carefully at him as he read it, and watched his face relax.

'Excellent, Excellent. Would you take dictation?'

'Sir, I have already drafted a reply, or rather, a letter to Mr Ward, if you would care to peruse it?'

Mr Pomfret read the letter carefully, and nodded. 'Couldn't have put it better myself. Come, let me sign it personally, pass me the pen and inkwell.'

The letter had contained confirmation that the Wards could be accommodated in the Pebbles, a building adjoining the White Lion, for the duration of the repairs to the vicarage, at a reasonable cost. She had relayed this intelligence to Mr Ward, in her draft, and bubbled inside at the praise from her employer.

'May I ask you to deliver this to the Woolpack, when you go home later? I know it is not one of your regular duties, but I am sure Mr Ward would like to see it as soon as possible. Make sure you give it into his hand, I do not want it to go astray.'

'Yes, of course, sir, it is no trouble.' She paused, and cleared her throat. 'Sir, if you are finished with instructions, could I ask you a pair of things?'

'Ask away.'

'Mr Temple announced that Mr Ward is to have an installation on Tuesday, and an induction on Saturday. Please, what is the difference, and why two ceremonies?'

'Ah, good question. Well, the installation is done by the bishop, in this case Mr Howley the Archbishop, and those who have the gift of the living, in this case the Dean and Chapter of our cathedral. Not the whole chapter, you understand, just a representative.'

Harriott smiled dutifully at his small jest.

'Mr Ward will have to travel to Canterbury for this; it is a private ceremony where he is installed into the cure of souls of the parish. But the induction, that is into the possession of the estate of the living, by which is meant the church and its contents, and the vicarage and the tithes and so on, this has to be done here, and I shall be part of it as churchwarden, though I am unsure as yet as to which clergyman will officiate.'

'So, sir, is that why the vicarage is dilapidated? Because it is the property of the incumbent during his tenure?'

'Indeed. I have heard some say that we, that is Mr Milsted and myself as churchwardens, ought to have seen to its repair, but I take offence at that: it is not in our remit to interfere.'

'I see. Thankyou, sir, sincerely. I do like to have things made clear.'

'As do I, Miss Curteis, as do I. Please carry on making my library more systematic, as you have been doing. Good morning.'

Harriott duly delivered her letter. Mr Ward was in one of the parlours with his wife, and the two smallest children. Harriott was struck with how welcoming both of them were, even before they knew of her errand. Mrs Ward was a tall, graceful person who sat engaged with needlework, and whom Harriott thought most beautiful. She wished she had seen a portrait of Admiral Nelson, so she could tell if there was a resemblance. Mr Ward had a slightly gingery head of hair, and an accent that bore traces of the same type of diction as George Bunn's, she thought, though far more refined. She watched as his face changed on reading the letter, and how he beamed as he passed it to his wife. After a short pause to admire the baby, she left, and went home to her chores.

On the way home she met Richard Marshall, and in spite of herself, stopped to talk once he hailed her.

'Well, young Harriott, and how are you this fine day?'

Thinking his opening line a little clichéd, she nonetheless found herself running her eyes over his broad shoulders and powerful legs. 'I am very well, Richard. Done any ringing recently?'

'We have planned a short peal for Tuesday, for the installation of Mr Ward, though he will be in Canterbury for it, I understand. And another, longer one on Saturday, for his induction here. Why don't you come up and watch us? You could bring us refreshment, if you liked.'

She was sorely tempted. She imagined the scene, with thirsty ringers grateful to her, and Richard taking her off somewhere afterwards, and . . . 'I expect I'll be cleaning my hair, or washing my teeth, or something, Richard. Thanks but no thanks.'

'Another time, maybe?'

And Harriott set off again, but with a tell-tale spring in her step. It did no harm to be on the receiving end of admiration.

'You know how stuck we have been over how to disentangle all the stories we've been told by the people at the theatre?' Stephen was grinning broadly as he came in to the Curteis' house that evening, quite early, and paced up and down. 'Oh, I ought to ask, is Mary around?'

'No, she's busy on an errand of some sort.'

'That's a shame.'

Harriott nodded, and frowned slightly, not having seen him in this kind of mood often.

'Well, I was weeding the flowerbeds behind Mrs Croughton's house, the ones right under the windows, and my sister Sarah came out to beat some mats, you remember, she's a maid there now? So naturally I got up and had a few words with her. And then, one of the guests, a Miss Clarke, she said her name was, walked out from the rose garden and spoke to us. Naturally, I took off my cap, and expected some commonplaces, before she moved on, but she stopped, and she asked us about ourselves.'

'First thing she said was, "Are you brother and sister?", well people do say we look a bit alike; and then she asked us where we lived, and how things were at home. It wasn't at all like I'd have thought: she seemed really interested, and Sarah told her about the chickens, and how Thomas always forgot to shut their coop up, and how Father had built Mrs Croughton's kitchen garden wall, the one across the lawn, or rather, mended it when it fell down a couple of years back.

'So then she explained how she works for the Foreign Office, whatever that is, in London, and so does her brother and his wife. She said they are staying with Mrs Croughton for a few days, their children are of an age, at least their younger ones are. Then, she and Mary, that's her sister-in-law, go on to visit friends in Rye with the children, but she said George, I suppose he'd be Mr Clarke, has to go back to work because of planning the coronation, he's more-or-less in charge of the overseas guests, under the Minister. There are a lot of foreign dignitaries they have to invite.'

'Where's all this going, Stephen? Get to the point.'

'Yes, all right. Well I was just standing there, sort of baffled about what she was saying, but then she wanted to know what I did when I wasn't at work, and I said, well, um, at the moment I'm trying to find out who killed this lady in the theatre, with two of my friends. I didn't mean to, it just sort of came out.'

'Really? So what did she say to that? Ladies aren't usually interested in that sort of thing, I believe.'

'Well just the opposite, actually. She got me to tell her all about Miss Burton, and our list of suspected persons, and how difficult it is to make any sense of it all, and she said, she once had to deal with that sort of problem, years ago, except the body was in a college chapel. And what she did was to write list after list, trying to see if people in one list were also on other lists, and gradually narrowing it down to just a few people.'

'I've been trying to do that.'

'Yes, I know, and you're very good at it, and I told her so. And she said, it was important to know just when the person was killed, and I said that's part of the trouble. But she said, what turned it around for her with her mystery was just one little bit of information, that she found almost by accident. And then she could chase after that, and more came out, and then suddenly it all became clear. So not to give up, and keep finding out more, and eventually it will come to a head, and we'll know who did it. And once we know who was the only person who could have done it, we'll know why as well. Motive, she said, is often most mysterious, and not to be too bothered about that at the beginning.'

'Really? She solved a murder mystery herself?'

'Yes, she was quite young, she said, about our age. And then she smiled a little smile to herself, and sighed.'

'That makes me feel a lot better, if ladies can do that sort of thing, and work in real jobs, and so on.'

'Yes, I thought you'd see that. And she was such a pleasant lady, talking to us as if we weren't just servants. She was wearing a gown cut just like your dark blue one, except it was silk, I think, and it was rose pink: she saw Sarah looking at it and asked her if she didn't think the latest sleeves were ridiculous, being so big, and Sarah didn't know what to say, being only fifteen, and not liking to say she loved them, although naturally she couldn't have such a gown herself.

But Miss Clarke saw her expression, and said, she was entitled to her own opinion, and if she liked the big gigot sleeves, then that was all well and good.'

'What an unusual lady.'

'I thought so, but then I've not met many to compare. But she had a mind of her own: I liked that.' He rubbed his nose, and looked away.

'So, are you saying, we just have to press on, and make more lists?'

'That's what she said. And keep talking to different people, and seeing where what they say doesn't quite match up, and try and work out who is telling the truth.'

Harriott nodded. 'You said she works for the Foreign Office?'

'Yes.'

'That means, I think, she must be what they call an intelligencer. Or spy. How exciting!'

Stephen chuckled. 'And she talked to little old me and Sarah. What a world.'

'We will do as she says. Keep on, keep trying.'

Monday evening passed with the two of them visiting the theatre and finding nobody in, except Mr Carpenter who was grumpily sweeping the stage, and moving scenery flats. He told them to clear out, as he was just about to lock up and go to his dinner, which was late, while at the same time staring openly at Harriott's bosom, which made her most uncomfortable. Seeing nothing there for them, they left as instructed, and Harriott, having no other good ideas, invited Stephen back to her house for dinner too.

Over the meal, Mr Curteis talked at length with Stephen about the new Imperial press he was thinking about buying, and showed him the pamphlet. This led on to discussing the cooking range, and then of course the newssheet had to be found, and the merits of the invention considered. Once the meal was over, he took Stephen into the print shop, and showed him the problems with his old press, how it was worn, and which parts tended to bind, and how the way it worked was slow, and asked him what he thought. Stephen tactfully said it depended on the price, and how much printing was likely to come his way, because it was no good having a fast press if there wasn't enough work for it. Also, it would only be a good investment if he was able to work for quite a few years yet, unless he thought Harriott would take over his business. Harriott, left out, dealt with the dishes and sulked.

On Tuesday late afternoon, Mary had a surprise for Harriott. She was working in the Bells when Mary arrived, on the arm of whom but George Bunn! She looked slightly flushed, but proud at the same time, and Harriott got someone to cover for her at the bar while she heard all about it.

'I didn't want to tell you, because, well, you know, you saw George first,' said Mary, turning to look up into George's face.

'No, don't think of it,' Harriott said. 'We hardly had a chance to get to know each other, it was that murder that put a stop to our meeting, wasn't it? Is that where you've been when you've been "busy", as you put it?'

'Yes; George has Tuesday evenings, and a half day on Friday, he got off a bit early today, and we thought we ought to tell you, now things are more settled between us.'

'I'm so pleased. George, Mary is lovely, and so kind. She's my best friend in the world.'

'I know that, I'm a lucky man. She's been telling me all sorts of things about what you've been doing after that night at the theatre.'

Harriott looked at Mary, frowning, and then her face relaxed. 'Of course, we could do with some more ideas, another set of brains.'

'Brains? Not me: Mary says you have brains for the lot of us.'

'Stephen too,' protested Harriott. 'He's very bright.'

'Now look, Harry, when do you finish?'

Harriott stepped out of the door to look at the church clock. 'In about twenty minutes, or so. If that clock's telling the truth for once. Why?'

'Because two things: George has realised we never looked at the chest the body was found in, did we? So we ought to do so, as soon as we can. But before that, George wants to meet Mr Collins at the White Lion, and hear his stories of the War, and so I thought we could go together, and then perhaps on to the theatre.'

'Alright, I'm happy with that. Warning, George, I'm not sure how many of those stories are true. Maybe all, maybe none.'

'We'll wait here for you, then.' Mary and George sat down in a window to talk, heads close together, while Harriott finished her duties. Once she had done so, she quickly ran through what Stephen had told her the day before for them, and Mary was suitably surprised at the condescension of the lady to her hostess' servants.

In due course the three of them made the short journey down the High-street to the Lion, and on the forecourt met with Stephen, on his way up from work to find them.

'Hello, girls; hello George. What are you doing here?'

'I'm with Mary,' he said, diffidently.

'And I'm with him,' said Mary, proprietorially, taking his arm.

Stephen looked from one to the other, and nodded in comprehension. 'Good, good. I take it you're up to speed with our little puzzle?'

'Well, I'm doing my best. But it's a bit complicated.'

'I'll say.'

'We're just going in here for George to hear about Corunna,' said Mary. 'He's very interested. In anything to do with the war with Napoleon, really.'

'Excuse me for butting in: did someone say Corunna?' came a voice from behind them. 'Who knows about Corunna here, may I ask?'

It was two ladies, out for a walk, parasols all correct, and hats so large they almost blotted out the sun.

Stephen pulled off his cap rapidly, and made a little bow. 'Miss Clarke, I apologise, we didn't see you. Are we in the way?'

'No, not at all. But Lady Mary and I were just out for a little walk, and we heard one of you mention Corunna. Might you introduce your friends?'

'Er, yes, of course. This is Miss Harriott Curteis, and this Miss Mary Exall; and this is George . . . I'm afraid I've forgotten your last name, George.'

'Bunn,' he said, blushing. The girls curtsied deep.

'I am Miss Rose Clarke,' the lady said, 'and this is my sister-in-law and best friend, Lady Mary Clarke. We are staying with Mrs Croughton for a few days. But perhaps Stephen has already explained?' She smiled at them all.

Harriott was the first to find her voice. 'Miss Clarke, we were just going to see if the landlord here, Mr Collins, would tell our friend George about his time in the Peninsular War. He says his bad knee is a wound he got at Corunna, but I am not sure how truthful his stories are. We have heard stories before from others, sailors for example, that have been found to be pure fabrication, or at least exaggeration beyond any resemblance to truth.'

'Astute woman,' said Miss Clarke. 'But, I must know, now I have heard this, just what he has to say. Do you not think so, Mary?'

'Absolutely, Rose, absolutely, if you wish it. Perhaps our new friends will introduce us to Mr Collins?'

'Capital idea. And you must join us for some refreshment, all of you. We can bespeak a private room, can we not?'

So within a few minutes the four young people and the two ladies were seated in a comfortable room, and tea and ale and, for Mary, port wine, were brought. Mr Collins seated himself cautiously on an upright chair, and prepared to tell his tale.

'First, Mr Collins,' said Miss Clarke, 'in which regiment did you serve?'

'Sergeant Robert Collins, First Guards, First battalion, Ma'am.'

'That's good. And where were you in the battle?'

'I was right by Sir John Moore when he got hit. He'd brought us up to the crest of this hill, and sent the second battalion down to attack the French centre while we gave covering fire from a distance, then he went back to fetch the Highlanders that had begun to retreat, to have them reinforce our unit. Then, just at the point when he had got back to our position with 'em, he was knocked off his horse by a roundshot from a Frenchie cannon. I got hit on the knee by a stray bit of shrapnel from it, the Frenchies put all sorts of rubbish in with their balls, so I couldn't do anything to help him, but he was a goner the moment he'd been hit, I could see that from where I was, lying on the ground. His arm was near off, and his chest and that was a real mess. Poor fellow, he was one of the few good 'uns.'

Miss Clarke turned to Lady Mary. 'That fits with what we know, doesn't it?'

'All correct, Rose.'

'Now, Mr Collins. Did you have much to do with the other regiments there?'

'There was a mort of units, all muddled up half the time during the retreat. Well, we'd been marching for more'n two weeks, it were dreadful. We got ourselves sorted before the big show, though, all right. Let me see, well . . . We was all in the snow, like, so you went with whoever could make the same pace as you. Cavalry were faster, of course, so they covered our backs, and the Light Brigade too. And the cannon, they slowed us, too. So, let me think, we were with the 1st and the 50th foot at times, and some of the 51st; the Highlanders kept to themselves mostly, but they were around and about. Cor blimey, they weren't half good in a scrap. Then, well, there seemed to be bits of half a hundred regiments, to be honest, Ma'am, I can't recall which now.'

'I see. And did you get to know any of the officers of the other regiments?'

'Not so's you'd say, make friends, Ma'am, it's not like that between non-coms and officers, you understand. But we had to deal with them, yes.'

'So you were, what, a sergeant I think you said?'

'That's right, Ma'am. And I'd have made staff sergeant if it hadn't been for this blasted knee, begging your pardon, ladies.'

Miss Clarke paused. 'Now, did you by any chance come across an officer, I think he was still with the 51st regiment, called Blackburn?'

Harriott heard a slight intake of breath from Lady Mary.

'Blackburn, eh? Let me see.'

'He was a captain, but acting major, because of casualties, I understand. Tall, dark brown hair, brown eyes?'

'I can't bring to mind . . . did he make it out on the ships?'

'No, sadly, no. He died on the slopes of a hill called Monte Mero, I have been told.'

'I wonder . . . but no, it was all too confused, and over twenty years ago. Sixteenth January 1809, I'll never forget that date. Sorry, Ma'am, but I can't say I did meet him.'

'Well, thankyou for trying. And for not inventing a story just for me.'

'Did you know this Captain Blackburn, then, Ma'am?'

'He was my fiancé.' She dabbed at her eyes with a small kerchief. But you are right, it was a long time ago.'

There was a pause. Mr Collins shifted in his seat. 'Is that all, ladies?'

'Yes, thankyou, all for now. But might you be willing to talk to our young friend Mr Bunn on another occasion? He is most interested in the War.'

'Righty-oh, Ma'am.' He levered himself to his feet with difficulty. 'You're staying with Mrs Croughton, they said?'

'Yes, but only for one day more.'

'I'll be sure to let her know if anything else comes to mind, like, about this Captain Blackburn.' He hobbled to the door, and took his farewell. 'Everything to your liking, ladies?'

'Perfect.'

CHAPTER 12

THE SEEKER

'DID ANY OF YOU NOTICE that scar across the bottom of his throat?' asked Miss Clarke when he had gone.

'He says, if anyone asks,' said Harriott, that it was from the knife of a Spanish woman who was defending her house when the soldiers went on a rampage and started pillaging and looting and, I am ashamed to say, er, raping.'

'So I have heard. Captain Blackburn's last letter was full of it; or rather, I deduced as much from what the censor had left.'

'I'm so sorry, Miss Clarke.'

'Well, as Mr Collins said, it was a long time ago. But I felt I just had to see, in case he knew him. As you will realise, I never married after his loss, and . . .' She broke off, and sniffed.

'There, Rose, I'm here.'

'Thankyou, Mary. Of course. But I have had a good life.'

The young people sat not knowing what to say. Eventually George said, 'You work for the Foreign Office, Miss Clarke?'

'Yes, I am a cryptographer. That is to say, I invent and break codes and ciphers. It involves a lot of mathematics, which is why I do it, I love it.'

'Oh. Really? I . . . well, I can't really manage sums, much. Beyond money, and that.' George twisted his cap in his hands.

'No, it is unusual. But Lady Mary here, she is fluent in languages. How many at the last count, Mary?'

'Don't. Please don't, Rose.'

'It was twenty-one last I heard.'

'Nothing like so many, really, no.' Lady Mary fluttered her hands in denial.

'I should like to do something important like that, some day,' said Harriott. 'Not just stay in little old Tenterden, nice though it is. And Stephen here wants to manage a great estate: he's a gardener, but he knows all sorts of things about soil and plants and machinery and so on.'

'Good for you, good for both of you: I hope you can achieve your ambitions,' said Miss Clarke. 'Now, have you enough in your glasses?'

They all said they had, not wanting to break the moment.

'I'd like to hear some more about this mystery of yours. If I'm not interfering, that is. It's been a long time since I had a mystery to solve that didn't involve codes.'

I thought Stephen had told you all about it, Miss Clarke?'

'No, I only explained a little bit, not all the details.'

Harriott sat back and thought. 'I don't know I can explain properly,' she began. 'It's all so muddled.'

'Start at the beginning and carry on until you come to the end, then stop,' suggested Miss Clarke.

'Yes, Harriott, you're always so clear, really,' said Stephen.

'Well, it all started when they found a body in a chest on the stage of the theatre, during this play we were watching,' she began.

Harriott drew her story to a close, and looked over at Stephen. 'Have I missed anything?' she asked. 'It's all so complicated, isn't it?'

'Not a thing,' he said. 'Like I said, you're always so organised when you explain something.'

'Excellent,' said Miss Clarke, who had listened to the whole story without even one interruption. 'May I ask a few things now?'

'Of course.'

'First, when do you think this poor lady actually died?'

Harriott looked at Stephen. 'We don't really know, which makes it so hard to know who to look for. It must have been after say, one o'clock on the Thursday.'

'No, more like almost two: the actors saw her fetching her gown from the green room about one thirty,' corrected Stephen.'

'Oh yes. And, well, nobody seems to have seen her after that. But the chest was put on the stage at maybe five or six, by Mr Carpenter.'

'Yes, but we only have his word for that,' said Stephen.

'Not really, Mr Gregory said it wasn't there when they finished on the stage at five, so it must have been after that.'

'Unless someone is lying, which they would if they were guilty.'

'Granted. So she might have died at any time really, until eleven the next morning.'

'If it was that late,' put in Miss Clarke, 'where was she in the period between two o'clock, when she fetched this gown, and the next day?'

'You're right. And we know she didn't turn up for work at three, at the Plough, or go there later to explain why she had been detained. So, we think, sometime between two and six on the Thursday is the most likely.'

'Good. It would be most useful to narrow that down further, if you can think of a way to do it. Now, who are your main suspects? By which I mean, people who could have been in the theatre between those hours.'

'Mr Higgins the American,' put in Mary quickly. 'He had met Miss Burton the night before in Honey-lane, and I think they must have had a row. I believe he'd followed her from America, and wanted her and she rejected him, so he was heartbroken. And then he went to look for her the next day, after she'd got back from Stone, and he found her and foully stabbed her to death!'

'Very well, Mr Higgins. Who is, if I understood you, not in Tenterden at present to allow you to question him?'

'No, that just makes one more difficulty,' admitted Harriott.

'What about . . .' said Stephen, then stopped, and shook his head. 'It can wait.'

'Then there's Mr Cousins,' said Harriott. 'He was around and about, all the time, and he knew her, and took her into the theatre that day by the back door, so he'd know about the broken lock, and he's a nasty piece of work, in my opinion. And he's from London.' She paused, realised what she'd said, and added, 'I'm so sorry, ladies, I didn't mean that . . .'

'No offence taken, and you're right, probably: London is full of miscreants. So, I don't remember if you said this earlier, why is this no-good Londoner here in Tenterden?'

'We don't know. He's been here over a month, and he goes out at least four times a week on horseback to other villages and towns, and nobody knows why.'

'What is his Christian name?' asked Lady Mary.

'Daniel. Daniel Cousins. And he wears the most horrid waistcoats,' said Mary.

Lady Mary turned to Miss Clarke. 'Rose, could it be? From the Home Office?'

'It might. It might indeed. Girls, is he, how should I say, rather forward with the ladies?'

'Absolutely,' said Harriott, immediately. 'And he has a long nose and a very good opinion of himself. Mary and I don't like him.'

'You know, I think we might know him,' said Miss Clarke. 'If it is him, he works for the Home Office, and I should think . . . What Bills are being prepared at the moment which would require visits to the countryside, Mary?'

'There is the Electoral Reform Bill, I suppose. Would that need assessments in the shires? It is going to upset a good number of people, so I think they would keep the details quiet. And of course Mr Wilberforce's bill to abolish the owning of slaves, which has been going on for ever, but I believe it is about to become law, soon, maybe in a year or two, is it not?'

'Dear William: he has laboured over this project for so many years. Hmm, not either of those, I think. What about our friends from Clapham who are trying to restrict the hours children are allowed to labour?'

'Yes, but why would someone come out to Tenterden for that?'

'Indeed. Of course. The only other legislation I have heard rumours about is something to do with poorhouses. The idea is to save money, or make it more efficient, or reduce administration, by combining several parishes into one great big poorhouse.'

'Which will of course increase administration, no doubt, and cost more, and be less efficient.'

'Of course it will. Well, that could be the issue. They would want to make sure the figures the parishes send are true accounts, and not just fabricated to cover up fraud.'

'My father is clerk to the poorhouse here,' said Mary. 'I could ask him.'

'Oh, I apologise, I meant no slight. But if you could enquire, yes. So that is two people. Others?'

'All the players, particularly Mr Gregory, because he was on the stage practising his lines. But then, if he was doing that with someone, he'd have difficulty doing a murder, wouldn't he?' said Mary

'He'd have an alibi, yes,' said Miss Clarke. 'I see.'

'What's an alibi?' said George, who hadn't spoken for a long time.

'It means, someone is able to say they were somewhere else, so they couldn't have done whatever they are being accused of.'

'Oh. I see. I think.'

'And there's Mr Brooke, and Mr and Mrs Carpenter, and anyone else in the theatre company,' Mary continued, ticking them off on her fingers. 'Also, all the people doing deliveries.'

'Not the deliveries,' said Stephen. 'They were all in the morning.'

'Oh yes.'

'That is a lot of people. No doubt you have tried to exonerate them, as best you can. Anyone else?'

None of them could think of any further names. 'Another idea was, I think Mr Carpenter suggested it, that Miss Burton had been . . . selling her virtue, and the gentleman in question wanted to silence her as he thought she was going to tell people about him, or she was blackmailing him,' said Harriott, 'but it doesn't fit with what we know of her character. And also, it could be absolutely anyone, any man I mean, who . . . well, had that habit.'

'Very well,' said Miss Clarke. 'Now, what about the method?'

'We haven't gone into that, really. It must have been a long knife or dagger, but they searched for one, and found nothing. And Mr Carpenter told the inquest that all their stage weapons are wooden.'

'If the murderer has any sense, it'll be at the bottom of a well, somewhere,' said Miss Clarke. 'On the other hand, murderers don't always have much sense, fortunately for us.'

'So you think we ought to look for it?' asked Harriott.

'Yes, indeed, but I don't think you'll find it. Nevertheless, it would be silly not to look, and miss vital evidence. Now, what about the chest she was found in? You didn't mention that.'

'George just spotted that we hadn't looked at that, and he only joined us today,' said Mary, beaming at him.

'A new mind on the topic is always useful. Well done George.'

'We are going to look for it once we are finished here,' said Mary.

'Excellent. Well, you few, you happy few, you band of brothers, and as importantly, sisters: Go to it, and, like Caesar's spirit, rage for revenge for Miss Burton's death.'

'You're getting all Shakespearean, dear: I think it's time to go,' said Lady Mary.

Miss Clarke pulled a face at her, and laughed. 'You're right, as always. Come then, let us let slip these dogs of war, and allow them to solve their own puzzle.'

The two ladies departed, and the others trooped after them. Outside, they could hear the bells being rung up, their rhythms erratic and clashing. Miss Clarke paused, and fumbled in her reticule.

'I have a card in here somewhere with my London address. I should so love to hear of the outcome of this affair, if you would be willing to let me know. Or, in the faint case I might be of more assistance, you would know how to contact me.' She found out the card, and handed it to Harriott.

'You must allow me the honour of favouring my own sex,' she said to Stephen, as she passed it over, smiling. 'I mean no slight by it.'

'Come, Rose, come. Let these youngsters be. We must go and inspect the church; I believe it has a fine carved roof.'

The four of them stood slightly bemused in front of the Lion, watching the ladies depart. The bells one by one fell silent.

'I didn't know gentlefolk would behave in such a kind way,' said Mary. 'I thought they always kept themselves above us.'

'I too,' said Stephen. 'Seems like she is an unusual lady.'

'Anyway,' said Harriott, 'let's not stand around: we ought to get on to the theatre before it closes up, and find this old chest.'

The theatre was indeed locked, so they went around the back to the unsecured door and went in. The building had an odd, hushed atmosphere, with the dim light visible in the auditorium through the stage doors making it seem ghostly, as if spectres of players long dead might still tread the boards.

'Let's get these sheets away from the window, so we can see what we're doing,' said Harriott, practically, 'and then we need to try and recognise the trunk. Stephen you crouched by it on that night: what exactly did it look like?'

'I wasn't taking too much notice, I was more concerned about what was in it,' he said, rubbing his nose. 'But, I think it was about so high,' he indicated, 'and so long, and it had a curved top, you know, like a half barrel, but not so sharp a curve.'

'What colour was it? What material? Was it iron?'

'Wooden, rather pale, I think. And some straps or bands across the lid, maybe?'

'Good. Well, let's set to.'

Although there was a lot of stored material in the area, most of it was in boxes or piled up in heaps, rather than in chests. As they searched, the bells began to sound, rather muffled inside the building. It did not take very long to determine that the chest was not to be found here, nor when they widened their search, in the green room.

'Where else could it be?' asked Mary. 'Unless they burnt it, because of, well, you know.'

'It could be a bad omen,' said George. 'Aren't players very superstitious?'

'I think they are,' said Stephen, 'so are you saying they might have got rid of it for that reason?'

'Well, maybe.'

'Where else could we look?' said Harriott.

'On the stage?' Mary went and checked. 'Nothing,' she called back

Stephen stopped and thought. 'Didn't they take the body to the town mortuary in it?' he asked. So, maybe it's still there?'

'I rather think they did,' said Harriott, remembering the inquest. 'At least, Dr Bishop seemed to say as much in his evidence.'

'Well, let's go there and see,' said Stephen.

As they left the building, the sound of the peal for Mr Ward's installation became louder, and louder still as they reached the High Street. No, wait on, thought Harriott, was it his installation – or was it the induction? She had got herself muddled, which annoyed her. No, it was the installation into the cure of souls, that was right. The tenor bell boomed out behind, and she pictured Richard Marshall hauling on his bell-rope, stripped for the work, muscles moving rhythmically, and his back stretching up above a most attractive . . . well, it was better not to go there, she might get carried away.

It did not take long to discover the mortuary building was locked up, and enquiry at the nearby inn revealed it was only accessible by application to the Town Clerk. Harriott undertook to do this the next day, and they set off home.

As they went, Stephen explained to George about what they had to do next, and what George might be able to help with, being as he was only free at certain times. He was very supportive, she thought, and kind. And, in spite of how he had ignored her when he was talking to her father about machines, she liked how he knew things, and could understand these new inventions. She stood outside her house and watched him walk on. Mary in turn, once she had waved George off, watched Harriott out of the corner of her eye, and wondered.

CHAPTER 13

ALL THE WORLD'S A STAGE

HARRIOTT'S MORNING WAS TAKEN UP with copying out contracts and agreements for Mr Pomfret, to do with the rental of The Pebbles to Mr Ward, and then accompanying him in his carriage to get them signed by the lessor and the vicar. It was strange to be bowling into town at such a height, and being assisted down by the groom. She almost felt sorry she had not passed Stephen on the drive, so important did it make her feel.

The date for moving across to the new accommodation was set for the Friday; charwomen had been arranged to clean the place on the Thursday; and as Mr Pomfret finished his business with Mr Ward, she heard him say to the new vicar that his induction would be taken by Mr Temple on the Saturday afternoon, with himself and Mr Milsted in attendance. She wondered if she would be allowed to participate, as she thought the whole ritual fascinating, but she held her tongue, and just took notes as directed.

Being as she had fulfilled her hours, she was left in town when business was concluded, and after snatching a quick lunch at home, ensuring her father was not in need of her assistance, and changing her gown, she then went in search of the two charwomen that had cleaned the theatre on the day of the murder, which somehow had been forgotten. Well, they had only been there in the morning, but she felt she ought to be thorough.

The first woman was rather vague about the whole thing, and said she never took no notice of them theatre folks, she just did her work and took her pay and that was that. However, the other was more helpful when she ran her to earth at the Vine Inn, if rather loquacious. Disentangling the verbiage, it seemed that the two women had not seen anything untoward on the Thursday, they had given the green room a quick lick and a promise, being as it was occupied, then cleaned the stage, the boxes, and the galleries. The only thing of note had been Mr Carpenter swearing to himself as he removed the dance floor, words that a woman shouldn't have to put up with hearing.

However, she added that they had been called in again on the Saturday, because of the uproar on the night before, and because one of the gentlemen had complained that his box smelled, which it certainly had not the day previous. So, they had cleaned all through again, and sure enough, the box by the stage had smelled like a dog had been doing his business there, but they had given it a good going-over and spread herbs and it was all sweet as anything by the time they had finished.

Which box? Why, the furthest one to the right of the stage as you look at it. She expected one of the older ladies might perhaps have had a little accident, what with the shock of the body being found? Trials of old age, she said, it'll come to you too in time, young lady.

Harriott thanked her profusely, and took herself off to see Mrs Carpenter, while the matter was fresh in her mind. She didn't know what to make of it, but she would put it in her notes forthwith. Mrs Carpenter remembered the matter well: it had been Mr Haffenden that had complained, and Harriott could look for herself, but it was all fine now, she didn't know what could have happened, but there you were.

Next, she applied to the Town Hall for access to the mortuary. She was met with a blank refusal to allow her access. The clerk said she had no authority to be allowed entry; only official persons were permitted. Also, it was not suitable for a woman to see; and what had this chest to do with her?

Harriott felt rage swelling in her chest, tried to breathe more slowly, and paused to let her shoulders drop back down. She tried reason, explaining how she and her colleagues were trying to establish the murderer of Miss Burton, to no avail. She tried cajoling, almost begging, which was so foreign to her nature. No result. Then, as a last resort, she asked just who would be allowed to see the chest. Doctors, Town Hall staff, and the mortuary attendant, it seemed, and of course the clergy, were the only ones.

'What about the chest's owner?' she tried, forlornly, turning to leave.

'Well, that's another thing,' he said. 'Can't say we could deny the rightful owner. 'Sides, it could do with shifting, takes up space, it does.'

Harriott left the building, fuming; crossed the road back to the theatre; and sought Mr Brooke. Mrs Carpenter said he was due in some time in the afternoon, but she couldn't say when. Harriott decided she was not going to be defeated by that odious clerk, and that she would wait for the theatre manager. In the meantime, she would have another look around the place, and maybe talk to any of the players who might be present. Mrs Carpenter must be sure to tell Mr Brooke she wanted to see him, and not on any account to let him leave without fetching her.

She entered the theatre through the door from the cottage, and first went in the near-darkness to the furthest box, the one that had had the smell, enough to require an extra cleaning. It was quite dim even when she pushed through the curtains and stood looking out over the stage. She knelt down and made a careful search of the floor by touch, but found nothing. Perhaps she ought to fetch a light and see if there were marks? But then the charwomen would have erased anything that had been of note, and the murder was now nearly three weeks ago. It was a shame they had not started to investigate this calamity immediately, and been able to see the body, the theatre, the chest and so on before they had been wiped clean, as it were.

Feeling a little silly, she applied to Mrs Carpenter for a candle, and searched the floor for marks. It was hard to tell by the weak light, but there seemed to be endless stains of one sort or another on the floorboards, and scrape marks where chairs had been pushed back and forth. The sill, facing the stage, had its paint chipped and peeling in places, and all in all she could make nothing of it.

Keeping hold of her candle she inspected the other three boxes on that side, finding much the same excess of marks. Feeling frustrated, she did the same in all the others, to no avail. And then, thinking there would be no end to this job, she went upstairs, and opened those shutters over the gallery windows that were still obscured, in order to examine the stage more readily.

The boards were all dusty, and marked in various places with the remains of what looked like coloured chalks. Two boards, however, both near the Pit, stage left, looked a little different. They were slightly darker, only a touch, but she thought also a little less worn? What this might mean she had no idea, but it ought to go on her lists.

Now, where exactly had the chest sat during the play? Of course, there had been other performances since then, but she ought to look. It was difficult to judge exactly, and she had to trek back up the spiral stairs to the position where she had sat in the gallery with George, to get the right perspective. Then, back down on the platform she checked the place for blood marks. Surely there would be some sign, even after a thorough cleaning? There were none, which seemed a little odd, given what had been said about the poor condition of the chest, the nature of its contents, and the manner of Miss Burton's death.

As she stood up from this last, crawling, inspection, she heard Mrs Carpenter's voice calling her name. Brushing the dust from her gown as best she could, she made her way back into the cottage, and to Mr Brooke's office.

'What do you want, Miss Curteis? I am monstrous busy, we have a performance in Rye tomorrow and all is ding dong.'

'Mr Brooke, sir, I am most sorry to bother you, but I felt we ought to inspect the chest in which Miss Burton's body was found, to see if there might be anything that could point us to the murderer. I believe it may be in the mortuary building.'

'So why am I needed?'

Harriott felt herself blush. 'The clerk at the Town Hall will not admit me, he says I have no authority; but he will allow the owner of the trunk to see it.'

'Can it not wait? After all, the sad event was a long time past?'

'Well, sir, it could, but I feel we have lost so much time already, without finding the answer, that if you could see your way . . . It is only across the road behind the Town Hall, it should only take a few moments.'

'Very well: I shall gain your admittance, and then return. You will arrange for its transport back to us? We may need it again soon.'

'Yes, sir, of course, sir.'

Back at the desk in the Town Hall, she stood back, holding in her resentment at how deferential the clerk was to Mr Brooke. However, he took them both to the mortuary outbuilding, where Harriott found the chest, stacked away in a corner under a pile of winding-sheets. Mr Brooke promptly identified it and departed, ordering the clerk to send it over at his first convenience.

With the help of the clerk she extracted the chest, set it on the slab under the skylight, and opened it. There was still a stench, but she held her breath and pulled out the cloths, matted together with the dried blood. She wished Stephen had been with her, she found this all quite unnerving, but she persevered.

As far as she could tell the noisome clump was made up of a mixture of materials. There were some fairly large cloths. One was of figured silk, it seemed; the others plain but of various colours. She thought they might perhaps have been used as wall-hangings to suggest different types of rooms. Then, there was what appeared to be a wrap-around kind of skirt, and a horridly-clotted item which might have once been a bodice. Other than them, the chest was empty. As regards staining of the inside, she could not see much evidence of blood, other than a faint mark or two near one end. She did not know what to make of this, so, using all her charm she asked the clerk to fetch her paper and pen, and made a sketch of the marks. Perhaps Stephen would be able to see what this meant, she thought. And as an afterthought, she marked on her sketch an indication of which side the lid hinged, and made a rough estimate of the chest's size using her forearm length as a rule.

Seeing the clerk's impatience, she left the matter there, replaced the noisome cloths, and sought reassurance from the clerk that he would arrange for the chest's being returned to the theatre. After all, if Stephen thought of something she might have missed, they could have another look once it was back at its home.

Harriott thought she would go back and write up the new things she had found out, in her papers. She had hardly passed the tollgate and crossed Vicarage-lane when James Maynard appeared, coming as if from her own house.

'Harriott! Just the girl: I've been looking for you. I missed you on Sunday.' He grinned at her, the dimple on his chin deepening.

Harriott felt her heart bump, but at the same time a pang of guilt assailed her as she realised she was likely to leave off the mystery, if James proposed a conflicting activity.

'Well, James, I've been busy. I have work to do, and my father to look after. What is it?'

'Well, if you're too busy, I'll leave it. It's just that I thought you might like to come with me to Cranbrook tomorrow, there's a bit of a fête on there in the morning, raising money for something or other. It'd be a pleasant drive, and we could have a spot of lunch, and so on? I have to see a man about some machinery, but that won't take long.'

Harriott didn't need long to decide. Eight miles with James in some sort of carriage, along the pretty lanes, seemed too good to miss. And she wouldn't say no to a wander around stalls, and being generally looked after.

'You're in luck. I don't work Thursday mornings, but we'd have to be back for about three, I'm due in the Bells.'

'Done. I'll pick you up at nine then, in the gig, not Father's chariot. Weather looks set fine, we should have a splendid time.'

'I'll look forward to it. I shall wear my best gown, in your honour.'

'You will outshine anyone in whatever you wear, Harriott. Everyone knows that. Well, until tomorrow.' He walked off, whistling, and disappeared into the seed merchant's.

Harriott went into her house, and settled down with her papers. It was difficult to concentrate, though, with images of James' smile intruding. She could do with a break from the puzzle, anyway. But somehow, there was a nagging feeling at the back of her mind that something wasn't quite how it ought to be.

When Stephen came by the Bells that evening, she showed him her papers, and he said he thought he ought to have another talk with Mr Carpenter, to try and pin him down more accurately as to the times people came into the theatre, and just when he himself had been away, and therefore unable to observe any malefaction. She nodded agreement, and watched his back as he left, wondering whether she ought to tell him about tomorrow's expedition, and deciding it was no concern of his.

Later, as she was clearing up and the last of the men were being shown the door, Stephen came back.

'How did you get on?' she asked, as he leaned on the bar. 'Any luck?'

'Well, after a fashion,' he said. 'Any chance of a gage of porter, or are you done?'

'No, you can stay,' she said, pulling him a pint. 'What were you doing all this time?'

'Talking, and more talking. Seems the company is off in Rye, so Carpenter had less to do, and was a bit more chatty. I don't like the fellow, he's mean to his wife, and lazy, but I think I made a bit of progress.'

'Here you are. Do you want to go and sit in the window and tell me what you found?'

'Surely, if you're done.'

'So, Carpenter was done with his dinner, and hadn't left for the Harris Arms, and was inclined to be chatty, like I said. I think he'd had a bit of something liquid with his food, he was a bit slurred, nothing much, but you know?'

'I've seen drunkenness in all phases,' she said. 'So, what did he say?'

Stephen pulled out a bit of paper, with scribbled pencil notes. 'He reckons he finished most of his work in the Pit about twelve, had his lunch, and was back there around twelve thirty. I mean, I worked out it must have been about then from what he said about other people he saw, like Mr Brooke, and the boy from the chandler: he didn't keep track of the time. Cousins said he delivered Miss Burton to the theatre about twelve thirty, didn't he, so that fits? So that was when he went up to tidy the galleries, like he said before, with his bucket, which is when he saw Miss Burton arriving. Now, he said previously that he went out for a walk after that, but I don't think it was straight away. He seems to have been doing something or other around the auditorium for a while, because he now says he saw Miss Burton again, and this time she was wearing that high-waisted gown, that she was found in.'

'But, she was supposed to meet the dressmaker, Mrs Relph, at two, wasn't she?'

'Yes, that doesn't quite add up. He says she came onto the stage, and began practising some part or other, muttering lines, he said. So he went for his walk, because he can't be doing with the players rabbiting on when he has work to do, and then after a bit, I had to press him on this, he went to the Harris Arms, and sat there a while, before coming back about three thirty. What he did then was just to lay out costumes, and fetch properties, and then lastly when the other actors had left the stage, put the chest in place, hang the draperies, and set out the scenery flats that were needed. He says, and mind, he might have changed his story a bit, that he just dragged the chest from the backstage area, and it might have had anything or nothing in it as far as he knew, because he never lifted it, being on his own.'

'Really? So Miss Burton, or rather, her body, might have been in it already?'

'That's what he seemed to be saying. I mean, I don't entirely trust him, but why should he lie? He wasn't there for the time that seems crucial, which is from about half past one until half past two, he was in the inn or somewhere; and if he'd been drinking, would he notice if the chest was heavier than it ought to be? I mean, if he just dragged it without knowing or caring what was in it?'

'So, was the murder done in the backstage area, where the chest was?'

'I don't know. It seems a bit odd, to kill someone while they stood in a chest, doesn't it?'

'Oh, of course, I hadn't thought of that before. Now you mention it though . . . It isn't reasonable, is it?'

'No, and while we're on that, did you find the chest?'

Harriott summarised her search, and showed him her diagram. 'The cloths were saturated with blood; or rather, they had been, it was just a disgusting mess now; but there wasn't much on the bottom of the trunk, and what there was was in these places, which seems peculiar to me.'

Stephen examined the diagram, and sucked his teeth. 'Where were the cloths then?'

'Just bundled up over the whole of the bottom of the chest. Of course they might have been moved by the doctor, when he examined the body.'

'So why? . . . I mean, wouldn't the blood have soaked the bottom, if there was so much?'

'I don't know. The chest ought to be delivered from the mortuary to the theatre soon, you could look for yourself.'

'Anyway,' Stephen took a long pull of his porter, 'after Carpenter had told me all he could, I went along to the Harris Arms. You wouldn't believe how hard it is to get anyone to remember who might have been there three weeks ago. I had to ask so many people, and I got a lot of rudeness and nearly came to blows with one fellow, but eventually I found someone who knew Carpenter, he couldn't stand the man, he said, but he reckoned he had come in about half past two, and left about half past four, or thereabouts. He knew this because he had to move from his favourite seat when our man came over, and prop up the bar instead. He says Carpenter sat in the window and drank old ale one after the other, maybe four pints, and he doesn't want to cross him when he's in that sort of fighting mood.'

'Fighting?'

'He didn't say there was any actual violence, but he was just wary. Told me he, Carpenter I mean, beats his wife something chronic. He had a whole lot of tales about him, that I had to listen to, but I couldn't work out if any of it was true.'

'What a horrible man. Poor Mrs Carpenter.'

'Yes, but it means he was away for most of the afternoon, and I imagine he'd been wandering around before he went into the inn, where I couldn't say.'

'Did Mr Carpenter see Mr Higgins at the theatre at all; or Mr Cousins, after that first time?'

'No. But remember, Miss Brown said Higgins, if it was him, came in later, about mid-afternoon, if I recall?'

Harriott consulted her notes. 'Yes, she said mid-afternoon, that's right. It's a shame nobody can give us a more accurate time, isn't it?'

'Not everyone can afford a pocket watch, though, can they?'

'No. Maybe, when all these other inventions are made, they'll invent a clock cheap enough for us all to have one?'

'Maybe. Anyway, I think we're a bit nearer. Carpenter left maybe about one o'clock, walked around a bit, went to the inn about two thirty. Higgins would have come in about, what, two thirty or three? Or later? And why? And did he meet Miss Burton? Cousins, now, what was he doing? If he is really on government business about poorhouses, he might be free for the rest of the day, and have come back for some reason to see her? And then, have you seen that sheet, *Lady Susan*? She's suggesting what Carpenter said originally, that we ought to be looking for a man patronising the brothels for our murderer.'

'You don't want to take much notice of gossip sheets,' said Harriott dismissively. 'People will print any old rubbish.'

CHAPTER 14

ARE YOU GOING TO SCARBOROUGH FAIR?

JAMES MAYNARD CALLED FOR HARRIOTT promptly at nine. She climbed up into the gig, taking his hand even though it wasn't necessary, and arranged herself comfortably beside him. Her sleeves were a bit of a nuisance in the narrow seat, but there was just about enough room, and she leaned back and sighed in anticipation.

Along the High-street they trotted, past the West Well, and turned down the hill towards Goodshill. James began to point out all the fields they passed which belonged to his father, and what plans he had for next year.

'I'm to be in charge of the arable,' he informed her, 'while Father keeps to the livestock. I'm going to sow some new crops, see how they do.'

He slowed to indicate various sites of planned innovations, and how other fields needed drainage work, the clay being most unforgiving. Then, as they passed the farmhouse, he explained how they were planning to extend the animal housing, and make a new shed for an engine to help with ploughing, if the new machinery being developed was as good as people were saying.

Harriott just looked at the scenery, and wondered what it might be like to live out of town on a farm, and whether it was something she might consider. James himself was lovely, and most engaging, but . . . well, was that life what she wanted? She settled for taking covert glances at his shoulders, he being focussed on keeping the horse under control, and at his profile, which was most appealing.

They passed Park Gate, and into Brogues Wood, and then by degrees through Forsten Green and Chequertree to Golford. James was very good at identifying some of the birds that shot out of cover in the woods with the passing of the vehicle, and telling stories about friends who farmed at various points along the road.

Eventually they made their way carefully down the steep hill past the mill into Cranbrook town, and left the gig at the George. James went to see his man about ploughing machinery, and Harriott went over to look over the church, rather than just wait outside.

She had inspected everything worth seeing in the building, and toured the graveyard, but there was still no sign of her host. Gravelled for something to occupy her, she began to look in the shop windows nearest the churchyard, and eventually after almost an hour, James reappeared, still talking to the mechanic. He waved to her, but stood for near on five minutes before he came over.

'Sorry about that, I didn't think it would take so long, but it seems these engines are not going to be available for a while yet. Something to do with patents, and problems with the linkages, and pressure in the boiler, and things like that, you wouldn't be interested, I'm sure.'

Harriott frowned at hearing this, but held her peace. 'So, can we go to the fête now?'

'Surely. Just let me speak to Mr Jonas in the seed merchants.'

At least James didn't stay long in the merchant's, and then they walked together up the hill to the fairground. There were stalls, and games of chance, and tests of strength, and so on, all the things one might expect of a country fête. He bought them both pastries, and they wandered around eating while seeing what they might like to try.

James decided to try his skill at bat-and trap, and Harriott was left on the side to watch, her sleeves preventing proper athletic movement.

The same was true at the Aunt Sally, though James was inordinately proud when he finally dislodged the target and presented his prize of an orange to her with great ceremony.

After all this exertion they went back to the craft stalls, and the haberdashers, the grocers, and of course the agricultural implement sellers. When this entertainment was exhausted, they retired to stand near the platform erected for the performance of the town band, and stayed awhile to listen.

'When this is over, would you like to go to an inn for lunch, or buy something here and make a pic-nic?'

Harriott looked around the field. 'We could sit over there, in the shade,' she suggested. 'Would you buy suitable viands, and some lemonade or something, and I will go and claim a place?'

He nodded, and she found a spot, and waited. Waited for longer than she had imagined necessary, until she found herself agitated enough to get up and pace around. At last James appeared, contrite, explaining he had met a man who knew about the best way to fertilise soils, and had to speak with him. He brought as a peace-offering pies, sweet pastries and lemonade, and an opened bottle of ale, and they sat back down.

As they ate, the band struck up into music for dancing and a few couples took to the more closely-scythed areas and tried out their steps. Harriott was content to watch, as she was both hungry, and unsure of making figures on such uneven ground. Her caution was justified as several of the dancers stumbled and one even fell when performing a swing, to the accompaniment of much laughter.

'Did you go to the Aid dance a few weeks ago?' Harriott asked, thinking back to the beginning of their puzzle. 'The one for that poor fellow who got killed under the cart wheels?'

'Jem, you mean? Yes, I was there. They raised a fair bit for his widow, that they did.'

'Was it well-attended?'

'Place was full, had to stand out half the time, there wasn't space for all of us to make figures.'

'You must have seen the poor lady who was killed, she was there. Miss Burton, I mean.'

'Don't know who she might have been. I was with my friends, didn't take notice of others.'

'She came with a man called Cousins, who had a fancy waistcoat. London man. She was very short and shall we say, solidly built.'

'No, didn't see her. 'Sides, we were making great inroads into the ale, that night.' He paused to munch on his pie. 'Are you interested in agriculture? There's so much to learn, I love it.'

'Well, we do need farms, I like to eat.'

'No, I mean, running the place, improving things, like yields, and trying new varieties, and so on.'

'I can see how much you love it, James.' She tried moving a little closer to him, but he was looking over at a display of cattle, across the way.

'Do you mind if I go and see those beasts? Father will want to know about them.' And he was off.

Harriott, disappointed, finished her pie, drank some lemonade, and then, seeing it was there, had a few deep draughts of the ale.

Before half past one it was time to leave, as she didn't want to upset Mr Paine with lateness again. It was only with difficulty she managed to get James away, and what with a delay getting the horse into harness, and paying for stabling, and so on, they were not on the road before two.

On the trip back, she tried to switch the conversation to matters other than farming, but James seemed to lack interest in other things. For instance, she told him a little about her work for Mr Pomfret, but he didn't really think women ought to be doing men's work. At the Golford toll, he spent an age trying to find the correct coins, which further agitated her. And then once they were moving again, she tried to tell him about some singular advances in printing presses, but he somehow manoeuvred the topic around to new types of ploughs. And as for their investigations, she finally realised it was best to not mention them, and sat back and concentrated on willing the horse to go faster.

The church clock was already striking the hour of three when they reached Westwell, and she hurried down from the gig outside her house, giving only a sketchy farewell and thanks, rushed inside to change, and arrived panting at the Bells, apologising almost as she entered the saloon, and taking her place behind the bar to a frown and a shaking of the head from the landlord, a wagging of his finger, and a promise of a telling-off to come.

She kept herself busy at the bar, and didn't dare slip off to the kitchen to see Mary until Mary came out, on her way home. She kept on serving, while Mary stood behind her and talked a little about her day, and a lot about George. It seemed he had begun work on the wherries on the rivers, but got bored with the same runs every trip, and found a berth on a coaster. This went fine, as they sailed to Harwich, and down to London docks, and the north Kent coast, but after they left Margate the wind got up and by the time they put into Winchelsea he was so seasick he left his crew and tried his luck in the town. There he went from house to house and eventually at one, the master told him his visitor might be wanting a footman, and that's how he came to be in Tenterden. Isn't that amazing? Mary said.

She carried on talking about George, saying a few things about how he had enjoyed meeting Mr Collins, and why he was so interested in Napoleon, and so on and so forth. When there was a lull in her chatter, Harriott decided she ought to say something.

'Why is it,' she asked, 'that all the really attractive men have a drawback? I don't mean George, I mean the other ones.'

'You're asking the wrong person, Harry, I've never been good with finding men, until now anyway. But, maybe, do you think perhaps the ones you like have lots of girls after them, so they think they can treat us how they want?'

'You're probably right.' She sighed. 'I do like a nice tight bum on a man, though. And broad shoulders. And he has to be tall, the taller the better.'

'You'll price yourself out of the market with those demands. How many young men are there in Tenterden anyway? Forty of the right age if you're lucky, and lots of those will be labourers, that you wouldn't really get on with, or already taken. Why are you asking? Have you had another disappointing time?'

Harriott hesitated. She didn't really want to say anything, it was all too fresh, but well, this was Mary. 'Can you see me as a farmer's wife, looking after the chickens and ducks, and feeding everyone when they come in from the fields at all hours?'

Mary laughed. 'Not in a hundred years, Harry. You'd be bored silly in a month. Unless the farmer had the most amazing rump and the equipment to go with it, and even then . . .'

Harriott sighed. 'I do believe you're right, Mary. Well, I suppose I just have to keep looking, in other places; maybe I need to look beyond Tenterden?'

'Maybe. But when will you get the chance? We don't have reasons to go much further than a few miles, or the money for coach tickets. I suppose we could head off on horseback, but sidesaddles scare me.'

'Oh well. Talking of coach tickets, have we anything else we need to ask Mr Cousins? And did you ask your father about him?'

'Yes, I should have said earlier. He did come and inspect the accounts and the admission books, and he talked to the warden, and even the cook and some of the inmates, and made a whole tranche of notes in a big book. And he was very close about why he was there, just showed a paper with his authority from London, and wouldn't say anything more.'

'How was his manner?'

'Father didn't really say, I don't think men notice these things much, but I could tell he didn't want him there, he felt it was interference, and he could run things perfectly well as they were.'

'Did he get any idea of how long Mr Cousins would be here?'

'Not that he said. Why? Do you think I ought to nip into the Woolpack and check he hasn't left already?'

'Maybe. Wouldn't do any harm. What are you doing next anyway?'

'Helping Mother with dinner, and then sorting laundry.'

'If you could: wouldn't take a moment. And if you happen to see him, is there anything we need to ask him?'

'I hope I don't: he's creepy.'

'So he is; but he's one of our main possibles.' She thought. 'You could ask him who he was at the play with on the Friday? We never did think to ask. And you could . . . well, you could say someone saw him at the theatre in the afternoon, and why didn't he mention it?'

'Did they? Who said so?'

'No, nobody said. It's just a way of getting him to cough up the truth.'

'I don't like falsehoods, I don't think I could . . .'

'No, never mind, I've seen you trying to lie, you go all red and anyone can tell. Leave it at asking about his lady friend on Friday, then.'

'All right. I'll see you tomorrow.'

At Morghew, Harriott broached the subject of the induction with Mr Pomfret, once she was sure he had approved all she had done, and had finished instructing her.

'Sir, I wondered . . . will you require me to attend the induction tomorrow?'

'No, that won't be necessary. It is a simple ceremony, just myself, Mr Milsted and Reverend Temple. Mr Ward is the one who leads, by touching all the elements of his new property. A symbolic touching, you understand. I shall not be here in the morning, though, as I have business in Ashford at my bank: the ceremony is not until three. You may continue with your usual duties.'

'Sir, if I may make bold, would it be permissible to attend the ceremony, to observe? It sounds most interesting.'

Mr Pomfret frowned. 'It is not usual, not usual at all. Why should you wish such a thing?'

'I am always looking for ways to enlarge my understanding, sir.'

'I see.' He pursed his lips. 'Well, I see no reason why you should not. But keep silent, and sit somewhere out of the way. We are gathering outside the porch to begin with the ceremony of the church key, and then progressing around the sacred stations.'

'Thankyou kindly, sir. I shall be invisible to you, I promise.'

Mary came by after she got home, to say that Mr Cousins had left, the morning previous, which was a relief, in a way, but it meant that they had now lost both their main suspects. She herself was off to see George, unless Harriott had any more investigations for her. But, given that all the theatre company were away in Rye, that left almost nothing they could do on the mystery, and so she wished her well, and waved her off feeling . . . well, not quite envious, she hoped, but something like. Wistful, maybe, that sounded better?

Which meant Harriott had no excuse for leaving the household tasks that she had been putting off, undone any longer. With a sigh, she fetched out the flatirons and put them to heat, collected the enormous pile of clean clothes, and set to.

In the evening while working at the Bells, she sent Stephen to have a look at the chest, which ought to have been delivered to the theatre. He did as she asked, but learnt nothing new. He said the company were not expected back until the following Thursday morning, as they were going on to Hastings before returning late on Wednesday. All in all, it felt a let-down from the progress they seemed to have been making, and the praise they had received from Miss Clarke. Stephen stayed in the inn for quite a while afterwards, chatting to her about this and that, in between her serving customers, and trying to be encouraging, but she felt quite flat.

Saturday was routine until the afternoon. She made sure she was in the church well before three, and wore her black gown the better to stay invisible. She wished she could have been outside for the beginning of the ceremony, but that was not possible. However, she could hear the words of Mr Temple, and the scrape of the key in the lock, as they gave over the possession of the church to Mr Ward. Then the four of them came in, and moved around the building laying hands on the font, the lectern, the pulpit, the altar, and the sacred vessels, before moving to the vicar's seat. Before sitting, Mr Ward was handed the sally of the sacristy bell, and tolled it slowly. There was surely some meaning in the number of strokes, which she counted carefully, but Harriott could not discern what if anything fourteen might mean.

Then, Mr Ward took his seat, and the curate spoke some words over him, which Harriott could not hear. Mr Ward replied more audibly, but whatever he said appeared to be in Latin, which she could not understand. Just then, she heard a scraping noise at the back of the church, and turned to see Richard Marshall standing up, walking to the tower steps, opening the door and going up to the bell chamber. She was briefly tempted to follow him, given that he had invited her to observe previously, but sank back down as she realised what such a visit would suggest to the man. And how she did not wish to be another of his conquests, however exciting that might be at the time.

In church on Sunday Mr Ward took his seat in the chancel, but the service was led by Mr Temple, Mr Ward only leading the prayers of penitence. The Ward family were not to be seen, but Harriott thought they might well have been in one of the chancel pews and not visible from her gallery. Afterwards, the four of them met in the churchyard by Stephen's holm-oak sapling, which he inspected and pronounced it to be taking well.

'What next?' he asked. 'What can we do now?'

'There's nothing to do,' said Mary. 'Everyone's gone away.'

Harriott sighed. 'Well, there's one or two things I thought about while I was finishing the ironing this morning. Nothing much, but I suppose we could look for the knife or dagger, couldn't we?'

'We can't go fishing in all the wells thereabouts for it, can we, if it was thrown down like Miss Clarke said,' objected Mary.

'No, but we ought to look through the property box when the company gets back.'

'The property box?'

'Properties are what they call the things they use on stage, like weapons and books and, well, small things you can carry, not like chairs and chests and things.'

'Oh.'

'And they'll have taken it with them I should think. We could scout around the green room, I suppose, while there's noone around.'

'I don't like going in there on my own, it's creepy and dark.'

'Why don't you and George do that on Tuesday evening when he's off then?'

'Oh yes, rum notion, it would be so romantic with just the two of us in the half-light.' She smiled up at George, who looked at his feet.

'We'll have to have a look at this property box on Thursday, then, Harriott,' said Stephen. 'That could be your job, you're free once you've done your housework. And then you could work through the list we made of the actors, and see where they all were between one and three that Thursday. See if they had what Miss Clarke called an alibi.'

'Don't forget Mr Brooke,' put in Mary. 'I know he says he was at home, except when he was called in to pay those people, but was he?'

'I don't want to go and question his wife, does anyone else?' said Harriott.

'If he's the murderer, he'll have made sure she knows what to say anyway, won't he?' said Stephen. 'I would, if I was him.'

'She isn't part of the company, is she?' Mary frowned. 'How could we find out where he was at that time?'

Nobody knew. Feeling rather at a loss, they split up, George to return to work at Morghew, Harriott to her chores, and Mary to walk back with George before she was due in the Bells' kitchen.

'What are you going to do, Stephen?' asked Harriott.

'I'll see if Mr Assister is at home, and spend time reading his soil book. I've not had much chance for a while.'

'Oh. Well, goodbye for now.'

CHAPTER 15

GOOD NEWS

THE NEXT FEW DAYS FELT rather Hum Drum to Harriott. True, she had her work at Morghew, and was making good progress with the library in between dealing with correspondence. Mr Pomfret informed her that he and his sister would be away for a week or more in the near future, he wasn't able to say when just yet, but when he was gone she could concentrate on getting the books fully arranged. Apart from sorting the post and replying to the few she could deal with herself, she could have all the books out of their shelves while she ordered them if she liked.

She met with Mary at the Bells, but didn't see Stephen at all. She supposed he was reading his soil book in the evenings, but it felt odd not to have him around. And on Tuesday evening when Mary was out with George, she had only her sewing to occupy her, a task she hated, and put off whenever she could. Mary did put her head around the door late that evening, to report her search of the green room had been unproductive, but disappeared immediately, and, sighing, Harriott bent again to her mending. Surely there was something else she could be doing before Thursday?

On Wednesday she laid out a sheet of paper with a list of all the actors she had heard of, with space to write what they were doing at the relevant time. That felt a little better, but still . . . they needed to know more about Mr Cousins and Mr Higgins. How could they find out anything when they weren't around?

On Thursday morning she had to help her father set the print for Lady Susan's latest issue, which left her frustrated at not being able to get on with the questioning of the returned actors. As she composed, and set the type on the forme, she was struck with an idea.

'Father? I know I can't know who Lady Susan is, but how does she get her gossip? Do people pass it on, or does she find it all herself?'

'No, people leave messages for her, don't you remember me telling you? They leave it at the Queen's Arms, anonymously if they like, and she may or may not publish it.'

'I see. Could anyone put an advertisement in the sheet? I mean, I just had an idea about asking for anyone seeing two of our men, around the theatre that Thursday after lunch.'

'Don't see why not. She might charge a shilling or so, but . . . look see, why don't you write something, and put it in now. I have to show her the proof before we print the whole lot, and so I can always take it out if she objects.'

Harriott paused in her typesetting, and quickly made a form of words to suit. She set it in the correct typeface, and locked up the forme. 'There, all done, Father. Shall I make the proof?'

The proof was made, she took it to the table to read it through for errors, marked them up, found out the correct letters and replaced them, and then printed the new version.

'Father, can you check this? I want to get to the theatre, I have some people to see.'

'Go on with you. Is it Stephen Fuggle you're meeting?'

'No, he's at work. I'm just going to talk to all the actors.'

'Oh. I see. Well, I'll see you for lunch, will I?'

'Maybe. Depends on whether I can find all the people easily.'

Harriott was working in the Bells that evening, when Stephen came in. 'Good day to you, stranger,' she greeted him. 'What have you to say for yourself?'

'These new plants, Camellias, like acid soil, such as peat; and so do rhododendrons,' was his retort. 'They also need it to be well drained, and don't like the frost, depending on species.'

'I didn't mean that, idiot. I meant, have you found out anything for our mystery.'

'No, we decided you'd see the actors and go through the properties, and report. Any joy?'

'A little. Look, take this list and go through it. I've noted down what everyone said.'

Stephen took some light ale and the paper over to a window table, and applied himself to it. He pulled out a pencil and made a few marks, and sat back at times, as if in thought. Harriott carried on serving, and rebuffing a couple of men who were getting a bit frisky with her, in her usual way. After quite a time, Stephen came back to the bar, and waited until there was a break in demand.

'Excellent job, as a start, Harriott, and so clear. Someone will be offering you a job as a clerk, soon.'

Harriott pushed him playfully on the shoulder. 'Idiot, like I said. What do you think?'

'So, the properties are all clear, nothing in the way of a weapon that could hurt anyone. And most of the actors have good alibis, because they were together a lot of the time, I see. But why did you rule out Mrs Robberds? She went out saying she was going to put dinner on, before two.'

'She was with others in the green room when Miss Burton came for the gown about one o'clock or a bit later; and she was there sewing a costume when Carpenter came back from the Harris Arms at four or so, with the Gregorys and Mr Bosworth. And I thought if she was doing dinner, that would take up the rest of the time.'

'But not all of it, do you not think?'

'Well, maybe, but. . .'

Stephen ran his finger down the list. 'Everyone else looks more or less accounted for. Well, not Miss Brown, we know about her, she was in her cottage in Honey-lane, and went in for something she'd forgotten mid-afternoon, when she may have met Mr Higgins, but some man she didn't know anyway. But seeing as she lives alone, she has no alibi. You've put her down as sewing a gown, that isn't evidence of anything, is it?'

'No, though she showed me the gown, and it is nearly finished. She has very good taste, the sleeves are fashionable, but not so large as to get in the way. I'm beginning to wonder if my red stripe was a mistake.'

Stephen shrugged. 'Not my field of expertise, though you do look lovely in it. Anyway, I think we can rule out the Rolands, I saw him when we began all this, and he was still unwell two weeks after the murder. And he's quite old, not really up to doing a bit of stabbing.'

'Well, I wanted to do this as well as I could, but I didn't like to go and visit him. He could have done it, but I agree, it's not very likely.'

'And I think this chap at Boars Isle, Sharpe, we haven't come across him, have we?'

'No: he's only someone they call on occasionally. Hadn't ever met Miss Burton, they thought. I didn't want to walk all that way to try and find him, it didn't seem worth it.'

'So, what about Mr Brooke? You haven't put much by him. Just that he was called in for a while around lunchtime to see to payments, but was at home the rest of the day. And do we really want to go and question his wife, even supposing Mrs Carpenter would give us the address?'

'No. It's rather awkward, isn't it? So, we have Mr Cousins and Mr Higgins, who are both now in London; Mr Brooke and Miss Brown, both of whom I doubt very much are murderers, though you never know; and Mr and Mrs Carpenter. We can't find them alibis, because they were around all day.' Harriott wrinkled her nose in thought.

'Mr Carpenter was in the Harris Arms from about two to four, and out walking around before that,' said Stephen. 'And Mrs Carpenter seems to have been in her cottage all day seeing to ticket sales, and Mr Brooke, and making her husband's meals, and so on.'

'I can't believe it's her,' said Harriott. 'She doesn't seem the type.'

'She had plenty of time in between to nip out and do a bit of stabbing, though,' said Stephen, with a mischievous grin. 'She's probably a dab hand with the carving knife. Besides, what do either of us know about the type of person who kills someone?'

'Actually, now you mention it, the weapon could be a kitchen knife of some sort, couldn't it, rather than a dagger or sword or whatever? Which would take her to the top of the pile.'

'It might. So, we're still stuck, aren't we?'

'We would be, but I had an idea this morning. You know that dreadful *Lady Susan* gossip sheet? Well, I thought an advertisement in it might help us find anyone who saw Mr Cousins or Mr Higgins around the theatre after about one o'clock. So I got one put in.'

'What a genius you are! I bow to your brilliance.' Stephen swept off an imaginary hat, and bowed deeply.

Harriott giggled, and told him not to be so silly, while glowing inside at the praise.

'When does the rag come out?'

'Fridays, I think. Which is tomorrow. I asked for people with information to bring it to me here or at the print shop, we'll have to see.'

When she returned from Morghew the next day, Harriott found a letter, post-paid, waiting for her. How unusual, she thought, taking it from her father. She sat down at the kitchen table without bothering to change her gown, and considered it.

Who would write to her post-paid? And on such fine paper? She slid a knife under the seal and opened it, looking first for the signature. It was Miss Clarke! Whatever next?

She rapidly read through the letter. Miss Clarke expressed her gratitude for introducing her to Mr Collins at the White Lion, and hoped that they had made progress with their mystery. She said that as soon as they had returned to London from Rye, she had made enquiry at the Home Office, and ascertained that Mr Daniel Cousins had indeed been sent to Tenterden to gather Poor Law information, and that he could be found for questioning if Harriott wished.

Hoping that she was not treading on their territory, she had taken the liberty of enquiring after their Mr Higgins also. She had deputed this task to her brother Sir George, who had enquired at a few gentlemen's clubs which might allow Americans, or theatrical types, and had discovered the man was known. Further enquiry had revealed he was currently working as an actor in a lesser-known theatre, the Coburg, in north Lambeth, to some known as the Waterloo Bridge district. She went on,

"*If you wish, you could come up to London to further your enquiries with these gentlemen, as I am sure there are questions you would like to pose, particularly to Mr Higgins whom you have not met, as I understand it. However, being as it is unsafe and indeed improper for a woman to travel alone by public coach, you may wish to be accompanied by Stephen – I apologise, I misremember his surname.*

If you and he were amenable, we should be delighted to give you both rooms at our house in Kennington, and pay for your coach travel up to London. I have not approached these gentlemen myself, so the ground is fresh for you. We would be able to meet the Tenterden coach at Charing Cross, and provide transport within London, as I imagine you are unfamiliar with the metropolis.

Please let me know if you are able to visit: I know there may be difficulties in securing leave from your work. If you can, please send me the date of your travel and I shall arrange payment for your tickets."

She set the letter down as if it were glass, and sat back in her chair, taking a deep breath. Then, leaning forward again, she reread it slowly, in case she had mistaken the meaning. But it still said the same. London! She had never had a hope of visiting: coaches were so expensive, and where would she stay, what would she do? But this offer, it beggared belief.

'Father, look at this.' She held out the letter to him, her hand trembling. 'Go on, read it immediately, please. Such news!'

Mr Curteis read it through once, and then again. He looked up at her, puzzled. 'Who is this lady? And why is she offering this?'

Harriott explained about the Croughtons, and the visit to Mr Collins, and how Miss Clarke had once solved a murder mystery herself. 'And isn't she thoughtful, she does what she knows we could not do ourselves, which is to say finding out these men, and leaves what we can do with help, to us.'

'Do you really think you ought to go? London is a most dangerous place, I hear.'

'I would not contemplate it alone, no, Father, but she says I should travel with Stephen, and that will be quite safe, I consider. May I go?'

Mr Curteis sighed. 'Of course, if you think you must. But do be careful, people are not always what they seem. You read of terrible tales in the papers.'

'These are friends of Mrs Croughton, though: surely she would vouch for them?'

'I expect so. I shall call on her tomorrow, and ask her to reassure me about the people who have invited you. A father must be allowed some caution concerning an only daughter.'

'I shall have to see if I can get time off from Mr Pomfret. How long would we be away, do you think?'

'It takes the coach ten hours to London, so two days will be taken up in travel. And you will want to be there at least two days, maybe three?'

'I see. Well, I shall ask Mr Pomfret tomorrow morning, and see if he can spare me.'

'When are you going to tell Stephen, then?'

'I don't know. Ought I to go back to Morghew and find him now? Or will after he has finished work be sufficient?'

'I should go to tell him now. Then he can ask Mr Ducksbury about the chance of taking time off for the visit, and also talk to his other employers if he has such.'

'Good idea, he is at Westwell tomorrow, Father. Oh, it's so exciting!'

Mr Curteis smiled benignly at his daughter, and added, 'I'll see about Mrs Croughton giving him leave when I go and ask about these Clarke people: I know he does work for her. She's a fair woman, I'm sure she'll be obliging.'

Harriott stopped, her face fell. 'But, father, I forgot. Who will look after you if I go?'

'Don't you worry about that, I'm not completely incapable. And I shall take the opportunity to go and eat with Mr Exall, if he will have me, on occasion. He's always asking.'

Harriott threw on her everyday gown and hurried back to Morghew. She found Stephen in the orchard, inspecting the progress of the fruit. With a nod to Mr Ducksbury, who was scything the grass around the trees and raking up windfalls, she called him aside.

'Whatever do you think I've had in this letter?' she said, still panting from her haste.

Stephen stretched himself, and grinned at her flushed face. 'Good day to you, Harriott.'

'Yes, alright, but see! A letter from Miss Clarke.!' She waved it at him.

'Really? Whatever about? Is she wanting us to ask Mr Collins further questions about Corunna?'

She looked at him through half-closed lids. 'Are you bamming me?'

Stephen stuck out his tongue. 'Come on, out with it – or do you want me to read the thing? I'm all over dusty, though.'

'I've a mind to go straight back home, if you're going to be like that.'

'Settle yourself, I'm just pleased to see you.'

Harriott pouted, but gave in. 'She says, would we like to go up to London to interview Mr Cousins at the Home Office, and Mr Higgins, who she has found in a theatre near Lambeth. She will pay for the coach and give us rooms in her house when we are there. And have us taken around in her carriage, it seems.'

'Really? Let me see.' He wiped his hands on his breeches, and took the letter.

'Is this true? Not a dry Bob?'

Harriott paused, considered. 'How can you say that about such a lady?'

'No, I believe you, I was just taken aback at the offer. Will you go?'

'I shall, but I would need an escort, being vulnerable as a woman, and mindful of the dangers of coach travel. Would you come?'

Stephen raised his eyebrows comically. 'Would I like to be King of England?' he said. 'Mr Ducksbury, do you think I might have leave for a few days, to take a trip up to London, to stay at the house of a grand lady and see the world?'

Mr Ducksbury laid aside his rake. 'What's all this? Hobnobbing with the quality, you say?'

'You overheard what Harriott said, I know. Might it be possible?'

'Hmm. It's not a good time, with all the beds needing weeding, and the watering and so on, and I don't know what Mr Pomfret would say, nor Mrs Croughton. But, well, I'll have to have a think about it. Anyways, will Mr Pomfret spare Miss Harriott? Seems to me he'd be needing her here to keep his business running smoothly. And what about her work at the Bells?'

Harriott's shoulders dropped. 'Please, Mr Ducksbury, don't talk like that. It's a such a good opportunity, for both of us. And it might be very good for Stephen, if we can arrange to look over a big estate, and speak to important gardeners there. He might be able to bring back some new ideas for you.'

'That's true enough, so it is. Well, like I said, I'll think it over. When would you be wanting to go?'

'I don't know. I'll have to ask Mr Pomfret when would be convenient.'

'Or least inconvenient,' said Stephen. 'You could offer to work other mornings, to make up, I imagine.'

'I'll speak to him tomorrow. And you can check at Westwell with Mr Hobbs tomorrow too, I don't think we'd be gone more than five days, so it'd be only one day you'd miss there, if any.'

Stephen passed back the letter. 'Do you think you could stand being with me for that long? But I suppose you'll have chance to meet all sorts of fancy men up in the capital.'

'Stephen! What do you take me for?'

'Sorry, couldn't resist it. No, I'm all for the trip, it'll be prodigious fine. I'll square it with Mr Hobbs like you say.'

CHAPTER 16

PERSUASION

THE NOTICE IN *LADY SUSAN* bore fruit immediately. Several people came to the Bells that very evening, and on Saturday afternoon, explaining how they had seen Mr Cousins in this place or that, at this time or the other, he being conspicuous by his waistcoats and his long nose down which he was prone to observe the world. Unfortunately, most of them were sightings of the wrong week, or the wrong place, or simply inventions, as far as Harriott could tell.

One woman from the butchers next door to the theatre back entrance did say she had seen him with a short woman going into the building at around lunchtime on the Thursday in question, as she was out the back sweeping the yard at the time; but this only confirmed what she already knew. Then there were notes left at the Curteis' house, of similar varying quality and, to be truthful, legibility. None seemed to be of use to the investigation. However, on the Saturday evening, a knock at the door revealed a man of unkempt appearance, who pulled off his cap at her opening it and asked if there was any reward for information, as he was in dire need. She said, cautiously, that there may be, depending on what he knew.

The gist of the man's tale was that he was in Honey-lane about three o'clock by the church clock, not that that was reliable, mind, he said, and never mind what he was about, but he was there quite a while, in the corner by Jackson's-lane, waiting and that, when he saw a man with a fancy Benjy and a long handle going in to the side door of the theatre. He hadn't read the gossip-sheet himself, not being educated, but he'd been told about it, and he thought she'd like to know, because it sounded like the cull she was after.

Harriott tried not to show her excitement at this news, and told herself it might not be the right man, or the right day, like all the other informants' intelligence she had received.

'I'm sorry to be ignorant,' she said, 'but what is a Benjy, and a long handle?

'A Benjy's what they call a waistcoat, Miss; and an 'andle's like, your nose, ain't it?'

'I see. What day was this?' she asked. I mean, what date?'

'It was a Thursday, Miss,' he said, 'I dunno the date, not taking notice of that sort of thing, but it was the day after the Aid dance for poor Jem as got crushed by that cart, that's for sure.'

'Are you certain about the time?'

'Well, Miss, I knows about those sorts of things, see, it comes in useful in my line of occupation.'

'And what might that be, sir?'

'Never you mind, Miss. Anyway, I sees him and he was in there about 'alf an hour, and then he's off, face like thunder, and that's the last I see of 'im. That day, at any rate.'

'You have been most helpful, Mr . . .?'

'Just call me Jack,' said the man. 'Now, about that reward?'

Harriott fished in her pocket and found a shilling. 'Will that serve?' she said.

Jack tapped the coin on the doorpost, and pocketed it. 'Now, Miss, if you want to hear the other part, you'll need to cough up another couple of them grunters. Fair's fair?'

Harriott hesitated. Then, propelled by curiosity, she found out a half crown, and handed it over. This disappeared as quickly as the first coin.

'See, after this feller left, there was another went in. He'd been 'anging about at the end of Honey-lane, down where the fields start, waiting, out of sight, as he thought. I reckoned he didn't want to meet this other cove, that's what I was thinking. Anyway, he sees him leave, and then he comes up the lane, and goes in the same way, all furtive-like. He'd have made a terrible sneaking budge, anyone would have seen what he was about at a glance. Anyway, he was in there a bit less time that the first flat, about a quarter of an hour mebbe, and then he comes out, just after this broad had gone in. I know 'er, she's from one of them cottages down the lane, but she ain't in the trade like most of 'em, so I hear tell.'

Harriott nodded. Miss Brown, no doubt.

'So, anyway, he wasn't carrying nothing when he went in, but when he came out he had somethink bulging his pocket. Couldn't tell what, but it was only about so big.' He indicated something around a foot long. 'The broad was only in about two or three minutes, and then she was back to her cottage. That's when I had to go, and I didn't see nothing a'rter that.'

'Is that everything?' asked Harriott. 'Was there any other thing you noticed that seemed odd?'

'No, nothink. Well, there was people in and out of the other door, Theatre Cottage they calls it, most of the time, but they'd have been seeing about tickets and that with Mistress Carpenter, I should think.'

'And what was this second man like?'

'Couldn't really say he was much out of the ordinary, really. Smart, but not like a gent; wouldn't interest a knuckle.'

'Sorry?'

'Knuckle? A pickpocket, you might say. His clothes weren't top drawer, though he looked smart enough, and he wouldn't have had anything much in his pocket book.'

'And his face?'

'Lean, I'd say, like he needed feeding up, and he wore a queer sort of tile, like a low topper, but straw, with a curly-curly brim.'

'I see. Did you hear him speak?'

'Not a dicky-bird. He never met nobody, and he was off back down past the Bells as soon as he were out of the door.'

Harriott considered. This sounded all correct, it fitted with what others had said, and it was hard to see how "Jack" could have invented it.

'Would I be able to contact you again, if I needed you to tell this to the authorities?'

Jack shuffled his feet. 'Not me, Miss, I don't hold with them 'thorities. But if you wanted to see me yourself, on the quiet, like, ask for me at the Queen's Arms, and they'll see you right.' And with that he was off, shambling down the street and disappearing into Mockbeggar-lane. Harriott went inside, to make notes, to be sure she remembered this intelligence correctly.

Meanwhile, Harriott had had her interview with Mr Pomfret. She had thought long and hard about how to phrase her request, and finally decided to play on his sense of justice as a magistrate. Once he had given her her instructions for Saturday, she began,

'Sir, I have a request to make.'

'Yes?'

'You will recall I attended the inquest on Miss Burton with you in your rôle as magistrate, some weeks ago?'

'Indeed.'

'Well, I and some friends were at the theatre when the body was discovered, and we felt the crime ought to be investigated, in the absence of an official force.'

'I recall you spoke to me about the Metropolitan Police at the time.'

'Yes, sir. Well, we have made progress, but our two main suspects have both left for London. In fact, one left before we even realised he might be involved: we have never met him.'

'Go on, you interest me.'

'Now, your neighbour Mrs Croughton had visitors last week, the Clarke family, I do not know if you are acquainted?'

'Only by report: I have not met them. I believe Sir George is a baronet?'

'Yes sir. His sister, Miss Clarke, spoke to us about our mystery, and has offered to pay for our coach travel to London, that is for me and Stephen Fuggle, who works in your garden. Further, she has said she will accommodate us in her house while we question the two gentlemen. I should have said, she and her brother Sir George have made enquiries, and discovered where they are to be found.'

'Really? Miss Clarke came to speak to you?'

'Yes, sir. She first spoke to Mr Fuggle, in the Herenden garden: he works there as well as here. She is a very unusual lady; she is involved with many political causes, such as the abolition of slavery. Also, I believe she solved a murder mystery herself when she was young. And, she works for the Foreign Office as an intelligencer.'

'How singular. I must make acquaintance with Sir George and his relatives when he next may visit. You know of course that Hester Croughton is my cousin.'

'Yes, sir, indeed. Now, I should need to be released from my duties for about five days, to allow time for the journeys, and for finding and questioning these gentlemen. Would you allow that, in the cause of justice?'

'Hmm. What would become of my correspondence, then? And, why does not Sir George make the enquiries for you?'

'Well, sir, Miss Clarke is a singular woman, as you said. She wishes to aid our investigations, not take them over. And as regards the work: I am aware of that difficulty. I could attend on the days I am not usually here, both before and after the visit, to make up the time, but there would necessarily be a gap.'

'Hold hard, I must think. I am to be away in Canterbury on business soon, and staying with friends. Harriott my sister is accompanying me. I think I mentioned it to you. I shall be away from . . . let me consult my diary.' He moved to the desk. 'Yes, from Monday week until the Saturday: I think I could spare you at that time for such a worthy enterprise. Would that suffice?'

'That would be splendid, sir. It is most kind of you, but I believed your public spirit would be sufficient to obviate any deficiency in the management of your business dealings.'

'You will let me know when the dates are confirmed?'

'Of course. Also, Stephen Fuggle needs leave from his tasks in the gardens.'

'I am sure that will be allowable also for such an endeavour, certainly as far as I am concerned.'

Stephen appeared that evening in the Bells, quite late. She fell over herself to tell him the news, and he began to tell her his at the same time. After a few moments, they both stopped, and Stephen deferred to her. 'Ladies first,' he said, with a deep bow.

Harriott told him about "Jack" and his report of the clandestine visits of their two men to the theatre, and why she believed him. Then she said about her permission to have leave from Morghew from the 30th, and how she had obtained it for him too. Stephen looked admiringly at her, and grinned broadly.

'And I spoke to Mr Hobbs, and he's fine with it, I'll just lose the money for the day; and now I've just got to ask Mrs Croughton. London, here we come!'

Harriott danced a little jig behind the bar, and then remembered Mr Paine. 'I'd forgotten, what about my work here? I can't leave the bar unstaffed for a week. And I haven't asked Mr Paine about it. I bet he'll say no. Oh, bother.'

Mr Paine clambered out of the cellar, and said, 'What was that about leaving the bar unstaffed, Harriott? Surely you're not going to desert me? I can't have you missing work, not now, when we're so busy.'

Harriott's face fell. 'But, Mr Paine, it's very important. It's about Miss Burton, that was murdered, and we've been offered our fares, and a place to stay in London, and . . .'

'Go on with you, girl,' he grinned. 'I've heard all about it from Dick Ducksbury, he was in earlier, and told me how you've been consorting with the nobs, and everything. He's fixed for his young lad to help him out when Stephen here's away, he says it's about time he started work, he's fourteen soon. So 'course you can go, I wouldn't stand in the way of something like that.'

'Oh, thankyou so much!' She rushed over and gave him a hug, then sprang back in embarrassment. 'I'm so sorry, I was just so overcome.'

Mr Paine didn't look offended, he just smiled, and wiped his hands on his apron. 'When does this come off, then?'

'We haven't arranged it yet, but we hope a week on Monday, for four or five days.'

So, that was that. The next few days passed in great excitement. Harriott wrote her letter to Miss Clarke that very evening, and took it to the receiving office first thing on the Monday. She spoke to the agent at the Woolpack, and he said that payment at the end of the journey was quite in order once he received notification it had been authorised. She booked their places there and then, deciding that they should travel outside, so as to cost Miss Clarke less, and because the weather was fine, and furthermore she had heard it could become intolerably stuffy inside coaches.

Miss Clarke's reply came on the Thursday, confirming that they would be met from the coach on the following Monday, and taken to her house in Kennington, and that she had arranged for their fare to be paid. Then there was the question of what to take with them: Harriott was constantly changing her mind about which gown to wear on the journey, and how much linen to pack, and whether she ought to wear the red stripe or the dark blue when she went to see the men. Stephen was more sanguine: he packed his Sunday suit, and a spare shirt, and he was done.

When Mary and George heard the news after church on Sunday they were of course jealous. Well, not George so much, being as he was of a nervous disposition concerning the big city; but Mary wished it was her travelling, although at the same time she was glad she could stay in familiar territory, and see George. Also, she was pleased for

Harriott, and secretly wondered how her being with Stephen for five days would work out. Would Harriott see what had been under her nose for so long, or would she still be oblivious?

Harriott had to put up with a lot of chaffing in the Bells from customers who had heard of her visit, with offers to come with her instead of Stephen, and suggestions of places she could visit while she was there, such as the more disreputable parts of the East End, so as to broaden her education. James Maynard came by, and offered to take her on another trip before she left, to the market in Headcorn, but she declined.

She worked at Morghew on the Thursday in addition to her usual times, and made sure all the correspondence was dealt with by staying late on the Saturday. That evening while writing out Mr Knowles' sermon she told him of the visit, but said she ought to be back in time to help him next Saturday, all being well. She could not be sure, though, and for that she apologised in advance. Mr Knowles wanted to hear all about the trip, and was pleased that something was being done to bring to book the killer of poor Miss Burton, and told her not to worry. If she did not appear, he would know why, and he would just manage with what he had.

In the service the day before the departure she was on thorns, worrying that she was coming down with a summer cold, or that she would oversleep, in spite of having booked the services of the knocker-up, and the fact that her father was always awake by dawn. She hardly heard Mr Ward's first sermon, and hurried home to make sure she had completed all the household tasks she had been procrastinating for so long, so her father would not be too incommoded by her absence.

The morning came; she was dressed and ready before six; she took a cup of chocolate to sustain her, but could not face any solid food; she and her father carried her box along the High-street to the Woolpack, and saw to its stowing on the coach roof; she paced, while running through the things she ought to have taken. She checked her pocket again for the small but vital items she might need. Money, of course, she had taken what she could, but it was very little. Her penknife; a comb; a kerchief, with several more packed in her box. Her bonnet was tied on securely, but she checked it anyway. And where was Stephen? Surely he had not slept in, after all this? Would her father have to come with her if he did not appear?

'Hush, calm yourself child, it is still early, near on twenty minutes until departure time. And look, who is that coming? Is it not Stephen?'

With relief she ran to meet him, then stopped short in sudden shyness. She took a deep breath.

'Stephen! You're here!'

'Er, yes,' said Stephen looking around as if he might have expected to come with a party of others. Aren't we going someplace today?'

'Yes, well, I know, but I've been so . . . distracted, but now, you're here.'

'All present and correct, Miss. And I have brought some sustenance for the journey.' He held out a paper package tied with string. 'I hear they rook you shamefully in the coaching inns, and only stop for a few minutes.'

The coachman saw to stowing his small bag safely, and then attended to the other passengers who were gathering. They watched him as the team of horses was hitched to the vehicle. 'Better use the facilities in the Woolpack,' he called, 'there won't be another chance for a couple of hours.'

Harriott shook her head in puzzlement, then nodded in comprehension, and took herself off to the retiring room. And then, it was time to mount the heights of the coach, and perch precariously as it seemed to her, on the narrow bench, with her feet dangling, supported only by a thin board.

'This feels very unsafe,' she said, trying to sit back further into the backboard. 'It's so high up, isn't it? I don't know . . .'

'It'll be fine, Harriott. You can hold on to me if you're worried.'

She harumphed a little at that, but as the coach began to jolt its way out under the archway to the High-street, the horses' hooves clattering on the cobbles, she clutched Stephen's arm nonetheless. Looking anywhere but at him, of course. It was a solid and reassuring arm, to be sure. She looked up at the church clock as they turned and gathered speed: it incongruously read ten minutes to three, so she could only assume they had left on time.

Along the turnpike they rolled, through the gate and past her house, past Westwell, then turned down the hill towards Goodshill. She remembered the last time she had been driven down here, with James, and how different this journey felt. The coach was slower than his gig, of course, even six horses could not pull such a weight with ease. The lurches unnerved her as they crossed the little bridge at the bottom of the dip, and she clutched Stephen's arm the tighter.

They took the turn by the Castleton's Oak beerhouse at speed, and before she knew it they were coming into Biddenden. It was only as they rolled along Headcorn High-street that their pace slowed, and Harriott risked loosening her hold on Stephen's sleeve. As soon as they reached the George, men raced out of the inn, some unfastening straps and buckles, and leading the spent horses to oats and hay, others harnessing fresh animals. Two people climbed onto the top by the driver, and within a couple of minutes they were off again, and tilting dangerously as they took the sharp corner by the church.

She found conversation difficult, with the noise of the wheels on the road, the jangling of harness, and the wind on her bonnet. She had to lean in close to speak to Stephen, and felt a curious reluctance to do so, his smiling face somehow unnerved her. She had thought to talk to him about what they might expect to see in London, but she somehow felt awkward.

The journey now led into places Harriott had never visited. The whole company had to climb off the coach for the ascent of the very steep hill into Sutton Valence, and walk up. Once they were back in place, the coach continued, stopping only for turnpike fees and changes of horses at one inn or another. She recognised they must have reached Maidstone by the size of the place, and ventured down as the coachman shouted there would be a twenty-minute stop. Barely had she seen to the calls of nature, though, and people were clambering back up and they were off again.

Beyond Maidstone the country was alien to her. One village after another passed, with signboards that meant nothing in her world. She and Stephen shared his pies, drank his ale, munched on early apples, and watched the world go by. No calamity had befallen the vehicle, and she gradually became used to the motion, so was able to sit without holding on to her friend, unless at places where the road was in poor repair and the jolting more violent.

The man on the other side of Stephen occupied the time by chatting to him about the government, and what they ought to be doing to help country folk, and agriculture, and how the country depended on its rural workers, but she could hear almost none of what he said, and gave up. Instead she watched the gradual change of the scenery, the different types of houses as they neared their goal. And at last, larger buildings began to appear, and then became more and more packed together. Surely this must be their destination?

But no. The coach sounds changed, and Harriott swivelled to see why. They were crossing a great river, ten times wider that the familiar Rother, unidentifiable objects floating in its eddies. How could men have built a bridge across such a swirling expanse? She clung on to Stephen once more, the height of her flimsy perch over the brown, sullen water terrifying her.

They crossed the bridge without incident, turned along the bank past yet more enormous piles of stonework, and within a few minutes turned in and stopped. They were at last at their destination. The coachman twisted around and reported: 'Ten hours dead, ladies and gentlemen,' and there was great applause.

Harriott and Stephen descended, stiffly, and waited for their baggage to be unloaded. She looked around at all the grand buildings, and inhaled the somewhat unwholesome air: London!

CHAPTER 17

LONDON CALLING

HARRIOTT STOOD WITH STEPHEN, THEIR bags at their feet outside the inn, feeling lost. Harriott, in spite of herself, moved a little closer to Stephen, and looked here and there for signs of someone coming to meet them. Everywhere there was movement and bustle, and people yelling out unintelligible calls, which she guessed must be about the wares they had to sell. There were the smells of fish, and horse manure, and a musty kind of tang which she supposed must be from the great number of coal fires in the place, and dust from where buildings were being knocked down nearby. There was a great drabness of colour in the buildings, and the dirt seemed to have even penetrated the brightest colours of the clothes of the people.

She was tired, and hungry, and to be honest, overwhelmed with this new place. Stephen must be feeling the same, she thought, he's never been to such a big place either. But he was looking around him, with a fascinated expression, and gazing up at the grey stone and rather dirty white marble, and even the piles of manure on the roads with equal interest. She clutched at his arm once more.

'Might you be Miss Curteis and Mr Fuggle?' came a voice from behind them. They turned, to see a short, cheery sort of man, with bowed legs and gaiters, beckoning as they nodded, and leading them to a light, low-slung four-wheel open carriage. Their baggage was stowed, and they mounted, the groom sitting in front and setting off with hardly a pause, clicking to his pair and wafting a whip around without much purpose other than for show, as the horses seemed to know where to go on their own.

He kept up a commentary on the buildings they passed: the Admiralty, the Foreign Office, where Sir George works, the Treasury, the Palace of Westminster; then they passed over Westminster Bridge, Harriott trying not to show fear this time; and he indicated Astley's theatre, and then the new Bethlem lunatic asylum as they turned south. The buildings seemed to go on and on, street after street. Eventually, well, quite quickly really, Harriott supposed, given the pace of the carriage, they left the main road and drew up at a moderate mansion, with a pretty garden full of evergreen shrubs. The groom helped them down, collected their bags, and showed them into the building.

Harriott did not know what to expect, not one whit. She thought Mary, who read books about romances among the gentry might be in better case than she, by knowing the proper etiquette, and modes of address. Stephen, however, seemed unbothered by everything, and admired some of the bushes as they walked to the door, saying he thought they might be some of the newest camellias, just getting established.

Then she remembered, and told herself off: she had been used to being in Mr Pomfret's residence for some weeks now. But it was quite different, she found, being a guest rather than a servant, and such a long way from home. She halted just inside the entrance and looked around her at the elegant hallway. Stephen was forging ahead not realising she had stopped. The groom had handed their luggage to a footman, who was disappearing down a corridor, and returned to his horses. Stephen had moved forward and was greeting someone she did not know. Realising she was out of place, she hurried on, and joined him.

'And you must be Miss Curteis,' said the man. 'I am Sir George Clarke, Miss Clarke's brother. You are most welcome.'

Harriott curtsied, knowing that was the right thing to do, but rather lost for words, unlike her usual self.

'I think Harriott is most tired from the journey, sir. Would it be in order for her to go to her room?'

'Of course. Those stage coaches are very uncomfortable, I believe and know.'

'I'm fine,' she said, feeling anything but fine.

Stephen gave her an appraising look. 'Harriott, come on, you need a rest. Trust me.'

Reluctantly, she followed a maid to a comfortable room, threw herself on the bed and was asleep within minutes.

It was dark when she woke, disoriented. She sat bolt upright, shaking slightly, then saw a glimmer of light from an unfamiliar doorway, and remembered. Rapidly she rose, brushed down her skirts as best she could in the dark, and peered out into the corridor. Following the sound of voices, and the gleam of candles, she descended the stairs and found herself in a dining room where Stephen sat at supper with Miss Clarke and several children or young persons, with what seemed like a good time being had by all.

She hesitated on the threshold. Miss Clarke noticed her first, and rose.

'Do come in, Miss Curteis. Are you rested? We have finished our meal, but you must be hungry after the journey. I think my brother's brood may have left you a few crumbs.'

Harriott looked down at her travelling gown. 'I do apologise: I should have changed, but there was no light.'

'Don't think of that, my dear. Come and seat yourself by your friend. He can help you to the dishes that remain.'

Harriott did so, still having to stifle yawns, and began to nibble. She found she was really quite hungry.

'Miss Clarke was just getting up to date with our problem,' said Stephen. 'She though it important to have a clear picture of how each of our two men might have perpetrated the crime, if indeed either is guilty.'

Harriott frowned slightly on hearing the word "perpetrated", but concluded Stephen had been learning from his hostess.

'And how are you setting out the circumstances of Mr Cousins' guilt, then?' she asked.

'I was just about to begin.' Stephen turned back to Miss Clarke. 'Well, Mr Cousins took Miss Burton into the theatre at around half past twelve, and they looked around the stage, before he left her. She went to the green room, and he went out by the back door. However, he told us he left her at the door: this other account is from Mr Carpenter.'

'Who is . . .? Remind me?'

'The caretaker, who says he saw them from his position in the gallery where they would not have observed him.'

'Surely it must be the caretaker who did the crime?' put in the oldest child. 'He was probably lying. And he would be there all the time, and he wouldn't be a gentleman, would he?'

'Hush, John, and let Mr Fuggle speak,' said Miss Clarke. 'Besides, just because someone isn't a gentleman doesn't make them bad.'

'That's not what they tell us at Shrewsbury, Aunt Rose.'

'So,' Stephen continued, 'Cousins leaves, and goes somewhere, but returns about three o'clock, and spends almost half an hour in the theatre. What was he doing? And why did noone see him? Mr Gregory was on the stage rehearsing at that time, and the others in the green room. Did he go to meet anyone? And whereabout was he? Does he have any witnesses as to his movements? Or was he committing the murder?'

Harriott frowned. 'If he was murdering then, where was Miss Burton from about one o'clock until three? And why did she not meet her dressmaker at two; or go to her work at three?'

'Indeed. But Cousins does not know of these times and appointments, and he may reveal new information as a consequence.'

'Excellent,' said Miss Clarke. 'But supposing him to be the murderer, could he have taken Miss Burton before her gown fitting, and returned to cover his tracks in the later period?'

Stephen rubbed his nose. 'If he did, then where was the body in that time?'

'In the chest, of course,' said John, who had followed the reasoning closely.

Miss Clarke frowned. 'If I may observe, it is a little odd to kill someone while they are standing in a chest, is it not? And surely the blood would splash everywhere, including on the murderer?'

Harriott nodded. 'That has puzzled both of us. I have no answer for it.'

'Also,' mused Miss Clarke, 'why would Miss Burton be by or in the chest when he returned after less than an hour's interval?'

'Maybe they were playing a game, and he got her to stand in the chest?' suggested young Rose, the middle child.

'Hmm,' murmured Harriott, 'well, possibly . . .'

'Anyway, what about Mr Higgins?' said Miss Clarke. 'Is he a better suspect?'

'I don't know,' said Harriott. 'We haven't met him, so we do not know what kind of a man he is. Also, if he had killed the lady, why did he stay for the performance the next day and then leave immediately on the following morning, and not depart before?'

'Let us think this through, then,' said Stephen. 'He had a chance meeting with Miss Burton late on the Wednesday, after the dance, and it might well have been confrontational. At least, that is what Mr Cousins suggested. We believe he may have been in love with her, from knowing her in America. Then, he tries to find her the next day, but he is prevented, as she has gone on a trip into the countryside with Cousins. Perhaps he sees her with him on their return at lunchtime, and tries to think of how to meet her again. He comes to the theatre later, perhaps that is when he buys his ticket, do you think? Then he sees Cousins entering, and is jealous. He waits at the end of the road until Cousins leaves, letting his anger fester and feed upon itself. Once the coast is clear, he enters, kills her, and hurries away.'

'The same objections hold,' said Miss Clarke. 'He would have had to kill her earlier, and be returning to cover his tracks. Fifteen minutes is a very short time to kill and conceal a body. On your supposition, he would have had to have a conversation with her before, that led to him thinking his suit hopeless, and then rather than turn his weapon on himself in despair, put her out of this world in anger. And in this case again, where was she for the two hours before?'

'Also, where did the weapon come from?' said John.

'We have no idea,' said Stephen. 'Mary, that is, our friend Mary, with George whom you met, had another careful search around the theatre for it before we came to London, and found nothing. And we have looked all over the stage boards and in the back stage area, and found no bloodstains. It is a puzzle indeed.'

'I still think it was the caretaker,' said John. 'He was around all the time, and could have killed her at one o'clock, then hidden the body in the chest.'

'He could . . .' said Harriott, slowly, 'but . . . why would he?'

'And, where did he get the weapon? And anyway, he was out of the theatre from about one or one thirty until three thirty or four, walking, or in the Harris Arms. And he says the chest wasn't heavy when he put it on the stage after Mr Gregory had finished rehearsing,' said Stephen.

'If he was the murderer, then anything he says may be a lie,' Miss Clarke pointed out.

'And all these times are so vague,' said Harriott. 'It is infuriating. Our church clock is forever going wrong, and nobody has a pocket watch that keeps good time, and most people don't even have that, so they are most vague about when things happened. It is very frustrating.'

Miss Clarke's eyes seemed to lose focus. 'I remember a time when all the clocks in a large town kept their own times,' she said, 'and they each ran slow or fast at different times, so one never knew . . . Well, it was a long time ago.' She sighed.

'Well, Rose and Charles, time for you to go to bed, I think,' said Miss Clarke. Your parents will be out until late at the Danish ambassador's dinner, so it falls to me to make sure you are asleep when they return. Off you go. And John, you go too, but you have another hour before retiring.'

The children left the room, and Harriott, still eating, watched them go. Stephen turned to Miss Clarke.

'Have you a programme of events for us, Miss Clarke? Or, should I say, when have you arranged for us to meet our men?'

'Mr Cousins, first thing tomorrow, about ten. My groom will drive you two and Sir George to Whitehall, and leave you at the door of the Home Office. Mary and I are quite occupied all day, so the carriage will wait, and take you to show you the sights. Miss Curteis, are you interested in seeing the shops?'

'Harriott, her mouth full, had to swallow quickly. 'Miss Clarke, of course, anything you feel would be useful. We have no money, though.'

'No, but one can gaze in the windows, can one not? Which reminds me, why did you travel outside on the coach? I would happily have paid for inside seats.'

'We did not want to put you to extra expense, Madam. Also, the weather was fine, and, well, we are not the kind of people . . .'

'I understand. Well, thankyou for your concern, and perhaps you may accept inside tickets if the weather is poor for your return.'

'May I ask, Miss Clarke, what gown would be suitable for our visit to Mr Cousins? I have a dark blue one which only has slightly puffed sleeves, I wear that when I work as secretary to Mr Pomfret; and I have a red-striped one with demi-gigot sleeves which is much more in the fashion.' She remembered. 'I fear though that you do not like the current wide silhouette, from what Stephen told me.'

Miss Clarke smiled. 'You are correct, but what I prefer is not at issue. Mr Cousins, from what you say, and what I have learned, is most keen on the latest fashions, even if somewhat . . . extreme in his tastes? However the dark blue might be more . . . serious, and engage his taking you more seriously.'

'Harriott looks wonderful in either,' said Stephen. 'You know, wear whichever makes you feel more confident, I'd say.'

Harriott paused. 'I think . . . I think I'll decide tomorrow, if I may?'

'Indeed. We breakfast at eight. After your visit and your sightseeing, you are at leisure. Dinner is not until six thirty, because of our work. We have arranged for you to see Mr Higgins early on Wednesday afternoon, when he will be arriving at the Coburg for a read-through of a new play, we are told. Are there any other things you wish to do in Town?'

'If it is possible, I should like to visit some gardens, and speak with the Head gardeners.'

'We had thought you might enjoy the Vauxhall Gardens, they are still open for another few days of the season. We had planned to go on Wednesday evening, as it gets towards dark, but they open at five, so if we go early you may be able to find some of the men to consult with at that time.'

'Vauxhall gardens?' said Harriott.

'Yes, they are a pleasure garden, with displays of fireworks, and music, and various places to eat, and what is the best thing from my point of view, the rich and the less well-off mingle and share the same enjoyments. They light the whole place with thousands of lanterns, it can look quite magical.'

'Excellent,' said Stephen. 'And would it be in order to speak with your own gardener? I saw some new imported camellias as we arrived.'

'Of course, he will be in tomorrow and Thursday.'

In the morning, wearing her striped gown, and with her hair arranged most becomingly with the help of Lady Mary's own maid, Harriott sat with Sir George and Stephen in the carriage, feeling rather awed at sharing the vehicle with a baronet. Stephen looked most smart in his Sunday suit, and with his shoes polished to a mirror by the boot-boy.

He looked quite at ease, whereas she held her hands firmly on her lap to stop them trembling, and tried not to look up as they crossed the long bridge again.

They were admitted at the door of the Home Office without any problem. As they left, Sir George spoke to them,

'I nearly forgot to say. If Mr Cousins proves difficult, or refuses to answer your questions, please don't hesitate to bring my name into play. You may tell him that I am on excellent terms with Sir Robert Peel, and it would go badly for him if he were to be difficult. But I trust your own abilities will make this information unnecessary.'

'Sir Robert Peel?' queried Harriott.

'He is the Home Secretary, he is Mr Cousins' ultimate superior.'

'I think I have heard of him,' said Stephen. 'Did he not sponsor the Metropolitan Police Act last year? But I thought he was Mr Peel?'

'He only succeeded to the baronetcy in May,' said Sir George. 'You are well-read, sir.'

Stephen smiled, and Harriott thought how pleased he must be at the praise.

In the building they were shown up promptly to Mr Cousins' office. As the clerk withdrew, and they sat down, Mr Cousins looked up from his desk and visibly stiffened.

'What is the meaning of this? I was told I had an appointment with persons who wished to speak with me about matters concerning the new Poor Laws.'

Stephen smiled. 'Well sir, in a manner of speaking, we are here relating to that issue. Or, more precisely, your presence in Tenterden recently on that business.'

'I see no reason to continue this conversation. I have nothing to say to you.' He stood, and moved from behind his desk.

Stephen made no move, other than to sit back in his seat slightly. 'No? Well, sir, you might find it to your advantage to change your mind. It is unfortunate that you have been concerned in the matter of a murder, to be sure, but it would be advisable for you to cooperate, to establish your innocence, or people might think you had something to hide, might they not?'

Mr Cousins stopped in his movement towards the door. 'I have nothing to hide. Now, leave my office, if you please.'

Harriott spoke up, addressing as it seemed the air rather than the man himself. 'You may not realise, sir, but you were seen entering the Tenterden Theatre at around three o'clock on the day of Miss Burton's murder, the Thursday, by a reliable witness. You were observed to spend half an hour there, when you had not mentioned this fact previously.'

Mr Cousins turned, and seemed to hesitate.

'And if I say I do not believe you?'

'Then we shall be the more convinced of your guilt, sir. One falsehood tends to incline one to expect other lies may have been told.'

Mr Cousins considered, then returned to his desk, sat down, and leaned forward, glaring at Harriott. 'What is the nature of this reliable witness, then?'

'I am not at liberty to say, sir. Perhaps you would again give us your version of events of that day? And could you start with your taking Miss Burton to the theatre at around twelve thirty, after your trip to the countryside?'

'I have already told you about that.'

'Yes, sir, but you may wish to reconsider the story you told.'

'Why so?'

'I shall not explain why: just this time, try and tell the truth, if you please.'

Mr Cousins sat back, and frowned. 'It is a long time ago; I cannot remember clearly.'

'I am sure that is not the case, sir,' said Stephen. 'Such important events must be burned into your memory.'

Mr Cousins, shifting in his seat, took several breaths, and addressed himself solely to Stephen.

'I took Miss Burton to the theatre by the rear door, as you said, about twelve thirty, by the church clock, though I am told that timepiece is quite unreliable.'

Stephen nodded. 'It is indeed, sir.'

'I did not consult my pocket watch at the time, so I cannot be more accurate. I left her at the door, as I said.'

Stephen raised his eyebrows, and saw Mr Cousins flinch.

'No, I misremember. I may have gone in a short distance, for a few seconds.'

'Really, sir? Why enter if only to leave straightway?'

'No, I did not leave straight away, I think, I possibly accompanied her to . . . yes, I did, I now recall, she wished to show me the auditorium from the stage.'

'Was there anyone else in the auditorium at this time, sir?'

'No, none that I could see. There were a few things on the edge of the stage, as if someone had been working, and before you ask, that damned chest was not present. We stayed on the platform for . . . perhaps ten or more minutes, while she told me about the play and the songs she would be singing.'

'Thankyou, sir. And then?'

Miss Burton went to find a gown she needed altering, and I left, by the way I had come in.'

'Did you not go with her to find the gown? Or any other thing, while you were there?'

'I . . . I may have stayed with her a little while in the area behind the stage. I . . . well, I think you will have realised, I was trying to advance our intimacy, but she was having none of it.'

Harriott spoke up. 'Were you attempting this by force, sir, as on other occasions?'

Mr Cousins, with a visible effort, ignored this jibe, and said, exclusively to Stephen, 'You may have found women unreasonably obdurate yourself, sir: well, Miss Burton was as inflexible as iron, while giving the appearance of feminine compliance. And even having taken gin earlier had not altered her resolve.'

'Yes, sir, why do you think she agreed to the spirit, being normally an abstainer?'

'I believe it may have been due to meeting an old flame the night before, and being conflicted about her feelings. However, that is only my supposition, and it did not help my own suit one whit.'

'I see. And how long might you have dallied in the back-stage area?'

'A matter of fifteen minutes, perhaps. Then she went to what she called the green room and I departed.'

'Thankyou. And after that?'

'After that? Why is that relevant? She surely met with colleagues in that green room, which absolves me of having murdered her then and there?'

'Just continue, sir, if you would be so kind.'

Mr Cousins adjusted his cravat, and seemed about to refuse. Then, thinking better of it, he said, narrowing his eyes,

'Are you working with the Metropolitan Police, then?'

'No, sir. We do however have the support of Sir Robert Peel, in our enquiries.'

Mr Cousins looked puzzled at this, and took out his watch to consult it. Replacing it, he continued,

'I spent the next period of time in my room at the Woolpack, looking over my notes.'

'Did any of the staff see you enter the Woolpack, do you think?'

'I spoke to a barmaid, yes; and no, I do not know her name.'

'And then?'

Seeing Mr Cousins hesitate, Stephen raised his eyebrows again.

'And then I left to enter the theatre by the Honey-lane door in pursuance of an earlier engagement,' he said, in rather a rush.

'I see. And can you tell us the nature of the engagement?'

'It was private.'

'I understand that. But unfortunately, where murders are concerned, privacy must often be breached.'

'I cannot speak.'

'I see. You are protecting a lady, I imagine.'

Harriott found herself drawing a quick breath, in surprise.

There was a pause. 'I was . . . I am, I mean.'

'She would be able to give you an alibi, you realise?'

'What is that?'

'Evidence you were elsewhere at the time.'

Mr Cousins considered this idea, and frowned again. 'Since you put it that way, I was to meet the lady in the small room just before the staircase, which is used for storage, on a . . . romantic basis.'

Harriott shook her head. To take one woman out to the Black Ox and then pursue his suit in the theatre, knowing he had another appointment later in the same building. Really! She was quite glad Stephen was making the questions, she might not have been able to keep calm.

'And the lady's name?'

'Sarah Mace.' He made a grimace.

'Did you go further into the theatre than this storage room?'

'No. Not any further.'

'And was your encounter satisfactory?'

'It was not.' Mr Cousins' face coloured at the memory. 'She wanted payment, when she had led me to believe she was enamoured.'

'I see.' Stephen kept silent, and put out a restraining hand when Harriott drew breath to ask another question.

'We met in that unusual place because she said she could not meet me at her home, it was too inconvenient, and she wanted to be private.'

Stephen waited.

'It seems she was just a common doxy. If I had wanted that I could find far superior in London.'

Harriott found herself balling her fists, and admiring Stephen's restraint.

'So, I left, and she departed by the back entrance. I insisted on that, so we were not seen together. I do not know what she may have done after that, and I do not care.'

'And you?'

I returned to my lodgings, and got on with my work.'

'No doubt you were seen again at the Woolpack at that time?'

'No doubt: there is always some busybody about.'

Stephen turned to Harriott, and said, 'I think that is all, sir, unless my colleague has any other questions?'

Harriott shook her head. It seemed, if this was all true, that Mr Cousins could not be the murderer. Which was oddly disappointing. Then she remembered. 'Oh yes, Mr Cousins. You attended the play on the Friday, did you not? I saw you there. With whom did you consort that evening?'

'A friend. Why is this relevant?'

'A lady friend?'

Mr Cousins inclined his head. 'Indeed.'

'And her name?'

'A Miss Ann Barton, since you press me. Is there anything else?'

'Only, sir, that we may return later in the week if our other investigations bring up information we should require you to clarify or corroborate.' She smiled sweetly. 'I trust you will be as welcoming as today, if such is necessary?'

CHAPTER 18

EVERYBODY LOVES YOU WHEN YOU'RE DEAD

THE GROOM, WHO TURNED OUT to be also called George, was waiting for them when they left the building, and seemed pleased to have the job of taking them around the capital, to show it off to its best advantage, as he said. First, they were driven past Charing Cross, where they recognised the inn at which their coach had arrived, and wondered at the works going on to the north where most of the buildings had been demolished. George told them there were grand plans afoot to build this and that, monuments and new headquarters buildings, and even an Art Gallery, but that progress seemed to be held up for lack of funds. He then headed on, towards a very opulent street called Piccadilly.

As they sat in the carriage as it made its way through a press of traffic, looking this way and that at everything new around them, Stephen asked Harriott, 'Do you know this Ann Barton that Cousins mentioned?'

'Yes indeed, she is a friend, perhaps not a close friend, but still. I must warn her about Mr Cousins, although she may already have realised. But the other, Sarah Mace, I do not know. She must be one of the ladies of Honey-lane.'

They were deposited by a most grand building they were informed was Burlington House, to wander along an arcade full of shops showing the most amazing goods, never seen in such a place as Tenterden. When they had filled their eyes with such treasures, George directed them across the road to Mr Fortnum and Mr Mason's grocery shop. Shop was hardly the word, thought Harriott, as they wandered the floors, and tried to decide which were the most tempting provisions.

George then drove them to the end of Piccadilly to admire the recently-completed Green Park arch, which faced the screen at the entrance to Hyde Park. He told them it was in honour of the Duke of Wellington, whose London house adjoined Hyde Park, and was to have been ornamented with statues and other sculpture, but King George had spent so much on his new palace that they had run out of money. Harriott thought how much their own George would have loved to be with them, to see these monuments to the war in which he was so interested.

Stephen asked to be set down, so he could visit the two adjacent parks, and he and Harriott wandered around for about half an hour. Stephen spoke to people whenever he could, discovering that both parks as well as St James' had been renovated during the building of the arch, as additional monuments to the victory over Napoleon, and asking many questions about the planting to anyone who appeared to be working there.

Next, they were taken to see the recent additions to what George called the Queen's House, as that had been its name under the late King George. He told them people were supposed to call it Buckingham Palace now, but old habits died hard. They admired St James' Park, with its newly-remodelled lake and islands, and winding walks, and Stephen was lucky enough to find the head gardener, whom he subjected to innumerable questions while Harriott admired the waterfowl, and wondered about where they might find lunch.

No matter, George took them by a devious route to a most smart shop in a square on the far side of the Green Park, where the proprietors were expecting them and advised them to choose whatever they liked, it was all paid for. Embarrassed, Harriott simply selected a small pastry, but Stephen chose more robustly, and soon she found she was joining him, and yielding to the blandishments of the waiter to finish with their signature ice creams or sorbets.

'Miss Clarke likes to be able to do this for us,' Stephen whispered to her, 'she is someone who does not think her money is hers only. I have heard of such people, but never thought to meet one.'

By the time they had finished eating, and had made sure George had also had sustenance, it was time to return. As George said, it was exhausting being in the big city for the first time, and Miss Clarke had been most insistent he should not keep them out too long.

There were more sights to see as they returned by a different route, along the Strand, turning past the grand edifice of Somerset House, and over the Waterloo Bridge which the stage coach had crossed the day before. Harriott found herself getting used to the size of the river, and the height of the bridge, and was less nervous this time. George again pointed out the landmarks, including the Coburg theatre they were to visit on the following day, and the Bethlem Hospital they had seen before.

On their arrival, tea was served, and then Harriott retired to lie down a while. She was surprised how right George had been, it had been a most tiring day. She took off her gown, and decided to wear the blue to dinner, because she wished to appear sensible and serious in front of her hosts.

On coming down to dinner at the sound of a gong, she was surprised to find noone in evening dress. She had felt she would be out of place, having no such gown, and realised this was yet another of Miss Clarke's kindnesses. She was seated by Stephen, and also next to the eldest child present, John, who was full of questions about their problem, and wanted to know just what Mr Cousins had said, and what sort of a gentleman he was, and whether he had the air of a murderer.

Harriott answered him as best as she could, but was unable to make an unbiassed judgement of his general character, so unpleasant was her emotional reaction to his presence. She turned to Stephen for support.

'What do you think about Mr Cousins, Stephen? Does he have the character of an evildoer? I just find him repulsive.'

'Well, I can understand that, since he seemed to display no morals at all in his relations with the female sex. But, I believe I found him rather pathetic, what with all those unnecessary lies. I cannot see how he could have murdered Miss Barton, assuming the Woolpack can confirm his account of returning there, and Miss Mace their assignation, or at least, if he did, how he could have covered his trail effectively.'

John leaned forward, excitedly. 'Could he not have waited in the back stage area on his first visit, until she came out with her gown, the one that needed altering, and killed her then? The chest was there at the time, was it not?'

Lady Mary raised a finger. 'Come, John, let our guests decide for themselves.'

'No,' said Stephen, 'John is right, he could have hidden, waited until she had changed, and then done the deed in that little time. It depends on when he was seen at the inn, but the problem is, or one of our problems anyway, the times cannot be fixed with any certainty, with the unreliability of the clocks.'

'So,' said Miss Clarke slowly, 'he might have killed her by the chest, and hidden the body in it. And then what? Just left the building as fast as he could?'

'There would be blood everywhere, though,' said John. 'Buckets of blood, all over the floor, all over him, and everything. It would be tremendous, like Ivanhoe, or one of those books.'

'I do apologise, John is going through a rather bloodthirsty phase. I am sure Sir Walter was not quite so graphic in his descriptions.' Lady Mary though, could not prevent a smile coming to her lips.

Stephen frowned, and rubbed his nose. 'I agree, there would be a right mess. But there's something else, something you said, I can't quite put my finger on it, that is important.' He sighed. 'Never mind, it might come to me if I don't try too hard.'

The rest of the evening was spent in discussing the sights they had seen, and making plans for the next days, once they had seen Mr Higgins and visited the Vauxhall Gardens. Stephen said he would speak with the Clarke's gardener after breakfast, and Harriott was claimed by John, who wanted her to spend time with him explaining all about how printing worked, because he was monstrously interested in machinery, and hoped he would be allowed to go to the opening of the new rail-way in Manchester in two weeks' time with his older brother, if his father would fund the journey. William was away at the moment visiting one of his schoolfriends, but he should be back in a few days. No matter that they ought to be at school by then, it would be very educational, did she not think? And not too far to travel from Shrewsbury? Surely Miss Curteis would support him against his father?

On hearing Stephen wished to see anything related to gardens, Sir George suggested he went to see the flower and produce market at Covent Garden, though warned him to be wary of pickpockets and ladies of the street in that area. His groom would be sufficient protection; though he suggested it was not a suitable place for a lady, unless she was most determined.

Harriott said she would prefer to visit something a little more sedate, if she would not appear too timid by doing so, and Lady Mary suggested the collection of paintings in the late Mr Angerstein's house in Pall Mall, from his own collection and that of Sir George Beaumont, which were supposed to be the beginnings of a national Art Gallery to be built at Charing Cross. Miss Clarke said she would accompany Harriott if she liked, as she had only seen them once, and had not had long enough to view them properly. To this Harriott assented with gratitude. She felt most unlike herself here in London, she who was normally so independent had been nervous of the river and its bridges, and glad of the company of Stephen, and even of the protection his presence afforded.

'How will you manage this programme, which I take you to be planning for Thursday, Rose?' said Sir George. 'We have only the one carriage.'

'Easily, Doddie. We shall travel to the market, and leave George and Mr Fuggle to make their inspection, and then I shall take the reins and go with Miss Curteis to Pall Mall. They can walk back towards us and we can meet at Leicester Square, and have some lunch at Jaunay's Hôtel, which as you know I adore, and hand back care of the phaeton to George.'

'Of course, Rose, but do not frighten Miss Curteis by your driving.'

Miss Clarke stuck out her tongue at her brother, and he raised his eyebrows at her. She laughed, and turned to Harriott. I am afraid I shall be needed at the Foreign Office that afternoon, so you will have to amuse yourself once we have eaten. But by then you will have a better idea of what you want to see, I am convinced.

'You know, Stephen,' said Harriott, as George drove them northwards to the Coburg Theatre, 'I think young John is holding a flame for me. He detained me on the subject of printing for far longer than I could hold forth, and then proceeded to tell me all about locomotives, and how wonderful Mr Stephenson is, and how he is going to be a great engineer when he is old enough.'

'I am not surprised, Harriott. You are eminently . . . how may I put it delicately . . . alluring, shall we say?'

'Surely not? I am just me.'

'Do you not possess a mirror? Do you never regard your face, your figure? And do not people envy your self-possession, your fire?'

'Well . . . I suppose Mr Paine at the Bells does, about the last one, any case. He says I bring in the customers. Shame he doesn't pay me extra for it.'

'And have you no admirers in Tenterden?'

'Well . . . yes, I do, you're right, but they all seem to have a fault. Too little consistency, or rather, too much a roving eye; or else too little ambition, being content to stay farming or what ever occupation they may happen to be in, without wishing to better themselves.'

'I see. So, maybe you ought to encourage young John? He has ambition and to spare.'

'Stephen! He is only fourteen.' She caught sight of Stephen's face, and realised he was bamming her. 'Oh, stop it, come on. Remind me of how we shall proceed with Mr Higgins.'

Stephen smothered his laughter, and assumed a mock-serious expression. 'I think the first thing will be for you to seduce him with your beauty, and render him as glazier's putty in our hands.'

'Stephen!'

'Oh, alright. I believe it depends on how he greets us. Sir George told me we can use his position at the Foreign Office as a persuasive tactic if we have need, as he is an alien, and liable to be deported at whim.'

'Is he really?'

'No, possibly not, but he may not know that.'

'Are you happy to be party to such a deception?'

'In the cause of justice, is it not permissible?'

Harriott considered. 'I do not think so, no.'

'Very well, we shall just have to use your charms, then.'

Harriott punched him playfully on the shoulder. 'Idiot.'

'Now, let me tell you what the Clarkes' gardener, Mr Tinsley, told me. Well, apart from most useful information about recent plants that have been developed or imported, and are likely to be the rage soon, that is. He has a friend who works for a large estate out in the countryside, not far away, in a place called Stockwell, and he says he can arrange for me to visit on Friday morning. Also, he told me about Mr Tradescant's botanical garden not far to the south of the Vauxhall Gardens, and I am so excited hoping I may be able to visit this too.'

The Coburg Theatre was a solid, blocky building softened by

a full-width portico bearing the grandiose inscription, “Licensed Pursuant to Act of Parliament of King George IV”, and above it high on the front wall, “Royal Coburg Theatre”. Stephen said it looked as though it was trying too hard to compete with Drury-lane and the other patent theatres. Harriott argued that if it had “Royal” in its name, it must have a patent. Stephen frowned, rubbed his nose, and said he thought she must be correct. Harriott sat back, pleased, as they drew up by a side entrance.

The two of them were admitted, and shown to a small bare room, to await Mr Higgins. There were just a dozen or so hard chairs, and, stacked around the walls, wooden frames supporting canvas painted with a plethora of scenes, no doubt for use on the stage. Mr Higgins entered after a few minutes, clutching a script and a straw top hat with a curled brim, saying as he did to someone behind him that he had thought the read-through was not for another forty minutes, and stopped as he entered on seeing the two strangers.

Stephen moved towards the door and closed it gently. ‘Mr Higgins, I presume? Thankyou for meeting us. My name is Mr Fuggle, and this is Miss Curteis. Won’t you sit down?’

The man looked this way and that, puzzled. ‘Where are the others? Are we not reading through *Don Pedro*?’

‘I apologise, but I believe the read-through will take place a little later this afternoon. We wish to ask you a few questions, that is all.’

Mr Higgins looked from one to the other. ‘Are you from the Police?’

Harriott could see he was trembling.

‘No, but we have the authority of the Foreign Office behind us,’ continued Stephen.

Mr Higgins looked yet more alarmed. ‘What’s the meaning of that?’

‘Nothing, sir, just as long as you will cooperate.’

He looked again rapidly from one to the other, then slowly sank down onto the edge of a chair. Stephen and Harriott took seats a little distance away.

'We understand you took a trip to Kent recently, to Tenterden?' opened Stephen.

Mr Higgins started. 'How . . . if maybe I did, what is that to you?'

'While you were there, a young lady was murdered.'

'I was never there. You cannot accuse me of this. I'm no stupe.'

'There is a signature of a Mr Higgins in the book of the White Lion inn, and the agent at the Woolpack recalls selling a ticket for the Saturday stage coach back to London to a man of your description.'

'Surely there are other Mr Higginses who might have visited this place, what did you call it?'

'With an accent as distinctive as yours, sir, and wearing a hat like the one you are carrying?'

His face fell. 'Perhaps I did make a visit, then. But I did not kill anyone, no way!'

'No, sir, we are not accusing you, simply gathering information about the death of Miss Burton.'

His face crumpled, and he took a couple of deep, erratic breaths. 'Poor Philly. Poor, poor Philly.'

'We hope you might be able to help us find her murderer, sir.'

He sat up at this, his face set. 'If I can assist in that endeavour, sir, I shall be well content.'

'Excellent. Now, perhaps you could give us an account of your movements between arriving at the White Lion quite late on the Wednesday evening, until you left on the Saturday coach?'

Mr Higgins paused, and thought. 'Let me see. After I was shown to my room, and I may say having knocked my head on those old beams a couple o' times, I took the advice of the chambermaid and went to look at the theatre, to get my bearings, as it were. It was dark, of course, but there were a few oil lamps in the streets, and I asked some passers-by to direct me. When I got to the entrance, which by the way I thought rather unimposing, cheap even, for a theatre, I waited, as there were sounds of a heap of voices, and of music, coming from the building. After a fair few minutes, people started emerging, and then

I saw Philly coming out on the arm of a . . . gentleman, I guess I ought to call him. I was filled with jealousy, and called to her. She looked shocked, and then asked who it was, and I said something about her having forgotten me already.'

'So then she told the man to go away, because she needed to speak with me, and after a few protestations he did. I don't know where he went, but it was towards the High-street.'

'And what happened next?' said Harriott, seeing Mr Higgins had stopped talking for the moment, and feeling she ought to contribute.

'We talked. Just stood there in the street and talked. Well, on my side it was more pleading, begging even, but she was obdurate. I got myself ready to pitch a fit, I was so frustrated, but I kind-of held it in, knowing it'd only make things worse.'

They kept silent, and eventually he controlled his breathing with an effort, and began again.

'I don't know how long we stayed there, back and forth, but it felt like an age. Anyhow, at length, she told me straight, it was hopeless me following her around, on the chance she'd change her mind, and the best thing was for me to high-tail it back to London, and forget her. She just turned and went, and I didn't dare follow her, for fear of . . .'

'For fear of?' said Stephen, tilting his head to one side.

Mr Higgins face flushed. 'No, I meant, I was frightened she might do me harm. I know what you're thinking, that I was going to say, that I might attack her, but I would never do that, not Philly. She was everything to me. You have to believe me.'

Harriott smiled at him. 'And then?'

'You have to believe me, she was much more powerful than she looks, and I'm a timid kind of fellow, and not strong.'

'Yes, sir. So . . .?'

'I just went back to my inn, I was about tuckered out, what with the trip, and the upset of how she was with me, and all that.'

'How about on the Thursday?' Harriott found herself beginning to feel sorry for the man. 'What did you do then?'

'I woke up late, and took my breakfast, and then just kind of wandered around. I went to the theatre again, spoke to a fellow who was delivering some beer, he said he hadn't seen her in the building, he'd been right through to the back and that, to the green room if you know what that means?'

'We do,' said Stephen. 'That'd be Mr Wickens: Harriott, he never mentioned meeting Mr Higgins when we spoke to him, did he?'

'No, he didn't. I'll make a note to ask him again.'

'Well, he sure seemed a bit distracted by something when I spoke, so maybe, I don't know . . . Anyway, after that I just kind of moseyed around, took a walk to the edge of town, kind of kicked my heels rather. Found a tavern up in some little place a ways out, called the Crown Inn, and they found me a meal, and the landlord, Mr Barham I think he was, if you want to check up on me, he didn't ask too many questions about my not drinking their ale, being as I'm teetotal, like Philly.'

'So that's why nobody saw him in town on the Thursday around lunchtime, Stephen.'

'Indeed. Do go on, Mr Higgins.'

'So after that?' He thought a while. 'I guess I went back to town, thought I might have another try at finding her. And I saw they had a show on the very next day, with Philly set to sing, so I bought a ticket, and as I came out I saw that fellow from the night before going into the side door, so I made myself scarce, went down the lane until he came out, and kept watch till he did.'

'How long was it before he left?' Harriott was trying to remember what Jack had said.

'Nigh on half an hour, I guess. So when the coast was clear, I went in the same way as he had, and tried to find my way around, but it was mighty dark, and there were some fellows on the stage rehearsing, or working out their movements, so I went on through and found a whole lot of junk stored backstage, and then someone opened a door, and I lost my nerve and scuttled out, and it was a good job it was dark because I had to pass a woman in the corridor, but she wouldn't have been able to see me much, I shouldn't think.'

'What was it you took from the theatre? Something you could fit in your pocket?'

Mr Higgins coloured. 'How d'ye? . . . Well, I might as well come clean, now I've told you all this, I suppose. There was this little inlaid box just kinda lying there, and it'd cost me a deal to get the coach down to see Philly, and I've been in and out of work up here, so I thought if I took it, it'd cover a few bills, maybe. I regretted it once I got back to my room, and I only got a few shillings for it anyhow. But there it is.'

'And then?' said Stephen.

'I thought about trying to find the other fellow, but I didn't know how, though he stood out, what with his fancy vest and all, and I asked a couple of people about him, and then I lost my nerve, and went to my room and stayed there the rest of the day. I was banking on being able to see Philly in the show, the next night, and then trying to catch her as she was leaving. Oh, yes, I forgot to say, I'd scouted round the back after I'd given up on finding the other fellow, in case there was any kind of stage door, and thought that's where she'll be coming out, once she was done. But just as I was about to see if it had been left open by any chance, this lumbering fellow came along reeking of beer, and looking like he might be ready for a fight, so I shrank back to let him by, and he went into the building.

'What kind of time might this have been?'

'Well, maybe about a quarter after four or more likely a little later. I did keep looking at my pocket watch, being nervous, you see, but it didn't seem to agree with your church clock, so I'm not sure it was working right.'

'And then?'

'Well, I was about done up with my nerves, but I was just going to try the door, and take a look inside, when the drunk fellow came out again, carrying something, and so I skedaddled, double quick.'

'What was he carrying?'

'I don't know, I was too bothered by the look on his face, I just turned and ran.'

Harriott looked at Stephen, and took up the questioning. 'Very well. And you say you spent the rest of the day in your room. I see. What about on Friday?' Harriott thought that there was no way Mr Higgins could have done the deed, if his story about the Crown Inn was true, but she wanted to be thorough. Also, he seemed genuinely distressed about Miss Burton, unless he was a much better actor than his difficulty in finding work might indicate.

'Friday? Well, I kind of kicked my heels most of the day. Saw that fellow I was talking about, in the street, but funked going over to talk to him. Looked in the church, mighty dark in there with those galleries and tall pews, ain't it? Took myself for a walk, round and about, into the fields, over some little streams, that kind of thing. Anything to kill time before curtain – well, I know you don't run to curtains in your little theatres, but you know what I mean.'

'And then I was in the crowd, wishing the first play to be over quickly, so I could hear Philly sing, she's got . . . she had, a wonderful voice, you know . . . and then they opened that blessed chest, and well, it threw me, totally threw me. I was up in the gallery, stage right, you see, and from where I was I could see directly into the chest, and when I saw it was Philly . . .' He began to sob.

Harriott realised that Mr Higgins must have been seated quite close to her and George Bunn at the performance. And of course she hadn't noticed him, not knowing who he was.

After a few moments, he made an effort and continued. 'I didn't know what to think. I remembered the row we'd had two days before, and feared whether anyone had heard us, and what people would say, and I thought the jig would be up if I didn't get away, so as soon as I could get out of the place I rushed over to the coaching inn and got me a ticket on the stage the next day, and spent the night imagining they were coming for me, all mixed up with heartbreak over poor

Philly, and I didn't sleep one whit, and then I was up and out and at the inn for the coach before it was light, and didn't calm down until I saw the smoke of this city again. And that's the truth.'

Harriott looked at Stephen again. 'Is there anything else?'

'I don't think so. Thankyou, Mr Higgins, you've been most helpful.'

'Is that all? Really?'

'That is all.'

'And might we sympathise with you in your loss?' added Harriott. 'Although it seems, she was never yours to start with.'

'No, she always said I was too timid for her, you're right there.' He sighed. 'But another thing, may I ask, how did you track me down to this theatre? London's a big place.'

'Our colleagues asked at the clubs which cater to Americans, and to actors, and from there it was simple.'

'I see. So if I ever did want to commit a felony, not that I would, I ought to cancel my membership, would you say?'

'They might still remember you at the club, though, Mr Higgins, might they not? I should not advise such a course.'

CHAPTER 19

STREETS OF LONDON

THE WHOLE FAMILY AND THEIR guests set off on foot for Vauxhall at about a quarter before five, excepting Miss Clarke, who apologised, but she was leading a Bible study in Clapham and could not excuse herself from it. It seemed the Clarke household possessed season tickets for the garden, which gave Harriott some comfort, as she was concerned about how much expense they were putting them to, on her and Stephen's account.

Once arrived, and passed through the entrance gates, Stephen consulted the clerk in the office, and headed off on his own in search of the head gardener. The others ambled this way and that, admiring the planting, the maze of walkways, the booths, several as yet not opened, and the fine vistas towards towers and pagodas and such-like.

'Miss Curteis, are you satisfied with the progress of your enquiries?' asked Lady Mary, as they paused at a bed full of colour.

'I think they have taken us as far as they can in London,' she replied, 'although we still do not know for certain who might be the evildoer.'

'Are you not convinced of the guilt of either of the men you have seen?'

'No, not at all. Mr Higgins, whom we met today for the first time, seems too meek to commit a murder, and too in love with Miss Burton to have killed her, even in a jealous rage. Besides, we are coming to believe that the murder was committed between one and two of the afternoon, and if he is confirmed to have been taking lunch in the inn in Boars Isle as he told us, I think he cannot have been at the theatre at that time.'

'I understand. And Mr, what was his name, the other man, Cousins?'

'He likewise. If he can be confirmed to have gone back to the Woolpack Inn after leaving Miss Burton while she fetched her costume, he also could not have done the deed. Besides, there is another problem we have not addressed, of the complete lack of bloodstains anywhere in the building. Not to mention the absence of a weapon. Though that of course could have been disposed of, the question is, where did it come from originally?'

'I am sure you will solve these conundrums in due course. Meanwhile, there is the matter of your colleague, Mr Fuggle.'

'How so?'

Lady Mary made a delicate noise, which might have been a small laugh. 'How do you . . . How are relations between you, I should say?'

'He is a friend, of longstanding, and has been most helpful in this enquiry.'

'Tell me about him.'

'Well, he works as a gardener, but he has very superior ambitions. He reads widely on the subject, and on broader issues, and seems to me to be set for better things than might be found in Tenterden.'

'How has he found London?'

'He has adjusted to the city much more readily than I have. I have found it quite overwhelming at times, but he has taken to it as one born. And in our enquiries, when I have felt most hesitant, he has taken the lead, and persuaded the men to speak without apparent difficulty. I have been most impressed.'

'I see. He has shown a lot of interest in the management of gardens in this area, I know. And of course, is presently interrogating Mr Gye and Mr Hughes's chief gardener here, I imagine.'

The little group moved on, and Harriott looked curiously at Lady Mary. Why was she asking her about Stephen like this?

'It has been so very kind of you and Sir George to invite us both into your home, Lady Mary; after all we are only provincials, quite ordinary people.'

'We are glad to assist. Rose would say that everyone is equal, and that those with privilege ought to aid those without. She is quite a firebrand, you know, once she has a cause to espouse. She is pressing for reform, for example in the questions of restricting child labour, and assisting Mr Wilberforce in his final push for the abolition of slavery in the Empire.'

'I see. Well, we are ever so grateful for your help. But, we have really done all we need to do with our questions, so perhaps we ought to be leaving, so as not to impose any longer?'

'By no means. Mr Fuggle has plans to visit more gardens, I hear, and I am sure you would wish to spend time with him, visiting the sights, and perhaps hearing a little further about his aspirations?'

'I have not heard anything about what these various gardeners have been saying to him, so far. But, if you are content, I would like to stay another day. It was a very long and uncomfortable journey here, and it would be good to be here a little longer before facing the return trip.'

'I understand the need for chaperoning is not an issue outside the *ton*, so you are not restricted as we were when we were young. I recall, it was quite difficult for myself and Sir George to find any time to be together without an audience. I envy you that.'

'I assure you that we are most careful to keep to the proprieties in other ways. Noone would think we are anything other than friends.'

'Of course, I would not suggest otherwise. But he seems a most superior kind of man, do you not think? Now, let me show you the place where they are setting up the tight-rope for the performance of some amazing dancing set to music and accompanied by fireworks, once darkness has fallen.'

Harriott followed her hostess, and was soon buttonholed by John, who wanted to tell her all about the balloon ascent which was due at six thirty, when the air would be at its most still after the heat of the day. John had to cope with his sister pulling faces at him, but stayed manfully by Harriott's side until they visited a stand where an orchestra was just beginning a performance. He succeeded in finding a seat by her as they played, and tried to converse about music, with less success. Harriott had never heard such a great sound: all the orchestras in Tenterden comprised perhaps a dozen players at most, and this had nigh on thirty. It was quite overpowering, especially sitting so close to the instruments.

After the first piece was concluded, Stephen returned from his quest for information, and slid into a seat on the other side from John, who ceded possession reasonably graciously.

'There you all are. I thought I'd never find you in this crush. There must be near a thousand people here, or maybe more?'

'Was your visit successful?'

'Very much so. Mr Stevens, he's in charge, told me he's been here six years, and the work's a bit hit and miss, what with the gardens closing after the summer season, so he has to have other employment, they only keep a few men on part-time from September to April. But he knew about the Tradescant place, and said it was well worth a trip. He approves of how the Stockwell estate is managed too. But the most exciting thing is, he knows Joseph Paxton! Well, that is, he worked alongside him at Chiswick Gardens for a year before he came here, and then Paxton moved up to Chatsworth a couple of years later.'

'Who might he be? And what is Chatsworth?'

'The Duke of Devonshire's seat, up in Derbyshire. Mr Paxton began as a gardener's boy at fifteen, he got a place at Chiswick at twenty, and by twenty-three he was in charge of a huge estate like Chatsworth. I read all about him in Mr Ducksbury's paper, and I want to do as well as he has.'

Harriott looked at him carefully. 'I don't see why you couldn't, Stephen. You want it enough, I can see.'

'Anyway, as well as that, Mr Stevens told me about a lot of the new plants they've put in this year here, although the main emphasis isn't on the planting, but the layout, and providing narrow winding paths so people can disappear from their friends for a while and, er, get to know each other better.'

'Might that not be seen as a little immoral?'

'Well, he says that all the chaperoning that the posh people insist on means young couples can't . . . well, you know. So they come here and conveniently get lost together.'

He saw Harriott look uncertain, so he continued, 'Also, he said the owners spend most of the entrance money, and the profits from the food and drink, on the shows, like fireworks, and balloon ascents, like tonight, and musical extravaganzas, not so much on the actual gardens, which he thinks is a mistake, of course. But I did pick up some most useful tips about what new shrubs are coming in, and how to care for the latest azaleas, and camellias. They can be tricky if you don't know what you're doing.'

'I feel very ignorant, Stephen. I don't really know anything about plants. Might I come with you next time you go and see a garden and speak to people? I'd like to learn.'

Stephen's face lit up. 'That'd be topping. Real beneship. I'd love you to.'

He sat back and relaxed a bit. 'When this music is over, can I show you some of the bang-up new species they've just had in this year, he showed me some of them in the propagation shed, and told me where to find the full-grown ones?'

'Surely. If Sir George doesn't have other plans.'

Sir George returned with the two younger children who were carrying some sickly looking sweetmeats, and was quite interested to follow Stephen and be shown first *Berberis moranensis* from Mexico, a shrub with spiky leaves a little like Holly; then a new kind of harebell from Rupert's Land called *Campanula lasiocarpa*, which Harriott declared monstrous pretty; and finally, after taking a few wrong turns in the maze of paths, they found out several saplings of *Eucalyptus pulchella* from Van Diemen's Land, a kind of peppermint tree with white bark.

'How do you remember all these names?' asked Harriott. I couldn't hold that Latin in my head for a minute.'

'I write them down, and repeat them again and again, and picture the plant with the name drawn on it, and I don't know, it just sticks in my head. What do you think of these little trees?'

'The leaves look a bit like willow, but the trunk's all wrong,' she said.

Sir George was also impressed. 'Do you think I should obtain some of these new, what do you call them, species, for my garden, Mr Fuggle?'

'Sir, I do not know if they will thrive without expert care. They are so new in this country, and our weather is not at all like that of Mexico, I understand, for the *Berberis*. But the other two may do splendidly, in the correct soil, I imagine. And they would be a talking point for visitors, to be sure.'

Harriott stayed quite close to Stephen for the rest of the evening, to the chagrin of John, and found she was enjoying herself once the strangeness of the place had abated. True, there were crowds of people everywhere, but Sir George and Lady Mary made sure everyone was looked after, and she felt curiously protected next to Stephen. Odd, really, he was no kind of giant, only an inch or two taller than her, and not imposing physically. But he was comforting, safe, and dependable.

By the time they had seen the ascent of the balloon, made without a fire using a new gas that had to be generated to fill it, and eaten a splendid supper, and watched the unbelievable acrobatics of the high-wire performer, and marvelled at the myriad lanterns, gasped at the firework displays, and walked for seeming miles, she began to yawn.

'Time we all took ourselves back home: Charles is flagging, and Rose too,' said Lady Mary, gathering up her youngest, one to each hand. 'I should imagine you two are tired as well?'

Harriott admitted as such, and the party departed, having to weave through crowds that had increased rather than decreased as the night deepened.

'When do the revels finish?' she asked.

'Oh, in the small hours,' said Lady Mary. 'I am glad our house is far enough away not to be disturbed by the noise, except occasionally. I do recall once, though, they had a firework arrangement on the basket of a hydrogen balloon, and once it had run its course the balloon itself caught, and there was such a bang it rattled our windows, and made our butler drop his tray, which caused him great embarrassment.'

And so to Thursday. After halting near the great market at Covent Garden, and leaving the two men to explore, Miss Clarke took the reins and conveyed Harriott without incident to Mr Angerstein's house in Pall Mall. She conducted her through the various rooms of the collection, commenting on the artists represented, and lamenting the lack of more modern works, such as those of Mr Turner, who she particularly admired. To be sure, Harriott thought many of the paintings very dark, but was overawed by the grandeur of the place, and could not consider making any criticism at all.

She found herself wondering what Stephen would make of the place, and of the little snippets of information that Miss Clarke dropped from time to time, such as the fact that the street name "Pall Mall" had its origin in a game that used to be played there over a hundred years ago, by royalty and their friends. She wanted to ask him what he thought of the gardens depicted in the paintings, and also just to feel him near her, which was very strange, as she was under the protection of an important lady, and had by now become more accustomed to the crowds and noise.

Miss Clarke appeared well-acquainted with many of the other visitors to the gallery, and stopped to converse often, introducing her as a friend from the country, but Harriott nevertheless felt somewhat out of place, aware of her hair not being in the mode, and her best gown, though fashionably styled, not being made of the highest-quality materials, and of her being without jewellery. However, Miss Clarke included her in conversations, asked her opinion on subjects she might be expected to have some knowledge of, and praised her to others as being most capable when she explained about them attempting to solve their mystery.

The return journey to meet Stephen being only short, Miss Clarke drove by a circuitous route to show off more of the capital to her guest. There was a great square with its garden and up-to date frontages of great houses; the pillared sweep of Regent's Quadrant; small shops and great ones; narrow alleys and wide vistas, and eventually, she drew up by a neat hotel, competently saw the phaeton into the care of a groom, and led Harriott into a morning-room, where she ordered tea, and asked her what she now thought of London.

Harriott was somewhat lost for words, quite unlike her usual self. 'I . . . it is so unlike Tenterden, Miss Clarke, that I cannot really comprehend it properly. The number of great buildings, the crowds, the grandeur. I am, I fear, quite lost.'

'London is all those things, to be sure. But do you not find it dirty, and smelly, and noisy?'

'Oh yes, those things too, but then Tenterden has its share of dirt and smells, and rubbish in the streets.'

'I have not taken you to the poor areas, I felt it would not be right for a first visit, but many of our citizens live in abject poverty, and filth and degradation abound there in a way that is unknown in the countryside. I am doing my best, with others, to alleviate this sorry state of affairs, but it is a grindingly slow process. But enough of London, here comes our tea.'

Once they were served, she continued,

'Tell me about Mr Fuggle. Do you hold an attachment to him?'

Harriott was puzzled. Miss Clarke too? 'No, not at all. He is just a good friend, and he has been most helpful in solving our conundrum.'

'Oh. I see. I just thought . . .'

Harriott looked at her, trying to read what she meant. 'Why might you think otherwise?'

'Oh, no reason, I just . . . we old spinsters are prone to seeing romance whenever we can. I . . . as you know, I lost my great love, and want to see others happy in consequence.'

'Well, Stephen is a person with great ambition, he wants to be in charge of a great estate some day. He was telling me yesterday about a man whose name I misremember who achieved that goal by the age of twenty-three, a big place in Derbyshire, I think.'

'And you? Do you have ambition?'

'Yes indeed, but it is not so focussed as Stephen's. I want to move out of Tenterden, and see the world a little before I fix on an aim. You may not know, but I hold the post of secretary to Mr Pomfret at present, he is our most important landowner, a cousin of Mrs Croughton with whom you stayed, and mayor. I feel quite proud of this; and would wish to further my prospects in some way, though I cannot see how at present.'

'Well spoken, Miss. Secretary, indeed. I am pleased you are entrusted with such responsibility. We women have a long way to go in securing work appropriate to our abilities. And, if we are to raise children too, that is a most complex issue.'

'I have no urge to begin a family at present, I am too young, far too young.'

'Quite.' She looked up. 'Oh, there comes Mr Fuggle. I must just go and ensure George is catered for, and then we may go through to the dining-room.'

'How did you find the art gallery, Miss Clarke? Did you have enough time to view all the paintings?' asked Stephen once they were seated.

'Indeed, thankyou for your concern. Miss Curteis and I feel most uplifted by the experience, do we not?'

Harriott saw her grin, and realised she was not expected to agree.

'For myself, I thought the paintings were rather dark and, to be sure, somewhat dull.' She tucked a stray strand of hair behind her ear. 'On the other hand, I could well admire the skill of the painters, and the grandeur of the place. I am not sure though that I should like one on my wall, back at home.'

'George and I had a fine time in the market. I was glad of his company; Sir George was right, it is a rough place. But I saw fruits and vegetables I had never come across before, and flowers of all types, exotic ones and homely ones too. It seems violets are the coming thing, they were everywhere, even though we are at the end of the season. They are cultivated under glass, and one trader told me he makes much of his profit from them.'

'Did you get ideas for the gardens you tend in Tenterden?' asked Miss Clarke. 'I know Mrs Croughton is keen on having new plants to show off.'

'Indeed. I think we could make a bed of the new varieties of tulip, the variegated ones, and I found I had enough coins to buy a few bulbs to try out.' He patted his pocket in satisfaction.

'Excellent. And have you both decided how you will occupy yourselves this afternoon?'

Harriott looked at Stephen. He raised his eyebrows a little at her.

'If Harriott would be willing, I should like her to accompany me to Mr Tradescant's botanical garden. Mr Tinsley told me that his cabinet of curiosities was taken to Oxford many years ago, but the house is still there, and the garden is still cared for and open to visitors.'

Harriott glanced at Miss Clarke, to read how she viewed this suggestion. Encouraged, she agreed heartily, thinking it would make a pleasant change from the city, and feeling quite drawn to sharing in Stephen's enthusiasm.

After a most intriguing lunch, consisting of several dishes chosen by Miss Clarke as being likely to be unfamiliar to the visitors, and lively conversation about the merits of each one, they regained the carriage and George, left Miss Clarke at the Foreign Office, and were taken over the river at Westminster Palace, George explaining that the Regent's Bridge at Vauxhall, though a more direct route, incurred a toll. Also, it passed some most unpleasant areas, including the new penitentiary at Millbank.

They recognised a few places they had noticed before, and made out the top of the tower in Vauxhall Gardens after they passed the turn for the Clarkes' residence, but were then deposited by a small chapel in an area known as South Lambeth, and pointed on their way by George.

CHAPTER 20

COME TOGETHER

HARRIOTT AND STEPHEN CROSSED THE main road, dodging between carts, carriages and people on foot, and soon found their goal. Harriott thought the house looked a little dilapidated, but followed Stephen through a door in a wall into the garden where an elderly woman collected their sixpences and pointed them to the best route around, explaining that they kept up the place in memory of the Tradescants, but apologising that the garden was not to the standard it had been in the lifetime of its founders.

Harriott found the walled seclusion a welcome relief from the busyness of London, and was content to follow Stephen around, stopping when he stopped, and listening to his talking, mostly to himself, but occasionally to her, absently.

'That must be a tulip-tree, I think, *Liriodendron*. I'm not sure, but probably. The way it spreads, hmm; it's hard to tell, when you've only read about them, Harriott.' He moved on, looking this way and that. 'That one, now, that'll be one of those new Japanese Maples, I'm fairly sure. Yes, the pointed leaves, and the colour. Although they weren't here in the seventeenth century, they must be an addition. We ought to find some of those plants named after the Tradescants somewhere, you know them, Harriott?'

'No, what are they?'

'Well, let us look about the ground under this tree . . . no, that's one I don't know . . . and . . . there is one, look.'

'Oh, I know that, that's a spiderwort, we have those in our yard, they grow anywhere.'

'Some do, but this one's a *Tradescantia virginiana*, see the purple flowers. Mr Linnaeus named it for them, it was the first specimen of the type, they brought it to England from America about two hundred years ago.'

'How do you know all this, Stephen?'

'That? When I heard of this place I asked Sir George, and he let me look in his library. I found out about it in one of his books. There were drawings of some of the plants, it was wonderful. I stayed up far too long last night reading it.'

He moved on, identifying some plants, puzzling over others. A few had labels, but many did not. Harriott was pleased to know a mulberry tree, and some commoner plants like Michaelmas daisies and phlox. More, though, she was struck with Stephen's passion for his subject, and his joy in discovering new species. It rubbed off onto her: she found herself just loving being with him, and sharing in his discoveries.

Ivory dogwood, white jasmine, agapanthus: the names rolled past her as they proceeded around the place. Harriott stopped listening to the names, and just drank in the atmosphere, the regularity of the beds, the neat arrangement of the planting, and the care that the gardeners had taken of the collection, so long after the death of its originators. There were occasional other persons inspecting the planting, as they were, but very few.

'When did Mr Tradescant die, Stephen?' she asked eventually.

'Just after the Restoration, in the 1660s, I think. I may have misremembered the date, I've learnt so much new recently. That was the son: the father began the collection.'

Harriott calculated. 'One hundred and seventy years ago. That's such a long time.'

'We're very lucky the present owners want to keep up the place. But I would think in not too many years, London will have spread out beyond here, and people will be offering so much money for the site for building, that the garden will disappear.' He moved off to inspect another bed, and Harriott looked after him, thinking he was actually quite a good-looking man, strange she had never noticed it before.

She wandered off by herself for a little while, but grew oddly lonely, and found out Stephen again, who seemed to have circumnavigated the garden and was talking to the owner, who was bent over, weeding.

'Do you get many visitors?' he asked.

'Not as many as we used to. People want a show like over at Vauxhall, not to appreciate the plants. But we get a fair few, more on a Saturday afternoon, of course. It helps to pay for the upkeep, you see.'

'Do you take in new discoveries?'

'Just one or two, to provide a little colour, or a background. We felt we should mostly keep to the ones Mr Tradescant brought to England, there are quite enough of those to keep us busy.'

Harriott drifted away again, hearing the conversation as a buzz in the background, and wondering if she might ever have a place of her own large enough to keep a garden. If she did, she would build a small grotto to sit in and look at the flowers, and have lots of those spiky plants, with the pompoms, she liked those.

Eventually Stephen broke off with the owner, came to her and said he thought they ought to be getting on back to the Clarkes'. They thanked the woman at the gate, stepped out into the street, and looked around at the bustle.

'That was so marvellous, Stephen, I'm really glad I came,' she said.

'It was. I'm glad you liked it. I didn't keep you too long?'

'No, it was just right.'

'So, let us set off home. Would you care to take my arm?'

'Do you know the way?'

Stephen looked up at the sun. 'I think so. Sir George had a plan of the area on his table, I consulted it.'

Harriott slipped her hand in the crook of his, noting how he had taken the outside station, and they ambled companionably along, first past villas of the well-to-do, then fields that were full of produce: supplies for the markets of the city, Stephen said. After a while they came upon a vast open oval area, which seemed to be common land, surrounded by a road, which they crossed, pleased to be in something resembling the uncultivated countryside again. Once over this, they came upon an unpleasant smell from an area which a sign proclaimed to be a water works. Harriott thought privately this name must be a euphemism for what really went on there, but they gave the place a wide berth, and continued north.

Several buildings announced their function in bold lettering: there was a chandlers' manufactory, a school for licenced victuallers, a business in fancy metalwork. Also there were more shops, more people, and more traffic. She enjoyed playing a guessing game with Stephen concerning what occupation people they passed might have, or what secrets they might conceal. It was in high spirits that they reached their goal, and were admitted by the footman.

At dinner, she reluctantly asked if Miss Clarke had been able to arrange for their ticket back to Tenterden for the Saturday. Or, if the times suited, they could leave the next day, though she knew Stephen was keen on seeing Stockwell House, or rather its gardens.

'No, do stay until Saturday. The coach leaves at ten, my man tells me, so you would not have time to visit Stockwell before. Besides, you have earned a little holiday, have you not, with all your work on this problem?'

'Stephen has done most of it here,' she said.

'No, we did it together,' he put in. 'We are much better as a pair than alone, are we not?'

Harriott frowned, then fell silent, thinking. She did like being with Stephen, to be sure. But what did he mean?

Her thoughts were cut short by John, again wanting to talk with her about the rail-way opening, and whether she could persuade his father to sanction the visit he so very much wanted. His brother

William was expected back tomorrow, and he was sure he too would want to go, and if only Miss Curteis would use her charm, he believed his father would say yes.

Harriott smiled, and said she did not think it her place to bully his father. He was affronted, and denied ever having suggested bullying. Sir George, of course overhearing all this, intervened, and said he would look into the possibility, and find out about coaches from Shrewsbury, but it would need permission from his masters at the school, and he was not hopeful an exeat would be forthcoming. However, he could propose it as an educational visit, and other pupils might also wish to witness the historic event, so, well, we shall have to wait and see.

Their visit to Stockwell was marred by rain, the first for some weeks. The groom had fitted the phaeton with a hood, but it did not keep out all the weather, and although the rain was not continuous or heavy, it found its way inside nonetheless.

Descending at the great house, they raised the umbrellas thoughtfully provided by Lady Mary, and set off for the gardener's shed. Not so much a shed, they found, but a large building full of the latest equipment. Harriott, glad to be under cover, looked around the tools, sacks of seed, and piles of matting, and even saw a small plough, which surprised her. Stephen sought out the head gardener Mr Mitchell, who was expecting him, and was pleased to be consulted, especially when Stephen mentioned how Mr Tinsley and also Mr Stevens at Vauxhall had praised his work.

'Would your lady like to see around the house while we make our tour?' he said. 'I am sure our housekeeper would be pleased to show off her domain: the master is away at present. It is bad weather for viewing the grounds.'

Harriott was tempted, but for some reason found she did not want to leave Stephen's side when he was engaged in his passion. 'No, it is most kind of you, sir, but may I accompany you both? We have umbrellas, and the air is still warm. A little mud is nothing, is it?'

Harriott followed the two of them at a little distance, not wanting to interfere but staying close enough to hear the conversation and perhaps learn something new. She was glad she had taken Stephen's advice to wear her travelling gown, the one she wore for work at the Eight Bells, because even after a few steps through the rather long grass the hem grew heavy with water, though the ground was still firm underfoot.

The two men inspected some of the planting, the flower beds and the shrubs, but she was taken by something else. It was annoyingly not definable: just something she could see, or perhaps just feel, about how the whole garden was constructed. It seemed as if it had always to have been this way, with the curves of the swathes of grass and the shapes of the clumps of trees making a harmonious whole, somehow. It had rhythm, even though it didn't move, she thought, and was perplexed by the observation.

She didn't like to say anything about it, but after talking for some time about which species did well in the Surrey soil, and what its qualities and difficulties were, compared to the clays of Tenterden, Stephen and Mr Mitchell began talking about famous gardeners they admired. She didn't follow all the talk, but resolved to ask Stephen later about these men, and why he admired them. She remembered how he wanted to be like the man who had gone to Derbyshire, but they didn't talk about him: the names were Brown and Repton, she thought.

'How do you like the garden, Harriott?' Stephen eventually asked, as they completed their circuit.

'Very well, very well indeed. I feel as though the whole place is in harmony, if that makes any kind of sense.'

Stephen smiled at her. 'That is exactly what Mr Mitchell has been trying to achieve. He is an admirer of Mr Lancelot Brown, although the estate cannot support quite such extensive works as Brown achieved. But he has done a fine job, I believe.'

'Thankyou, it is good to be appreciated,' said Mr Mitchell. 'Now, perhaps you would like a cup of tea before you make your way home? It's about time for my break, and the lads will be coming in out of the wet for a while too.'

Harriott sat on a box near a little pot-bellied stove and watched Mr Mitchell with the kettle as her skirts steamed gently in the heat that reached her. Two other men and a boy came in, all with the unfamiliar accents of the city, and sat a little apart. Although the tea was rather weak, it was hot and reviving. Mr Mitchell explained they were given the used leaves from the big house, which saved them a deal of money.

After quite a short while, Mr Mitchell stood up. 'We'd best be getting on, now, Mr Fuggle, if you don't mind. Simon, you and James can carry on weeding those beds, there's no chance of scything today; and William, I think those shrubs over by the glasshouse ought to be clipped next, when you've finished the ones you're doing.' He turned to Stephen. 'You'll be knowing your way home, then, you two?'

'We will be set right if we just turn left at the gate and keep on going, I believe?'

'That's it: keep straight on until you see that new church with the tall cupola and the columns, then you're at the Oval, and that'll see you on your way. Give my best to Mr Tinsley, won't you?'

As they left the grounds, Stephen turned to Harriott. 'Are you alright to walk? It's only a couple of miles, I think, but there are carriages called hackneys around, maybe.'

'Of course, what do you take me for? Anyway, that'd cost money we don't have.'

'I was just thinking of you, that's all: it's wet and you've been out in the rain a long time.'

'I'm perfectly capable of walking, thankyou. And we can see more of London.'

Stephen stiffened, as if he had said the wrong thing, and although taking the outside on the pavement, didn't offer his arm. After a few steps, Harriott took it anyway, and said, 'Sorry, I didn't mean to be sharp, you were just being kind, I realise,' and leaned on him a bit, feeling him relax. 'You know how I like to be independent, normally, don't you?'

They made their way slowly along, splashing in puddles in spite of their care in placing their feet, and looking at the new terraces and some large villas set back from the road, and the occasional shop and even an independent chapel. It was odd to see how London seemed to be almost visibly moving south, the buildings becoming more and more densely packed as they walked north.

'Tell me, who is this man Mr Mitchell admires? Brown, wasn't it?'

'Lancelot Brown, yes. He was the great man of the middle part of last century, and although his style is not always appreciated now, he did design a huge number of great estates, and achieved a great fortune. His sons became a Member of Parliament and an admiral, and he purchased the lordship of Fenstanton in Huntingdonshire with his fees.'

'Do you hope to do likewise?'

'No, not at all, but I should like to make my mark, certainly. But that is a long way off, I consider. Anyway, let's leave that for now, come on, remember yesterday, what do you think of that man there with the cane? What secrets does he conceal, would you say?'

At length they reached the church Mr Mitchell had mentioned, a fine Palladian building, and feeling curious, they went in to look at the architecture for a short while. Then, thinking that it must be getting towards time for lunch, they crossed the roads by the Oval and were soon inside their destination and changing into dry clothes.

None of their hosts was in the house, so they ate with the children and their governess, a sensible woman of middle years. After the meal, the others departed to their lessons, and Stephen announced he would spend the afternoon in Sir George's library, to take advantage of an opportunity not readily available in Tenterden. Harriott accompanied him to find out a novel, and see if she could discern what Mary saw in the sort of romances she preferred. Passing over a number of stories by Sir Walter Scott, she settled on one called "Emma" which she had seen Mary reading, and decided to sit in the morning room which had a prospect over the garden, to read as much as she might before their hosts returned.

It was slow going, and she rapidly became irritated by how idiotic the heroine was in regard to Harriet, the simple girl she befriended. Nonetheless she persisted, unusually for her, hoping that the wretched woman would be brought to book by someone, perhaps by her neighbour Mr Weston, for her idiocy. Also, she was irritated by the father, who was so useless she would have slapped him rather than take any notice of him or pander to his ideas.

She put her book down after an hour or so in order to calm herself, and went to stand in the window to see if the weather was improving. It did not seem to be, and she wondered how wet they would get on the roof of the coach the following day. Then, her mind travelled to how Stephen was doing with his reading in the library, and then on to recalling his rapt face when he was exploring the botanical garden yesterday, and learning from Mr Mitchell this morning.

Would it be better if she read her book in the library? It would be more companionable, to be sure, but would it distract Stephen? Also, it was more comfortable in the morning room. But something drew her, and she had almost to make an effort to sit herself down again in the window alone and continue the saga of Emma's well-intentioned blundering.

The Clarkes had invited guests for dinner that evening, and Miss Clarke apologised to Harriott when she arrived home, that they would all be dressed in their finery for the occasion, but not to be concerned, her striped gown was lovely, and perfectly in the fashion, and if she felt at all uncomfortable not having an evening gown she could borrow some of her jewellery, if it would help. There was no need to feel so, but she knew people did, and so, . . . well, she wasn't putting it very well, but there it was.

Harriott heard the kind intention behind the words, and said she would like to wear a necklace of some kind, if that would not be an imposition, or making her seem to be acting above her station. After a series of exchanges about the proper etiquette, each trying not to offend the other, it was agreed she should wear a plain cross on a simple silver chain, and have her hair arranged again by Lady Mary's maid.

Stephen came down in his Sunday suit, his shoes newly polished, and appeared unmoved by the sight of Sir George and his guests in evening wear. However his face lit up on seeing Harriott, and he pretended to shield his eyes from the brilliance of her appearance. The maid had persuaded her to let her place little pearls in the hair arrangement, and she had allowed it rather than cause a disagreement.

On this occasion the children were not to attend, much to John's chagrin, which was something of a relief for Harriott, who was nervous enough about dealing with other elevated personages. She had practised her curtseying in her room before coming down, and tried to remember the proper address for titled persons, but still felt unconscionably apprehensive.

As it turned out, none of the guests was titled, nor indeed of lofty attitude. Miss Marianne Thornton, a young woman in her thirties, was one of Miss Clarke's friends from Holy Trinity, Clapham, and Mr and Mrs Sedgcombe, though living north of the river, were also involved with the struggle against poverty and in the reform of the prisons.

The conversation naturally turned on such issues, and all of the guests included both Stephen and Harriott in the discussion, inasfar as they were willing to express an opinion on matters about which they had never really thought overmuch. They were shocked to learn of a rising of the farm workers in East Kent that had begun only that last Saturday, when a threshing machine was destroyed, and that buildings and hayricks had been set alight, in protest at reducing wages and loss of winter employment to machinery.

Equally unexpected though was the reaction of their hosts to the rioting, which was to side with the dispossessed and not the landowners. Mr Sedgecombe wanted to know if Sir George could bring any pressure to bear on the Members of Parliament with whom he was acquainted concerning the question of wages; Miss Thornton was exercised about the chances of the new Poor Law Bill making any worthwhile improvements in the lot of the starving; Mrs Sedgecombe talked of making a visit to the county of Kent where all these disturbances had occurred, to speak with the workers to gather more information about their grievances, so as to present a more forceful message.

By the time the dessert was served, though, they had exhausted the topic for want of sufficient new information. Harriott and Stephen had not been able to contribute anything much, having been unaware of the plight of agricultural labourers, inasmuch as Tenterden was a fairly affluent area compared to some. Also, being in the town, they chiefly associated with townsfolk, other than when Harriott served labourers beer in the Eight Bells.

'But is there anything I could do to help this cause?' she said, at a lull in the conversation as the guests addressed themselves to an orange-pudding. 'I would like to find some work that would take me beyond the confines of my town, yet be interesting and useful.'

'Our societies, ones to alleviate poverty, improve the prisons, missionary societies and so on, are constantly in need of people to compile the information that is collected, and present it in a fashion that can be readily assimilated by those in power,' said Mrs Sedgecombe. 'And we need people to raise funds for the cause, and to write articles for our magazines, and so on. But they are not often paid posts, because we want to devote all our monies to achieving our goals.'

'Harriott is a private secretary to our largest landowner,' said Stephen, 'and her writing is the neatest I have ever seen. Plus, she is a printer's daughter, and knows all about the machinery of printing, and is most intelligent and diligent.'

'Capital,' said Mr Sedgecombe. 'We could do with people like you to help our cause. Are you Evangelical yourself?'

'Methodist,' said Harriott after a brief pause, being unsure of exactly what Mr Sedgecombe meant, 'though I attend the parish church with my employer at present.'

'No matter; we welcome all like-minded persons to our little army.'

'The difficulty is,' said Harriott, 'I have no other means to support myself. We are only here through the kindness of Miss Clarke and her brother.'

'Miss Clarke explained to us how you are solving a mystery,' said Mrs Sedgecombe. 'Would you care to tell us the story? Perhaps in the drawing-room over coffee?'

CHAPTER 21

BACK HOME AGAIN

In the morning the rain had eased, but clouds still shrouded the sun, and Harriott had to prevent Miss Clarke paying for an inside seat for them at the coaching inn, saying she had given them so much already, and she could not possibly accept, and so on and so forth. She felt a little unwell, and on edge, as she often did at these times, but she held her ground and insisted.

'Very well, Miss Curteis, I accept defeat. But be sure to write and tell me how the mystery turns out when you have solved it. I insist: it is too exciting.'

They waved as the coach rumbled back into the Strand, and made sure their blankets were secured in case of rainfall. Harriott, more used to the movement now, nonetheless felt impelled to hold on to Stephen's arm again, it felt good to do so, somehow, and he didn't seem to mind. Besides, she would far rather have spent the morning quietly, she seemed to have developed a sniffle, and had frequently to reach into her pocket for her kerchief.

'Did you finish that book you took?' he asked, as they crossed Waterloo Bridge.

'No, not even close, I was still on the first volume. I couldn't . . . it didn't . . . hold my attention, it seemed too annoying. I don't know why Mary liked it so much.' Privately, she realised her irritation might have been because of her courses starting, but she hadn't made the connection at the time.

'I had a grand time with the illustrated volumes of new plant discoveries, and the geology books. Sir George has a fine collection of most modern works.'

'He can afford them, I suppose.'

'I'm not sure he is all that wealthy. I mean, of course he is far richer than us, by a long way, but I understand from Mr Tinsley that his estate in Gloucestershire is quite small, and he has two boys at Shrewsbury School, which must cost something. Also, he believes Sir George gives a lot of money to the various causes his sister supports, as does she. He just has good taste, and the books he does possess are the most useful. Of course he may have inherited some of the older volumes from his wife's father: I gather he was a merchant in textiles, and successful. But Lady Mary has several brothers, so I am unsure about this.'

Harriott blew her nose again. 'How do you know all these things?'

'I talk to people. The footman, the cook, the gardener, and Sir George himself, when I asked him about the library.'

'I thought it was women who were supposed to talk all the time?'

'Maybe, maybe not. But I like to know things, and the best way to find out is to ask. Look, there's the Coburg Theatre again. I wonder how Mr Higgins is doing, whether he is still fearful about being arrested?'

Harriott thought he probably was, poor man. However, she stuck to her topic. 'Have you found out an opening for a gardener in a bigger place than Mr Pomfret's or Mrs Croughton's then?'

'Not yet. But I have made contacts, and will write to them in a month or so, to see if anything new has come up.'

Harriott was curiously relieved that he had not found new employment, but said nothing. She held on more tightly as the coach swayed around an obelisk in the middle of an open area her neighbour told her was called St George's Circus, and began wondering what the future would hold for each of them. It would be strange to be back in Tenterden, so much new had happened.

After a delay at Maidstone because one of the fresh horses cast a shoe while resisting being hitched, and this had to be replaced as there were no others available, they rolled into the familiar yard of the Woolpack at gone nine o'clock. Getting down stiffly, Harriott left her box to be called for in the morning, but Stephen took his smaller bag and they walked companionably down the High-street to her door, albeit punctuated by her repeated sniffing and nose-blowing.

'Well, goodnight, Harriott. See you in church. We can get together with Mary and George and see what's what, afterwards.'

'Goodnight.' She stood at the door, watching his shape disappear into the darkness, then turned and went in to tell her father all about their week in the big city.

Meeting in the churchyard, Mary was agog to hear their news, but even more so falling over herself to tell them what she and George had been doing in their absence.

'We made a lot of progress,' she said, holding out a paper. 'Look, we've talked to all the actors, and found out where they all were from the time Miss Burton got to the theatre until that evening.'

Harriott looked at the paper. 'Mary, you have surpassed yourself: I can't read a single word of this.' She grinned, slightly uncomfortably because of the soreness of her nose. 'Come on, let's go and find somewhere you can explain what your scribble means.'

Sitting in the back room of the Bells, Mary smoothed out the paper and explained.

'Now, you had found out some of this before, Harry, I know, but George thought we ought to check again, and make sure we knew where every one of the actors were during the whole afternoon, because these were the people who were in the building, and so they had the most chance to do the deed, isn't that right, George?'

'That's so. We checked up on those there alibis, didn't we, Mary?'

'And I thought it'd be a chance to see what kind of people they were, too, and see if they seemed likely to be murderers. Though I still think it must be that Mr Higgins, you know, the mysterious stranger.'

'Well, I . . .' said Harriott. 'No, that can wait, let us know what your spider's web says first.'

'So, Mrs Robberds came in to the theatre first thing, and was doing jobs of sewing and such in the green room until one-thirty, or a little after, it was just after Miss Burton had come in to fetch her costume that she left, she said. Then, she went home to cook dinner, and came back at four, until five. She was seen by someone or other in the green room all morning, and then again when she came back. You'd found that out, Harriott, already.'

'But in between, she says she went home to put something on for their dinner, and I spoke to Mr Robberds who told me they'd had a lovely stew that evening about five thirty, so she couldn't have been back at the theatre, or the stew would have had to have been on all day, nearly, and spoilt.'

'Couldn't she have prepared it earlier, and just nipped home to set it on the fire?' asked Harriott

'Not really, because she hadn't bought the meat until after two, I went and asked the butcher she goes to, he said he knew her well. So she hadn't time to be murdering in between, what with preparing the meal.'

'Wonderful. Mary, you're a treasure. I ought to have thought to do that myself'

'And anyway,' Mary continued, looking pleased, 'George and I both thought she was genuinely upset about Miss Burton, she's a bit of a mother to the younger actresses, you see, and wouldn't have done such a thing.'

'I'm not sure that's a reason to rule her out, but the timings are, I know.'

'And who's next? Oh yes, Mr Robberds, we went and spoke to

Mr Nailor, where he works, he was at the job all day, cleaning hides. Horrid job, I felt quite sick there.'

'Good for you again, Mary, I didn't go and see his employer, I thought he wasn't a likely one.'

Mary looked at her, she was speaking a little nasally. 'Are you alright, Harry, you don't look all that well?'

'It's just a cold; carry on.'

'Now the Gregorys spent all day together, I suppose they could have done the murder together, but I didn't think it likely. They were in the green room from about twelve to two, and on stage, Mrs Gregory was helping her husband with his movements for a new play, from three to five. In between, they went and got something to eat at the Harris Arms, and they say they didn't see Mr Carpenter there or on their way back. So he can't have arrived in the inn much before three, I don't think. And we checked with the Harris Arms, and they agree the Gregorys were there about those times.'

'The trouble is these times are all so approximate, aren't they?'

'Yes, and that church clock is worse than ever, it is stuck at half past three now, and they say they're going to have to raise a subscription to get it mended. Anyway, Mr Brooke: we wheedled his address out of Mrs Robberds, and I went to see his wife, when I thought he'd be out. She says he was with her all day except about an hour at lunchtime, and he was cross at having to go out, and when he came back he'd been hurrying, and he'd only been gone less than an hour. And, I said, was there anything different about his appearance, and she said not, so I think she'd have noticed if he had bloodstains, wouldn't she?'

'You've been wonderful, Mary, much more thorough that me,' said Harriott.

'Good work,' added Stephen. 'And George too, of course.'

Mary coloured slightly. 'So, Mr Bosworth was in the green room or on the stage all day. Remember he had an argument with Mr Gregory about wanting to practise his entrances? And we made a list of who saw him when, but,' she looked more carefully at her page, 'I can't quite make out all of them.'

'We covered the whole time, though,' said George. 'Mary's been right careful.'

'Excellent,' said Stephen. 'We can trust you, I know.'

'Now, Miss Chester's the same, she was in the green room all day and didn't go out, because she's playing Susan and it's a big part, she was going over and over her lines, sometimes with one actor and sometimes another: we made sure someone had been with her all the time. Besides, I can't see her stabbing a woman, can you, George? And why would she want to?'

'She might have been jealous,' said Stephen, 'though I can't see what of, or who of. Anyway, I agree with you, and if she didn't leave the green room that lets her out.'

George went up to Boars Isle and saw Mr Sharpe: he was working at the forge, he helps the blacksmith, he checked, and he was there all day.'

''S'right,' said George. He's in the Susan play, but he only plays a small part, so that's why he wasn't in to the theatre then.'

'The Rolands, being at home and Mr Roland ill, we couldn't think of how to check them, but he really was ill, we saw him, and he was still coughing fit to bust, he looks really poorly. He's a bad colour, Mrs Roland thinks it might be consumption.'

'Could we ask his doctor?' said Harriott.

'Doctors wouldn't tell you anything,' said Stephen, 'it's called professional . . . something, they don't talk about their patients, Dr Bishop told me.'

'And the last one is Miss Brown,' said Mary. She was at home alone sewing, except when she passed Mr Higgins in the corridor at about three thirty, and so we can't confirm that.'

'Mr Higgins said he did pass a woman as he came out, but didn't see her face,' said Harriott.

George piped up, 'Mary didn't say, but we asked if that was

everyone, and Mrs Robberds told us there are three other men in the play, but they live out at other places, . . .'

'Yes, Wittersham and Rye, I think,' put in Mary.

'. . . and so they weren't around at all on Thursday. They did come in on the Friday for the last rehearsal, though, I think. There are lots of male parts, you see, and even so they have to double up; but only two women's. The other women play the crowd scenes.'

'But we have shown Miss Burton must have been killed on the Thursday, haven't we?' added Mary.

'That's right,' said Harriott, 'or else we'd have to know where she was when she didn't keep her appointments.'

'Which just leaves the Carpenters, of the people in the theatre.'

'Yes. Do you think it was one of them?' asked Harriott.

'Not really, I think Higgins did it,' said Mary.

George looked at her, hesitantly. 'I don't know much about that,' he said, but I reckon Mr Carpenter is more likely. I mean, he was there most of the time, and he's not good to his wife, as I see it.'

Mary nodded. 'George might be right. We didn't go and see them, we didn't have time. But let's hear about your trip, before George has to go back to work. Mr Pomfret'll be wanting his lunch served in not so long.'

Harriott looked at Stephen. 'Shall you or shall I?' she said.

'You say,' he said, smiling. 'You'll put it better, in just a few words.'

Harriott paused, blew her nose again, took a breath, and then summarised the results of their visit in rather more than a few words, but without mentioning all the other things they'd done.

'So you see, Mr Cousins is clear of suspicion if we can confirm he went back to the Woolpack, and Mr Higgins if he really was at the Crown,' she finished.

Mary sighed. 'Oh, I did so want it to be Higgins. Well, never mind, it makes it more likely George is right, doesn't it?'

George got up and went to check the time with Mr Paine, who owned a pocket watch, which he had bought recently owing to the unreliability of the church clock. Returning, he said he had to go, else he'd be in trouble with the cook. 'But you'll fill me in, Mary, won't you, on Tuesday?'

'Of course. 'Bye, George.' She kept looking after him until he was out of sight.

'Now, what about the Carpenters?' said Mary. 'I don't like him at all, either, he's so bad-tempered.'

'Well, we have a few jobs to do first, then we can look into the Carpenters,' said Harriott. She pulled out a paper. 'See Mr Wickens to confirm he saw Higgins around the theatre late morning, and see if he has anything else to say about him. Check at the Crown with Mr Barham about Higgins' story of getting lunch there. Check at the Woolpack for Cousins' comings and goings. And try and interview Miss Mace, concerning her assignation with him in the theatre boxroom.'

'You'd better do that, Harriott, not me, so she doesn't get the wrong idea of why I was calling on her.'

'Very well, if you'll take yourself up to Boars Isle? Mary, can you ask about Mr Cousins in the Woolpack? See if he went back in about one o'clock, and left about three; and returned around three-forty? I'll see Mr Wickens and Miss Mace. How do you think ladies of the night occupy themselves in the day?'

'The same as anyone else, I imagine,' said Stephen. 'Right, I'll be off, and we can meet again when?'

'How about at my house at six, after dinner? Or you could both come and eat with us, if you like, at five. I have a pile of jobs to do for Father, having been away so long, and I must see Mr Knowles, and apologise for letting him down yesterday.'

At five o'clock they all sat with Mr Curteis and ate a filling stew, while he quizzed Harriott and Stephen about their time in London, and what the capital was like, and the people, and all sorts of questions, that Harriott thought she had answered the evening before, and during the day, but he wanted to know more, and hear Stephen's point of view, and so on.

Once dinner was over, the three of them sat around the cleared table and reported. Mr Higgins' story was fully corroborated by Mr Barham, Stephen said, and Harriott had found out Mr Wickens, who recalled saying something to an odd nervous kind of fellow, about some actress, but he wasn't too clear about the man, he'd been busy. Mary said the Woolpack staff had been most helpful, and Mr Cousins being so . . . noticeable, yes, he'd come and gone as he said.

Harriott said it had taken a while before she was able to speak to Miss Mace, but once the woman was disengaged, she had confirmed the meeting with Mr Cousins, with a few choice words about the ancestry and morals of her failed customer. It had been most instructive, going to see her, she said, with a slight wrinkling of her nose.

Which left just the Carpenters. Unless there was some unknown person who sneaked into the theatre unnoticed, that is. But where to start?

'Well, what about trying to work out where the murder actually took place?' asked Stephen. You know, if you stab someone in the back, they aren't likely to be standing in the chest at the time, and then fall backwards into it. And then you'd have to pull the dagger out, which would be awkward when they were in it. And the blood would go everywhere.'

'Yes, and all over the person doing the stabbing,' said Harriott, remembering what John had said in London, about his book "Ivanhoe".

'So, we could look for bloodstains, couldn't we?'

'But we already did that, I crawled all over the stage and all I found was a couple of boards that were a bit darker than the others. Well, there were chalk marks, which I suppose are for the actors to know where to stand; and scuffs and scrapes, and bits that were discoloured slightly, but nothing that could have been blood.'

'Why do you think those boards were different?'

'I don't have any idea.'

'Perhaps we could all go and look at them? In the daytime, with lanterns as well.'

Mary looked uncomfortable. 'I don't really want to see blood, you know. Can't I do something else?'

'Well, if you wanted to kill someone in our theatre, where would you do it, Mary?' asked Stephen.

'I wouldn't, it would be horrible.'

'Yes, but if. Go on, try and think.'

Mary screwed up her face. 'I'd want to do it . . . where noone could see me. And I'd do it as quickly as I could, and very quietly, and run away as fast as anything,' she said, shivering.

'Where would be the most private place then?' Stephen rubbed his nose.

'The boxroom where Mr Cousins met that woman, Miss Mace,' said Harriott promptly. 'She told me it's not the first time she's met a man there.'

'That's one place. Any others?'

'One of the boxes?' suggested Harriott. 'I remember going the wrong way the first time I went to look around after interviewing Mrs Carpenter, and the one on the right, by the stage, is very private and dark.'

'The one the Haffendens sat in?'

'That's the one.'

'We ought to have a look at that then too.'

'Remember, that was the place that smelt bad, they had to get the chars in again on the Saturday, didn't they? Well I already looked all over that one before.'

'We could have another look, though, now we're sure what we're looking for. But it's a bit late now and the sky's still overcast. We need to have better light for that sort of job. How early can you finish tomorrow?'

'I have to catch up with Mr Pomfret's work,' she said, remembering. 'I expect I'll need to spend the whole day there. And I have to see

Mr Paine, and find out what shifts he wants me to work this week, too.'

'Surely you could find an hour or so at five o'clock?'

'I have my father's dinner to get, remember? And lots of other jobs too. It was lovely to go up to London, but there's a lot of work to do to make up for being away.'

'I could go with you, Stephen, tomorrow, if Harry doesn't mind,' said Mary. She went to the window. 'I think the weather might be changing, the sky's already a little red at the horizon. And George isn't off until Tuesday evening.'

'No, why should I mind? You do that,' said Harriott, 'we need to get this whole thing finished, it's six weeks or more since the poor woman died.'

CHAPTER 22

DO YOU REALISE?

HARRIOTT ARRIVED AT MORGHEW EXTRA early on Monday, expecting a pile of post and other jobs waiting for her. She needed to work extra hours, but still finish as early as she could, she reckoned, what with having her father to look after, and Mr Paine requiring her in the Bells from six until they closed. But she didn't feel at her best, what with this cold.

George had stacked all the post neatly on her desk; and there were two messages with the letters, one from Miss Pomfret, who wanted her to make a fair copy of some notes she had been making, and one from Mr Pomfret, who said that having arrived back only late last night, and having business in the town first thing, he would not be meeting her until eleven, but that she should make sure all the letters were opened and sorted, for him to deal with once he returned, as he had several other meetings later that day, beginning with one at one o'clock with Mr Ward.

Harriott set to, opening all the correspondence neatly, bar one which was clearly private, reading each through rapidly, and setting them in piles. The first was of those that needed only a routine reply, leaving place for Mr Pomfret's signature. She left the writing of those for later, and instead made notes about the others so as to be ready and prepared for a rapid review of the relevant questions. The third pile was of a more complicated nature, where she did not know how her employer was likely to want to respond, and these she had not dealt with at all when he came by.

'Good morning, Miss Curteis. I trust you are well, and your visit to the capital went off satisfactorily?'

Harriott stood up as he entered, and curtsied. 'Yes, sir, very well. We found out all we needed to, and learned a great deal of new things too. But, you said in your note that time was short, may I first go through the list of questions I have about your correspondence?'

'Indeed. Once we are at leisure, though, I should be most interested to hear both about the two gentlemen you saw, and the progress of your enquiries, and also about Sir George and his household. Perhaps later in the week, eh?'

'Yes, sir. I shall stay late today, and come in tomorrow morning, and I hope I shall be caught up presently.'

They went through the letters, Harriott trying not to sniff as they did so. She noted her instructions, as usual; but of course there was a great number of instructions, and she worried that it would take her an unconscionable time to finish them all. However, Mr Pomfret seemed in good humour, and as he turned to leave, she asked,

'Did your trip to Canterbury go well, sir, if I may so ask?'

'Excellently, my girl, excellently. I made several new connections, and completed a transaction which should be most profitable. Now, I must go, the Reverend awaits me. I shall see you tomorrow, then.'

Harriott did not leave Morghew until gone three o'clock, and hurried home to get her father's meal ready. As she reached Brewhouse-lane, James Maynard hailed her.

'Harriott! Good to see you back, I missed you at church, you left before I could get out.'

'James. I'm sorry, I'm in a rush.'

'There you are, then. Well, I wanted to ask you if you would like to come and see our new bullock, Father's trying to improve the herd?'

'Not at the moment, James, I'm so busy. Another time, maybe?' and she hurried on.

While changing her gown, stoking the fire and putting the water on to heat, and finding where her father had put the salt while she was away, she thought about James. He looked the same, of course, but somehow, she hadn't felt the same as she normally did when she met him. None of that fluttering of her insides, and that urge to spend time with him. It was most odd. Still, he didn't have the ambition she wanted in a man, he was content to take over from his father when the time came, and stay in Tenterden. Anyway, she had lots to do, and not much time to do it in.

In the Bells, it all seemed back to normal, the same old faces, except, it didn't seem quite the same there either, somehow. She couldn't say why, or what was different, but it was. She fended off the flirtations of the usual men who'd had a little more than was good for them, and wiped tables and pulled pints quite as if she'd never been gone, but there was something.

Richard Marshall came in with his band of ringers, it being practice night. He looked the same too, but again, not. He came to the bar, grinning, and tried it on with her as usual, but she didn't feel tempted, not even a little bit. Not that she couldn't appreciate the breadth of his shoulders, or the roguish look in his eye, but he just didn't . . . well, he hadn't . . . she couldn't say what, but it wasn't there. Maybe it was that he was a bit too unsettled for her liking? Or maybe it was just her cold.

Mary then appeared, smiling and looking pleased with herself. Harriott looked for Stephen following her, but he wasn't there. She was disappointed, she'd got used to having him around when they talked of the mystery. Where had he got to?

'Harry, we've found out all sorts of things, me and Stephen.'

'Where is he then?'

'He went home, his mother wanted him to mend her table, one of the legs had come loose.'

'Oh.' She felt curiously resentful, as if his mother shouldn't have call upon him.

'Don't you want to hear? It's very exciting.'

Harriott shook herself, looked back at Mary. She must have looked distracted, or something. 'Of course. What is it?'

'Well, we both took oil lamps, and we first went into the store room, and had a thorough search there, because Stephen said he didn't think we'd been in there before. I should have said, we had to go to the Carpenters' to be let in, because the side door was locked, it not being a play night. And Mr Carpenter was there, grumpy as always, and Mrs Carpenter looked like she'd been crying. And he asked us what we were about, but Stephen just said, Investigating, and he tried to tell us we couldn't go in, but Stephen said we had Mr Brooke's permission, so we were going to look around, and he let us go, but he looked murderous. Oh, I didn't mean that, I mean . . .'

'I know what you mean, Mary. Go on.'

'Yes, well, I was glad I was with him, I would have run away if I'd been on my own, when Mr Carpenter was horrid. Anyway, there wasn't anything to find in the storeroom, and I thought what a horrible place to meet a man, but there it is; and then we went into the big room, and opened up all the shutters upstairs, so we could see better, and found the boards which you said were different, and then Stephen had a wonderful idea.' She paused, dramatically, and Harriott smiled at her and said,

'You have my full attention, Mary. And then . . .?'

'Well, Stephen said, what if the boards that were different were usually in the part of the floor that gets taken up, except if there are dances? So we set our lanterns so we could see, and he picked up the boards that are stacked by the side of the pit, and we looked at the top ones. We didn't have to move many, and we found it.'

'Found what?'

'Well, there were three boards that had a dark mark on, well, several marks, and we took them up on the stage and laid them side by side, and there it was.'

'What?' said Harriott, not sure if to be annoyed or to laugh at Mary's storytelling.

'A circle of dark something, about eight inches across, and Stephen said it looked like blood, that someone had tried to clean off, but had just smeared it a bit, and not got it very clean.'

'Really? Not a big patch, but a circle, like a ring?'

'Yes, that's it. And we thought and thought what might have made it, and we went into the backstage area and looked for round things about the right size, and then Stephen saw Mr Carpenter's bucket, the one he uses to carry his tools, and if he needs water for something, whatever he's doing. And he took it back, and it fitted exactly!'

Harriott was now excited herself. 'So, does that mean Mr Carpenter is our man?'

Mary frowned. 'I thought it did, but Stephen said it just means the murderer used his bucket, or one like it. But it must be him, mustn't it?'

'I don't see who else it could be, Mary. So what do we do now?'

'I haven't finished. Just as we were putting the boards back where they came from, Mr Carpenter came in, and asked us if we hadn't done yet. I think he saw us with the boards, because he looked all frightened, I thought, but then he just said, "Leave them boards alone, they're nothing to do with you. I've got to lay them tomorrow for a dance that's coming off on Wednesday, and I don't want them messed with."'

'Really? What dance is that? Are you going?'

'No; and I don't know. But don't you see, he'll have a chance to clean them better, if he's laying them tomorrow?'

'He will, won't he? Can we show them to anyone before that, so there'd be an official witness? I can't do it, I've got to go to Morghew.'

'Who needs to see them?'

'Anyone important. How about Mr Brooke?'

'Yes, well, I'll see if I can do that first thing tomorrow, if you like, I'll see who I can find.'

Harriott nodded, and served another customer. When she was free again, Mary continued,

'Anyway, after that, we went and had another look at the last box on the right, the one that Mr Haffenden had complained smelt. We looked and looked, but there wasn't anything to see. But Stephen said it would be a good place to do a murder, because of being at the end of the corridor, it not going through to the backstage, and because of the curtains around it shielding it from most of the rest of the room. He is clever, don't you think? Much cleverer than me.'

'Yes, he's got a good brain, but you're you, and you've got loads of good qualities, and you're my best friend. Anyway, that's why the Haffendens take that box, I suppose, it's more private.'

'Yes, I suppose so. But there weren't any bloodstains there; I know you looked before. Nothing. And it didn't smell either, but it was a long time ago.'

'Anything else?'

Mary shook her head.

'You have done wonderfully. Now all we have to do is to . . . well, work out how . . . I don't know . . . yes, what do we have to do?'

'I don't know. Miss Burton can't have been killed in that box, because there was no blood. Or anywhere else, we thought, because of the same reason.'

'We'll have to think, and come up with something. When are you meeting George tomorrow?'

'At five, at the Morghew gate: we were going to go for a walk, he wants me to show him the path down through Tilden Gill, if it's still good weather.'

'Hmm. And did Stephen say anything about what he was doing after work then?'

'Not exactly, no. Well, he did say . . . I think he'll be at Herenden tomorrow, won't he? You could call in and ask him on your way . . . no, you don't go to Morghew on Tuesdays, do you?'

'I will be doing tomorrow, like I said, there's a deal of work to catch up on.'

'Oh yes, you did say. Um, Stephen'd like to see you, I expect. He'll be in the front garden, weeding, in the morning, he said.'

'What, he told you where he'll be? Why?'

'Oh, no reason.' Mary looked anxious, and rubbed her knuckles together. Anyway, that's where he'll be, if you want to talk to him, I think. But I must get home, Mother will be wondering where I am.' She turned, and left hurriedly, Harriott looking after her in some puzzlement.

She wouldn't have time to go and see Stephen before she got to work tomorrow, though, would she? But then, the prospect seemed quite appealing, for some reason, as long as she didn't get her gown dirty. He had really done well this evening, and she'd like to tell him so, and yes, it was odd, she was kind of missing him being around, somehow.

Edward Wickens came in just then, and ordered four gages of ale. As she served him, she remembered the messing about in the Harris Arms that had torn her sleeve several weeks ago, and how much fun that had been, but somehow, now, she didn't want a repeat of that, not really. Even when he leaned over and tried to kiss her, she just leaned away, and shook her head. He was gorgeous, true, with that mop of curly dark hair, and those dark twinkly eyes, but not a patch on Stephen, really. Nothing like as intelligent, or reliable, or, well anything. Stephen had ambition, he was kind, he looked after her without making her feel second-class, he was fun to be with, without being too rowdy; he was just right.

Then, at last, it struck her. She had, without noticing it, fallen for Stephen Fuggle. No, she couldn't have, surely. What? . . . How? . . . When? It wasn't possible, was it? She'd known him for so long, and he was just, good old Stephen . . .

She examined her feelings carefully as she thought about him, pictured his laughing face, the way he moved, him rubbing his nose in thought. It was true, though, it was, however it had happened, she cared. More than cared, in fact. She felt it deep, deep down in her chest. She took a long, deep breath. How was she going to face him now? And what would Mary think? And more importantly, what on earth was she to do about it?

CHAPTER 23

INTERMISSION

HARRIOTT FOUND HER PACE SLOWING as she approached the Herenden gatehouse, she was a little out of breath for some reason. It would make a change to take that route to Morghew past Herenden, wouldn't it, and she could find out if Stephen . . . well, she could just ask him what he was doing that evening, couldn't she? At the thought, she felt herself blushing with embarrassment. No, she couldn't just yet, her feelings were too . . . she hadn't quite managed to . . . perhaps she'd see him after work, that would be better. She kept firmly to the left of the Rye-road, just in case she was tempted, and marched on.

Mr Pomfret's correspondence was a welcome relief, it occupied her mind fully, in a way she hadn't managed last evening after getting home. Her father hadn't said anything, though. Somehow, she'd felt he'd be able to notice there was something different about her, she felt so strange inside, surely it would show on the outside?

She couldn't care for Stephen in that way, could she? It wasn't reasonable. For a start, he wasn't tall enough, and he wasn't . . . well, roguish, like the men she usually went for. And she used to play hoops and jacks and that sort of thing with him when they were younger, and he had once broken her doll and she had slapped him in the face, and not spoken to him for weeks. And, to be fair, when she had been eleven she had let his chickens out by mistake, and the fox had got them, and he had been so upset. And, . . . he was just Stephen, not a . . . well, an object of love, not that sort of love, anyway.

She bent to the letters, glad to be able to concentrate on handwriting, spelling, order and method. She began to cough a little. Drat this cold! Mr Pomfret hadn't said what time he'd be in today, she hoped she'd be able to get all the routine replies finished for his signature by that time. And if she could make a start on the ones he'd dictated, making fair copies that is, it would be very good.

Mr Pomfret appeared late in the morning, followed by George bearing a tray with cups and a pot of tea. She looked up, surprised, and stood and curtsied. He'd never brought refreshments to their meetings before.

'Good morning, Miss Curteis. Hard at work, I see. But perhaps you might leave your papers and come sit over here, and take tea with me before we return to the grind of commerce? I find myself exceeding curious to hear about your trip to London, if you might indulge me?'

'Of course, sir.' Harriott set down her pen, wiped her fingers on a cloth, and made her way to the settee. 'I am making good progress, the regular replies are done and await your signature, and I have begun the ones you dictated.'

'Yes, yes, all in good time. Now, tell me about your investigations, and how they have turned out.'

Harriott took her tea, and sat on the edge of the settee balancing the saucer on her lap, hoping she was adhering to the correct etiquette. She had to stop for a while to think where to start, there had been so much happening.

'You arrived in London with Mr Fuggle yesterday week, did you not?' he prompted.

Harriott, at the mention of Stephen's name, felt she might have begun to blush, but found herself coughing again instead. She frowned in concentration, and decided to begin with the interview with Mr Cousins.

'Sir, on Tuesday last we were conveyed to the Home Office in Sir George's phaeton; well, Mr Fuggle sat with the groom, and I with Sir George, which was most condescending of him, and . . .' She paused again, feeling flustered. This was not like her, not one whit.

'Indeed.' Mr Pomfret sipped his tea, and she continued.

'Mr Cousins was rather taken aback by our appearance, and initially tried to have us leave the room, but Stephen, Mr Fuggle I mean, convinced him it would be to his advantage to be more . . . accurate in his recollections than he had been previously.'

'Indeed. A most superior kind of gardener's assistant, I perceive?'

'Yes, sir, Stephen is very intelligent, and has great ambition for the future. He handled Mr Cousins most skilfully, and we heard what we believe to be the truth, by the end of our interview.'

'Which is?'

'It appears that after spending the morning with Miss Burton, and her taking gin, when she is normally abstinent, he was nonetheless unsuccessful with his blandishments, even after going into the theatre with her at lunchtime, and being shown the stage, and having a further conversation with her backstage. She went to the green room to fetch a costume she wanted altering, and he left to return to his inn. He was staying at the Woolpack, and we have checked his time of return, as best we could.'

'I see. But he could not have killed her then?'

'No sir, she then entered the green room and was seen by several players, collecting the costume.'

'Of course. Carry on.'

'Mr Cousins was then observed to enter the theatre again at around three o'clock, and stay for half an hour. We have ascertained this was for a . . . an assignation with a lady of Honey-lane, and I spoke to the woman in question, who confirms his story. He then returned to the Woolpack, and this was also checked, and tallies.' She coughed again, several times.

'Are you unwell, Miss Curteis?'

'Sir, I do apologise, I have a little summer cold.'

'Very well. So, there was no time to commit the murder, or cover his tracks, even though he was twice on the premises? I see. And at what time do you believe the murder to have taken place?'

'Between one and two o'clock on the day before the body was discovered, sir, the Thursday, but all the times are extremely uncertain due to most people not possessing pocket watches, and the unreliability of the church clock.'

'Yes, I have noticed that myself.'

'I believe there is to be a subscription raised for its repair, sir.'

'Indeed? I must support that endeavour. Please remind me, later, when we return to our business.'

'Yes, sir. Now, Mr Higgins, the American, turned out to be a most nervous man, deeply in love with Miss Burton, who had followed her from New York, and then traced her by his contacts in the theatre world, to this town. He is presently working at the Royal Coburg Theatre by Waterloo-bridge.'

'Ah! A motive: the spurned lover?'

'Well, yes, and no, sir. We believe him too timid to have acted in such a way, and too in love with her. Mr Fuggle, Stephen, was able to persuade him to cooperate by mention of the Foreign Office, and describing how we could show evidence he had been in this town.'

'The Foreign Office?'

'Yes, sir, Sir George is as you will know very senior in that department, and aliens such as Mr Higgins are at the mercy of its rules. Or, that may not be the case, but he certainly thinks so.'

'Excellent. Well done, Mr Fuggle. And, no doubt, yourself, Miss Curteis, I am sure not all the success of your enterprise is due to your friend.'

'I think most of it, sir, is on account of Stephen: I found the big city most intimidating, whereas he adjusted to it without apparent effort. Anyway, Mr Higgins said he spoke with Miss Burton on the Wednesday evening and was repulsed; he made several tentative and unsuccessful attempts to see her on the Thursday, and at the time we think the murder took place he was eating his lunch at the Crown Inn in Boars Isle. He did enter the theatre briefly at around three-thirty, but he had not time to do much beyond steal a decorated box.'

'You have witnesses to all this, I take it?'

'Yes, sir.'

'So, you are satisfied you have eliminated those two men from your list of possibles? Who else remains?'

'We, that is, my friend Miss Exall and another, have shown that all the players have alibis for the whole of the period from twelve to five o'clock on that day, being at any time with one or other of the company, or at home with their spouse, or similar proofs. The only exceptions are Miss Brown, who was making a gown in her cottage in Honey-lane, except for one brief visit to the theatre at about a quarter before four, if I remember correctly. Then there is Mrs Carpenter, who was in her house, Theatre Cottage, selling tickets and dealing with other callers, apart from her household duties; and her husband, the caretaker, who is therefore our main and, indeed, only remaining, suspect.'

'And where was this man at the time?'

'He was in the auditorium in the morning, taking up the floor after the dance the night before, in preparation for the performance, and after lunch, tidying up; and then he says he went for a walk. After that he was in the Harris Arms, and returned at perhaps a little after four o'clock and continued tasks such as laying out costumes, and finding properties for the plays, until the stage was cleared.'

'Cleared?'

'By that I mean, by Mr Gregory and others: he was practising his lines on the stage until five o'clock. So, when they had gone, he did further tasks like placing the chest onto the stage in its correct position – and I may say he avers the chest was empty when he moved it – and then he went home before six, saying his back hurt, and falling asleep in his chair, before retiring to bed early.'

'If he was the malefactor, then you cannot trust his word.'

'No, sir, but the chest has a very weak base, and if anyone carried it laden, it would probably collapse. I heard they took it on a hurdle to the mortuary for that reason.'

'He might have dragged it, though?'

'Yes, I agree, he might. Now, there are two other problems we face. The murder was done by a single stab wound through the rear of the left chest into the heart, and we have found no place where a large quantity of blood was spilt, anywhere in the theatre, and noone with blood-stained clothing, or opportunity to clean or dispose of such clothing before being seen after the event.'

'A real difficulty, I admit. But the chest was full of stained cloths, was it not?'

'Yes, some of which appeared to be Miss Burton's regular garments; but we cannot see how such a murder could have taken place, with the victim standing in a chest, and allowing the stabbing, and yet not spilling blood elsewhere.'

'Yes. Good point.'

'The second objection is we can think of no reason Mr Carpenter might wish to kill Miss Burton. She had no money, knew no secrets we have been able to uncover, lived a blameless life, was a member of the Methodist chapel and an abstainer from drink, and a hard worker. Also, she hardly knew Mr Carpenter: most of the cast avoid him, especially the women, as he is so bad-tempered.'

'Hmm. So where next?'

'There are just a few odd things I haven't mentioned, sir. First, Miss Burton was found dressed in a costume of the 1810s and poorly-applied white face paint. Why would she have made up with face paint? The costume was because she was due to meet a seamstress for alterations, that is understood; but why make up, and only partially and poorly? Secondly, we have found three floor boards among those taken up from the area over the Pit, which when put together, show a dark imprint corresponding to a bucket used by Mr Carpenter to carry tools, water, and other such things, around the building. And two of the boards in the stage area are of a different shade from the rest, as if the soiled boards had been replaced by unstained ones at some time.'

'Carpenter, then, clearly.'

'Possibly, even probably, sir. But hear the last oddity. The box, stage left, occupied by Mr Haffenden and his family on the night of the discovery of the body, smelt . . . er, "as if a dog had done his business there", I was told. It had to be cleaned, and we do not know what this might signify. But we examined it and there was no trace of blood staining.'

'This is which box?'

'The one nearest the stage, sir, on the right as you view the stage from the audience.'

'I see. What do you make of this?'

'We do not know, sir.'

'Well, shall I have this man arrested, and brought to book?'

'We have no real evidence against him, sir, as yet. If he did kill her, where are the bloodstains? And why did he take such a risky course, in such a public place? And what possible motive might he have?'

'What sort of character does this man have?'

'Well, grumpy best describes him. He drinks heavily, I believe, and is on bad terms with his wife. He resents the company using part of his house as an office, although he is only living there because of his employment with the company. His interests seem to be chiefly drinking and avoiding work.'

'A ne'er-do-well, then?'

'He does have employment, sir, and discharges it well enough not to lose his job and his accommodation. And many men are grumpy and do not commit murders of others.'

'They do kill their wives, though, I have seen it often in my courts.'

'Yes sir.'

'Well, I wish you luck with the investigation. You are continuing in your quest, I imagine?'

'We are. We are so close to finding the truth, and yet. . .'

'It will come. It will come. And now, let us to our work, and get these letters dealt with. I can see that someone like yourself might be moving on to better things in due course, and I need to avail myself of your efficiency as much as I can before I lose you.'

By the time Harriott had finished the letters Mr Pomfret had dealt with, it was nearly four o'clock. She had found herself making mistakes, and having trouble remembering what she was going to do next, so everything took longer. She thought about going to see Stephen on the way home, but couldn't face it. And now it wasn't just embarrassment, she felt quite ill, actually, and her cough seemed to be getting worse.

By the time she reached home, and put the kettle on the fire, she felt quite unsteady. She made tea for her father, and took it into the print shop for him, but he took one look at her and marched her up to bed, instructing her to lie there and not move, and he would see to the dinner. She protested of course, but he was having none of it, and by the time she had drunk her tea, she felt so bad she couldn't have gone down and done her chores anyway.

Mr Curteis came up to see her with a little dinner, but she couldn't face it, and just asked for a glass of water.

'It'll be that bad air up in the big city,' he said, 'or the miasma rising from the river. It's a great river, I hear tell, and full of unhealthy stinks.'

'It is big,' Harriott said, in between coughing, 'and quite dirty, but . . . I don't know. I'll probably be fine again tomorrow, father.'

But in the course of the evening she felt worse and worse. She was first hot, and then cold, throwing off the covers and then huddling under them. She tried to eat some soup her father brought, but couldn't face it, after the first few spoonfuls, and then, mercifully, she fell asleep, rousing every so often from dreadful dreams, confusing ones, where everything seemed to be moving in impossible directions, and where she couldn't control anything, and she felt terrified almost all the time.

CHAPTER 24

STRANGE LITTLE GIRL

HARRIOTT OPENED HER EYES BLEARILY, and tried to sit up. What time was it? The daylight was too bright. Had she overlain? Surely she must be due somewhere . . .? But she couldn't remember what day it was, for some reason. She sank back into her pillows, exhausted by the effort, and fell asleep again.

When she next woke it was dark, or at least, twilight. There seemed to be some light from the corridor outside. Was that someone coming in? Who was it? Was she in danger? She struggled with the bedclothes, panicky, then felt a cool hand on her forehead pushing her down, gently, calmly. She subsided. How weak she was. Whoever it was, she couldn't fight it.

'There, there, Harriott, don't be frightened. It's only me, your father. And Mary's outside. Would you like to see her? You've been very ill, but all's going to be well, if you can just rest.'

Mary? Oh, yes, Mary. Wasn't there something she ought to be asking her? But what?

'Yes, please, can Mary come in?' Her voice didn't sound like her, it was all cracked, croaky.

A movement at the door, a light coming nearer. Someone sitting on the bed, by her.

'Harry, I've been so worried, but you do look better. Not . . . well, not quite yourself, to be fair, but better. I'm so relieved.' She rubbed her knuckles together.

Oh yes, Mary. Mary does that with her hands. Did that. Didn't she? Harriott coughed a few times, painfully, then sank back into blackness.

Was that bells? Church bells? She ought to be up and ready, she had to be in the servants' line to welcome Mr Pomfret. Harriott sat up suddenly, felt swimmy, sank back, and coughed and coughed. Oh yes. She was ill, someone had told her, she thought, a long time ago. But she felt so sticky and horrid, she wanted a bath, or at least a wash, if only she didn't feel so dreadfully weak. Perhaps she could try and get up?

There was a handbell on the chair there, it wasn't usually there. Ought she to ring it? Well, maybe she should.

Her father appeared, looking a bit grey, tired, and old. 'Harriott! You're awake again. I'm so glad. Do you think you could manage a little breakfast?'

'I'm not hungry . . . no, actually, I think I am, a bit. Could I have something to drink, I'm so dry?'

Mr Curteis fetched a glass of water from beside the bed, and she drank thirstily. Her lips were cracked, her throat hurt, but it felt better. She sank back, breathless from the effort.

'Now, how about a glass of warm milk? Or, could you manage some porridge?'

'Milk, please, first. And then, maybe, yes, porridge would be lovely.'

He left the room, and soon Mary appeared with her milk.

'Here you are, Harry, are you feeling a bit better now?'

'I'm fine, thankyou.' She took a long draught. 'No, I'm not fine, really, I'm feeling dreadful, but I'm . . . I don't know.'

'That's alright, Harry. Don't worry, you'll be alright, now.'

'What do you mean?'

'We thought we were going to lose you,' she counted on her fingers, 'three days ago, you were so ill.'

'What? What day is it now?'

'It's Sunday, you can hear the bells, can't you? You fell ill on Tuesday evening, don't you remember?'

'No, not properly, it's all like a long, confusing dream.' She rubbed her head, her eyes. 'I was doing . . . Mr Pomfret's letters, and . . . I didn't feel well enough to go and see Stephen, and . . .'

'He's been so upset you're ill. He's been in every day, but your father didn't think it proper to leave him in the room with you, so he stayed by the door, and he says Stephen was almost crying.'

'Why? Crying, over me?'

'Yes, Harry. He really cares about you, hadn't you noticed?'

Harriott shook her head, and took another drink of the milk. 'I can't . . . I don't know, what to, er . . .'

'No, it's alright, just lie back. I'll take that milk, and set it just here, where you can reach it, and go and see if the porridge is ready yet.'

Harriott was drifting, on a raft somewhere, out at sea, but it was very calm, very still. She opened her eyes, and instead of the sky she saw . . . Mary, wasn't it?

'Oh, good, you're awake again. Do you want any more of your porridge? I can heat it up again.' Harriott struggled upright. Mary pulled and pushed her pillows so she was comfortable. 'There, is that right?'

'Thankyou. I do feel a bit more myself, now. Is it still Sunday?'

'Yes, it's nearly seven o'clock in the evening.'

'Oh. Well.' She coughed. 'What was wrong with me?'

'You had a lung fever. A really awful one, you were so hot, then shivering, you were calling out, your lips were blue, it was awful.'

'Why, were you here?'

'Of course. I helped to nurse you, don't you remember? No, you wouldn't, of course. My mother helped, and Mrs Chambers, and all sorts of people came round. It came to what the doctor called a crisis on Thursday night, and after that you seemed to settle a bit, but you were still very ill.'

Harriott shook her head. 'I don't remember, I'm sorry. And I'm so sorry for putting you all to so much trouble. I'll be alright now, you can let me be.'

'I'm not sure about that. Dr Bishop says you aren't out of the woods yet, he means you need to rest, and get your strength back.'

'What, for a couple of days, you mean?'

'No, more like a week or two.'

'But what about my work?'

'That's all taken care of. Your father sent little Simon next door round to Morghew with a message first thing on Wednesday; and I told Mr Paine, so it's all dealt with.'

'Oh. But I ought to . . .'

'No you didn't ought. You'll be as weak as a kitten, after all you've been through. Look, Mr Pomfret came by and left his card for you, here it is: he signed it, "with best wishes for a speedy recovery".' She passed it to Harriott, who looked at it, not quite comprehending. It was signed, "Virgil Pomfret". 'But you won't be able to go to work for at least two weeks, Dr Bishop said.'

'Oh. We'll see about that. What I really want now is a good wash, a bath if possible. I feel horrible.'

'I'll see to that tomorrow morning, if you like. I'll put the water on to heat first thing, and get your father to bring up the tub, and I'll help you, and I'll change your sheets at the same time.'

'But we usually have the tub in front of the fire.'

'You won't be going downstairs for a day or two, Miss. Mark my words.'

Harriott sank back into her pillows. This was a different sort of Mary from the one she was used to. But she didn't have the strength to argue.

By Tuesday Harriott was definitely improved. She was sitting at the kitchen table in her undress in the late afternoon when Mary came in with George, carrying a basket with apples and a pie.

'Here you are, Harriott,' said George, 'these are from the cook at

Morghew, on Mr Pomfret's orders. You need to build up your strength, she says.'

Harriott took it, and smiled. 'Everyone's been so lovely. I don't deserve it. But, I've been longing to know, but Mary won't let me talk about it, how is our investigation going?'

'Er, well, it's not, really. We haven't had any new ideas, and Mary's been so busy looking after you, she hasn't had time. Stephen's been too worried about you to think about it either, so Mary says.'

'Where is he then?'

'He'll be along later, after he's finished work, he said. He didn't like to come by yesterday, once you started to feel a bit better, until you felt stronger, but he was here every day before, when you were bad.' Mary gave Harriott a look which she couldn't fathom.

Stephen, yes. She had to see Stephen, she wanted to see him, but she just didn't . . . she wasn't ready to . . . not so soon, she couldn't tell him how she felt about him, she just wasn't up to it.

'Perhaps in a day or two we can try and talk it all over and see what else we can think of,' she said, 'but just now my brain doesn't seem to be working properly.' She coughed, and spat something decorously into a kerchief. 'I'm bringing up this stuff all the time, it's not very nice.'

'It's better than what was coming up before,' said Mary, 'all frothy and red and bubbly, it was horrid.'

'Everyone's so glad you didn't die,' said George. 'You have a lot of friends, all over town.'

Harriott didn't quite know what to make of his statement, so she just took a sip of the water in front of her.

'Anyway, we won't stay long,' said Mary, 'we don't want to tire you. Do you want to go back to bed yet, if you do I'll help you upstairs?'

'No, not just yet. I need to get Father's dinner . . .'

'No you don't,' interrupted Mary. My mother's looking after him, he's fine. And she'll bring some up for you, when she comes round. Can't you behave like an invalid for a few days?'

'No. No, I can't.'

'Well we'll have to make you.'

'Another thing, I keep forgetting to ask, where did all the flowers come from? My room is full of them, and they look fresh.'

'Yes, Dr Bishop told us we couldn't bring flowers until you were much better, they take all the air, he said. But Stephen brought them yesterday, and left them with me, and I arranged them.'

'Stephen?'

'Stephen. He had permission from Mrs Croughton to take them from the garden, don't you worry, but it was all his idea.'

'Mrs Croughton? So it must be Monday or Tuesday. Or Friday: he works there on those days.'

'Yes, it's Tuesday now, he picked them yesterday. You really aren't yourself, are you? Come on, I'm going to take you upstairs, and put you to bed. You've been up long enough, and you need to rest.'

There was a knock at the bedroom door. Harriott didn't answer, she was dead to the world, breathing noisily, but with some colour in her cheeks: not the hectic red of her illness, not the pallor of when she was over the worst, but the beginnings of a healthy pinkness, though her face was sunken in, and her arms, laying on the white sheets, thin and feeble-looking.

Stephen stood by the bed, with Mr Curteis just behind him looking on. He tried to take in the fact that Harriott really was going to recover, going to be well again. He held more flowers in his hands, roses this time, and laid them on the chair by her head. His breath came jerkily, and he wiped his nose, swallowed a few times, and then turned away.

'She's right on the mend, lad,' said Mr Curteis. 'She's a bonny lass, she'll be back to normal before long, mind my words. And then, you'd better tell her, hadn't you?'

'Tell her?'

Mr Curteis raised his eyebrows at him. 'Harriott is the only person in this town I reckon, who doesn't know you've been in love with her for the last three years. Mary knows, her mother, most all of her friends. Even I could hardly miss the signs.'

'Oh. I'm sorry. I . . .'

'No need to be sorry, lad. It's me that ought to apologise, for her being so contrary as to prefer that James Maynard, and Edward Wickens, and all them other boys to you. Not that they're not nice enough lads, for the most part. But she's a singular girl, she needs someone special, and I'd wager that could well be you. I hear about things, you know, and I reckon you're going places. And Harriott would do well to stick alongside you when you do so, if she has any sense.'

'Might I hope? Do you think she might sometime care? I did think when we were in London . . .'

'I don't know, you'll have to ask her, but the way she talked about what you did together up there, it was Stephen this, and Stephen that, and saying how impressed she was with you handling them fellows that might have done the murder, and all the information you knew about gardens and that. Still, give her a few more days and then.'

'I will Mr Curteis. I will. And thankyou.' He turned, and they made their way downstairs. 'I'll look in tomorrow, same sort of time. Maybe she'll be awake?'

'We'll have to see.'

CHAPTER 25

HOW TO FIND TRUE LOVE AND HAPPINESS IN THE PRESENT DAY

On Friday evening, Harriott called a conference. Well, it was the first time George would be free, so all four of them could be together; and also the first time she had felt up to coming downstairs to sit for more than half an hour at a time.

They talked over the whole affair, ran through all the people who had been around at the right times, tried to think of who might have had a motive, people they hadn't thought of before, and got exactly nowhere. Then, George said he and Mary had been in to ask Mrs Carpenter about sharp knives, and the only ones she kept was a stubby little blade for paring, and a great wide one for carving, neither of which would fit the bill. And anyway, she had said, 'They was in my dresser all that day, and I'd have missed them if anyone had been about borrowing them.'

Harriott sat back into the cushions Mary had fetched to make her more comfortable in her chair. 'Oh well,' she said, 'It seems like we're stuck.'

'What did Miss Clarke say?' said Stephen, 'Keep on looking, and eventually something will come up.'

'I hope it will, but it doesn't look like it will,' she answered.

'Then tell us more about your trip to London, would you, Harry?'

'Haven't you heard enough yet? Surely, I've told you everything, haven't I? No, I know what I can tell you about, I've just had this letter, it came a little before you arrived, it's from Miss Clarke's nephew John. He's fourteen, and I think he has an attachment for me, it's a bit embarrassing.'

'Competition for you, eh, S. . . ?' Mary put her hand to her mouth, and blushed. Stephen to his credit, simply said, 'Can we hear it?'

Harriott, concentrating on finding the letter, took it out of her pocket, and smoothed it out. 'He managed to persuade his father and the school to let him and his brother attend the opening of the Manchester and Liverpool railway on Wednesday, he must have written this that very evening, before they returned to Shrewsbury, where they're at school. Anyway, I'll read it.'

"Dear Miss Curteis,

I thought you would be interested to hear that we did make our trip to the railway opening, all thanks to your encouragement and persuasion of my father. It was monstrous brilliant and splendid. We had three coaches, because there was William and me, and two other boys in our form, and three from the year above me. One of the brushers came along to keep it all proper, and two 'postors to keep us in order. We made sure we took lots of grot with us to eat on the way up, and we had a fine journey. Father met us when we got to the place, he said he had business in Manchester, but I think he was just as keen as we were to see the show.

We stayed in a little town called Newton-le-Willows, which is a funny name, isn't it? It is in between the big cities, as the Head Man said all the lodgings in Liverpool and Manchester would be taken, and he didn't want his boys to be led astray by the vices of the metropolises. Shouldn't that be metropoli? Anyway, we first went to see a huge viaduct over a canal at a place called Sankey, it's the biggest in the world, they said, it has nine arches, and is amazing high. And then we went along to the station at Parkside, where the engines were to stop to take on water, and found out a good place to see everything. Don't you wish you'd been with us? I do.

There were two tracks, laid quite close together, and William went and laid down between the rails to see how far apart they were, and got in trouble with the brusher for it. We waited and waited, and then at last we heard the engines coming. There were two, one behind the other on the left hand track, the Phoenix and the North Star, they were called, with carriages full as full with people, and they stopped just past the station to wait for the one on the other track, which was hauling the Duke of Wellington's special carriage and three others. He's the Prime Minister, you know, he's very important, so he had the most modern and most powerful engine, called Northumbrian. His train had a band in the first truck, but I don't know how he could have heard it over the noise of the engines.

Anyway, the Duke's train stopped, and lots of people got out and wandered around all over the place, on the station and the tracks and everywhere. Then, there was more noise, and a yellow engine appeared on the left track, it was called the Rocket, I found out later, and everyone cleared out of the way, when a man shouted. Only there were three gentlemen who didn't seem to realise what was happening. One of them got hauled up into the Duke's carriage, and one pressed himself against the special train out of the way, but the other was climbing up, half in the carriage, holding on the door, when it swung open and he was hit by the Rocket, and fell on the track, and his leg was all mangled up by the wheels. There was buckets of blood, it was monstrous amazing, I saw it all.

Anyway, the brusher made us all leave then, he said it wasn't the sort of thing boys should be seeing, and I think they took the man away, and I expect he died, because it was a real smash-up. But I'm really glad I went, and I think even more now that I might become an engineer, because it was so terrific, and everyone says this is going to be the future of travel, and when the engines get a bit better nobody will want to travel by coach, the trains will go as much as three times as fast, and it'll be much more comfortable and cheaper, but I don't know how it could cost less, because they've got to make the track and everything.

So, I'm out of space, but I thought you'd want to know about all this, and I do hope you might come and visit us in London again, in the holidays, or maybe we'll go and see the people at Herenden some time and I could see you then?

J Clarke"

Harriott laid the letter down, and coughed. 'Sorry about the schoolboy fascination with machinery and injuries, but I thought it worth telling you about. I know Stephen is keen on all sorts of mechanisms, aren't you Stephen?'

But Stephen was looking into the distance, and his lips were moving. He didn't seem to have heard her, or something.

'What's a Brusher, and that other word, a Postor or something?' said Mary.

'I don't know, but they're probably words they call the schoolmasters or the senior boys or something.' She coughed again, and turned back to Stephen. 'Stephen? What is it?'

'Buckets of blood,' he responded. 'Isn't that what he said?'

Harriott looked back at the letter. 'That's right. The man getting injured, he was a bit ghoulish about it. And he said something about that when we were at dinner, too, the second night, I remember.'

'Yes, that's what I was trying to place before, you know, but I think I've got it now. Look, the big problem with our mystery is that there is nowhere that was bloodstained, apart from in the chest, right?'

They all nodded.

'So, where was there blood near the theatre? In a bucket?'

'Outside the butchers, near the back door,' said Harriott, I fell over it, didn't I, and you . . . well, I fell over it.'

'So, what if, and it's still an if, Miss Burton was never stabbed after all, and the blood was animal blood from that bucket, and just put there to make it look like she was stabbed, and really she died some other way?'

'But . . . what about the stab wound in her chest?' said Mary.

Stephen paused, and thought for a few moments. 'Dr Bishop didn't do a post-mortem, did he? So we don't know how deep the cut went.'

'No,' said George, 'so you're saying it might have been made by a little blade, mightn't it?'

'Like Mrs Carpenter's paring knife?' said Mary.

'What about Mr Carpenter's penknife?' said Stephen, getting excited. Everyone carries one of those, and if you only want to make it look like a stab wound, that would be enough.'

'But what if there had been a post mortem thing, whatever you called it?' said Mary, 'it'd have been discovered.'

'Which means, doesn't it, that the plan wasn't thought through very well, surely?'

'Yes,' said Harriott, 'because it wasn't planned, it just happened.'

'So, Mr Carpenter kills Miss Burton somehow, and for some reason we don't know, and then he . . .' Stephen mused,

'. . . hides her body somewhere, . . .' Mary, bouncing up and down on her chair,

'. . . and then later, gets the blood in his bucket, and puts her in the chest, and soaks the clothes and things in the blood, and that's why there was . . .'

'. . . that ring mark on the boards, where the bucket stood,' concluded Mary, triumphantly. 'Oh yes, I haven't told you, I got Mr Ward to see them. I couldn't find Mr Brooke, but I met Mr Ward outside the Pebbles, just going toward the church, and thought he might help. I had to tell him all about the mystery, and he was quite willing to be a witness, and I showed him the stains on the boards, and told him what we think it means.'

'Brilliant,' said Harriott, and then was seized with another fit of coughing.

'You need to go back to bed, Harry,' said Mary, 'you've been up a long time. Come on with me. You men, you work out what we need to do next. I'll be down in a little while.'

Reluctantly, Harriott allowed Mary to take her upstairs, and undress her, and put her in bed. She coughed all the while, but the sputum coming up was less dark, that surely was a good sign. And now they'd solved the mystery, hadn't they? Well, maybe. She wasn't sure, she couldn't really think straight just now. She'd sort it out after a bit of a rest.

On Saturday morning Harriott woke up feeling quite a lot more like herself. She had a cursory wash, and dressed properly for the first time. Her gown hung off her, and her face looked so thin and drawn in the glass, but at least she didn't seem to be coughing so much, and she felt properly hungry at last. She made her way downstairs, holding on to the rail, and moving slowly, and sat down at the kitchen table to catch her breath.

After a minute or two, she set the kettle to boil, noting her father must have already banked up the fire, which ought to be her job. He didn't seem to be around: she put her head into the print shop and it was silent. He must have gone out, she decided. Which left her alone, with her thoughts. She had to decide what to do about Stephen. How she felt, and what she . . . what he . . . well, she just didn't know. It was so embarrassing, whichever way she looked at it.

She made a pot of tea, but there was no milk in the cool bucket, so she had to take it black. Eventually, she couldn't put off thinking any more. There was no getting away from it, she had fallen in love with Stephen, it was just amazing she hadn't noticed it before, there had been so many signs. It hadn't happened suddenly, it had grown over the days and weeks. Perhaps she should have realised when she wanted to hold onto his arm, even when the coach wasn't all that jerky? Or when she had so enjoyed playing the game of imagining what secrets passers-by concealed, with him? Or even, when she had been so happy to walk in the rain with him back from the Stockwell estate?

How did he feel? She couldn't say. Perhaps she could ask Mary, that would be the thing, it would be most awkward, but less so than asking Stephen himself, wouldn't it? She tried to think back about how he was around her, and really, she couldn't think of anything particular, only of him always being kind and helpful and complimentary to her. She'd finish her tea, and then toast some bread, if she could find where Father had put the toasting fork, and then see if Mary was at home. It'd be the first time she'd been out in the street, that would make her feel more back to normal.

She'd hardly finished getting her bread to brown when Mary came in at the back door, unannounced, like she always had.

'Harriott, you're up and dressed. Are you feeling better?'

'Not too bad, as long as I don't try and do too much. Would you like some toast?'

'Yes, please; let me take that fork and do it. You sit back.'

'I'm not an invalid, Mary.'

'Yes you are for the moment. Do as I tell you.'

Harriott sat back, and tried to think about how to broach the subject. She could say . . . no she couldn't. Or perhaps, something vague, like, How do you think Stephen feels about me? Maybe she could begin my asking how things were going between Mary and George, that might break the ice for her.

'So, Harriott,' said Mary, sitting back on her haunches, 'when are you going to realise Stephen Fuggle has been in love with you for the past few years? You're as bad as that Emma in the book I told you I read, with Mr Knightley. It's not fair on him.'

'Stephen?' she said, confused. 'In love with me? Surely not.'

Mary guffawed, there was no other word for it. 'Yes, Stephen, lamebrain. Why can't you see it? I know you like tall men, handsome ones, ones with big muscles, exciting ones, but it's not fair to keep being just friends when he's so . . . so utterly devoted to you. Can't you see your way to liking him a bit more, that way?'

Harriott couldn't speak. In fact, she began coughing again, she was so overcome. Stephen Fuggle in love with her? What?

'He was utterly distraught when you were ill, you know. And he brought you all those flowers, as soon as they let him, he kept on asking when you could have some. And, well, he kept asking me too if you were going to die, and what could he do to make you well, begging me to let him help in some way. And, you idiot, he's a far better man than that James Maynard, or Richard Marshall, or what's he called, Edward Wickens.'

Harriott couldn't stop the tears leaking out. She sobbed and coughed alternately, until she was so out of breath she put her head on the table and just shook. Mary carried on with the toasting, and let her be.

After a few minutes, she raised her head a little. 'I've been such a fool, haven't I?' she croaked, her voice not working properly. 'And now I've been so worried since I realised I'd fallen for him, and I didn't know what to do about it, and then I got ill, and . . .'

Mary stood up, and put the toast on a plate. 'Really? What a relief. Well, you'd better tell him as soon as he finishes at Westwell, hadn't you? Or do you feel well enough to walk down there during his lunch break?'

'I'm not sure. I . . . I'd like to, if what you say is true. But, well, can we try a few steps outside when we've eaten this, and see?'

Mary opened the Curteis' front door and pushed Stephen in. 'Go on, you. She's not well enough to walk down the road yet, but she's well enough to face facts. I'll be next door when you're done.' She shut the door behind Stephen, and he took a cautious step forward.

Harriott came out of the kitchen, her hands screwing up her apron. They looked at each other. Harriott smiled a half-smile, a nervous smile. Then, all of a sudden, she rushed up to Stephen and threw her arms around his neck, and hugged him as if she never wanted to let him go.

'I've been such an idiot,' she mumbled into the cloth of his shoulder. 'Can you forgive me? I didn't realise. I just . . . didn't know.'

Stephen stroked her hair, nuzzled into the curls. 'I know, I know, Mary told me. It's all alright, Harriott, it's all going to be alright.'

She sniffed. 'I should have known, I should have. And I thought I was quite clever, really, knowing about things, and being Mr Pomfret's . . . if I still am, after being away so long.'

'He'd be a fool to drop you, Harriott. An utter fool.'

'Really? Do you think so?'

'Of course. And now we've nearly solved the mystery, he'll be even more impressed with you. Like I am, only not in the same way, I hope. I couldn't bear to share you, you know.'

Harriott started to giggle. 'Mary asked me when I first began to work there, what he was like, and did I find him attractive, you know.'

'Oh, no, do I have a rival? I mean, apart from John Clarke?'

She dissolved into slightly uncontrolled giggles. 'Neither of them,' she managed, at last, 'though John might want to challenge you to a duel over me, I think. I expect there'd be,' she broke off to cough, 'buckets of blood if you did fight. Oh, but I couldn't bear the thought of you being killed. Please don't have a duel, won't you?'

Stephen said nothing, simply hugged her tighter. Then, there was a noise of steps behind, and Mr Curteis appeared, saw the scene, and left immediately, grinning. The two of them just stood there, embracing, and swaying slightly.

There was a knock at the door. Harriott reluctantly released her hold on Stephen's neck, and went to open it. Stephen stayed close by her side.

'Oh, Mr Pomfret! I'm so sorry I haven't been to work, I've been . . . but you know.'

He looked from one to the other. 'I see there is more news than you simply being on the mend. But that is not my business. May I come in?'

'Of course.' She stepped back, and led him into the parlour, sat down. Stephen sat by her, close. Mr Pomfret looked around him and took his seat.

'I understand from Mr Ward that you have now all but solved the mystery around Miss Burton's death,' he began.

Harriott looked at Stephen. 'Mr Ward?' she said, puzzled. 'Oh, yes, Mary asked him to look at the marks of the bucket on the stage boards with her, after you found them, I remember. It must have been just before I fell ill.'

'Indeed,' said Mr Pomfret. 'Now, the reason I have called; well, first to see that you are recovering satisfactorily, of course; but then to ask again if I ought to be taking steps to have this man Carpenter arrested? Mr Ward has been asking around about the crime, and he feels that the authorities ought to have been more energetic in investigating it. I am extremely grateful to you for what you have done, it has saved me considerable embarrassment.'

Harriott looked at Stephen, and took his hand. 'What do you think?'

Stephen frowned. 'We still don't have any proof, though, do we? Though I don't think Mr Pomfret will know about our new idea, about why there was no blood anywhere in the building.'

'What's this?' Mr Pomfret asked.

Stephen explained, simply and clearly. 'Even though that idea points more to Mr Carpenter, all we know is negatives. We have shown that none of the actors could have done it; nor Mr Cousins or Mr Higgins who we suspected at first, nor any of the other people who visited the theatre that morning.'

'I've just thought of someone,' said Harriott. 'What about Mrs Relph, the dressmaker, she was to meet Miss Burton to decide on alterations to her costume, so she was there at the right time?'

Stephen sat back, rubbed his nose. 'Why did we miss her? I've been stupid.'

'No,' she squeezed his hand, 'no more than any of us.'

'Why should such a woman want to kill an actress, and one who was going to give her work?' asked Mr Pomfret. 'Surely she wouldn't have the knowledge of the theatre to conceal her deed in that way, in any case? How would she know about the floorboards, and the bucket, and so on? And with this discovery, surely Mr Carpenter must be guilty?'

'I think, sir,' said Stephen slowly, 'that we ought to wait a little longer before acting. Harriott is not well enough to go and question people, but I will, with our other friends, and see if we can find any more proofs, or exonerate Mrs Relph.'

'I want this to be cleared up, Mr Fuggle. As soon as possible, it is not good for the town, and I am being pressed by Mr Ward and others to take action. When will you next be at Morghew?'

'On Wednesday, sir.'

'Could you not do your investigating before then, and let me know by, say, Monday, or Tuesday at the latest? It is most unpleasant in my position to have this unresolved.'

'Certainly sir, I will do my best.'

'Good day, then, and good luck.'

CHAPTER 26

DEATH OF A LADIES' MAN

THE FOUR OF THEM GATHERED again at the Curteis' after church. Mary and George had been to see Mrs Relph, and Stephen had cudgelled his brains all afternoon in the Westwell garden, and later at home, to no effect.

'Mrs Relph *could* have done it,' reported Mary. She was at the theatre when Miss Burton was changing into her costume, and nobody else was about in the auditorium: Mr Carpenter had left, and the players were in the green room.'

'But how would she have killed Miss Burton?' objected Stephen.

'Well yes. I meant, she had the opportunity to do it, really. She did go into the green room asking where Miss Burton was, we know that. But she didn't have anyone to say where she was after she left the theatre, she just went home, and got with her housework. But she is a small and quite elderly woman, over forty-five, I think, and we heard Miss Burton was very strong and fierce.'

'Actually,' put in Harriott, 'now we think she wasn't stabbed, that is a very big hole in our idea. How did she actually die?'

Stephen nodded. 'I've been thinking about the same problem. So I went and visited Dr Bishop again, he sends his regards, Harriott, by the way, and best wishes for a continuing recovery. I asked him, Just supposing the wound in Miss Burton's back was made by a penknife, to throw suspicion in the wrong direction, and the blood had come from the butcher's pail, could he think how she might have died without the stab wound that was the apparently obvious cause? He wasn't too pleased with the idea: I'd expected that, but I said, nobody had asked him to do a post-mortem, and if he had he would have discovered the real cause, would he not, which calmed him, I believe.'

'Doctors don't like being wrong, do they?' said Mary.

'Anyway, he hummed and hawed a bit, and said, it was possible she had been poisoned, of course, but there were no signs of burning around her mouth, and in any case she had white face paint on, which would protect from such corrosion. Or, she could have been strangled, or suffocated, or even drowned, he supposed. And then there was always the possibility she had died naturally, from a heart-attack or a seizure, but then why should anyone go to the trouble of making it look like a stabbing?'

'How would she drown in the middle of a theatre?' asked Mary.

'Quite: he said that was most improbable, he was simply listing ways people died without external violence being evident.'

George had been listening without saying anything. 'Face paint?' he said. 'Why was she wearing face paint?'

'We thought it odd too,' said Harriott. 'We didn't understand that part at all.'

'Why do ladies wear face paint, then?' George persisted.

'Well, to make them more beautiful,' said Mary, 'though I don't think it does, usually. Or on stage, so they look the part they are playing.'

'Harriott wouldn't need it,' put in Stephen, grinning, 'she's as beautiful as she could be anyway.' Harriott punched him on the arm.

'They use it to cover up blemishes, mostly,' she said, 'and to contrast with rouge, especially at evening functions, in the candlelight.'

Stephen slapped his hand on the table. 'That's it!' he cried. 'It was covering something up, that the murderer didn't want anyone to see.

He put it on, and not very well, because, I suppose, he wasn't used to doing it, to cover up . . .'

'What then?' asked Harriott, feeling his excitement.

'. . . marks on her face and neck, surely? Now, what would cause them?'

'Strangling, suffocation, that sort of thing?' said George.

'Yes, of course. And why would the murderer, no, lets call him his name, Mr Carpenter, have his hands on her face and neck?'

They all looked at him, puzzled. 'To kill her?' suggested Mary.

'No, well not deliberately, I don't think. But he might, if he was trying to . . . you know, have his way with her. And she would have resisted, being the forthright sort of woman she was, and strong, so he would have tried to subdue her, but somehow it went too far, and . . . well, she died.'

'Is that possible?' asked Harriott. 'I mean, the dying bit. I could easily believe Carpenter would want to rape a woman, he's revolting.'

'I'd better check with Dr Bishop. I'll go now.'

'Hang on a minute, Stephen. Let's just think. Is there anything else we've missed?'

They all thought hard. 'Nothing I can see,' said Stephen. 'Harriott?'

'No, not just now. Well, then, you'd better go, then you can tell Mr Pomfret the news, and maybe he will work out a way to prove it all. I can't see how.'

Stephen jumped up and ran out of the door. The others sat and talked and talked, trying to see if they had it all straight. Harriott got up and went to find her father, to see if they could all stay to lunch, and would he fetch it, as she really wasn't up to snuff just yet. He hugged her, and said Of course, and that she had a brightness in her eye he hadn't seen for ages, and what had happened, apart from Stephen of course, so she told him they really had solved the mystery now, and just now had to prove it.

Stephen was back before lunch was on the table. 'Dr Bishop says,' he panted, 'that if a woman was being prevented from calling out, and had hands on her mouth and neck, it could press on the . . . I'm not sure what he called it, something like carrots, but he meant the artery in the neck, and cause the heart to stop. Then she would die.'

'That must be it,' exclaimed Mary. 'We've done it!' And then, 'Well, you and Harriott have done most of it, I mean.'

'No, it was all of us,' said Harriott. 'Don't do yourself down.'

'Now let's go through what happened in what order,' said Stephen.

'We've just been talking about that,' said Mary.

'Very well, you take me through it.'

Mary blushed, and turned to George. 'Go on,' he said, 'you'll be fine.'

'Well, first, Carpenter would have seen Miss Burton on the stage with Mr Cousins, when he'd be up in the gallery.'

'No, I don't think that's right,' said Harriott. 'I've just thought: he said he was there collecting rubbish, but the chars had already been around everywhere and done that, hadn't they?'

'So he was lying,' said Stephen. 'He was probably somewhere else at that time, or if he was in the gallery, he was just doing nothing.'

'Alright,' continued Mary. 'And he probably heard Miss Burton saying she was going to fetch her costume, and change, and he thought, I wager she'll change in that first box, ladies often do, so he scuttled upstairs to get a good view from the left-hand gallery, . . .'

'. . . Stage right: where George and I sat on the night of the play,' put in Harriott.

'. . . to spy on her as she undressed. Then, when she came out and did what he hoped, he was so inflamed with passion, . . .'

'Lust,' put in Harriott.

'. . . lust, that he went down and around and found her still not quite fully clothed, because the gown was too tight and so on, and then he tried to have his foul way with her, and accidentally killed her.'

'Excellent,' said Stephen. 'I'm sure you're right so far. Then what?'

'Well, he would have been a bit shocked, wouldn't he? So, he'd want to think what to do.'

'And put his trousers back on,' added George.

'Well, yes,' Mary flapped a hand at him, 'but mostly to get away and think. So he went for his walk, and then feeling all churned up and frightened he went to the Harris Arms and had beer, to calm down, and that's where he worked out his plan.'

Harriott took over. 'On his way back from the inn he passed our timid Mr Higgins, and then again when Mr Higgins was trying to get into the building, he came out again carrying something, Higgins said.'

'The bucket,' Mary explained. 'To fetch the blood. Before the butcher disposed of it, you see.'

'And then he set that down somewhere, and waited . . .' Harriott.

'Did some jobs, like laying out costumes . . .' Mary.

'Then when they'd all gone, after about five o'clock, he fetched the chest, and set it on the stage, . . .'

'. . . got Miss Burton's ordinary clothes and the blood, and soaked them, put them in the chest, and then carried the body from the box where she'd died . . .'

'. . . which was why it smelled, because she'd wet herself once she was dead, I know that happens, I had to lay out grandfather, . . .'

'. . . and put the body on top,' finished Mary triumphantly.

Stephen clapped his hands. 'Of course. And then, he used the white paint to cover up the marks of his fingers on her face and neck, closed the lid, rinsed out his bucket at the well outside the back door, and went home.'

'And snored in his chair, because of all the beer, and the strain of it all,' finished Harriott.

'So why did he stay in bed all the next day?'

'To keep out of the way, in case he was suspected: he probably thought we would believe the death happened on the Friday, don't you think?'

'Not knowing about Mrs Relph, or Miss Burton's duty at the Plough. I see.' Stephen gave a great sigh. 'So, now what?'

'You go and tell Mr Pomfret, and he can decide. He's the magistrate,' said Harriott.

'What, now?'

'No time like the present.'

'Very well, I'll go as soon as we've eaten.'

'Can we come with you?' said Mary. 'I want to be in on this. George too?'

'I couldn't, not the master,' said George. 'He scares me.'

'George too,' said Stephen. 'And I wish Harriott could come but it's too far for her to walk just now.'

Mr Carpenter was arrested the following morning on Mr Pomfret's orders, by a deputation of men from the town hall, and was said to have put up no resistance, rather seeming resigned to the fact, according to the gossip that spread to the furthest reaches of the town by noon. He was confined in the town jail by the church, to await transfer to Maidstone, and then trial.

Mr Pomfret also ordered an exhumation, and examination of the remains with the face paint removed revealed signs of livid discolouration of the face and neck, albeit much deteriorated, in the possible shape of the fingers of a large pair of hands. Dr Bishop when consulted gave his opinion that such maltreatment, in a woman known to suffer from episodes of dizziness, and possibly fainting, might well stop the heart. A post-mortem was performed, but the internal organs were too deteriorated to provide any further information.

Harriott only heard all this intelligence at second-hand, much to her annoyance, wishing she could have been there to witness the outcome of all their efforts. But it was no good, she was still too weak, and had to rely on Mary's colourful interpretation of what she had heard from the folk at the Eight Bells, and third- or fourth- hand news from the mortuary staff via the stable man at the Woolpack. The whole affair was of course duly reported in *Lady Susan* at the end of the week in the most sensational of terms, and she was by then well enough to be able to compose the print for the article and set it in the forme, though sorely tempted to soften some of the more florid descriptions of events, and correct not a few errors.

Forced to sit at home, and think, Harriott began to have doubts about their deductions, and whether they had really found out the right person. She worried whether Mr Carpenter was clever enough to have worked out the plan to cover up what he had done, being as he was so lazy and most often drunk. After mulling on this for some time, she hesitantly told Mary about her concerns, but Mary reassured her that Mrs Robberds had told her that, now she knew how the crime had been carried out, she remembered the very same thing had been portrayed in a play they had put on some years before, which Mr Carpenter would have seen. Why she hadn't thought of it before she could not say, but there you were.

Carpenter was transferred to Maidstone jail on the Thursday, and a trial date set on the charge of murder. Witnesses began to be informed that they would be required to attend, to give evidence. Harriott had already been instructed by Mr Pomfret to write out in fair copy all the information they had collected, including the list of alibis, the timetable they had calculated, and their reasoning, for the use of the lawyers. She was able to do this at home, from her notes, being still too unwell to take much exercise. She asked Stephen to take it round to Mr Pomfret at Morghew on the Friday, and wondered if she would have to attend the trial, and whether indeed she really wanted to, now their work was to decide the fate of an individual.

Three days after the transfer had been effected, though, word came through from Maidstone early in the morning that Carpenter had managed to hang himself in his cell. The prison doctor had seen him and believed he had descended into melancholia following his arrest, and succumbed to despair. This intelligence was passed to Harriott by Mr Pomfret in person. He came to visit Harriott after church to inform her, and to repeat his thanks, though she also wondered if he also wanted to check how soon she would be able to return to work.

Nobody was much upset at the news of the death, even Mrs Carpenter, who asserted that "I knew he was a bad 'un, but I didn't know he was that wicked", according to Mary, via Mr Paine at the Bells, who had it from one of the charwomen at the theatre. Her main concern was whether she would be allowed to stay on in her cottage, now there was nobody to perform caretaker duties.

All in all it was a most peculiar week. Harriott couldn't decide if they had succeeded in achieving justice for Miss Burton, or simply caused more trouble all round. Was she responsible for Mr Carpenter's death? Or was it his own guilt that had caused it? But as Mr Brooke told her, when he visited to thank her, it is as well not to have a murderer in one's midst, and better to not suspect all one's colleagues with an unsolved mystery hanging over everyone like a sword of Damocles. And she had Stephen now, of course, which was a great and wonderful bonus; and she had been up to London, and seen so many things, and heard of opportunities that she might one day be able to take up.

Harriott and Stephen sat in the Pit waiting for "Black-eyed Susan" to begin. Harriott turned and waved to Mary, sitting with George in the gallery. There had been quite an argument as to who had which tickets, now they were each to sit with a different man from before, but Harriott, as she usually did, had prevailed. It had been quite a while since the first, curtailed, performance, to be sure, but Mr Bosworth, though recovered physically from his heart-attack, had not felt emotionally ready to revisit his role until some time had passed.

'I had a letter today,' said Stephen, nonchalantly, moving along the bench a little closer to Harriott.

'Oh, what was it?'

'You wouldn't be that interested,' he said, making an elaborate show of looking away.

Harriott punched him on the shoulder. 'Come on, out with it.'

'Well, it was only from Knole Park, near Sevenoaks, from the head gardener.'

'Really? What did he say?'

'Only that he would like to meet me, and if we suit, there is a post of second gardener available, which I might like to take.'

'No! Really? How wonderful. But . . . that would mean you would have to move away . . . and what about me? I couldn't bear for you to go so far.'

'Nor I, Harriott, nor I.' He leaned in and gave her a chaste kiss on the nose, given the public nature of the place. 'I wondered . . . well, you probably wouldn't . . . but I was thinking of hiring a gig, or maybe borrowing one, to go and look at the place, and might you come with me to see?'

'Would I?'

'I hoped so.'

'But, I mean, if you do suit, and leave Tenterden, then . . .'

Stephen moved closer. 'Well, I think there may be jobs up there for you, like you are doing for Mr Pomfret, don't you think? There are lots of big houses in the area, I've heard.'

'But that would be quite improper, wouldn't it?'

'Not if we were married, it wouldn't.'

Harriott jerked away. 'Stephen Fuggle, are you asking me to marry you, in the most unromantic way I've ever heard of?'

'Er, well, yes, I suppose so. I can't very well go down on bended knee here, there isn't room between the benches.'

"Tut! If you are inclined to preach, here is a milestone. I'll leave you in its company." The actors burst onto the stage, and began their argument with gusto. The candles were doused in the auditorium and the audience hushed. The two men strode to and fro and bickered; then there came a sound of doleful singing, and Susan entered. It was odd to see the actors they had met so often, now in their dramatic roles. Miss Chester looked the picture of a downtrodden victim of a rapacious landlord, and excited sighs of sympathy from all watching.

Doggrass raised his voice; he strode across the stage, and flung open the chest. The audience held its breath.

Then on with his diatribe, on with the play, on with the entertainment, on with life.

Harriott leaned over to whisper in Stephen's ear.

'Yes,' she breathed. 'Yes please.'